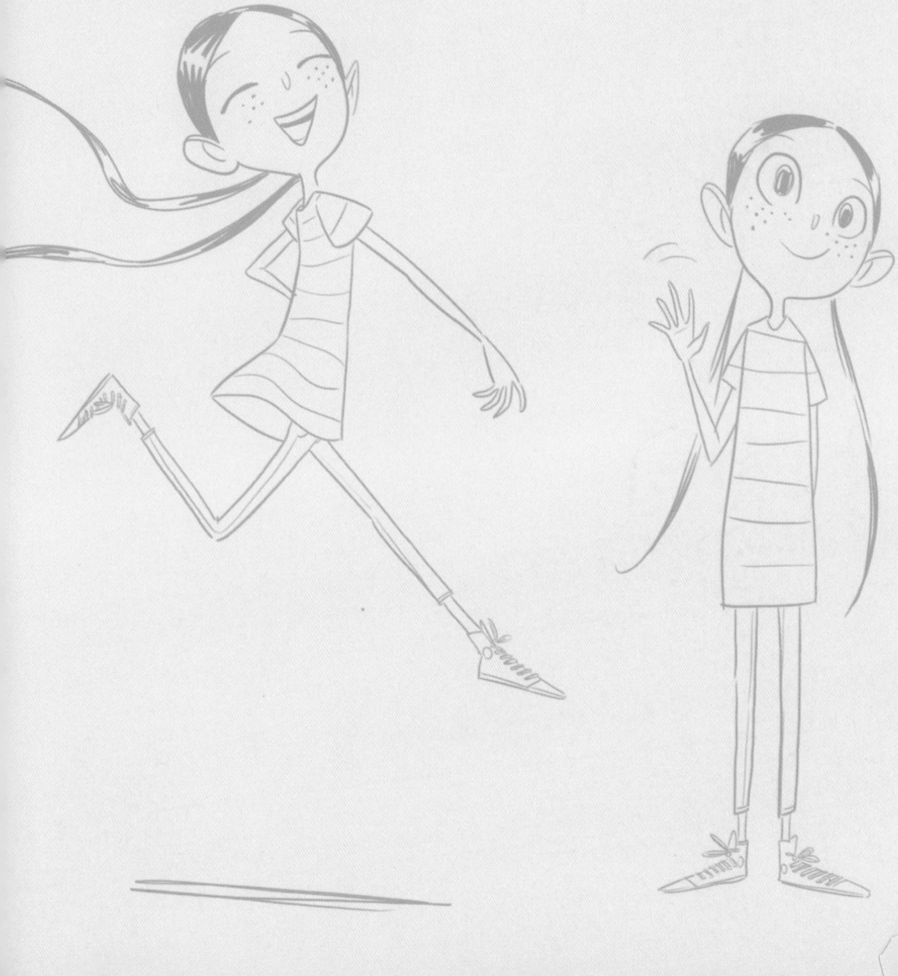

ELLIE in First Position

Passions aren't limited to a single country or a single language. That's why Elena and I are so happy that our little Electra is flying overseas, from Italy to America. We hope she brings each of you the energy and strength to pursue your dreams and inspires you to stand up to anyone who tries to tell you, "You can't do it." Electra never believed such nonsense, and look at her now! She's in your hands—in a new world, in a new life.

Thank you so much!
-Brian-

Original North American edition © 2023 Marble Press LLC
Text © 2021 Brian Freschi
Illustrations © 2021 Elena Triolo
Translation by Nanette McGuinness

Original North American edition published in 2023 by Marble Press, 245 Stonewall Rd, Berkeley, CA 94705
www.marblepress.com

Original Italian edition is titled *Elettra*, published in 2021 by Editrice Il Castoro Srl, Viale Andrea Doria 7, 20124 Milano
www.editriceilcastoro.it

This work has been translated with the contribution of the Center for Books and Reading of the Italian Ministry of Culture.

CENTRO
PER IL LIBRO
E LA LETTURA

This North American edition is published under exclusive license with Editrice Il Castoro.

Cataloging in Publication Data is available from the United States Library of Congress.

ISBN: 978-1-958325-00-1 (Paperback)
ISBN: 978-1-958325-01-8 (Ebook)

Printed in China

BRIAN FRESCHI   ELENA TRIOLO
TRANSLATION BY NANETTE MCGUINNESS

ELLIE in First Position

MARBLE  PRESS

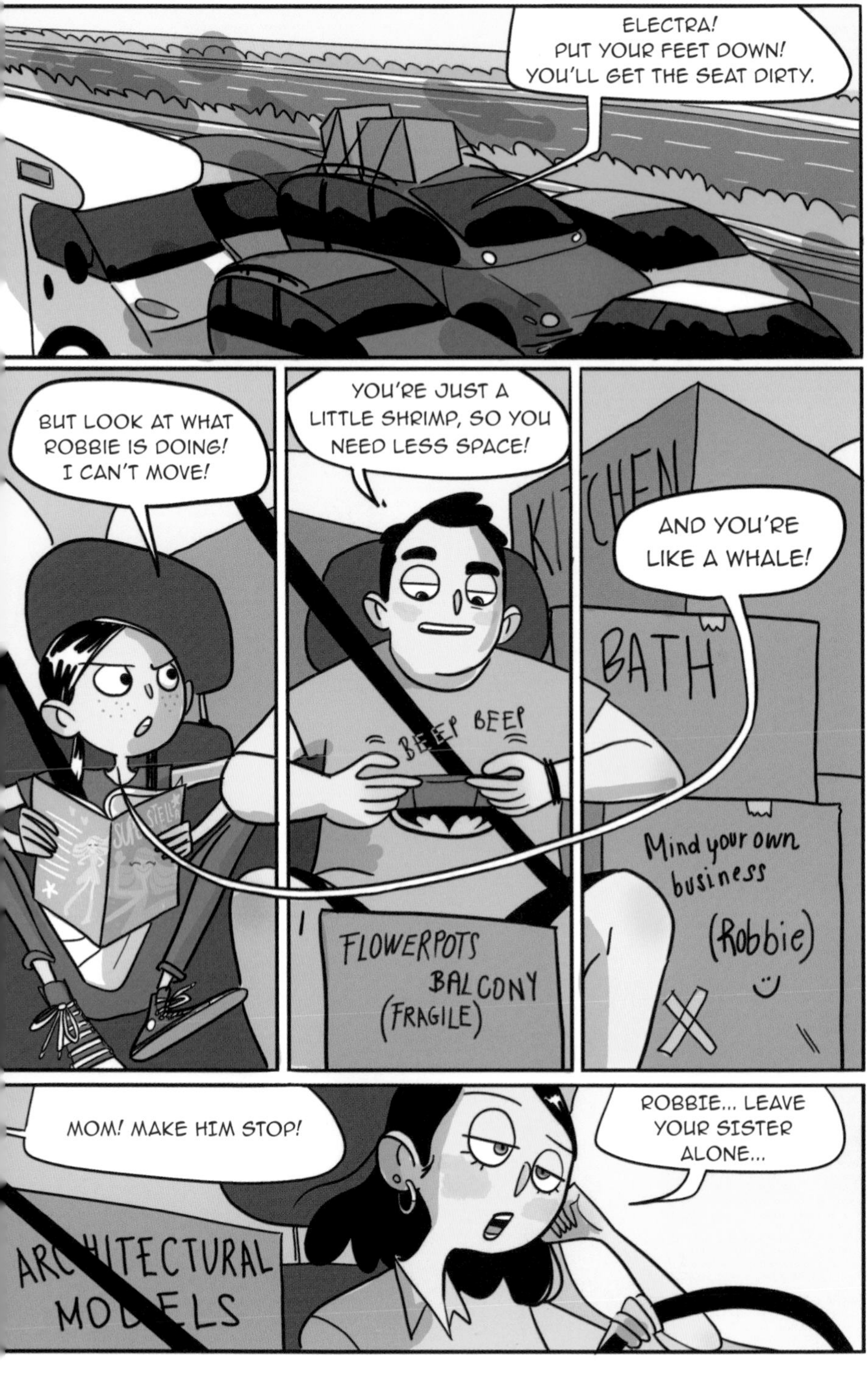
ELECTRA! PUT YOUR FEET DOWN! YOU'LL GET THE SEAT DIRTY.
BUT LOOK AT WHAT ROBBIE IS DOING! I CAN'T MOVE!
YOU'RE JUST A LITTLE SHRIMP, SO YOU NEED LESS SPACE!
AND YOU'RE LIKE A WHALE!
KITCHEN
BATH
BEEP BEEP
Mind your own business (Robbie)
FLOWERPOTS BALCONY (FRAGILE)
MOM! MAKE HIM STOP!
ROBBIE... LEAVE YOUR SISTER ALONE...
ARCHITECTURAL MODELS

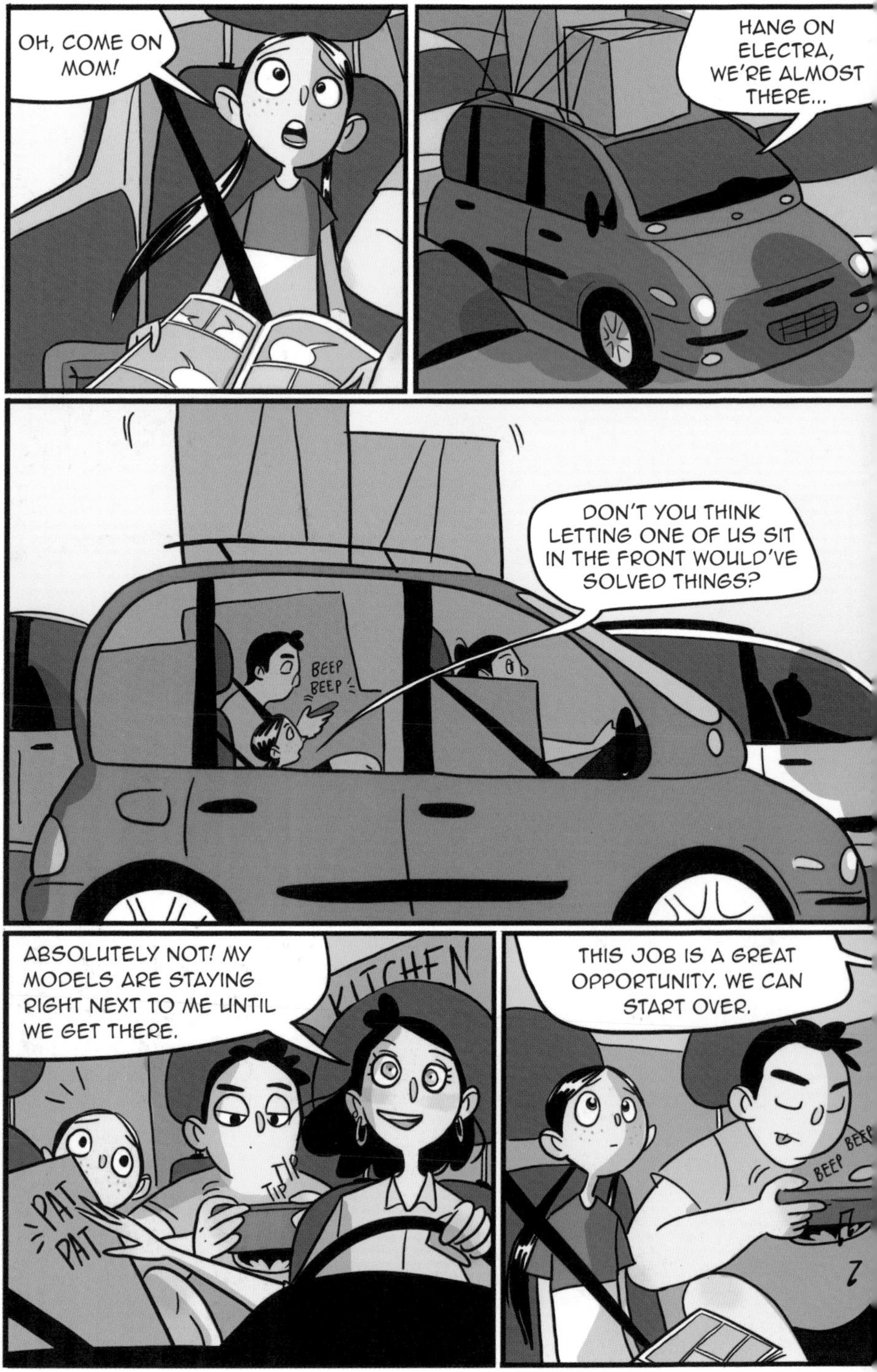
OH, COME ON MOM!
HANG ON ELECTRA, WE'RE ALMOST THERE...
DON'T YOU THINK LETTING ONE OF US SIT IN THE FRONT WOULD'VE SOLVED THINGS?
BEEP BEEP
ABSOLUTELY NOT! MY MODELS ARE STAYING RIGHT NEXT TO ME UNTIL WE GET THERE.
KITCHEN
TIP TIP
PAT PAT
THIS JOB IS A GREAT OPPORTUNITY. WE CAN START OVER.
BEEP BEEP

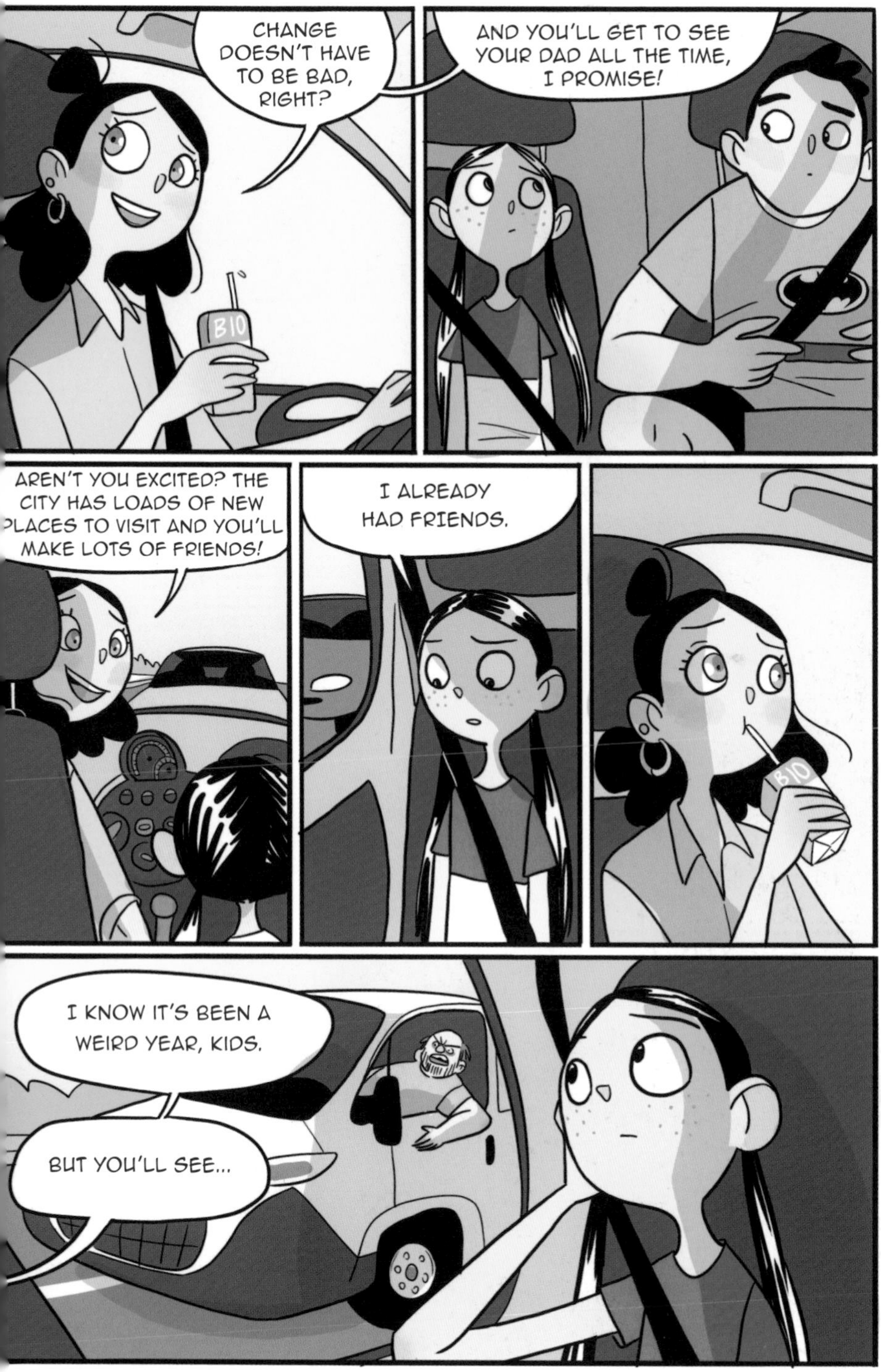
CHANGE DOESN'T HAVE TO BE BAD, RIGHT?
AND YOU'LL GET TO SEE YOUR DAD ALL THE TIME, I PROMISE!
AREN'T YOU EXCITED? THE CITY HAS LOADS OF NEW PLACES TO VISIT AND YOU'LL MAKE LOTS OF FRIENDS!
BIO
I ALREADY HAD FRIENDS.
BIO
I KNOW IT'S BEEN A WEIRD YEAR, KIDS.
BUT YOU'LL SEE...

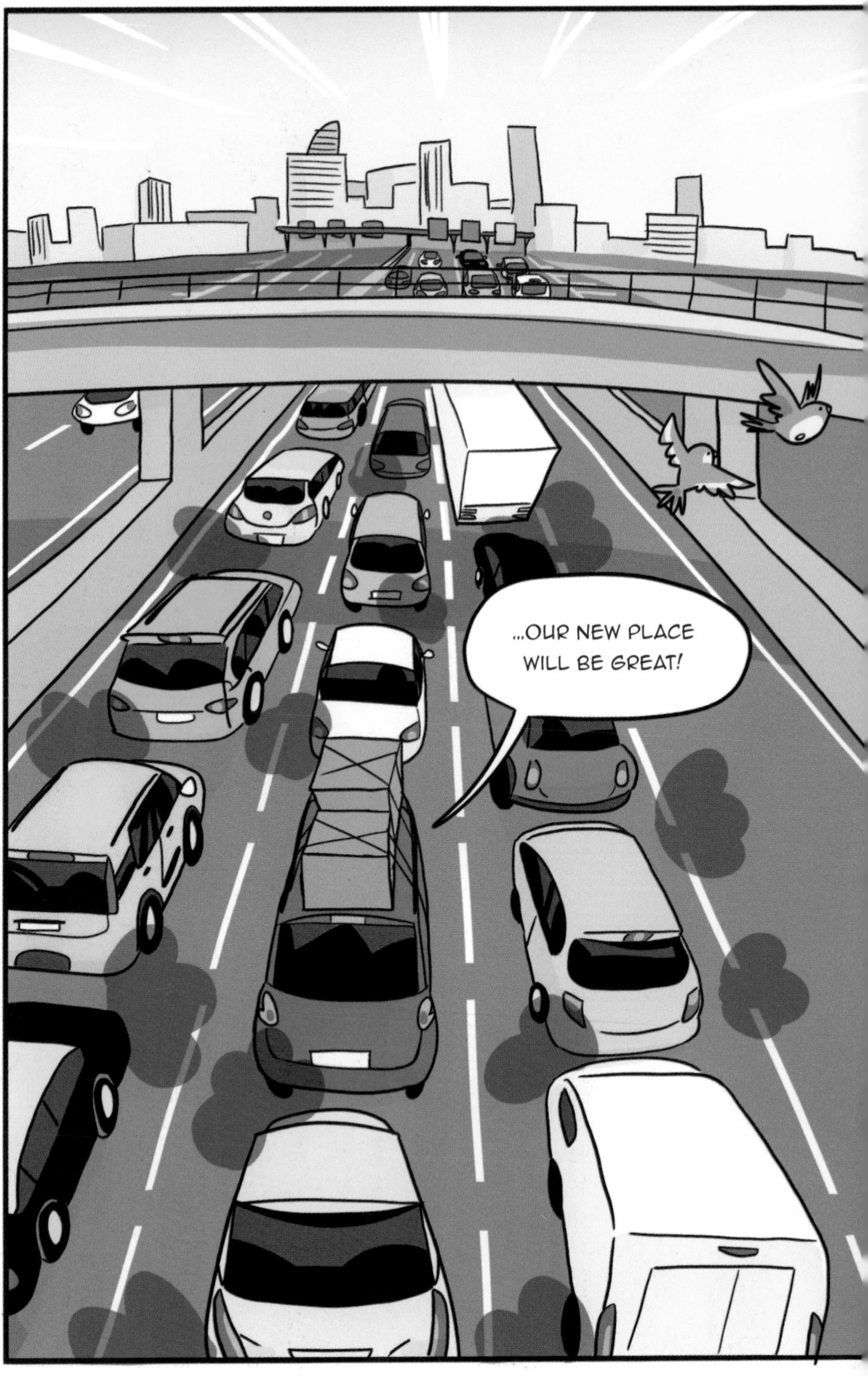
...OUR NEW PLACE WILL BE GREAT!

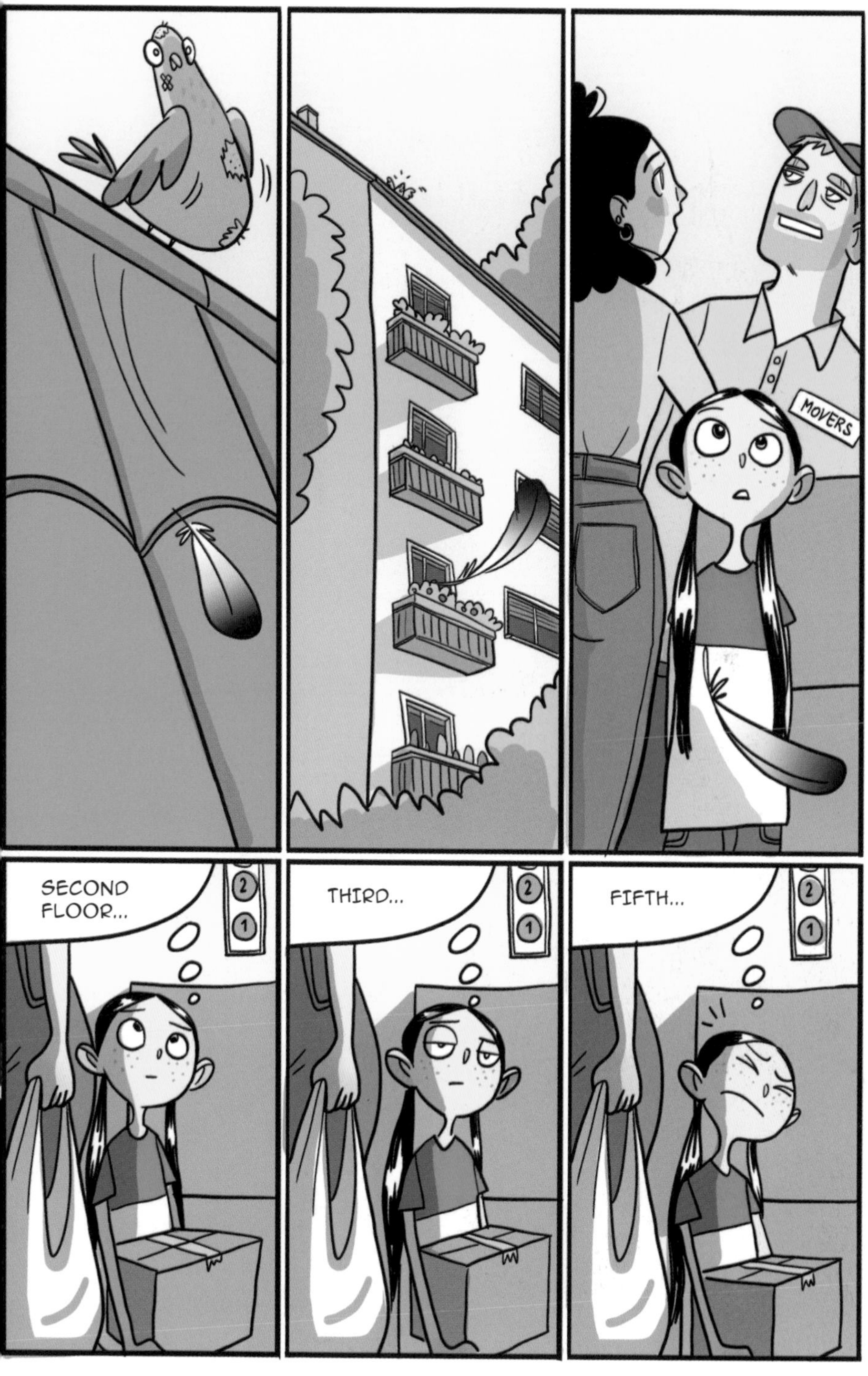
MOVERS
SECOND FLOOR...
THIRD...
FIFTH...

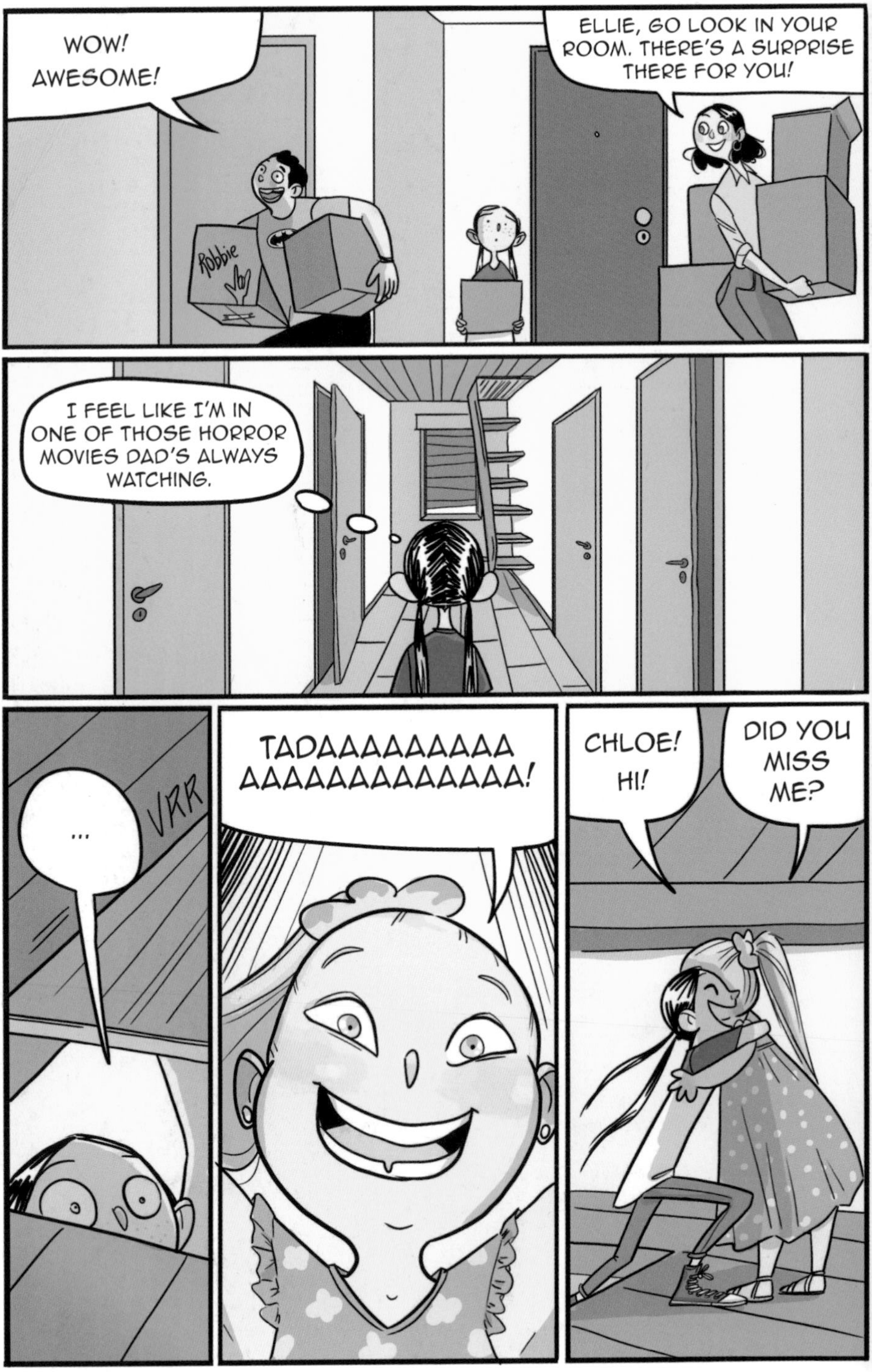
WOW! AWESOME!
ELLIE, GO LOOK IN YOUR ROOM. THERE'S A SURPRISE THERE FOR YOU!
Robbie
I FEEL LIKE I'M IN ONE OF THOSE HORROR MOVIES DAD'S ALWAYS WATCHING.
...
VRR
TADAAAAAAAAAA AAAAAAAAAAAAAA!
CHLOE! HI!
DID YOU MISS ME?

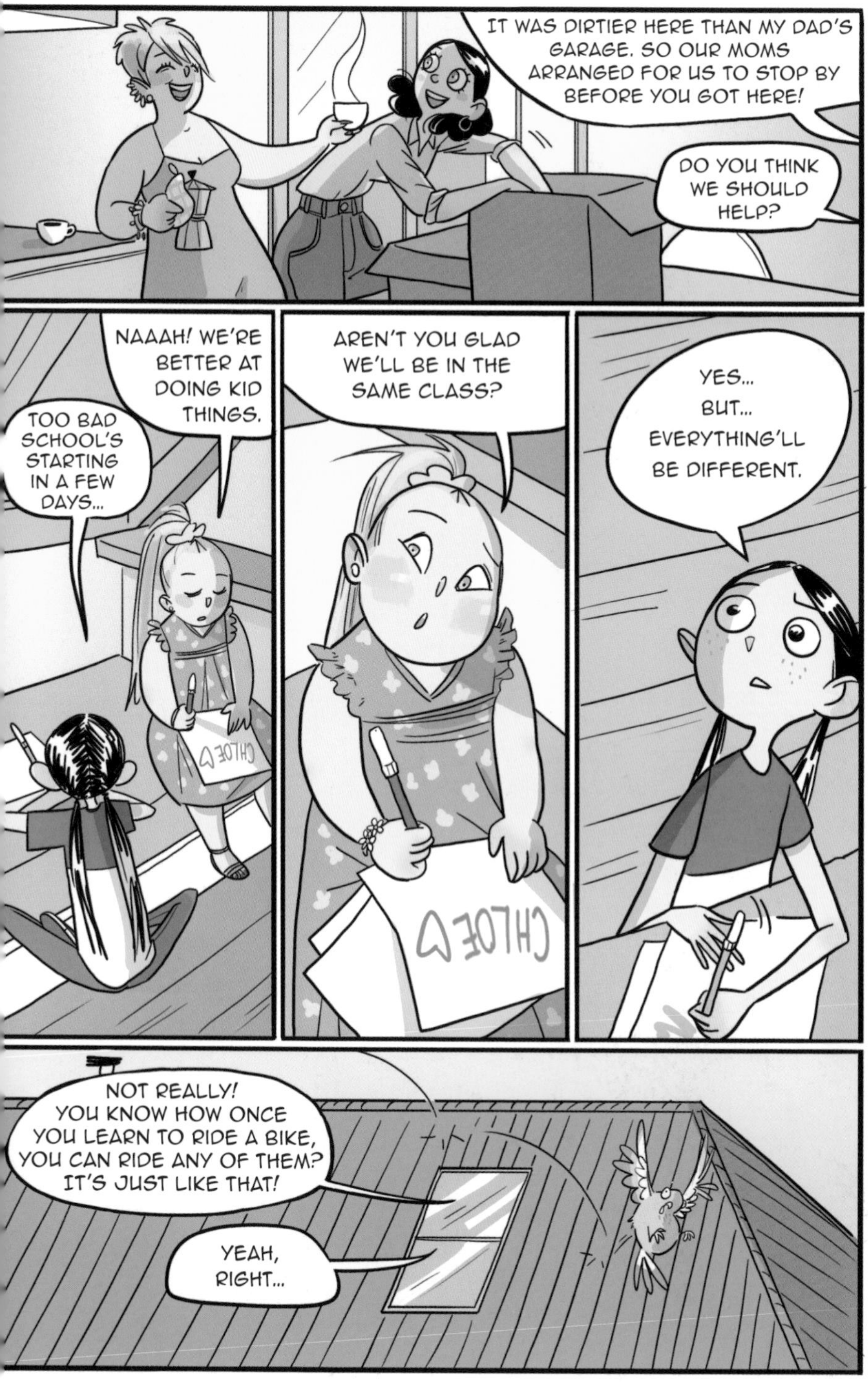

IT WAS DIRTIER HERE THAN MY DAD'S GARAGE. SO OUR MOMS ARRANGED FOR US TO STOP BY BEFORE YOU GOT HERE!
DO YOU THINK WE SHOULD HELP?
NAAAH! WE'RE BETTER AT DOING KID THINGS.
TOO BAD SCHOOL'S STARTING IN A FEW DAYS...
CHLOE
AREN'T YOU GLAD WE'LL BE IN THE SAME CLASS?
CHLOE
YES... BUT... EVERYTHING'LL BE DIFFERENT.
NOT REALLY! YOU KNOW HOW ONCE YOU LEARN TO RIDE A BIKE, YOU CAN RIDE ANY OF THEM? IT'S JUST LIKE THAT!
YEAH, RIGHT...

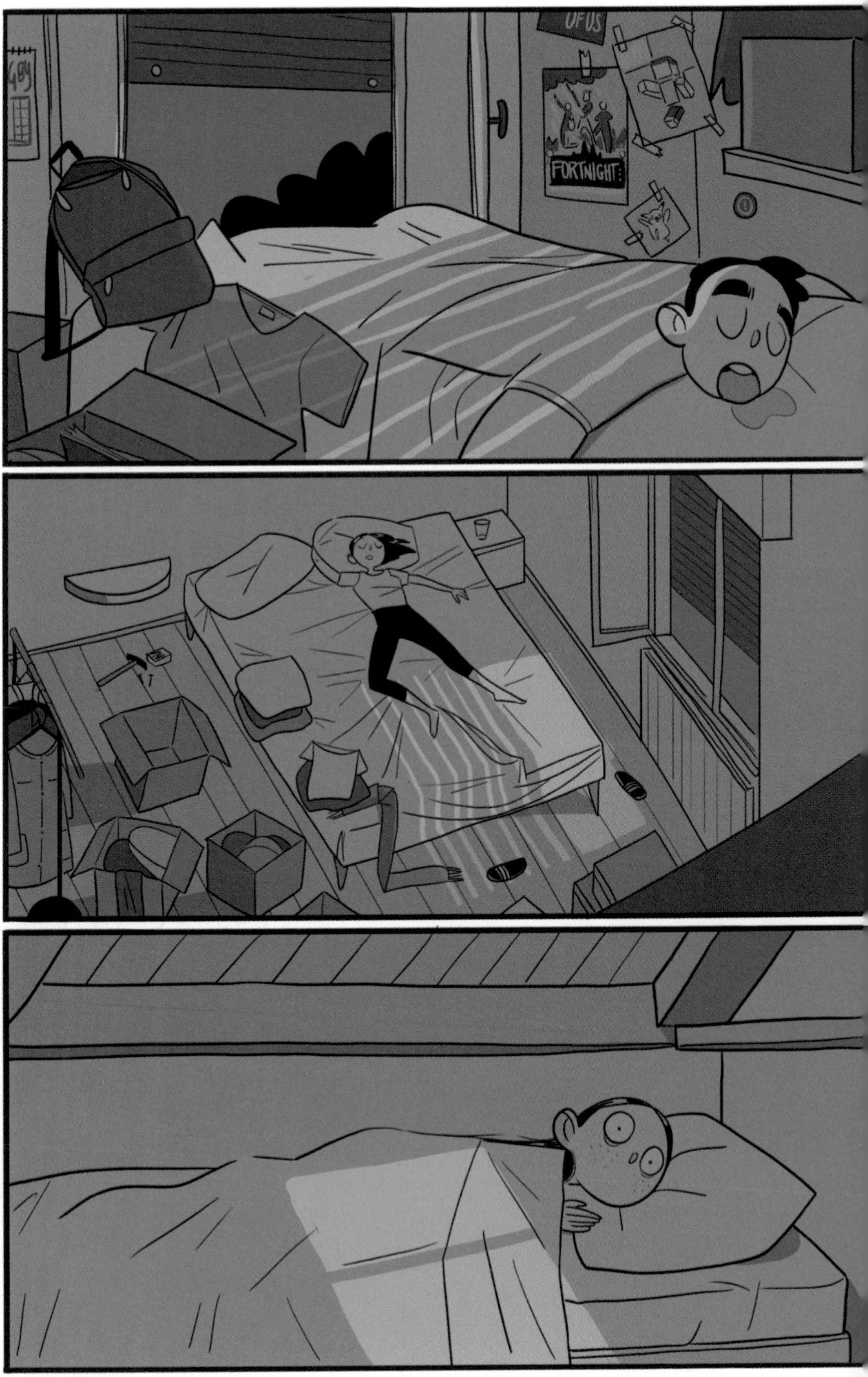
OF US
FORTNIGHT

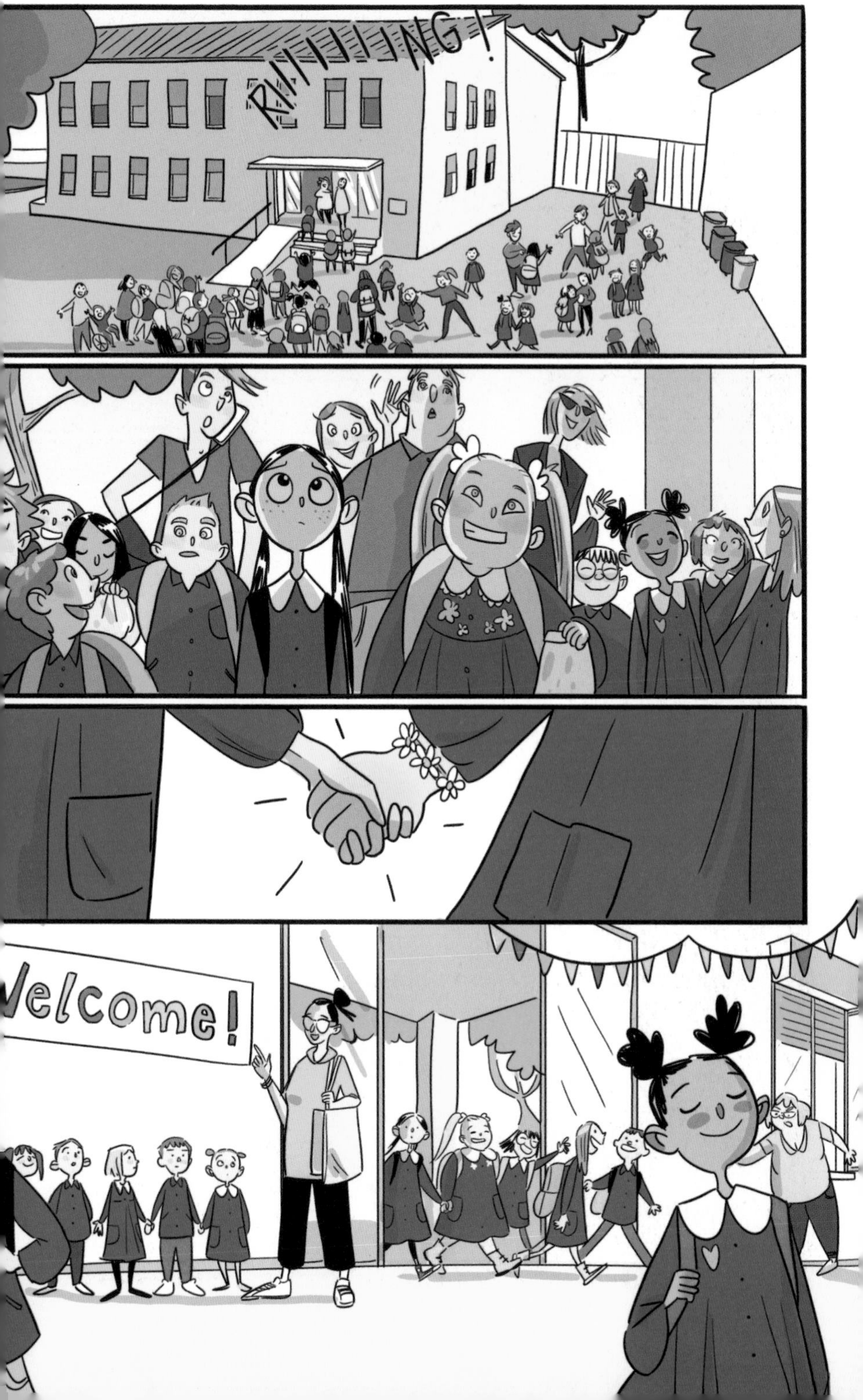
RIIIIIIING!
Welcome!

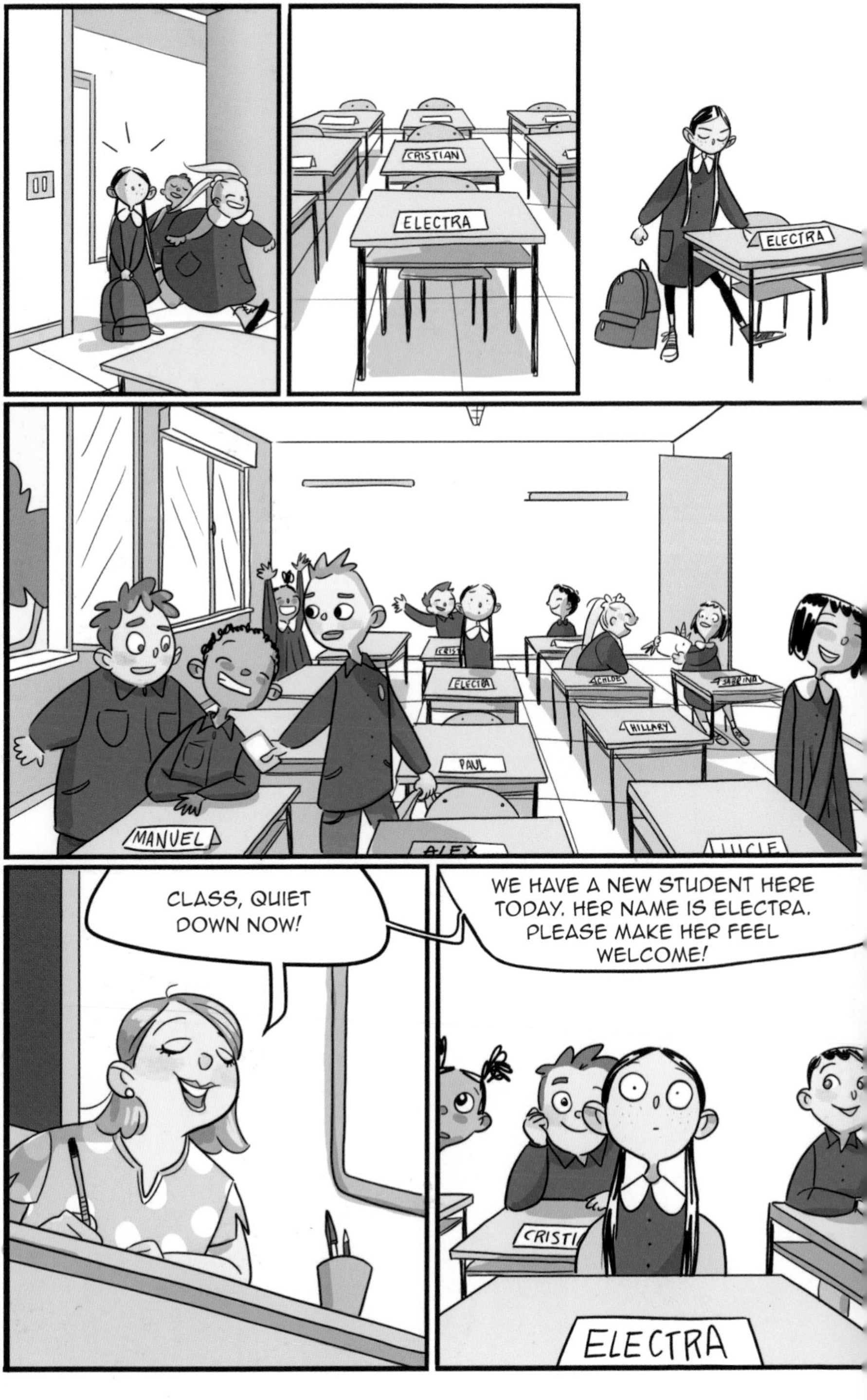
CRISTIAN
ELECTRA
ELECTRA
HILLARY
PAUL
MANUEL
CLASS, QUIET DOWN NOW!
WE HAVE A NEW STUDENT HERE TODAY. HER NAME IS ELECTRA. PLEASE MAKE HER FEEL WELCOME!
ELECTRA

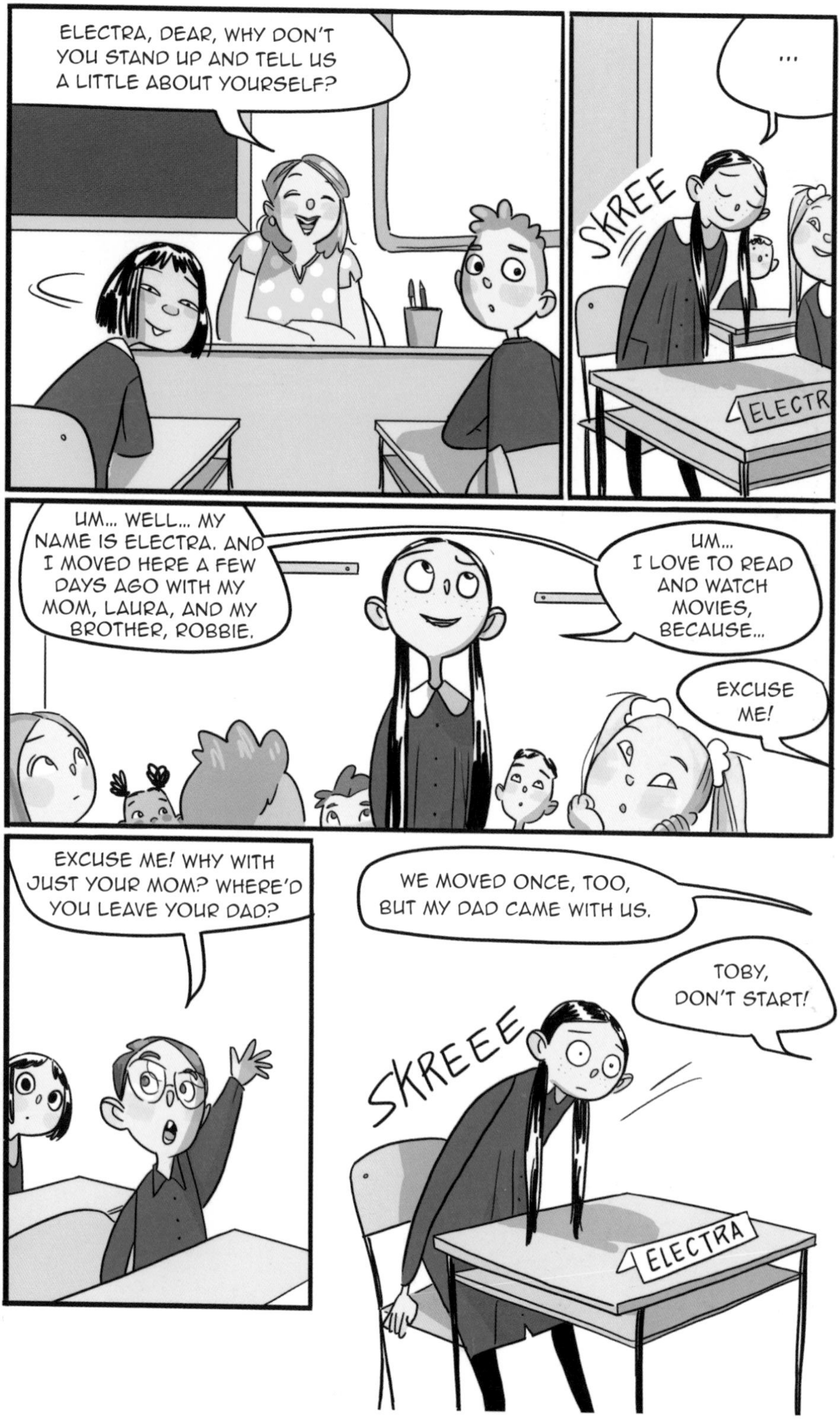
ELECTRA, DEAR, WHY DON'T YOU STAND UP AND TELL US A LITTLE ABOUT YOURSELF?
...
SKREE
ELECTR
UM... WELL... MY NAME IS ELECTRA. AND I MOVED HERE A FEW DAYS AGO WITH MY MOM, LAURA, AND MY BROTHER, ROBBIE.
UM... I LOVE TO READ AND WATCH MOVIES, BECAUSE...
EXCUSE ME!
EXCUSE ME! WHY WITH JUST YOUR MOM? WHERE'D YOU LEAVE YOUR DAD?
WE MOVED ONCE, TOO, BUT MY DAD CAME WITH US.
TOBY, DON'T START!
SKREEE
ELECTRA

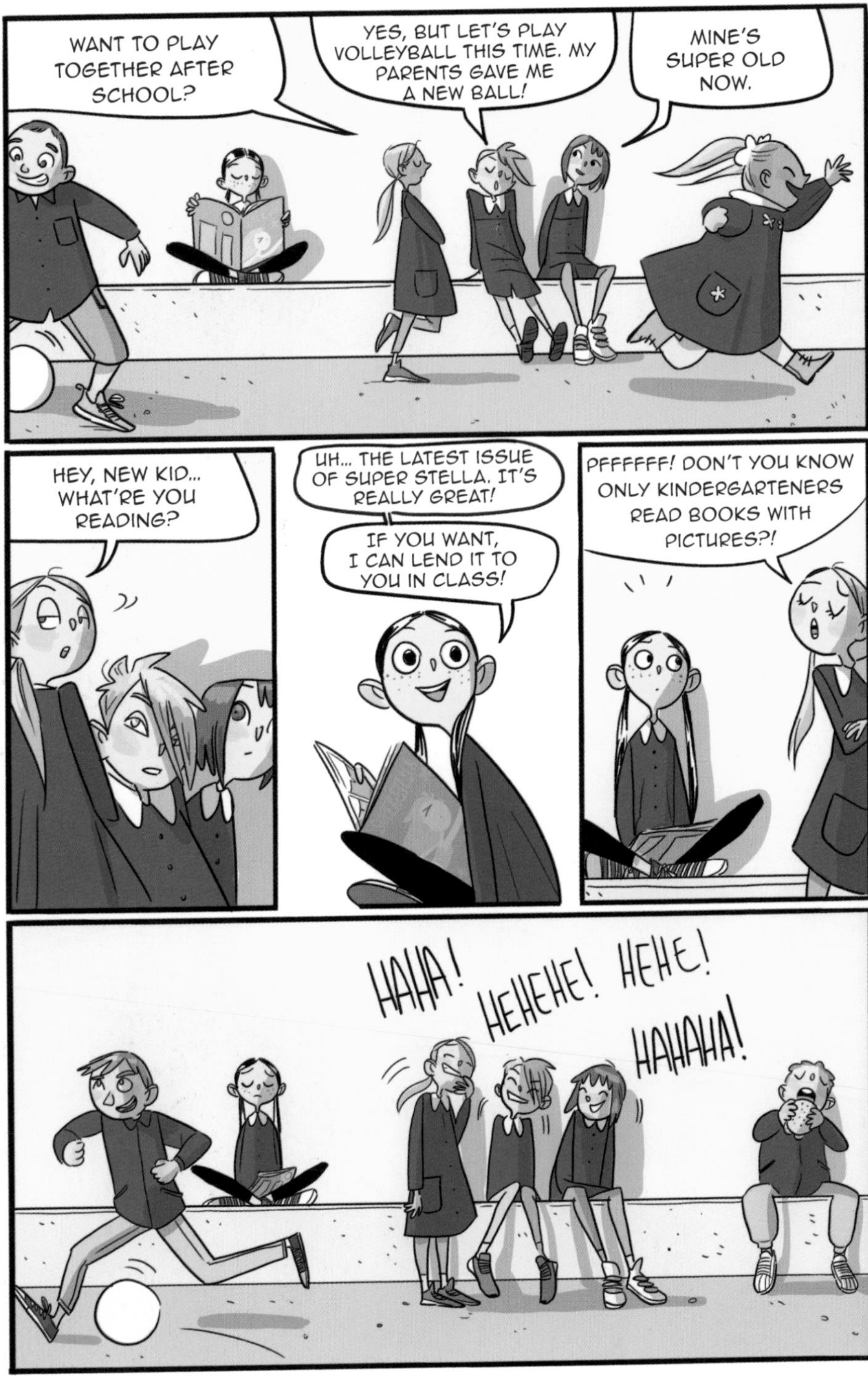
WANT TO PLAY TOGETHER AFTER SCHOOL?
YES, BUT LET'S PLAY VOLLEYBALL THIS TIME. MY PARENTS GAVE ME A NEW BALL!
MINE'S SUPER OLD NOW.
HEY, NEW KID... WHAT'RE YOU READING?
UH... THE LATEST ISSUE OF SUPER STELLA. IT'S REALLY GREAT!
IF YOU WANT, I CAN LEND IT TO YOU IN CLASS!
PFFFFFF! DON'T YOU KNOW ONLY KINDERGARTENERS READ BOOKS WITH PICTURES?!
HAHA! HEHEHE! HEHE! HAHAHA!

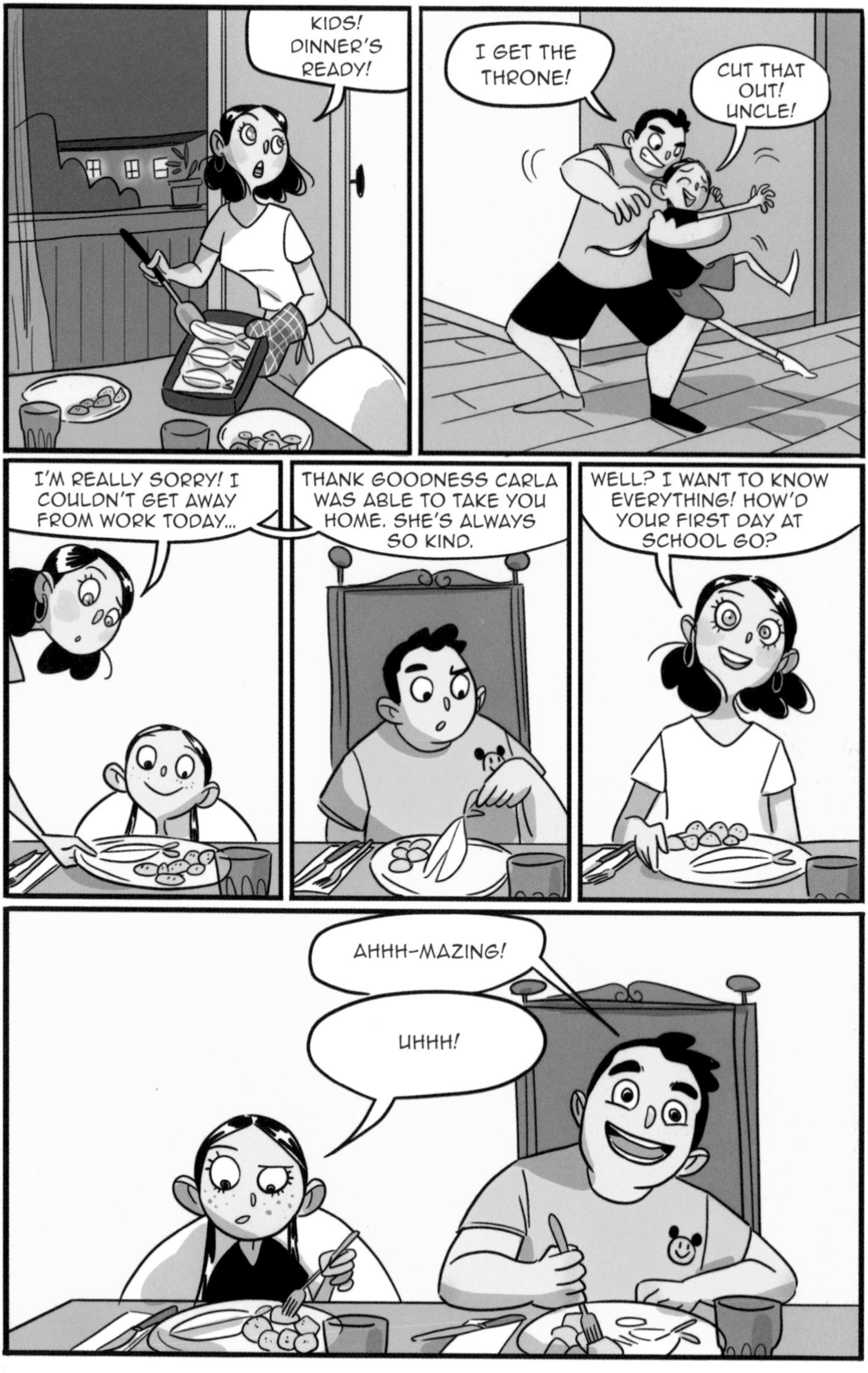
KIDS! DINNER'S READY!
I GET THE THRONE!
CUT THAT OUT! UNCLE!
I'M REALLY SORRY! I COULDN'T GET AWAY FROM WORK TODAY...
THANK GOODNESS CARLA WAS ABLE TO TAKE YOU HOME. SHE'S ALWAYS SO KIND.
WELL? I WANT TO KNOW EVERYTHING! HOW'D YOUR FIRST DAY AT SCHOOL GO?
AHHH-MAZING!
UHHH!

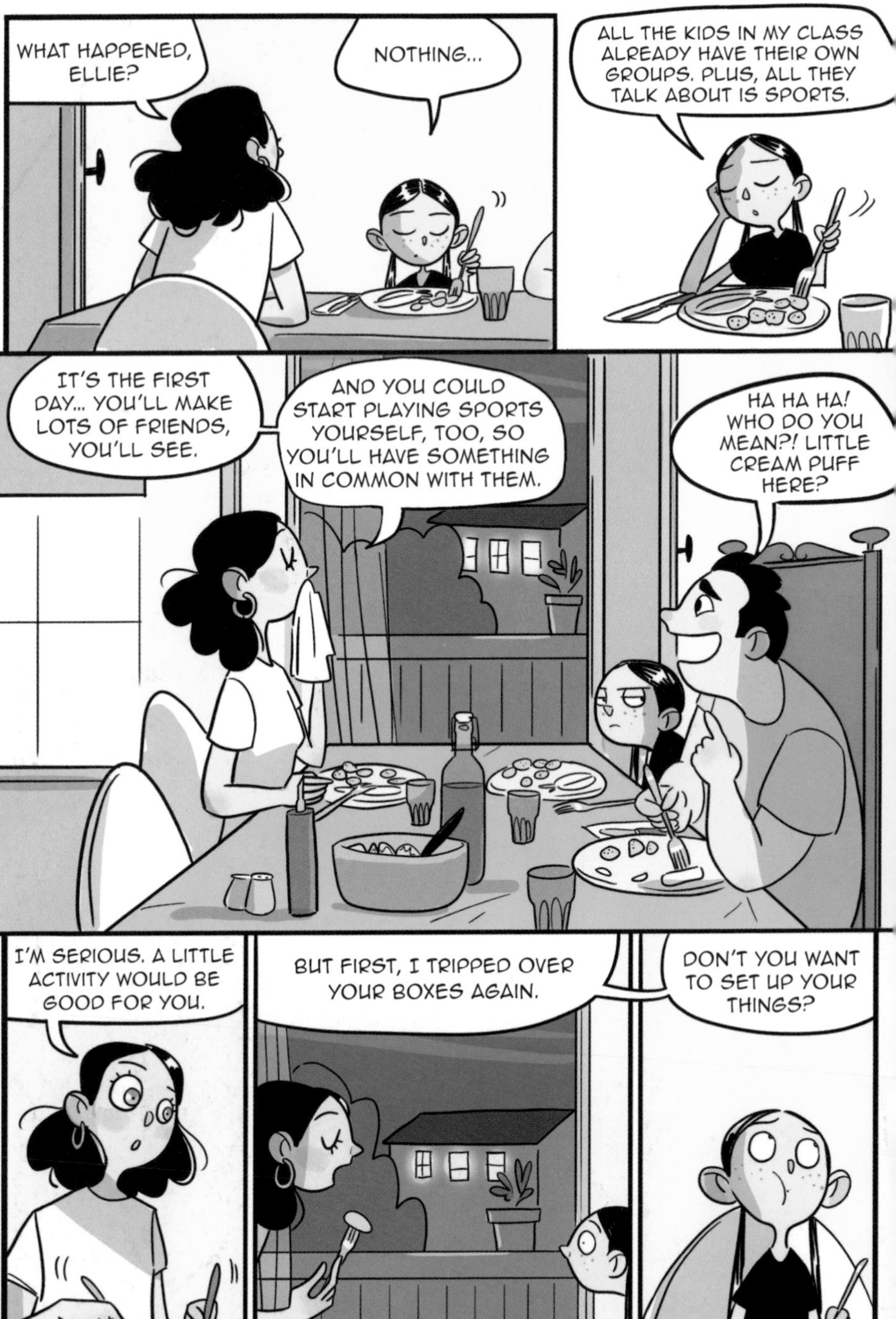
WHAT HAPPENED, ELLIE?
NOTHING...
ALL THE KIDS IN MY CLASS ALREADY HAVE THEIR OWN GROUPS. PLUS, ALL THEY TALK ABOUT IS SPORTS.
IT'S THE FIRST DAY... YOU'LL MAKE LOTS OF FRIENDS, YOU'LL SEE.
AND YOU COULD START PLAYING SPORTS YOURSELF, TOO, SO YOU'LL HAVE SOMETHING IN COMMON WITH THEM.
HA HA HA! WHO DO YOU MEAN?! LITTLE CREAM PUFF HERE?
I'M SERIOUS. A LITTLE ACTIVITY WOULD BE GOOD FOR YOU.
BUT FIRST, I TRIPPED OVER YOUR BOXES AGAIN.
DON'T YOU WANT TO SET UP YOUR THINGS?

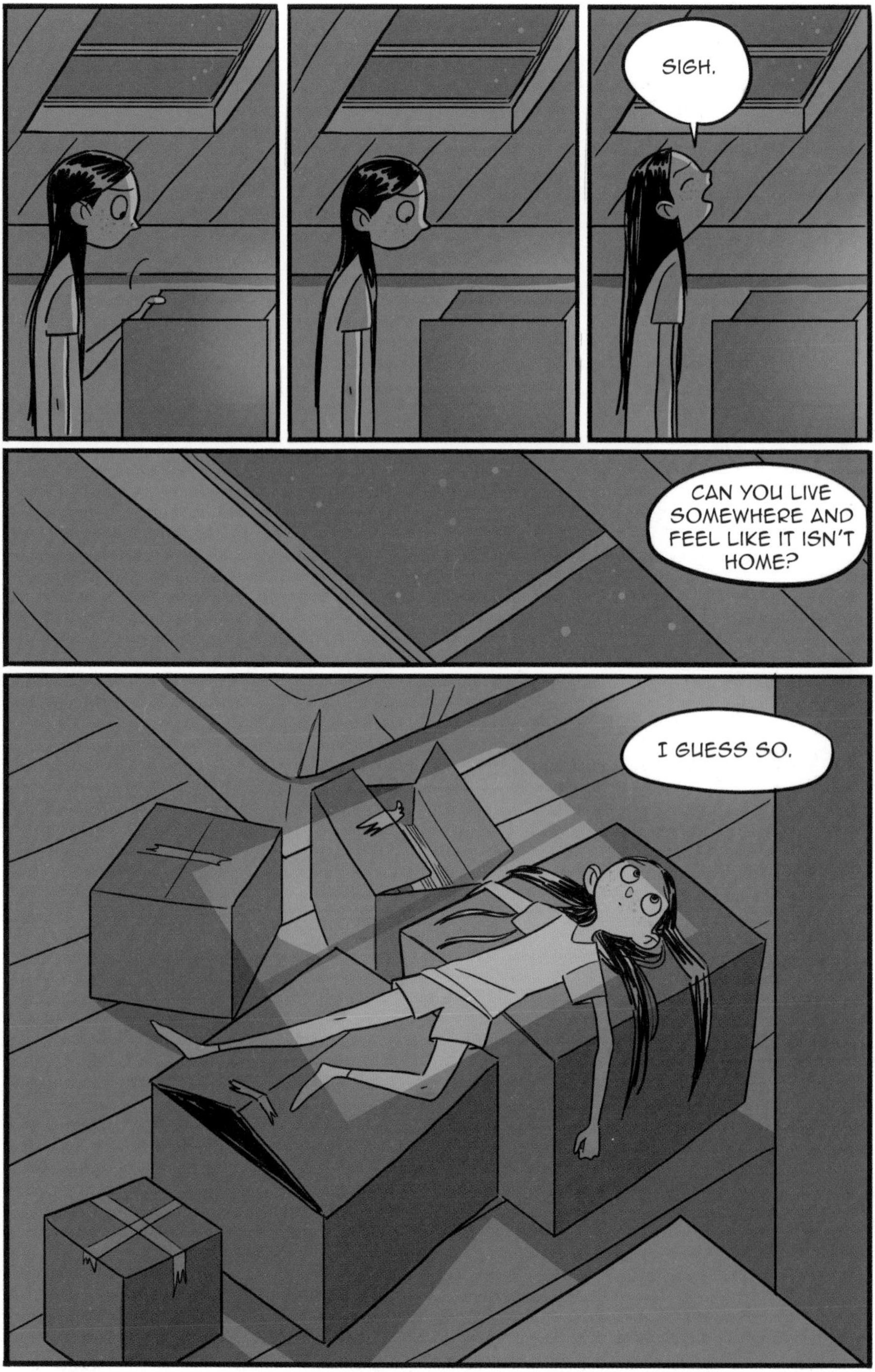
SIGH.
CAN YOU LIVE SOMEWHERE AND FEEL LIKE IT ISN'T HOME?
I GUESS SO.

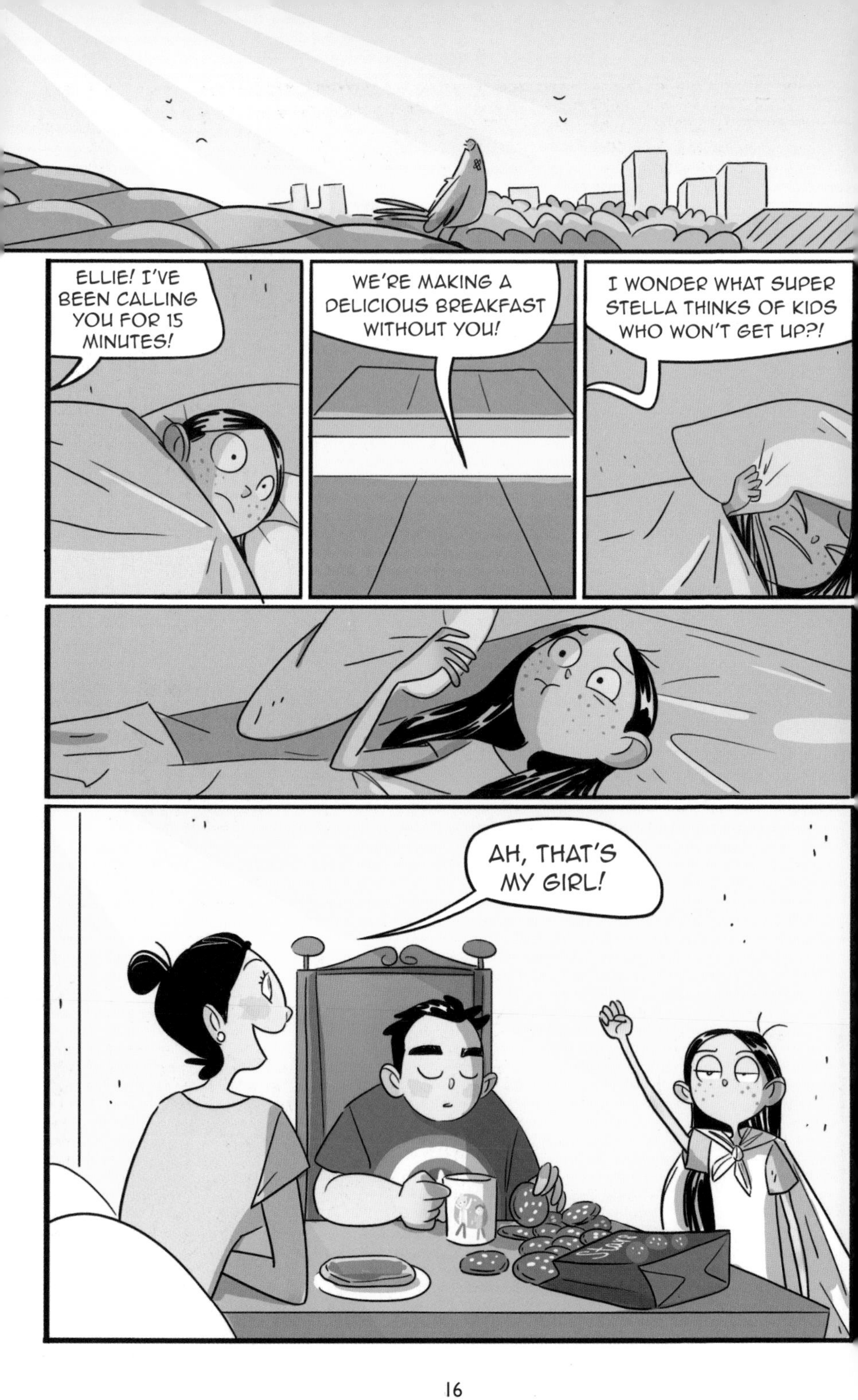
ELLIE! I'VE BEEN CALLING YOU FOR 15 MINUTES!
WE'RE MAKING A DELICIOUS BREAKFAST WITHOUT YOU!
I WONDER WHAT SUPER STELLA THINKS OF KIDS WHO WON'T GET UP?!
AH, THAT'S MY GIRL!

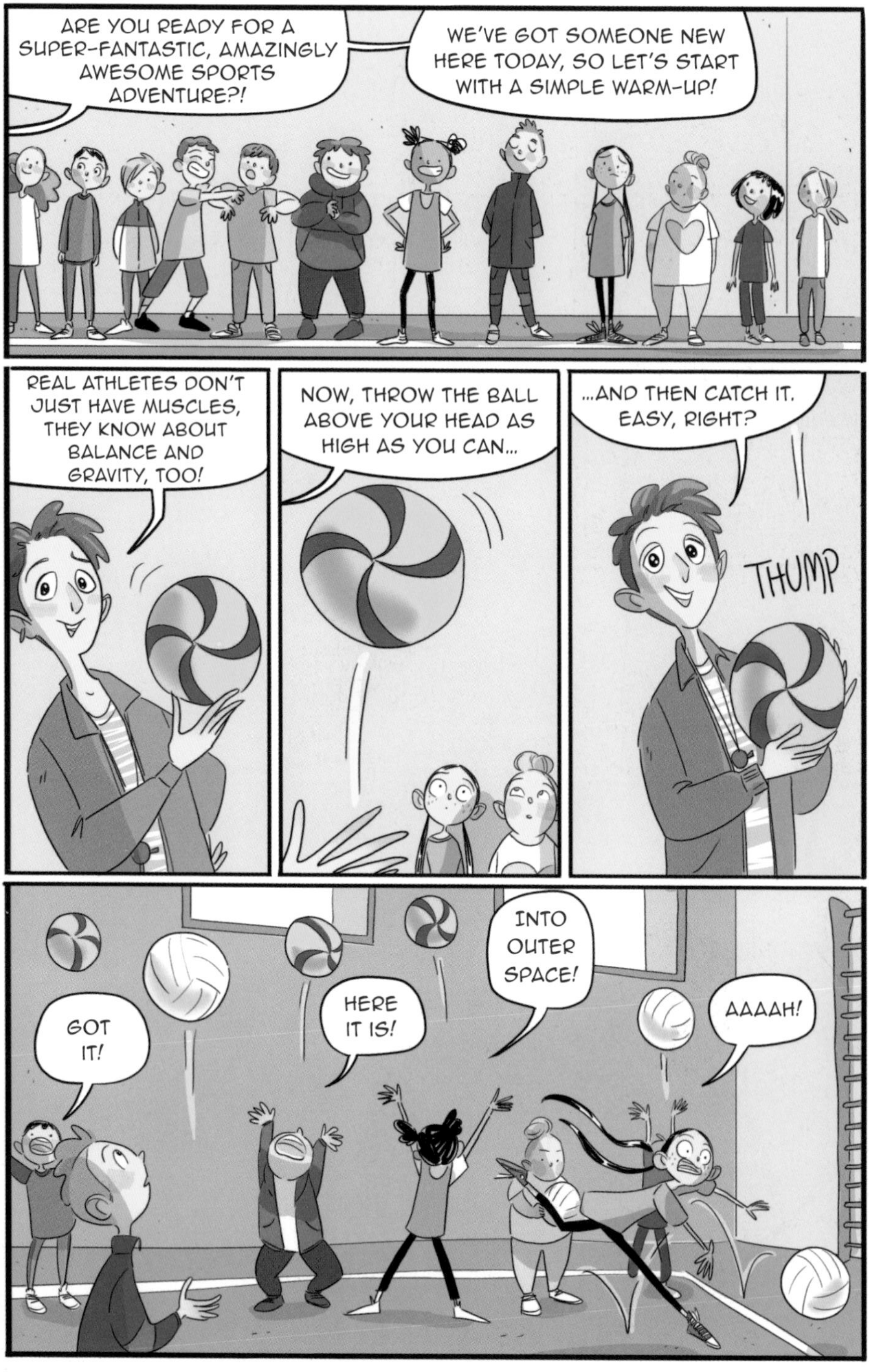
ARE YOU READY FOR A SUPER-FANTASTIC, AMAZINGLY AWESOME SPORTS ADVENTURE?!
WE'VE GOT SOMEONE NEW HERE TODAY, SO LET'S START WITH A SIMPLE WARM-UP!
REAL ATHLETES DON'T JUST HAVE MUSCLES, THEY KNOW ABOUT BALANCE AND GRAVITY, TOO!
NOW, THROW THE BALL ABOVE YOUR HEAD AS HIGH AS YOU CAN...
...AND THEN CATCH IT. EASY, RIGHT?
THUMP
GOT IT!
HERE IT IS!
INTO OUTER SPACE!
AAAAH!

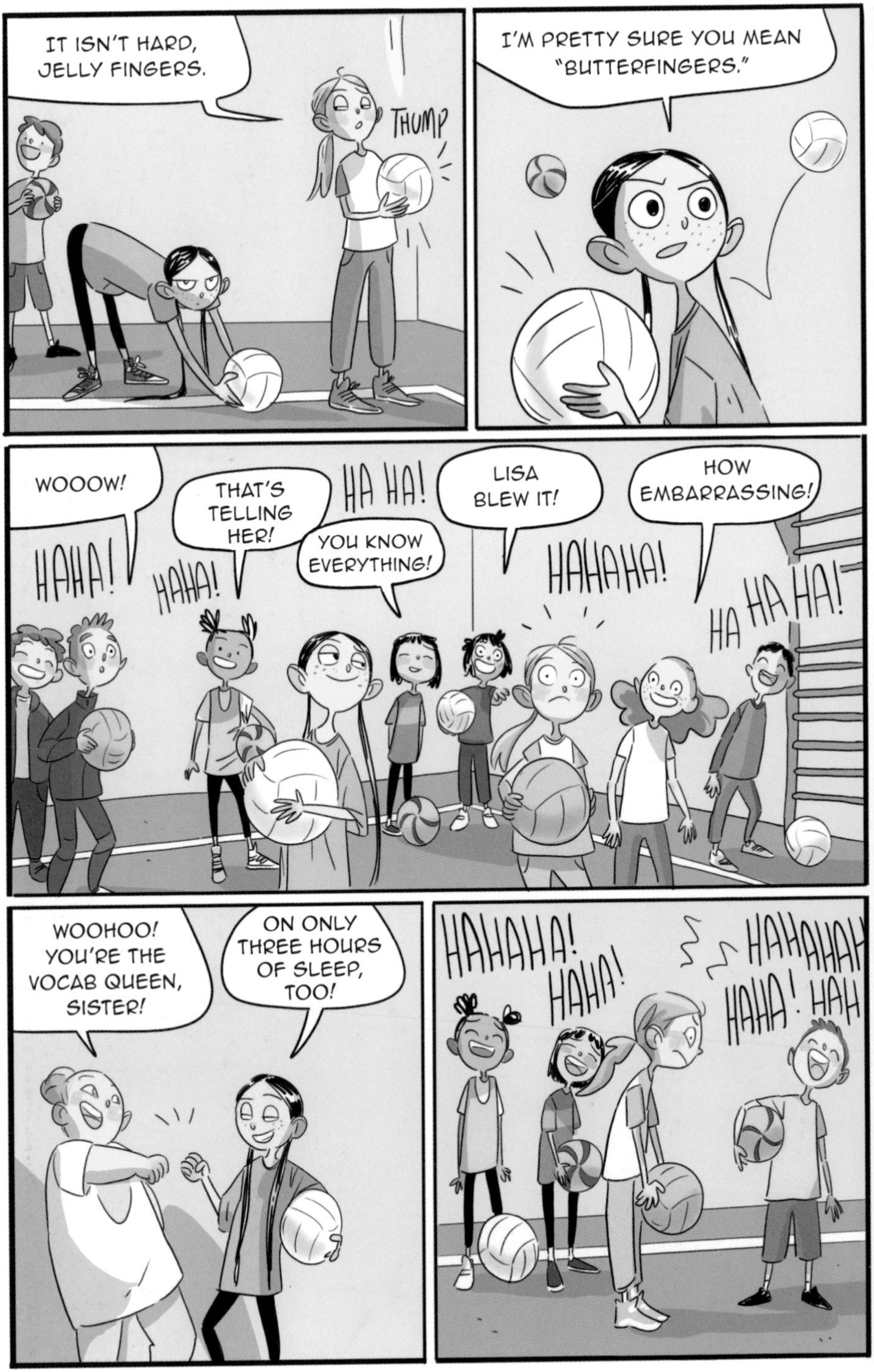
IT ISN'T HARD, JELLY FINGERS.
THUMP
I'M PRETTY SURE YOU MEAN "BUTTERFINGERS."
WOOOW!
HAHA!
HAHA!
THAT'S TELLING HER!
HA HA!
YOU KNOW EVERYTHING!
LISA BLEW IT!
HAHAHA!
HOW EMBARRASSING!
HA HA HA!
WOOHOO! YOU'RE THE VOCAB QUEEN, SISTER!
ON ONLY THREE HOURS OF SLEEP, TOO!
HAHAHA!
HAHA!
HAHA!

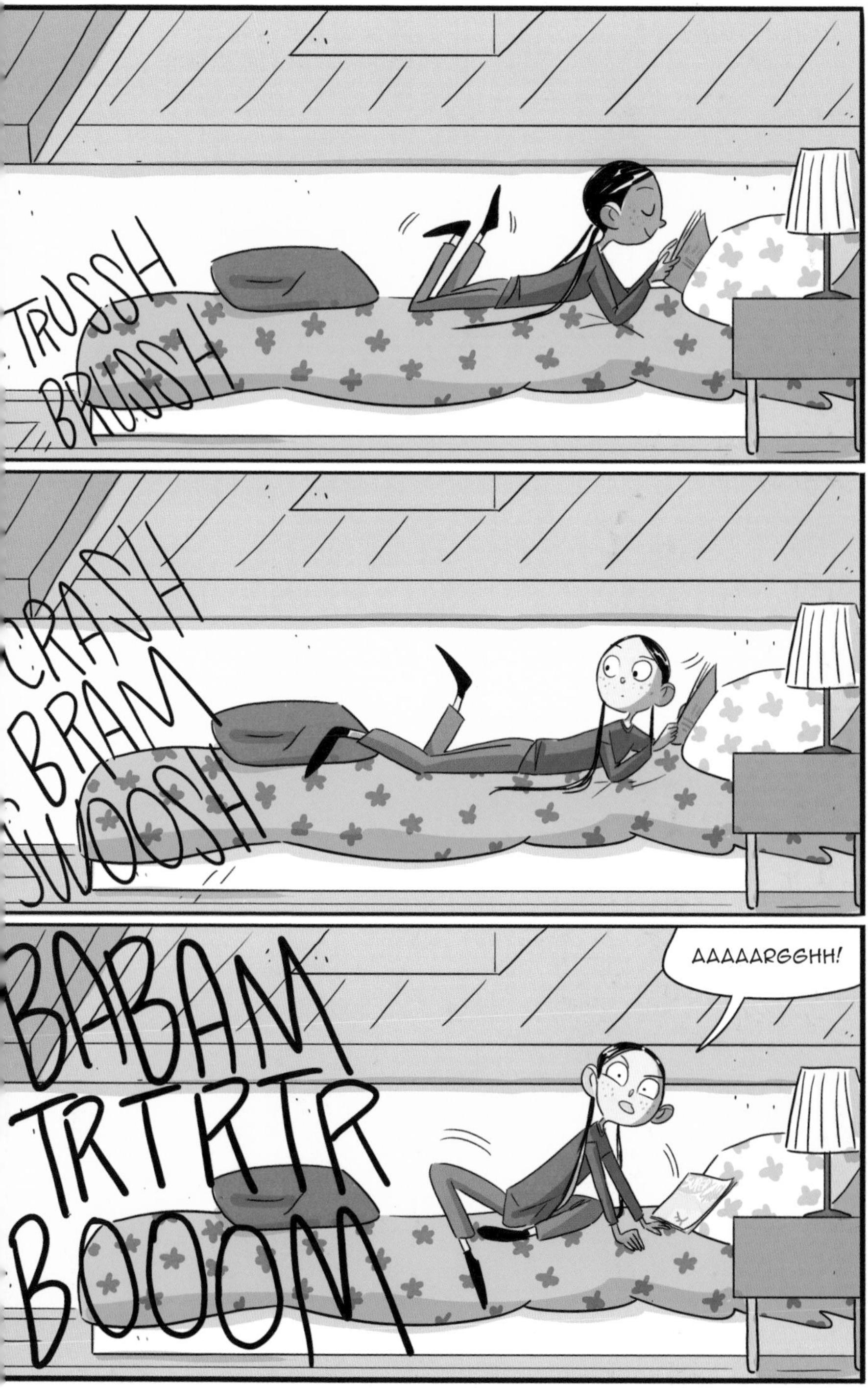
TRUSSH
BRUSSH
CRASH
BRAM
JUOOSH
BABAM
TRTRTR
BOOOM
AAAAARGGHH!

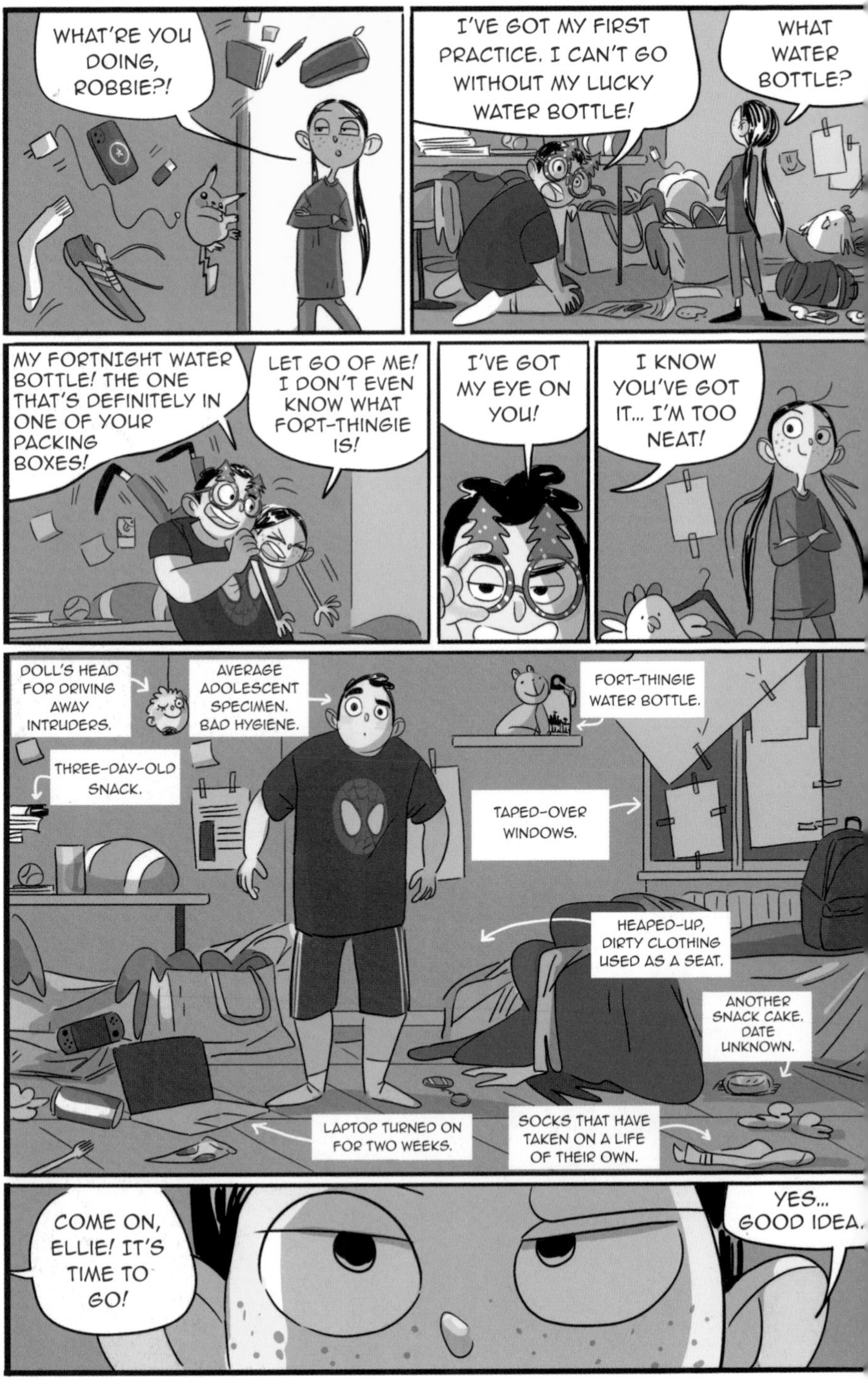

WHAT'RE YOU DOING, ROBBIE?!
I'VE GOT MY FIRST PRACTICE. I CAN'T GO WITHOUT MY LUCKY WATER BOTTLE!
WHAT WATER BOTTLE?
MY FORTNIGHT WATER BOTTLE! THE ONE THAT'S DEFINITELY IN ONE OF YOUR PACKING BOXES!
LET GO OF ME! I DON'T EVEN KNOW WHAT FORT-THINGIE IS!
I'VE GOT MY EYE ON YOU!
I KNOW YOU'VE GOT IT... I'M TOO NEAT!
DOLL'S HEAD FOR DRIVING AWAY INTRUDERS.
AVERAGE ADOLESCENT SPECIMEN. BAD HYGIENE.
FORT-THINGIE WATER BOTTLE.
THREE-DAY-OLD SNACK.
TAPED-OVER WINDOWS.
HEAPED-UP, DIRTY CLOTHING USED AS A SEAT.
ANOTHER SNACK CAKE. DATE UNKNOWN.
LAPTOP TURNED ON FOR TWO WEEKS.
SOCKS THAT HAVE TAKEN ON A LIFE OF THEIR OWN.
COME ON, ELLIE! IT'S TIME TO GO!
YES... GOOD IDEA.

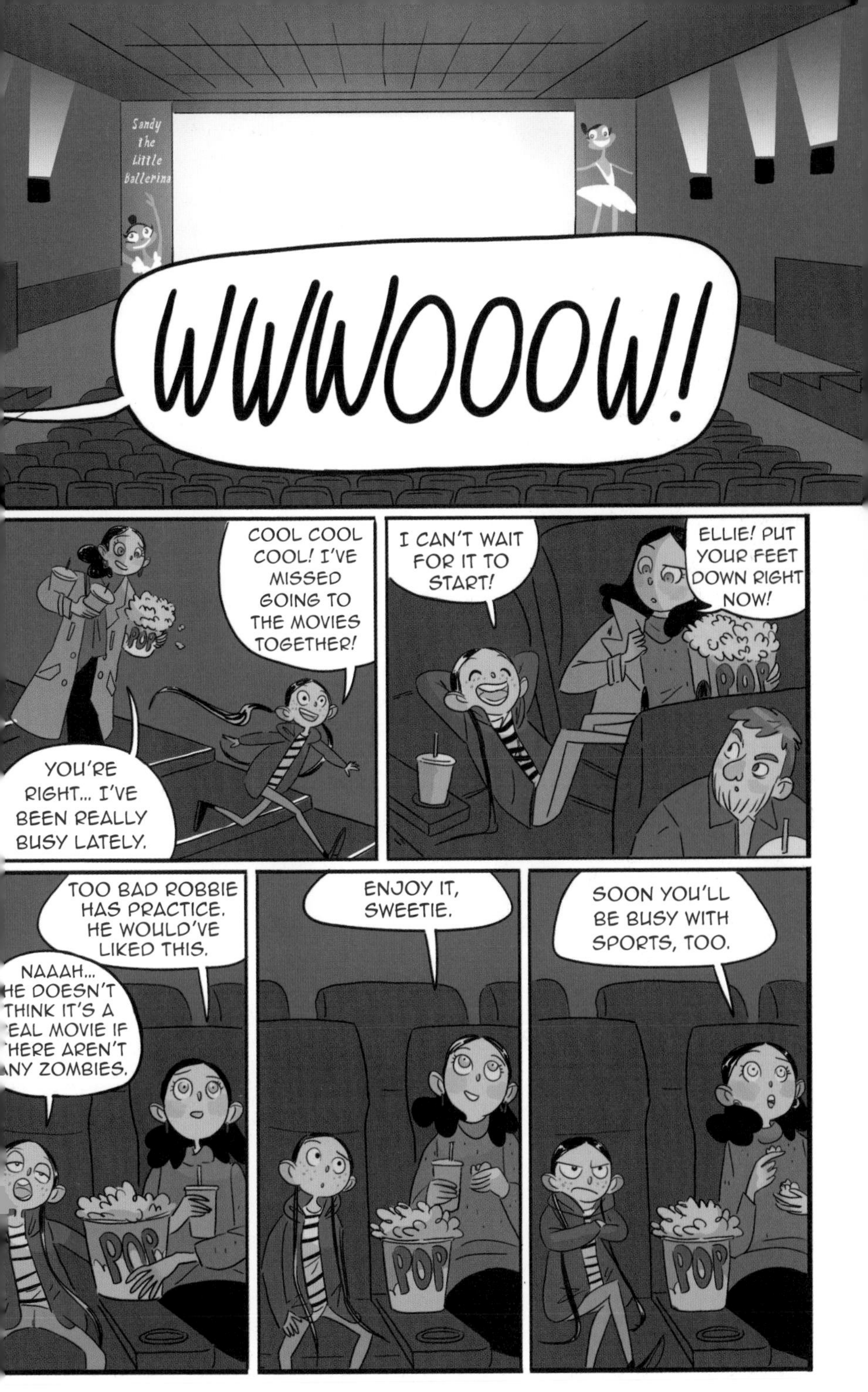
Sandy the Little Ballerina
WWWOOOW!
COOL COOL COOL! I'VE MISSED GOING TO THE MOVIES TOGETHER!
YOU'RE RIGHT... I'VE BEEN REALLY BUSY LATELY.
I CAN'T WAIT FOR IT TO START!
ELLIE! PUT YOUR FEET DOWN RIGHT NOW!
TOO BAD ROBBIE HAS PRACTICE. HE WOULD'VE LIKED THIS.
NAAAH... HE DOESN'T THINK IT'S A REAL MOVIE IF THERE AREN'T ANY ZOMBIES.
ENJOY IT, SWEETIE.
SOON YOU'LL BE BUSY WITH SPORTS, TOO.

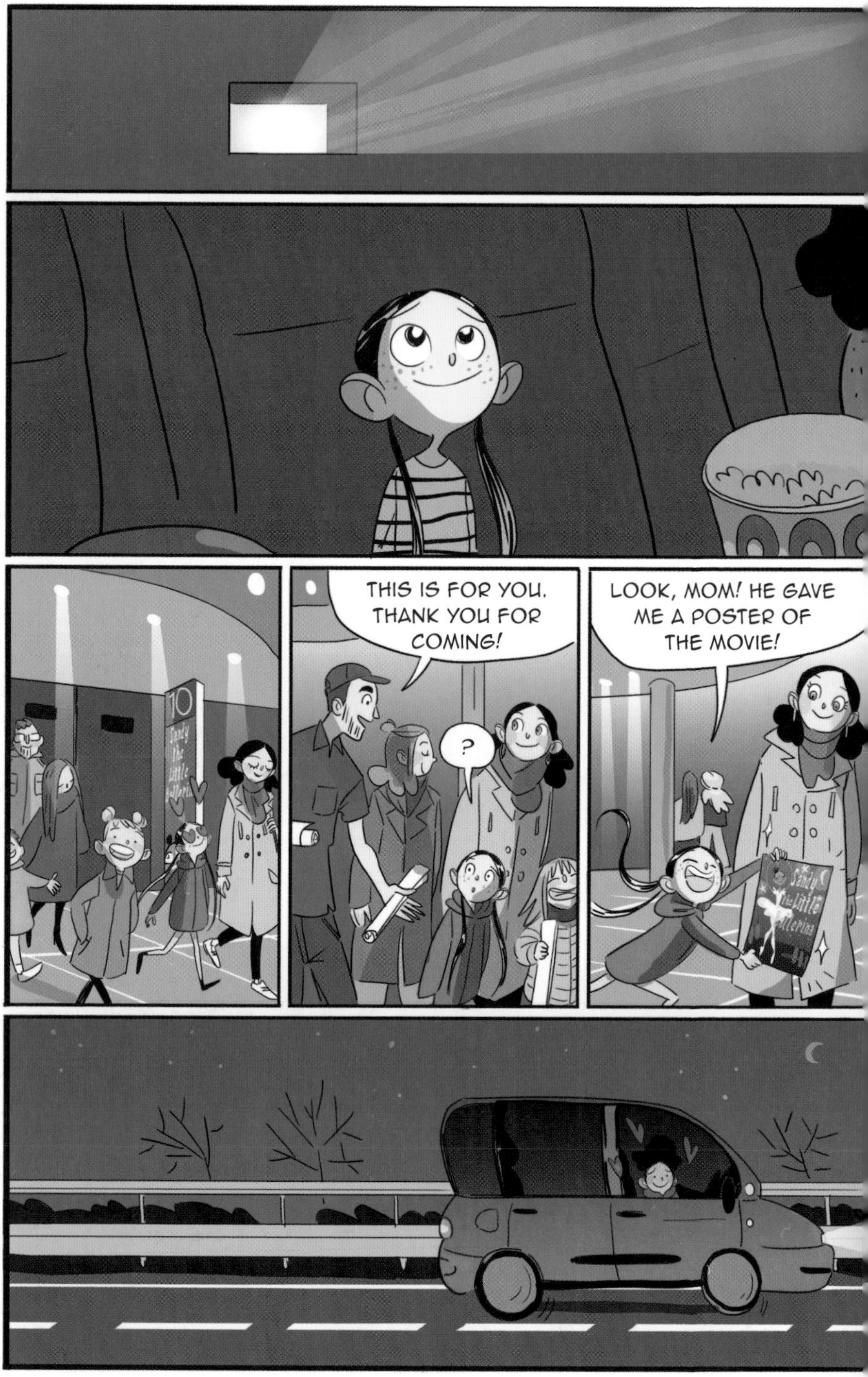
THIS IS FOR YOU. THANK YOU FOR COMING!
?
LOOK, MOM! HE GAVE ME A POSTER OF THE MOVIE!

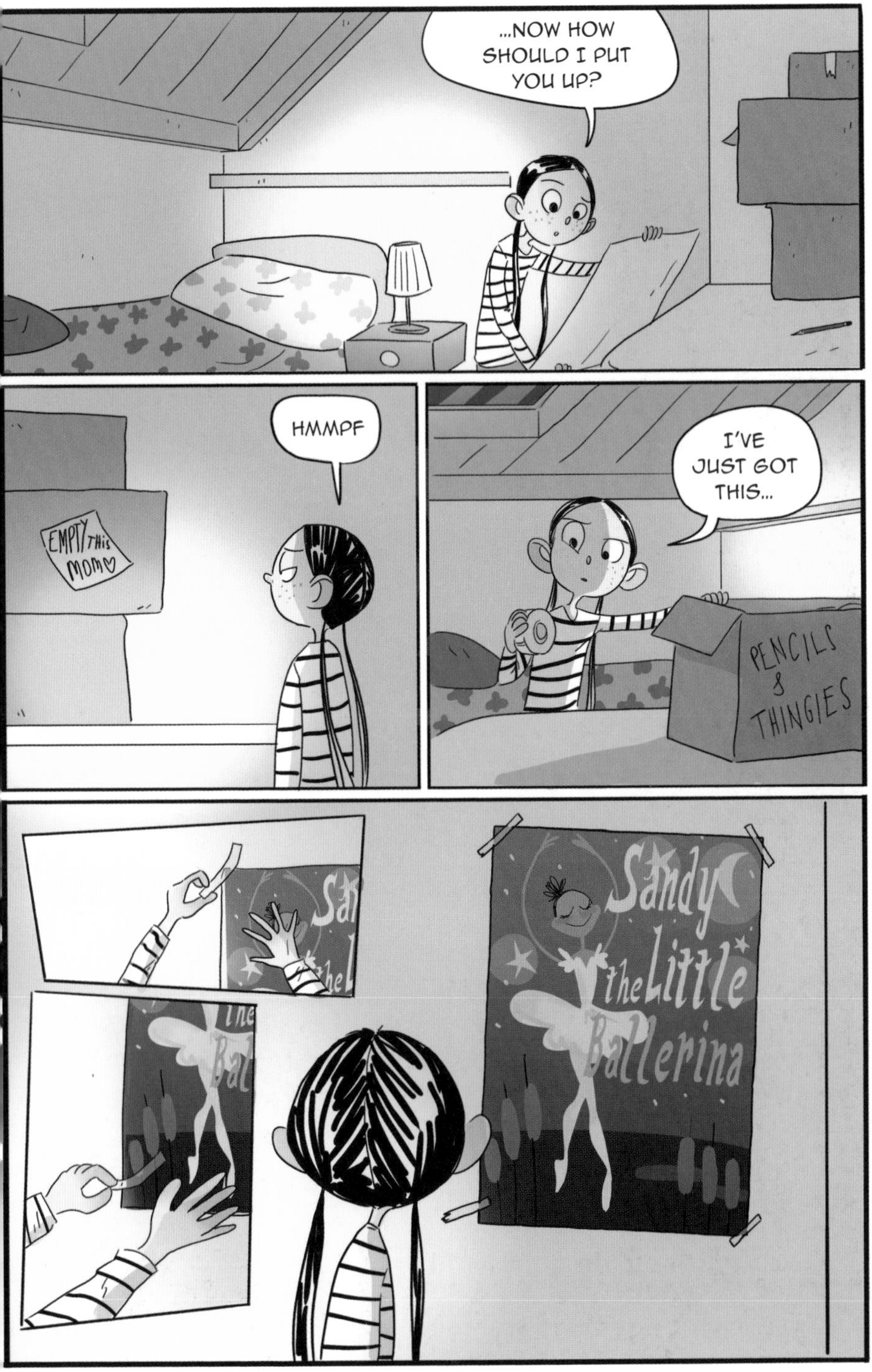
...NOW HOW SHOULD I PUT YOU UP?
HMMPF
EMPTY THIS MOM
I'VE JUST GOT THIS...
PENCILS & THINGIES
Sandy the Little Ballerina

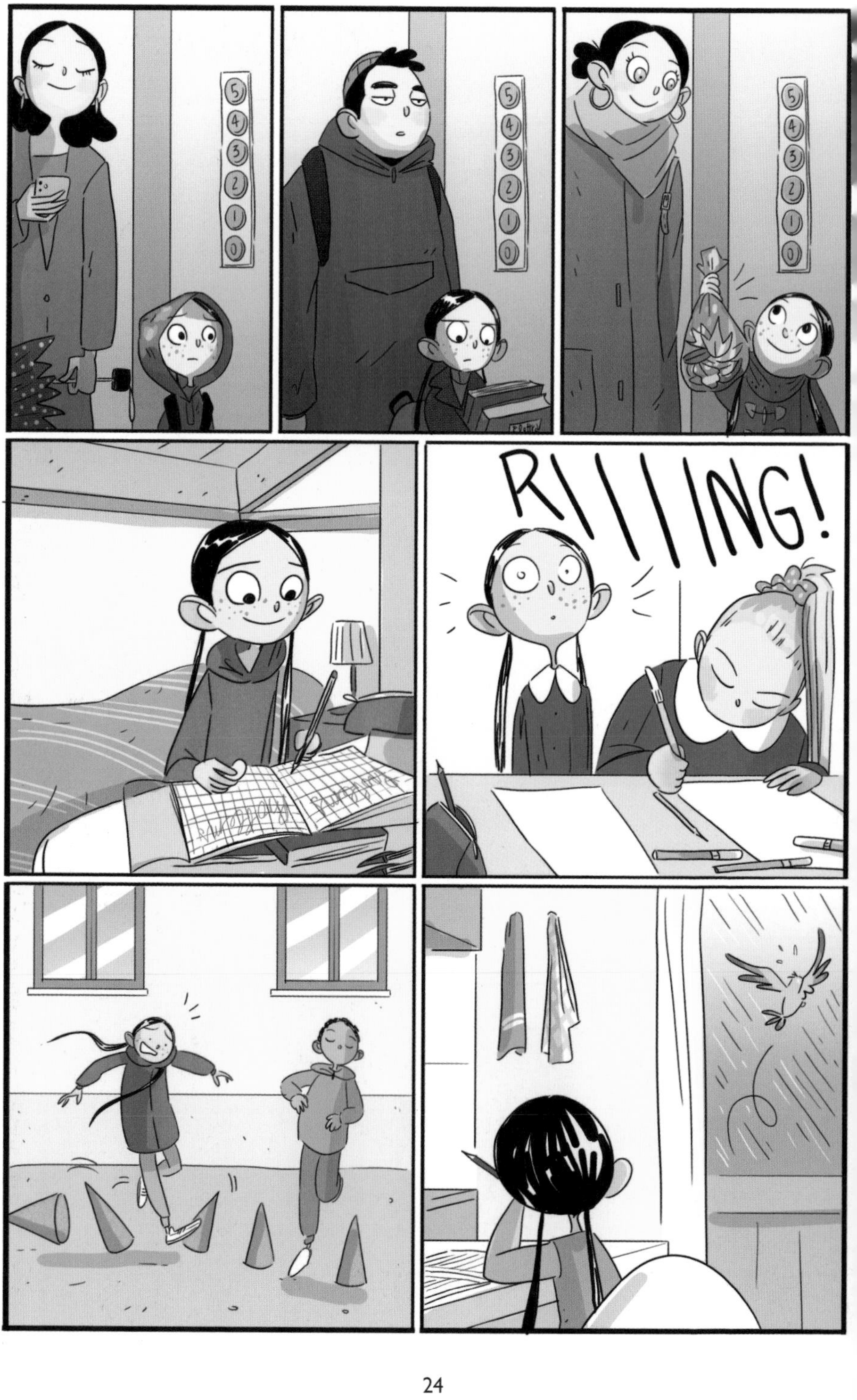
RIIIING!

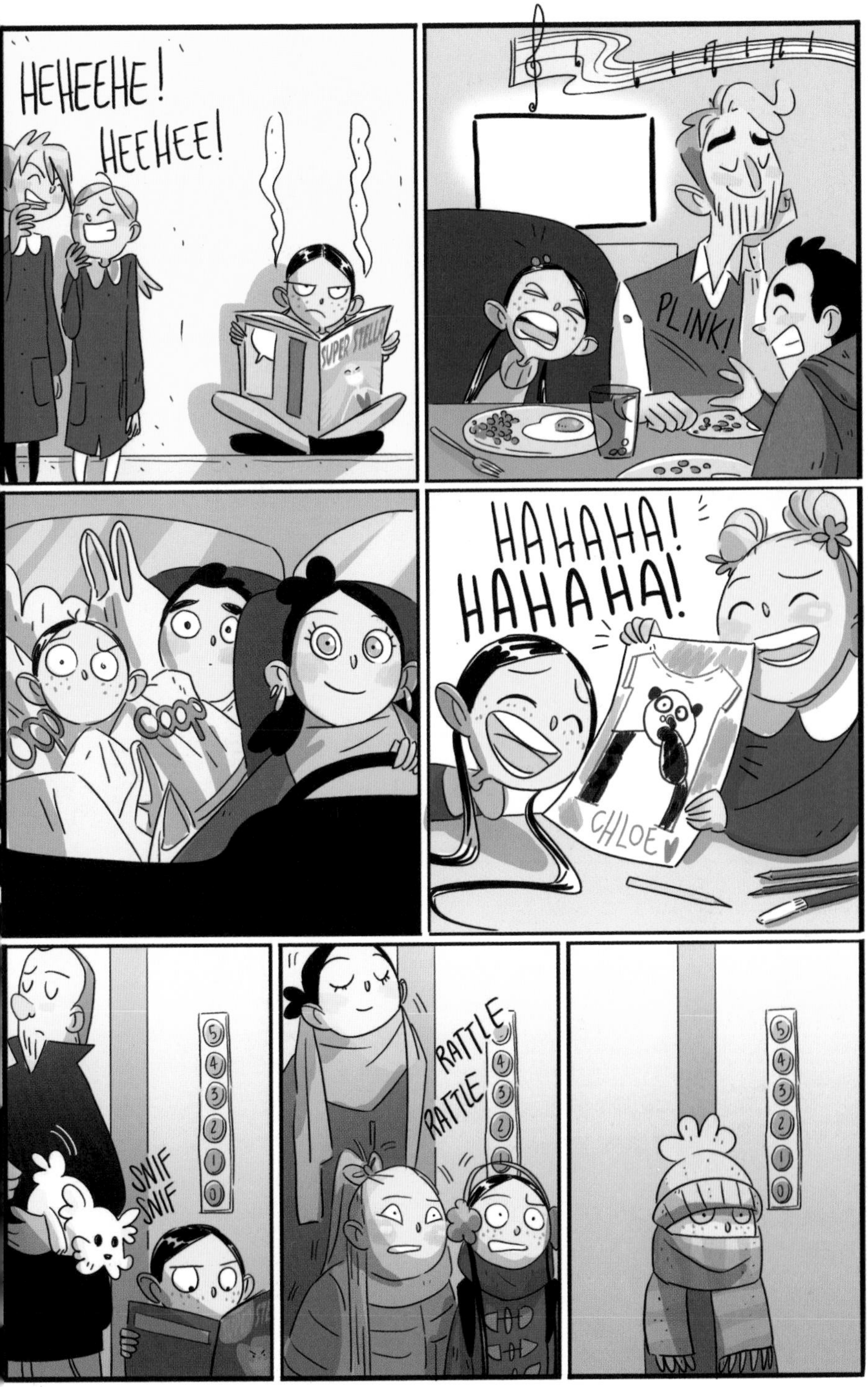
HEHEEHE!
HEEHEE!
SUPER STELLA
PLINK!
COOP
COOP
HAHAHA!
HAHAHA!
CHLOE
SNIF
SNIF
RATTLE
RATTLE

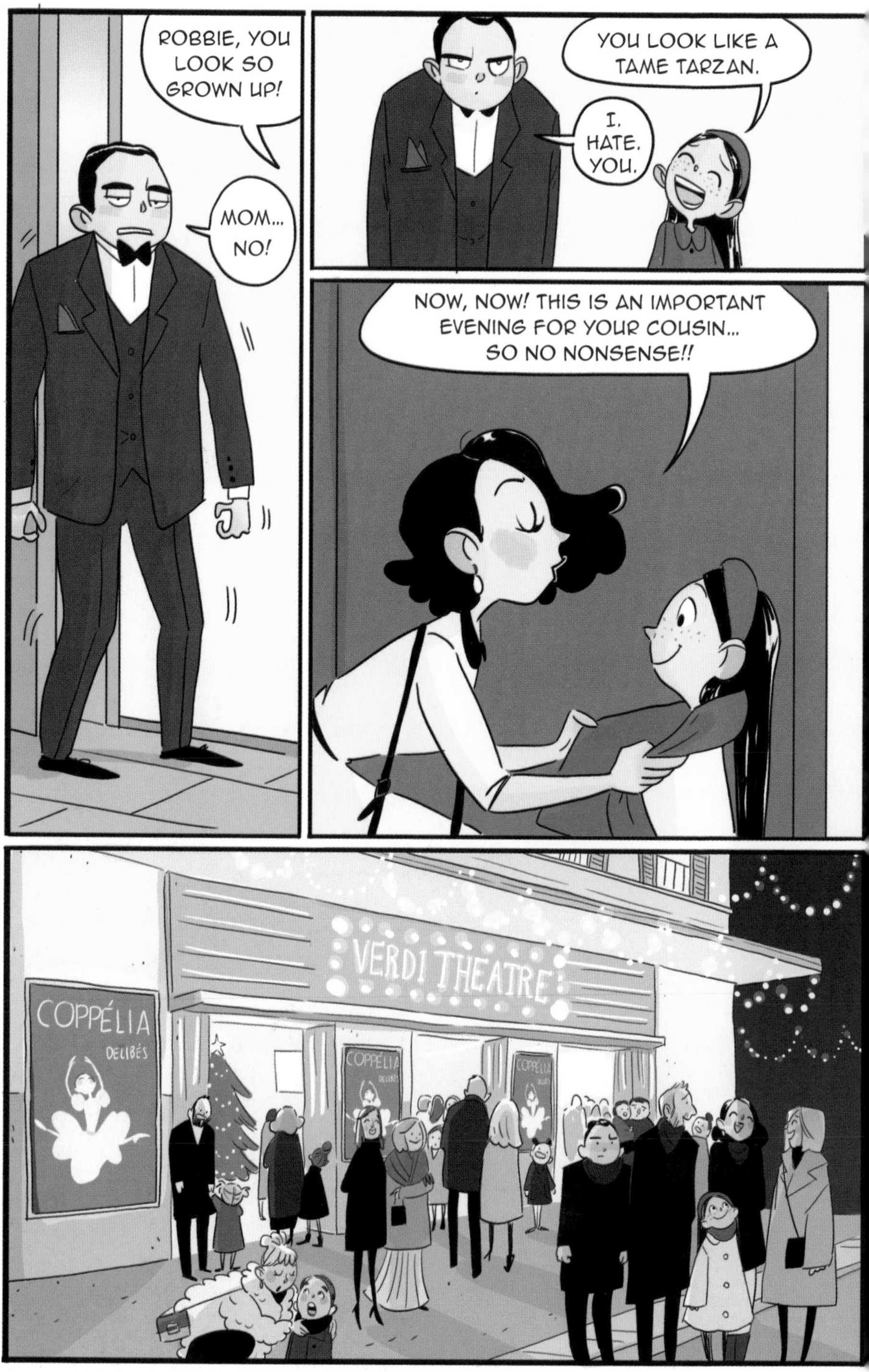
ROBBIE, YOU LOOK SO GROWN UP!
MOM... NO!
YOU LOOK LIKE A TAME TARZAN.
I. HATE. YOU.
NOW, NOW! THIS IS AN IMPORTANT EVENING FOR YOUR COUSIN... SO NO NONSENSE!!
VERDI THEATRE
COPPÉLIA
DELIBÉS
COPPÉLIA
DELIBÉS
COPPÉLIA

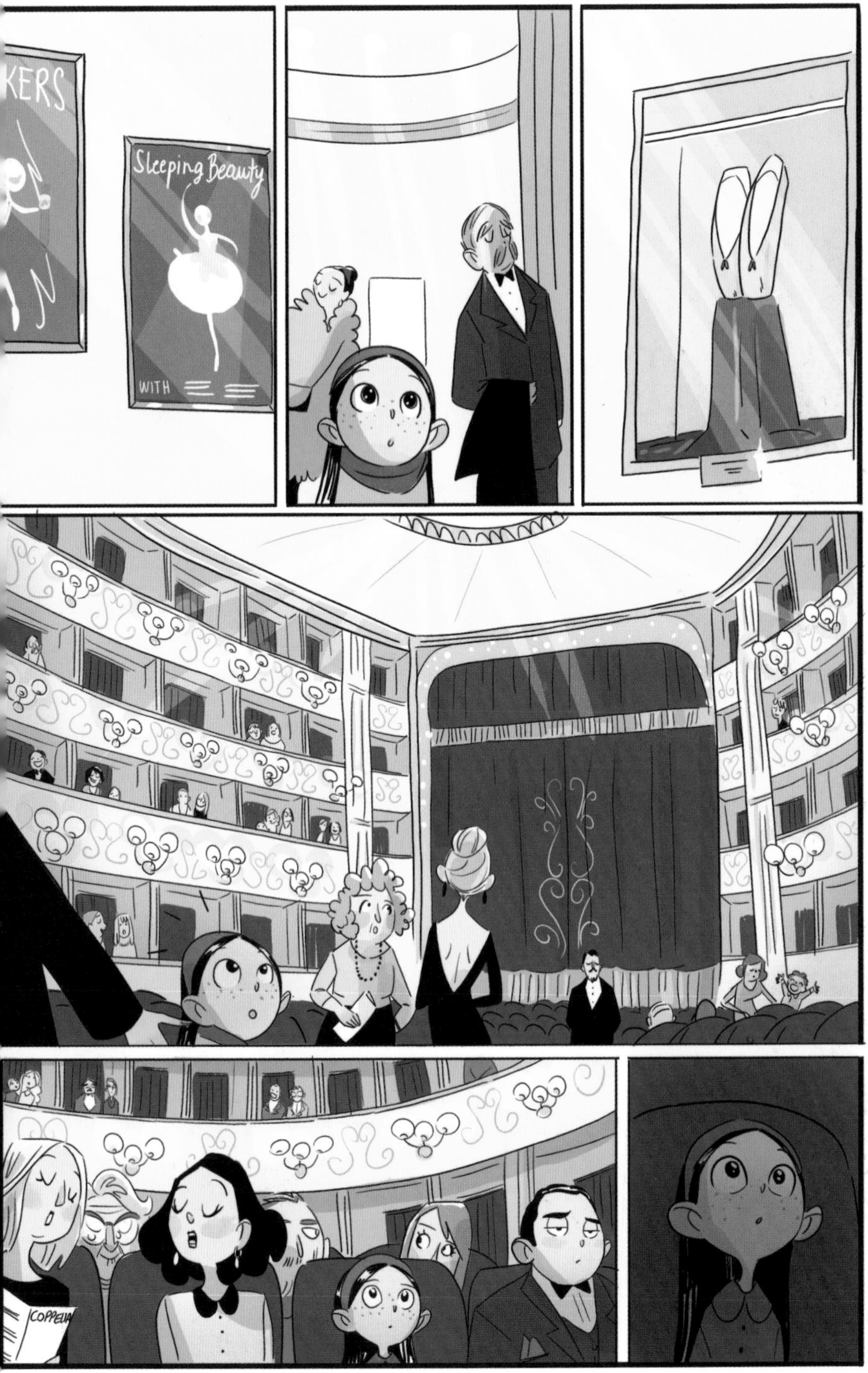
KERS
Sleeping Beauty
WITH
COPPELIA

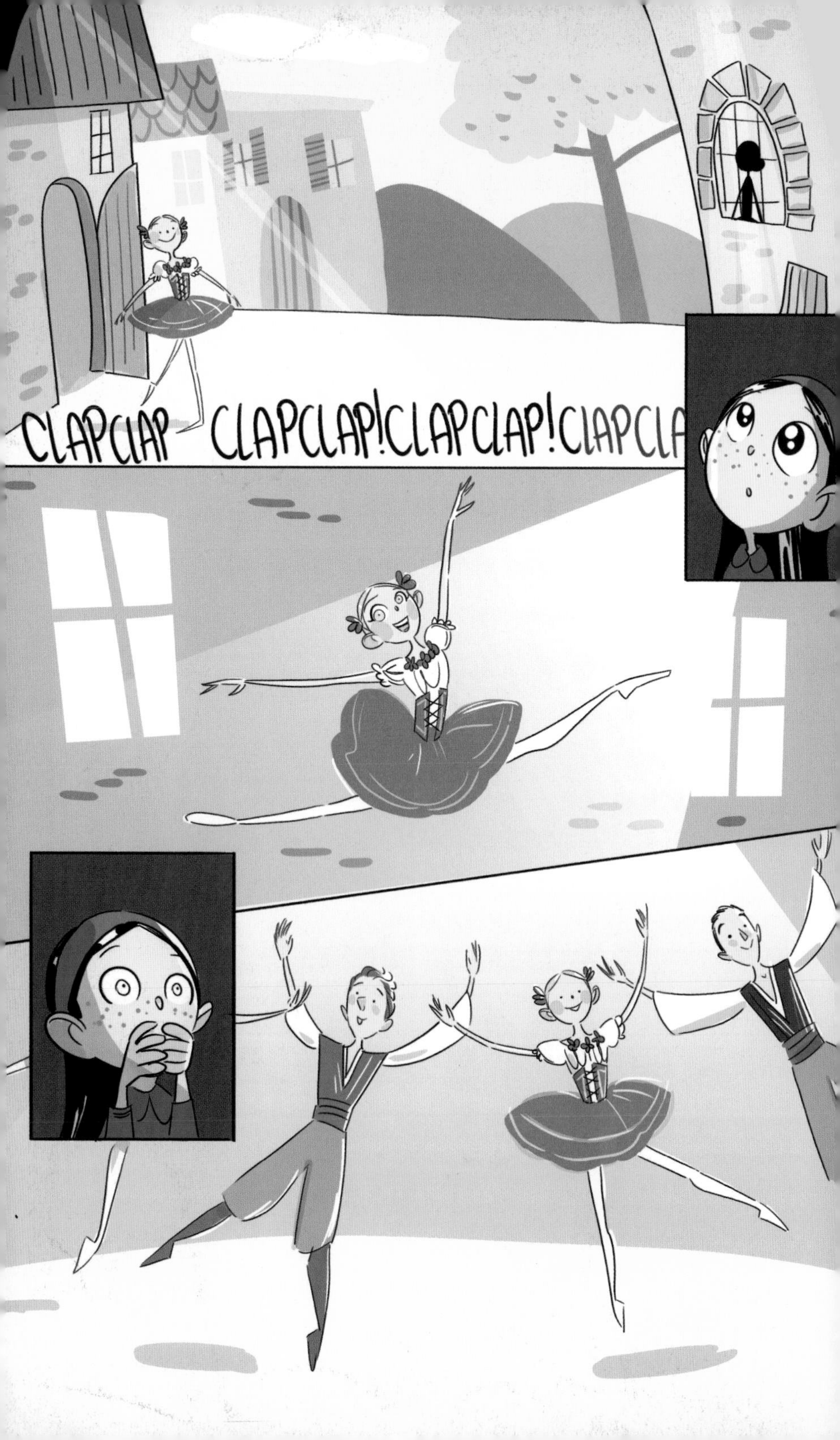
CLAPCLAP CLAPCLAP!CLAPCLAP!CLAPCLA

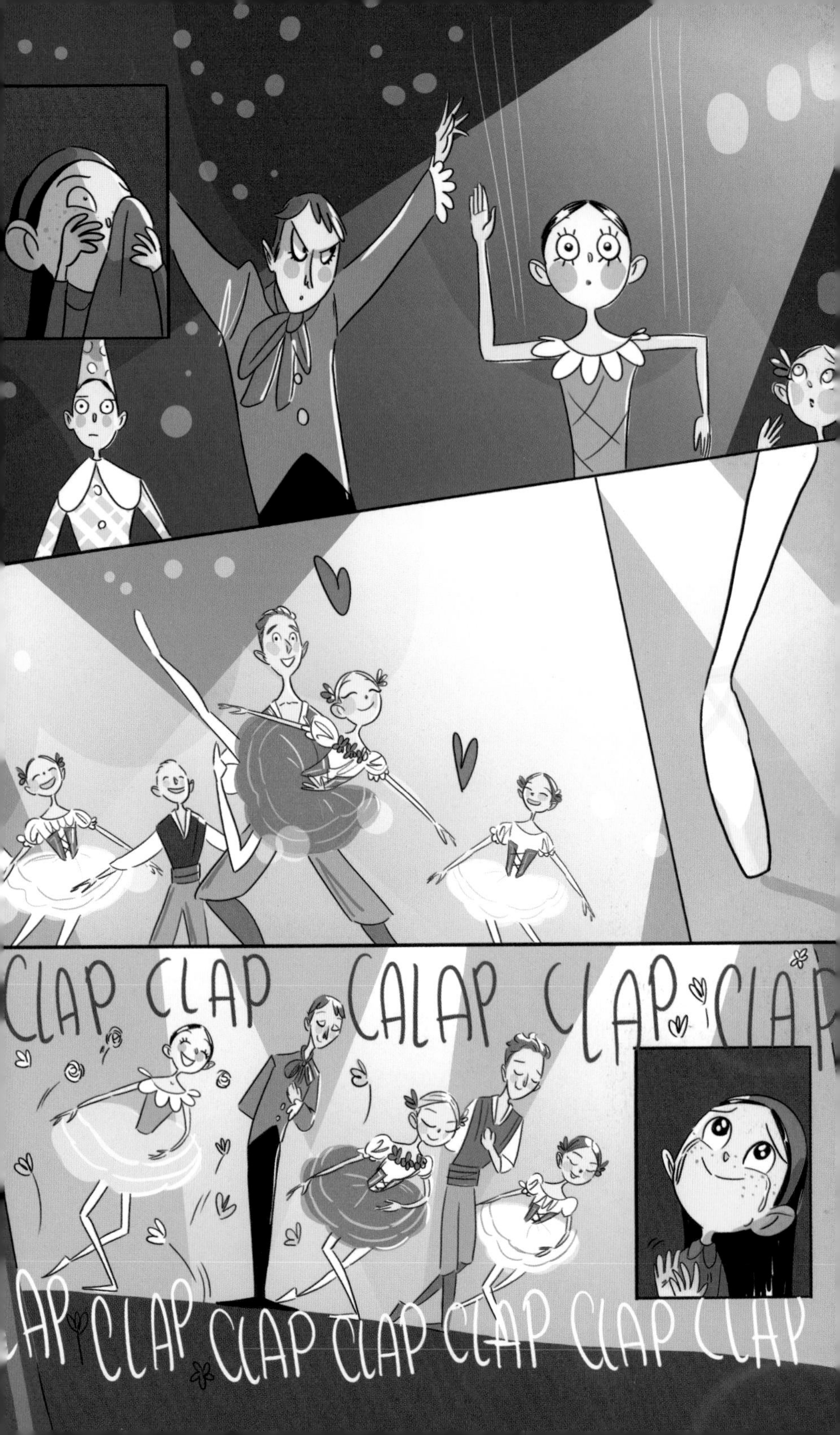
CLAP CLAP CALAP CLAP
CLAP CLAP CLAP CLAP CLAP CLAP

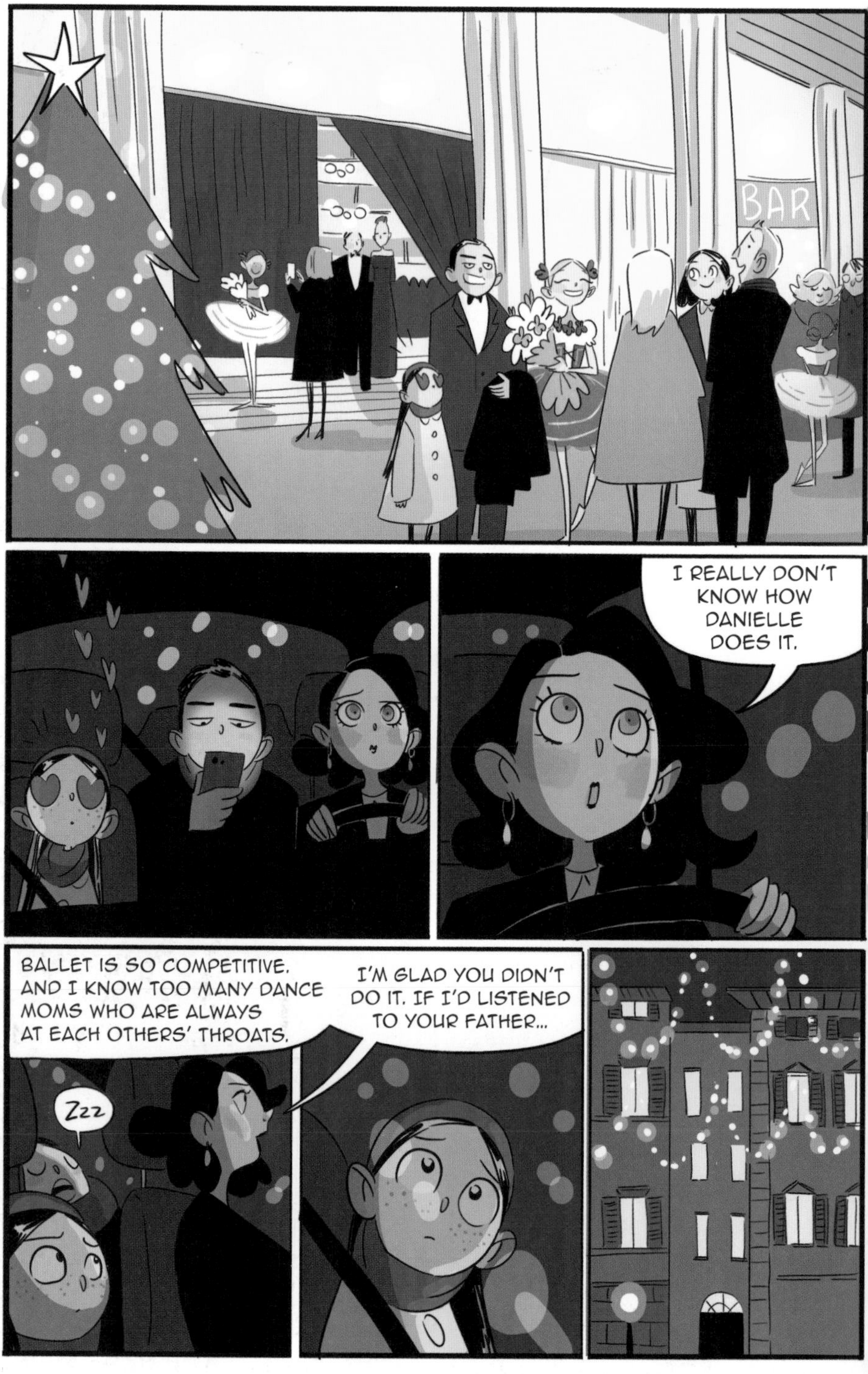
BAR
I REALLY DON'T KNOW HOW DANIELLE DOES IT.
BALLET IS SO COMPETITIVE. AND I KNOW TOO MANY DANCE MOMS WHO ARE ALWAYS AT EACH OTHERS' THROATS.
I'M GLAD YOU DIDN'T DO IT. IF I'D LISTENED TO YOUR FATHER...
Zzz

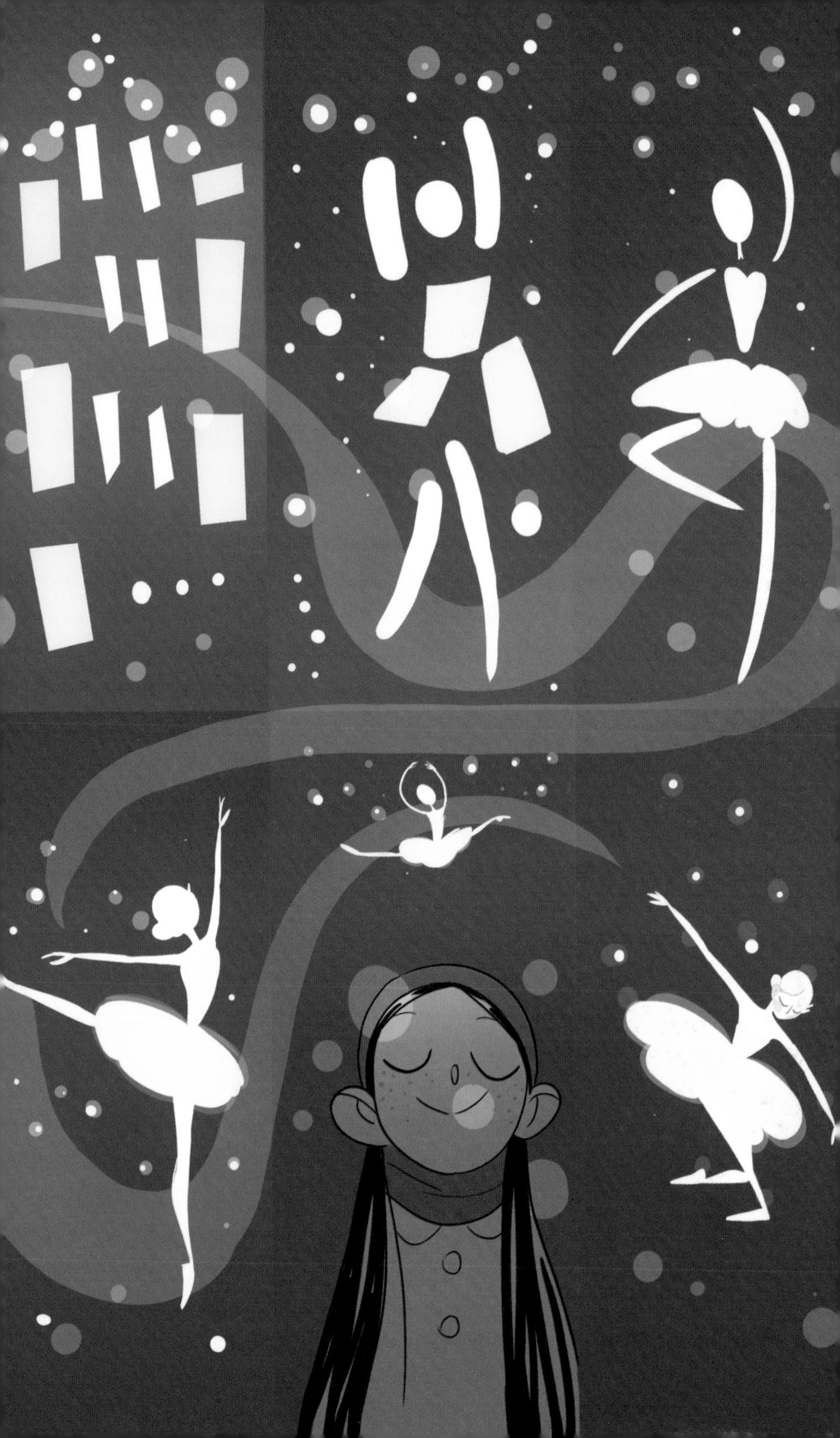

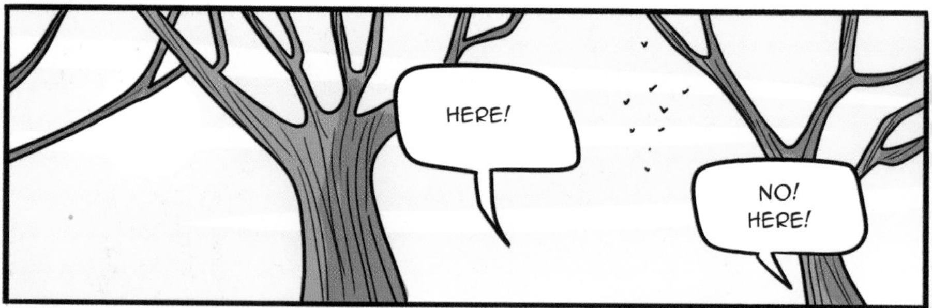
HERE!
NO! HERE!

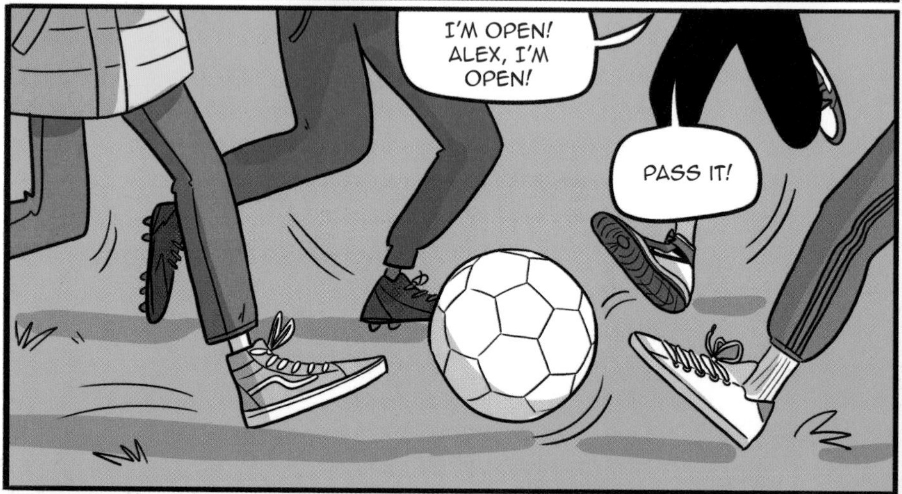
I'M OPEN! ALEX, I'M OPEN!
PASS IT!

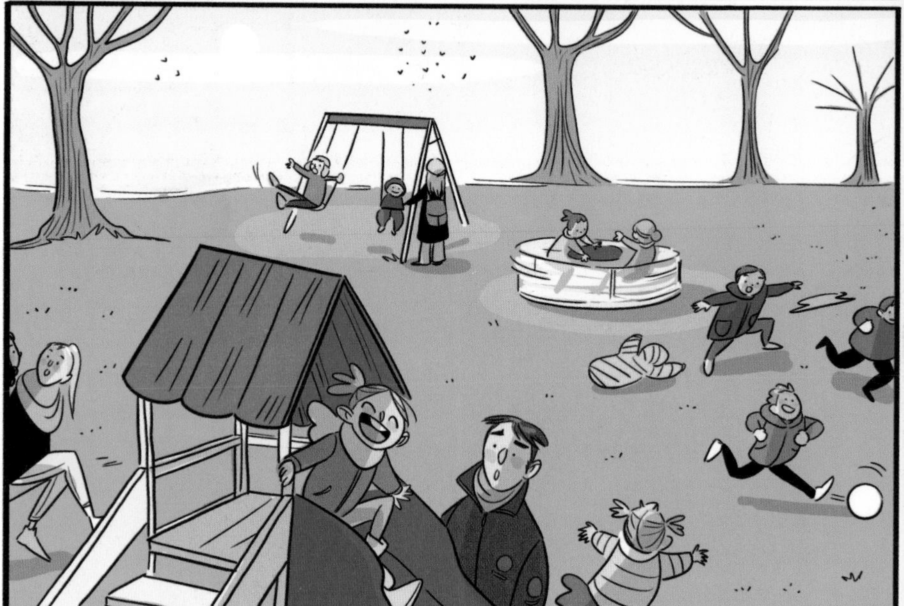

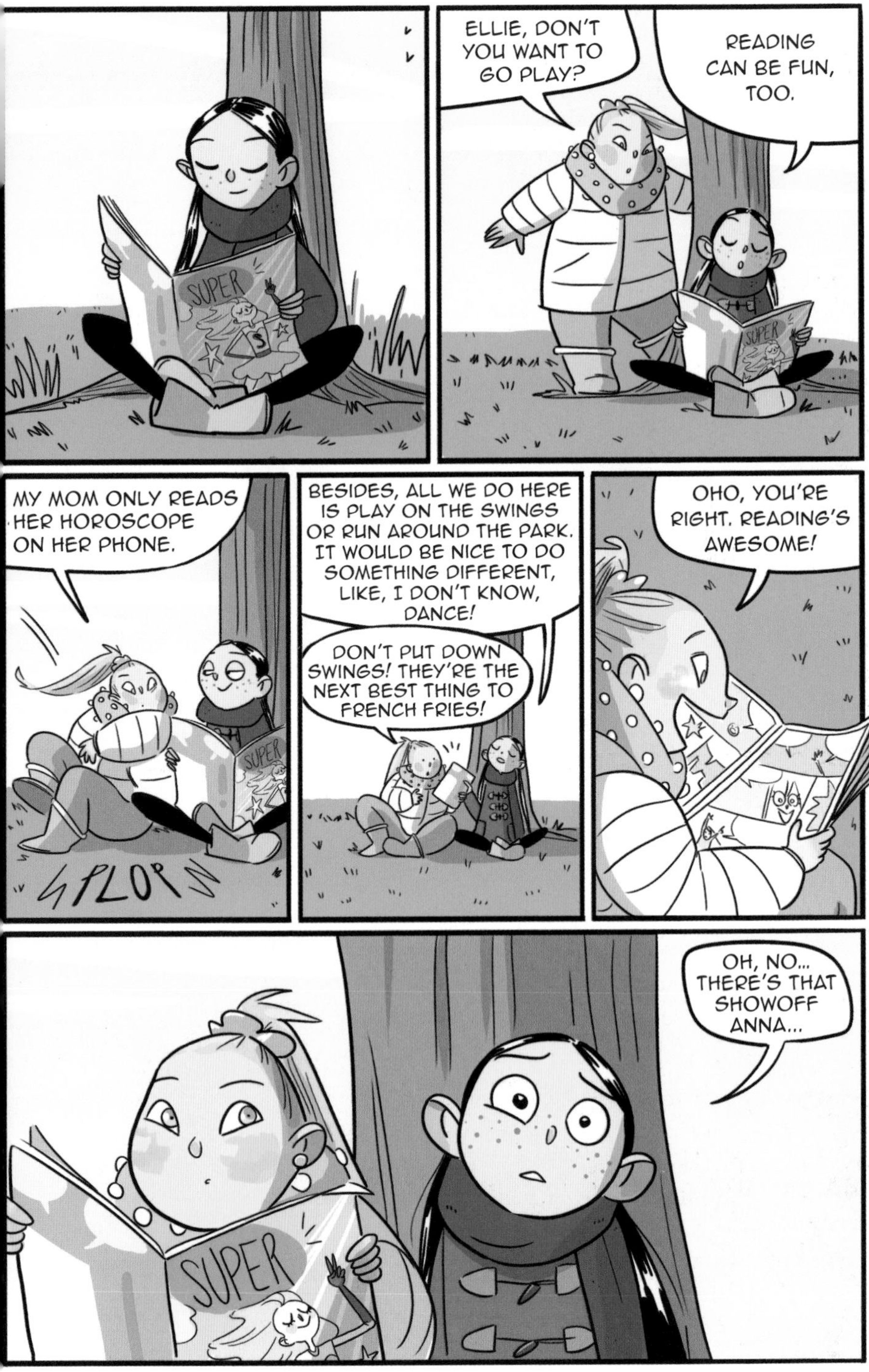
ELLIE, DON'T YOU WANT TO GO PLAY?
READING CAN BE FUN, TOO.
MY MOM ONLY READS HER HOROSCOPE ON HER PHONE.
SPLOP
BESIDES, ALL WE DO HERE IS PLAY ON THE SWINGS OR RUN AROUND THE PARK. IT WOULD BE NICE TO DO SOMETHING DIFFERENT, LIKE, I DON'T KNOW, DANCE!
DON'T PUT DOWN SWINGS! THEY'RE THE NEXT BEST THING TO FRENCH FRIES!
OHO, YOU'RE RIGHT. READING'S AWESOME!
OH, NO... THERE'S THAT SHOWOFF ANNA...

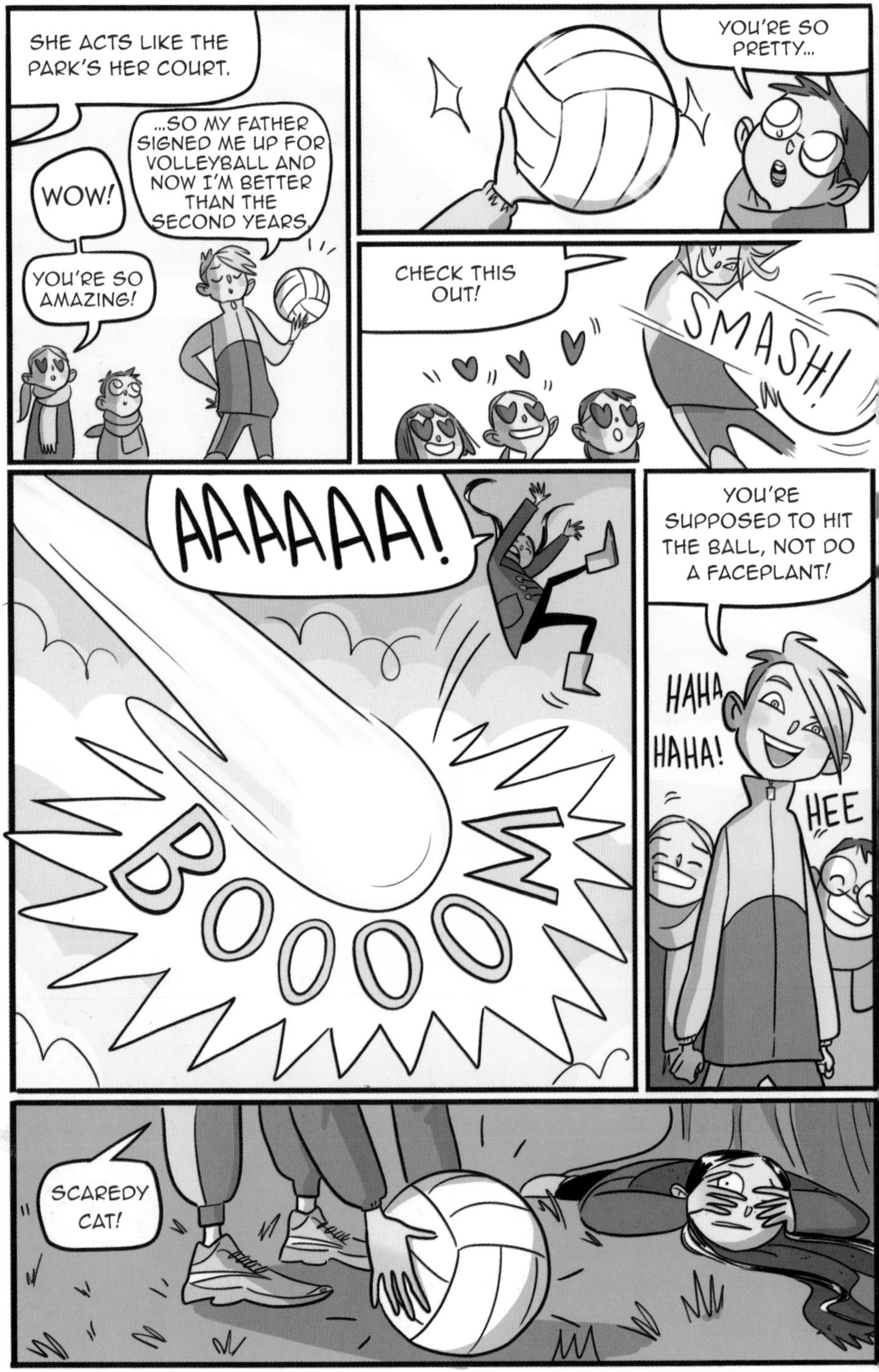
SHE ACTS LIKE THE PARK'S HER COURT.
WOW!
YOU'RE SO AMAZING!
...SO MY FATHER SIGNED ME UP FOR VOLLEYBALL AND NOW I'M BETTER THAN THE SECOND YEARS.
YOU'RE SO PRETTY...
CHECK THIS OUT!
SMASH!
AAAAAA!
BOOOOM
YOU'RE SUPPOSED TO HIT THE BALL, NOT DO A FACEPLANT!
HAHA
HAHA!
HEE
SCAREDY CAT!

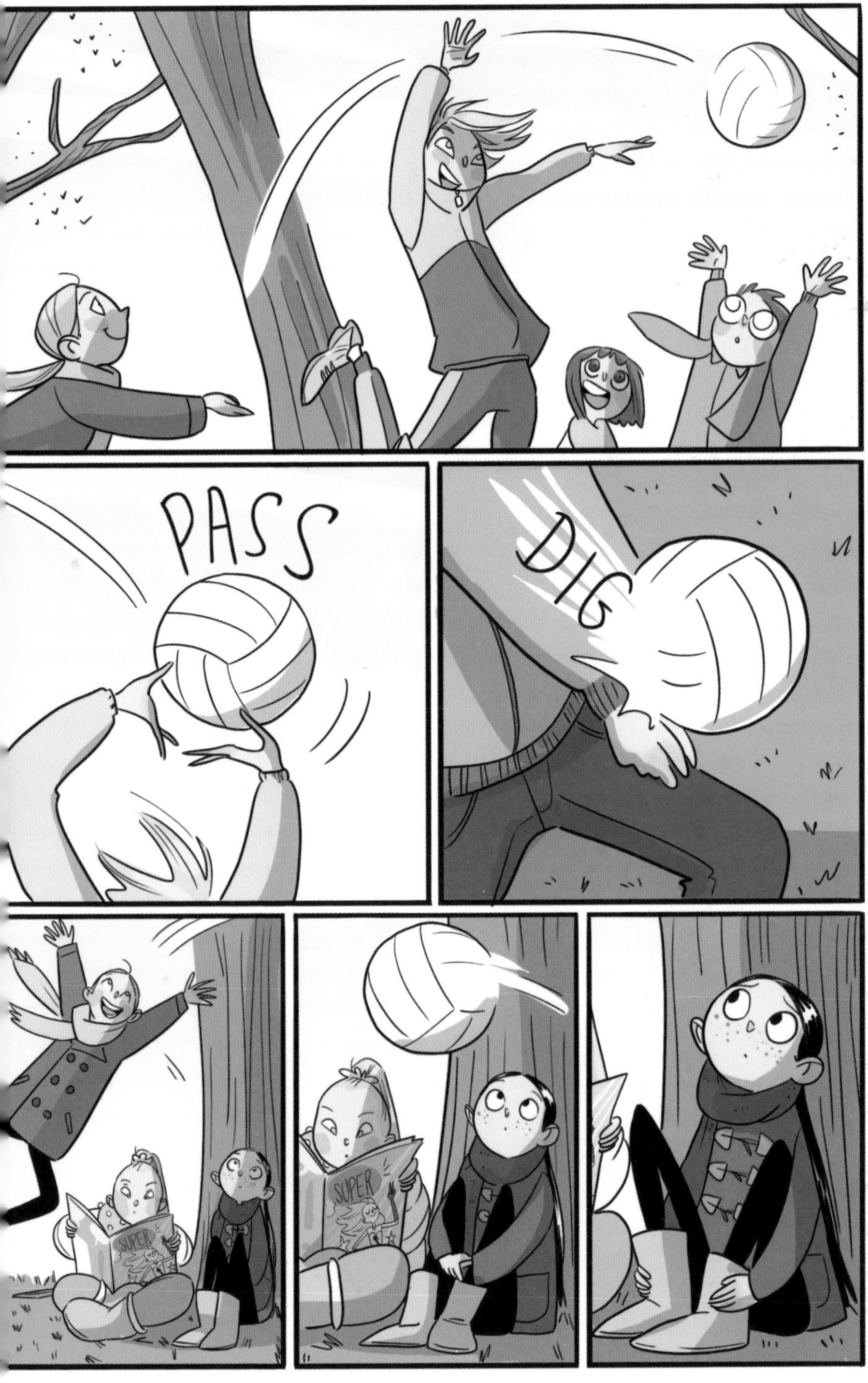
PASS
DIG
SUPER
SUPER

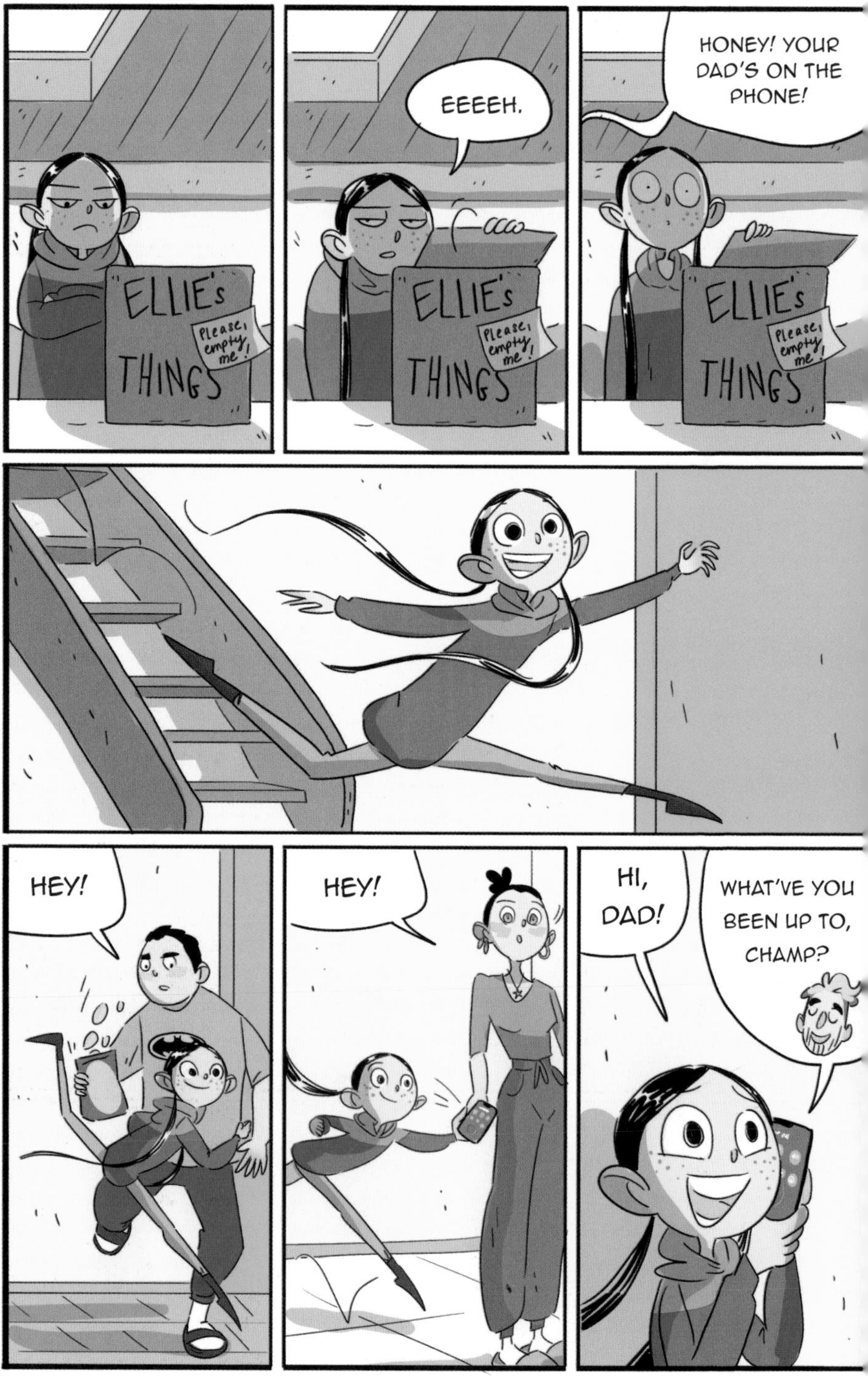
ELLIE's THINGS
Please, empty me!
EEEEH.
HONEY! YOUR DAD'S ON THE PHONE!
HEY!
HEY!
HI, DAD!
WHAT'VE YOU BEEN UP TO, CHAMP?

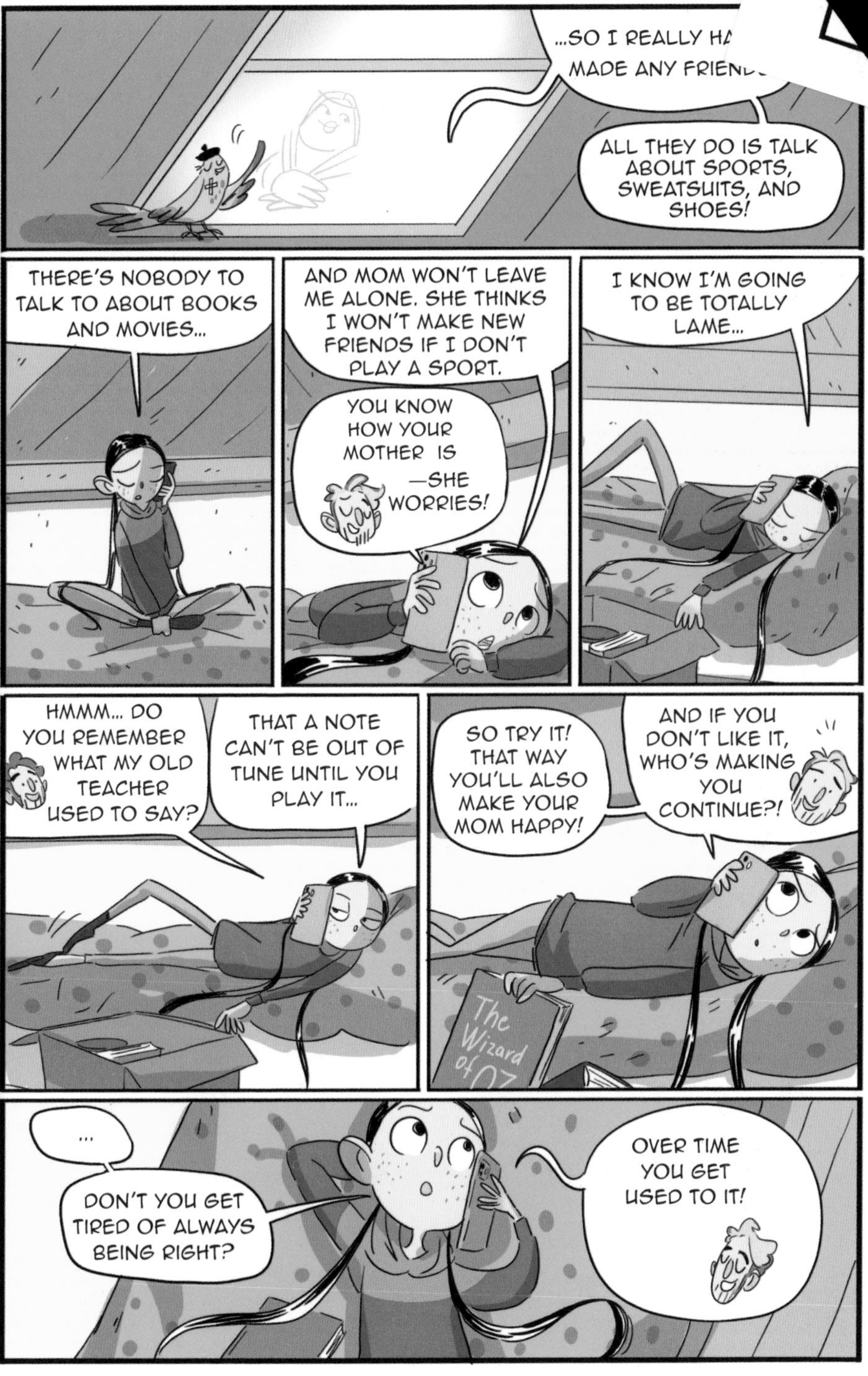
...SO I REALLY HA
MADE ANY FRIEN
ALL THEY DO IS TALK ABOUT SPORTS, SWEATSUITS, AND SHOES!
THERE'S NOBODY TO TALK TO ABOUT BOOKS AND MOVIES...
AND MOM WON'T LEAVE ME ALONE. SHE THINKS I WON'T MAKE NEW FRIENDS IF I DON'T PLAY A SPORT.
YOU KNOW HOW YOUR MOTHER IS —SHE WORRIES!
I KNOW I'M GOING TO BE TOTALLY LAME...
HMMM... DO YOU REMEMBER WHAT MY OLD TEACHER USED TO SAY?
THAT A NOTE CAN'T BE OUT OF TUNE UNTIL YOU PLAY IT...
SO TRY IT! THAT WAY YOU'LL ALSO MAKE YOUR MOM HAPPY!
AND IF YOU DON'T LIKE IT, WHO'S MAKING YOU CONTINUE?!
The Wizard of Oz
...
DON'T YOU GET TIRED OF ALWAYS BEING RIGHT?
OVER TIME YOU GET USED TO IT!

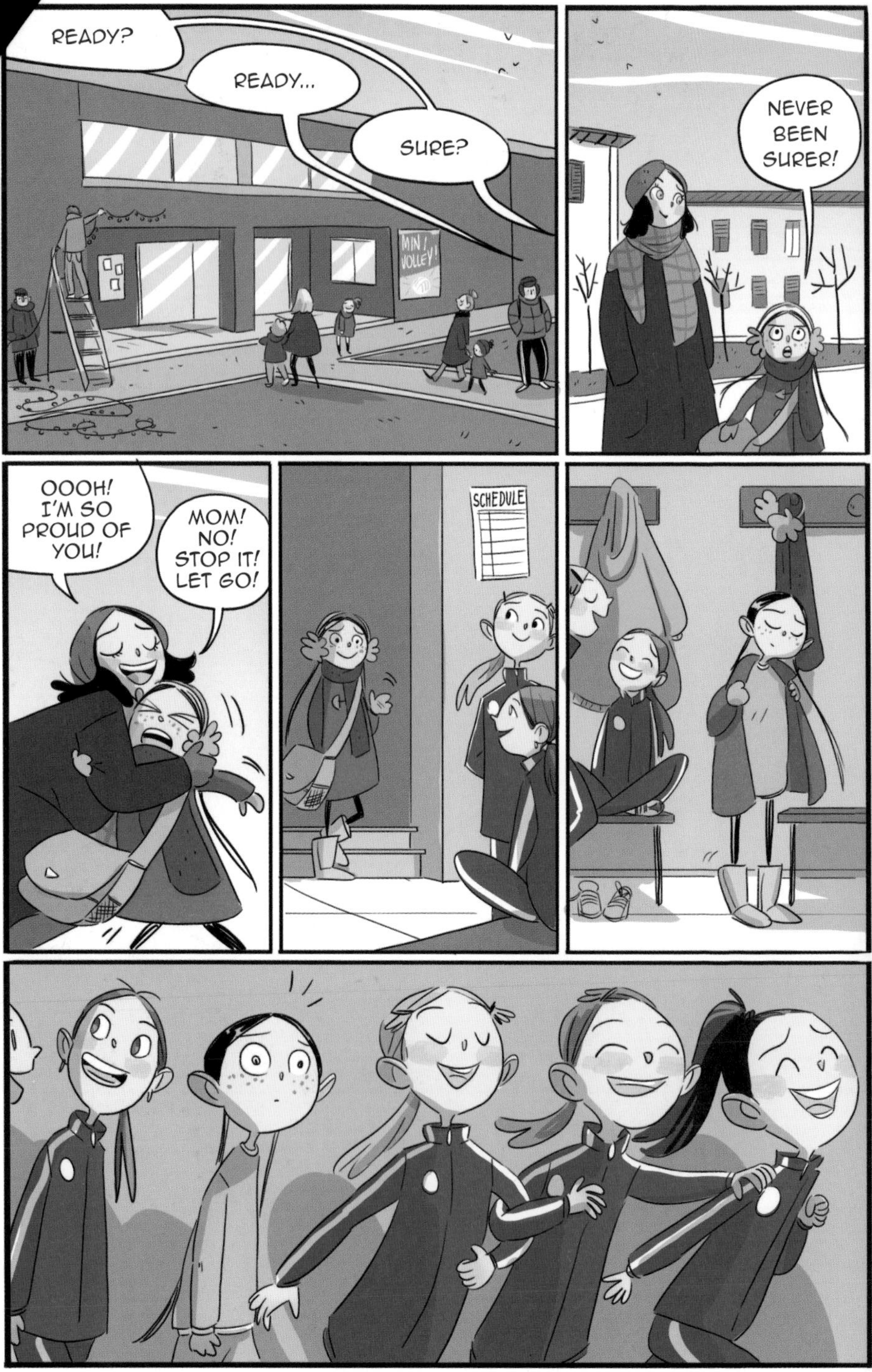
READY?
READY...
SURE?
MINI VOLLEY!
NEVER BEEN SURER!
OOOH! I'M SO PROUD OF YOU!
MOM! NO! STOP IT! LET GO!
SCHEDULE

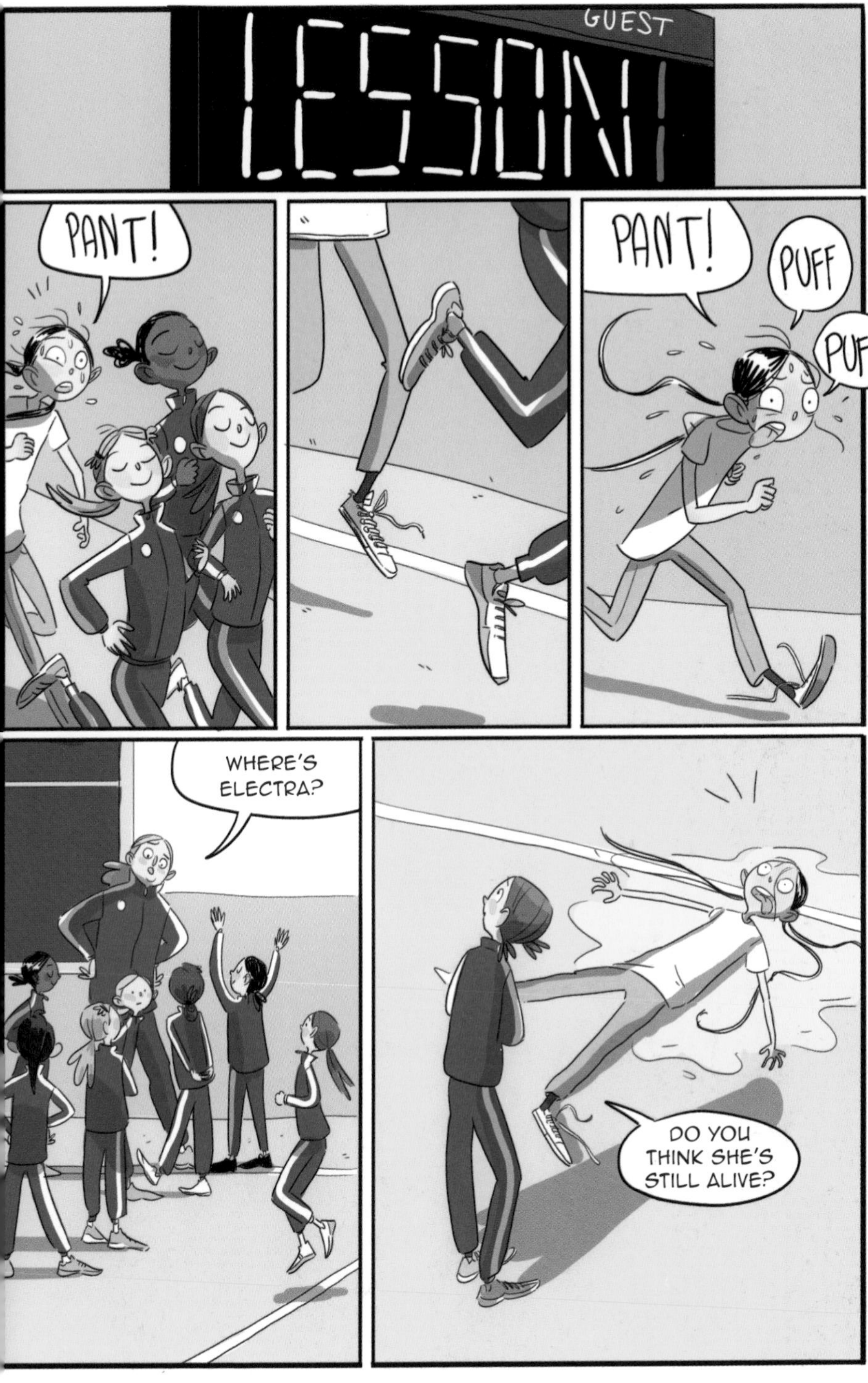
GUEST
LESSON!
PANT!
PANT!
PUFF
PUFF
WHERE'S ELECTRA?
DO YOU THINK SHE'S STILL ALIVE?

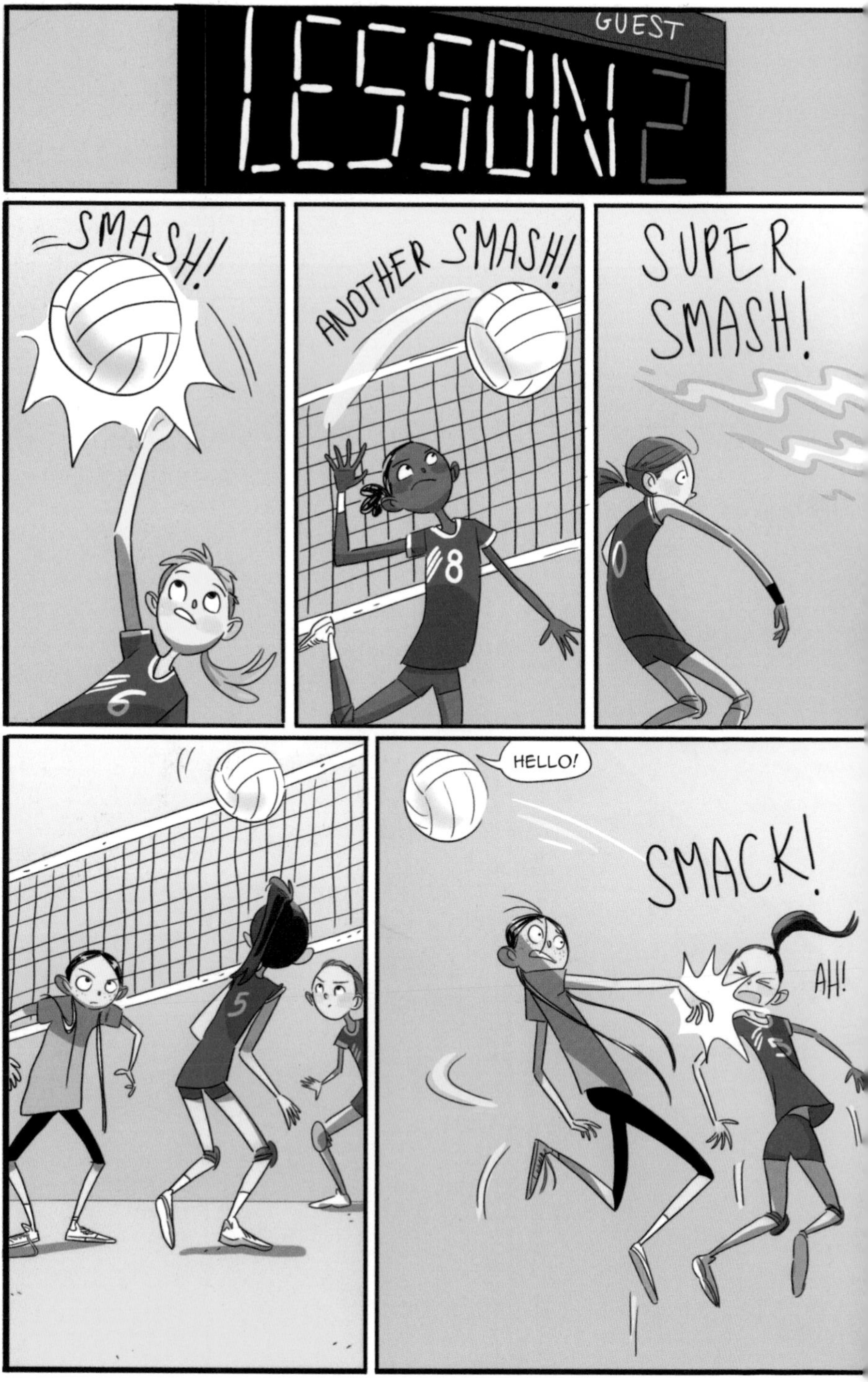
LESSON 2
GUEST
SMASH!
ANOTHER SMASH!
SUPER SMASH!
HELLO!
SMACK!
AH!

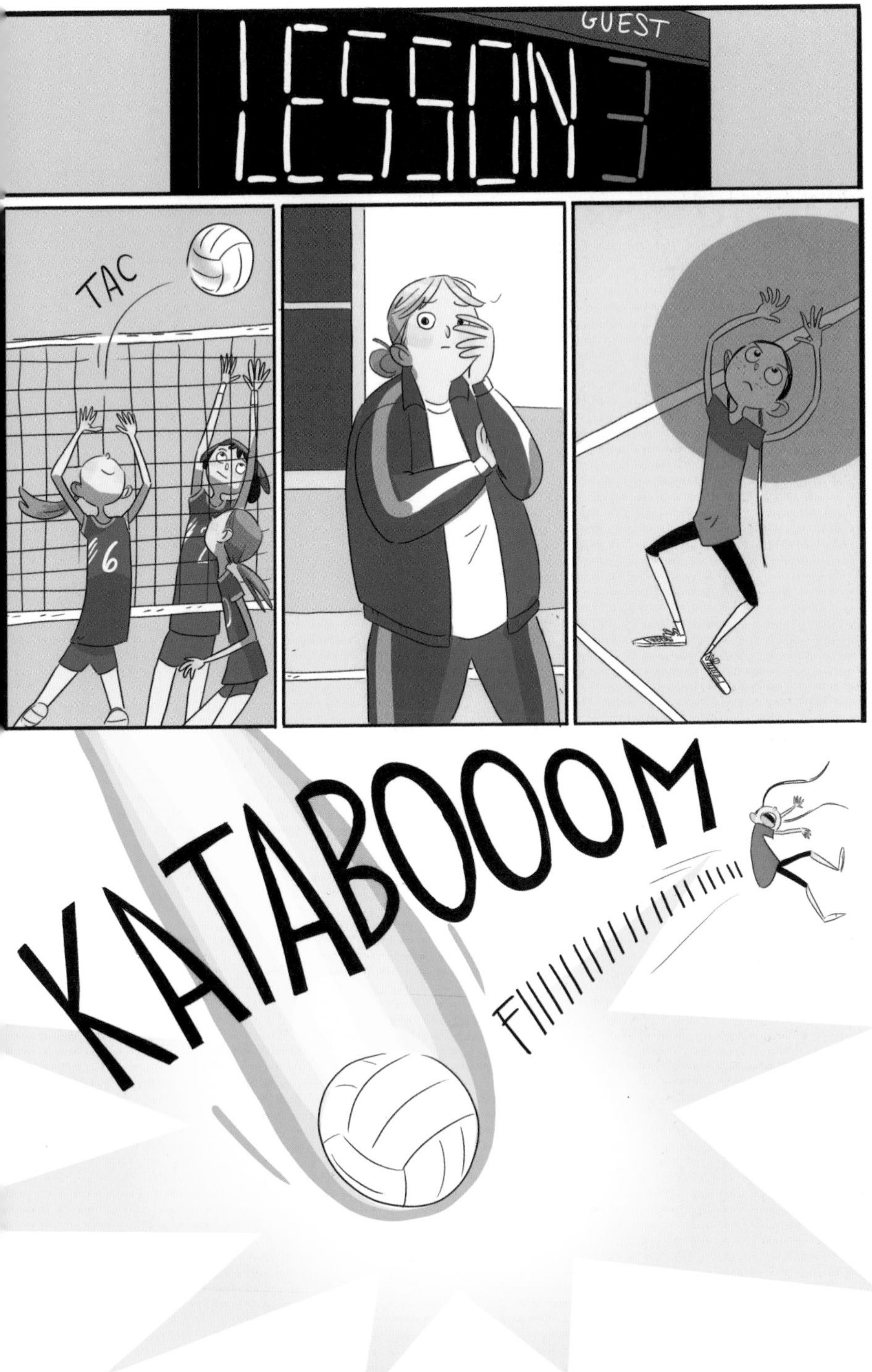
GUEST
LESSON 3
TAC
6
KATABOOOM
FIIIIIIIIIII

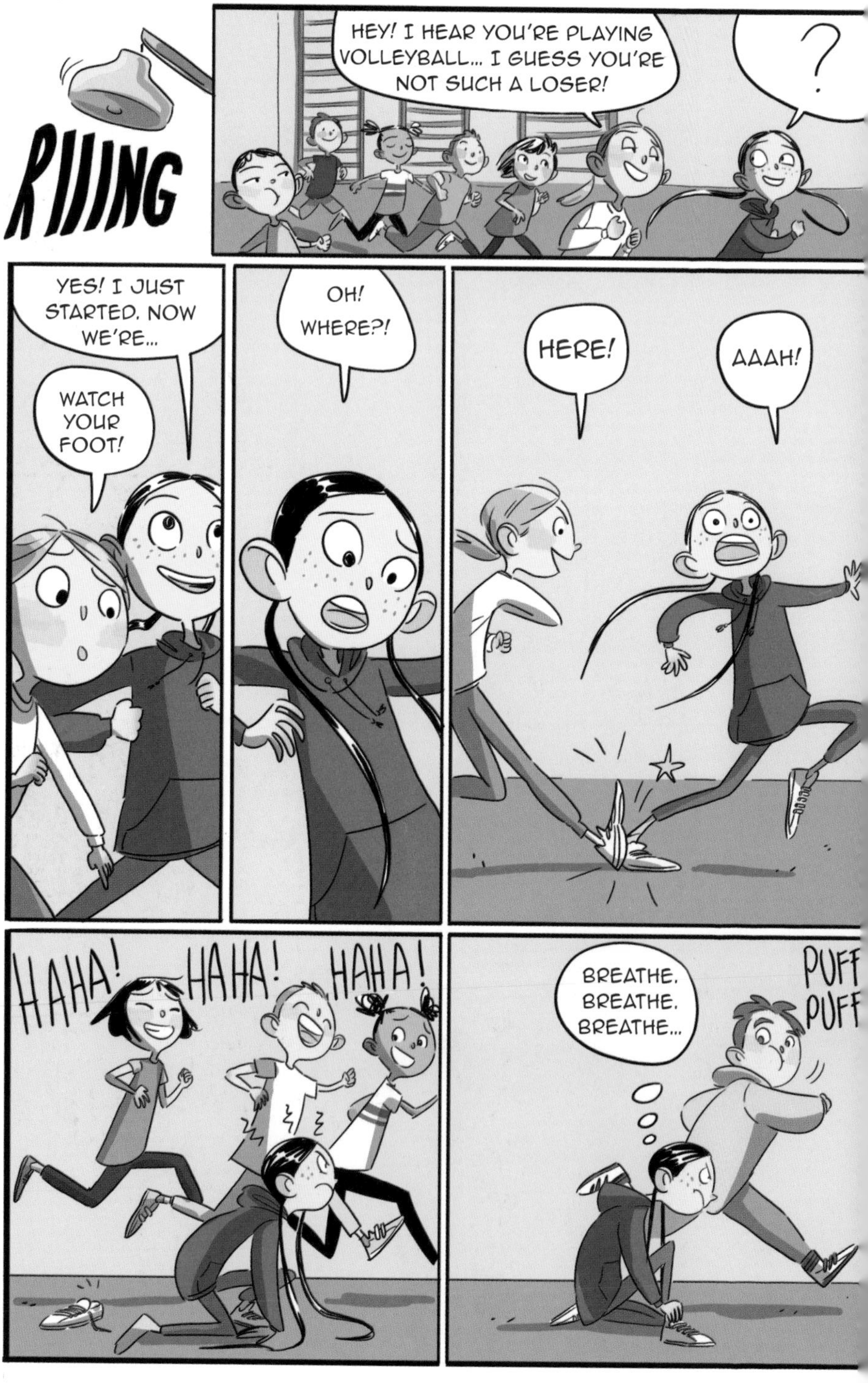
RIIING
HEY! I HEAR YOU'RE PLAYING VOLLEYBALL... I GUESS YOU'RE NOT SUCH A LOSER!
?
YES! I JUST STARTED. NOW WE'RE...
WATCH YOUR FOOT!
OH! WHERE?!
HERE!
AAAH!
HAHA! HAHA! HAHA!
BREATHE. BREATHE. BREATHE...
PUFF PUFF

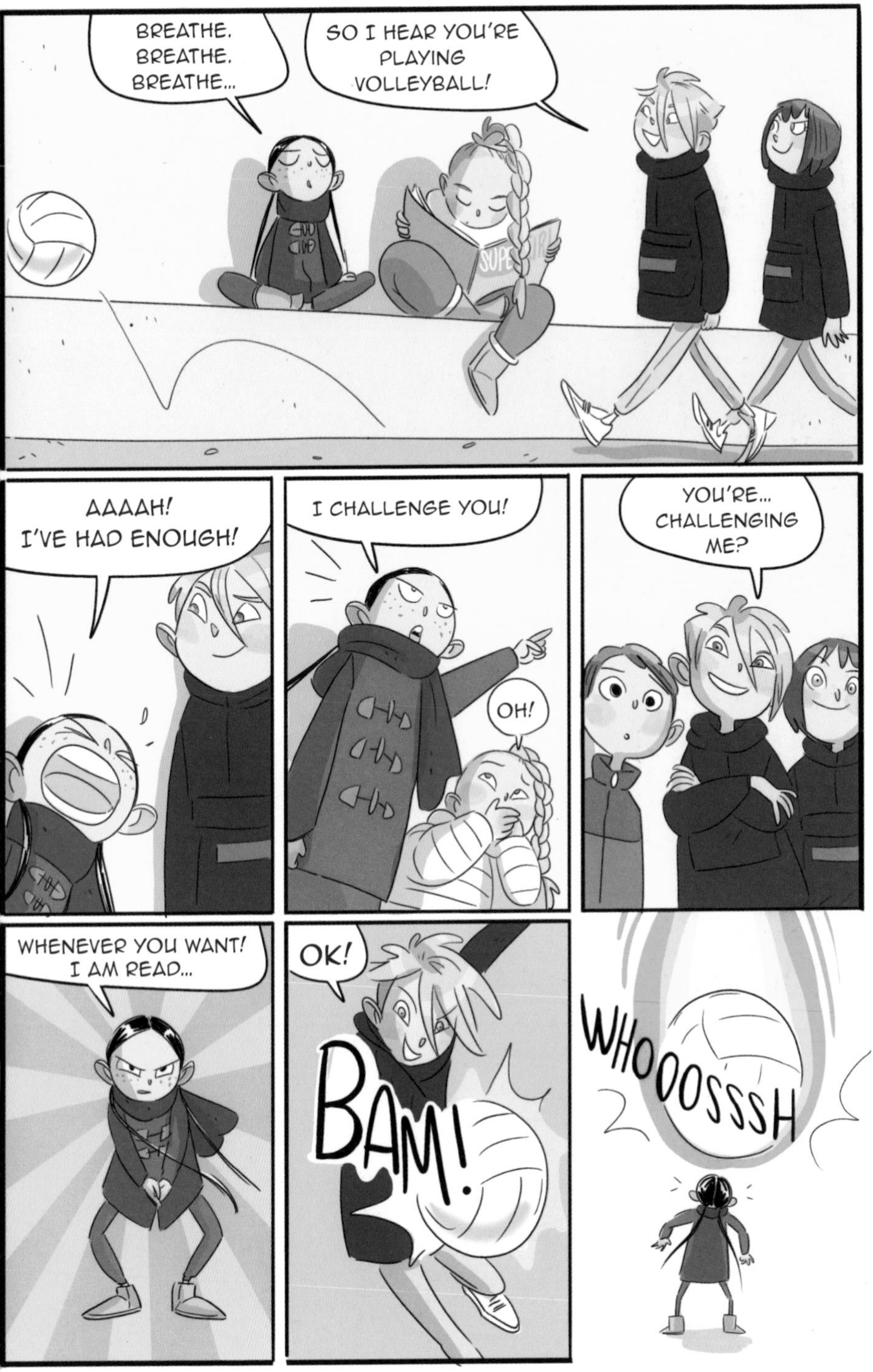
BREATHE.
BREATHE.
BREATHE...
SO I HEAR YOU'RE PLAYING VOLLEYBALL!
AAAAH! I'VE HAD ENOUGH!
I CHALLENGE YOU!
OH!
YOU'RE... CHALLENGING ME?
WHENEVER YOU WANT! I AM READ...
OK!
BAM!
WHOOOSSSH

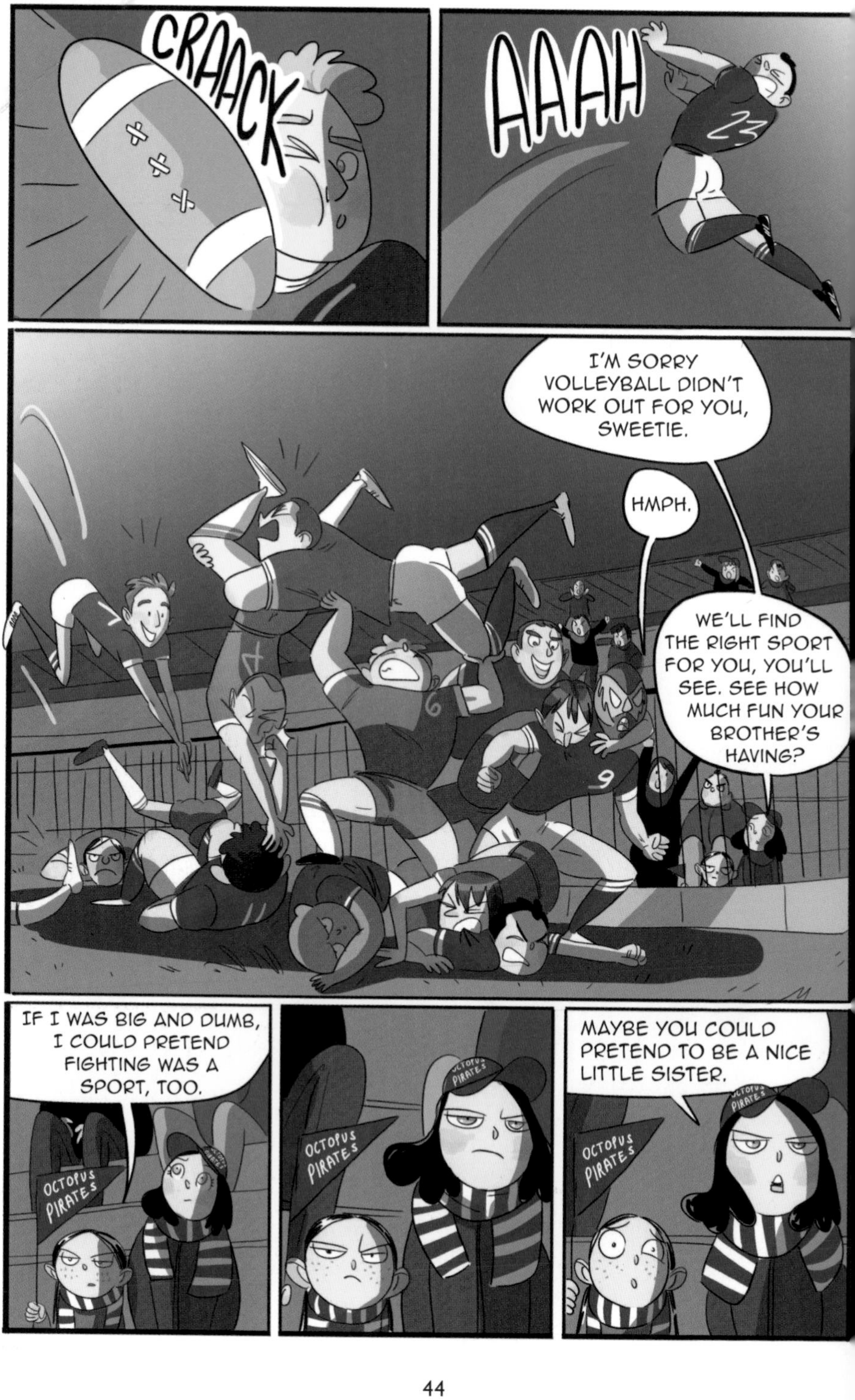
CRAAACK
AAAH
I'M SORRY VOLLEYBALL DIDN'T WORK OUT FOR YOU, SWEETIE.
HMPH.
WE'LL FIND THE RIGHT SPORT FOR YOU, YOU'LL SEE. SEE HOW MUCH FUN YOUR BROTHER'S HAVING?
IF I WAS BIG AND DUMB, I COULD PRETEND FIGHTING WAS A SPORT, TOO.
OCTOPUS PIRATES
MAYBE YOU COULD PRETEND TO BE A NICE LITTLE SISTER.

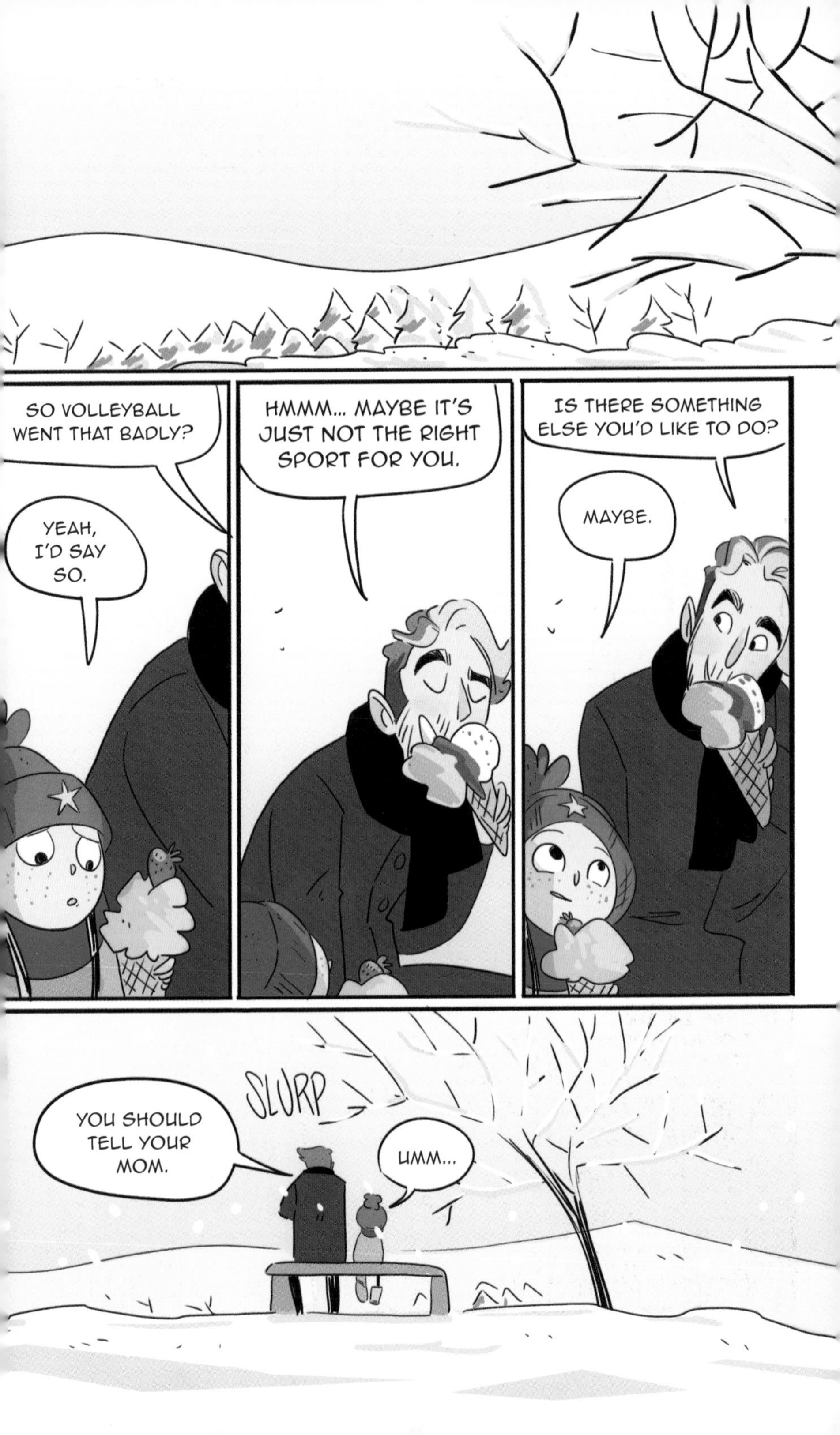
SO VOLLEYBALL WENT THAT BADLY?
YEAH, I'D SAY SO.
HMMM... MAYBE IT'S JUST NOT THE RIGHT SPORT FOR YOU.
IS THERE SOMETHING ELSE YOU'D LIKE TO DO?
MAYBE.
SLURP
YOU SHOULD TELL YOUR MOM.
UMM...

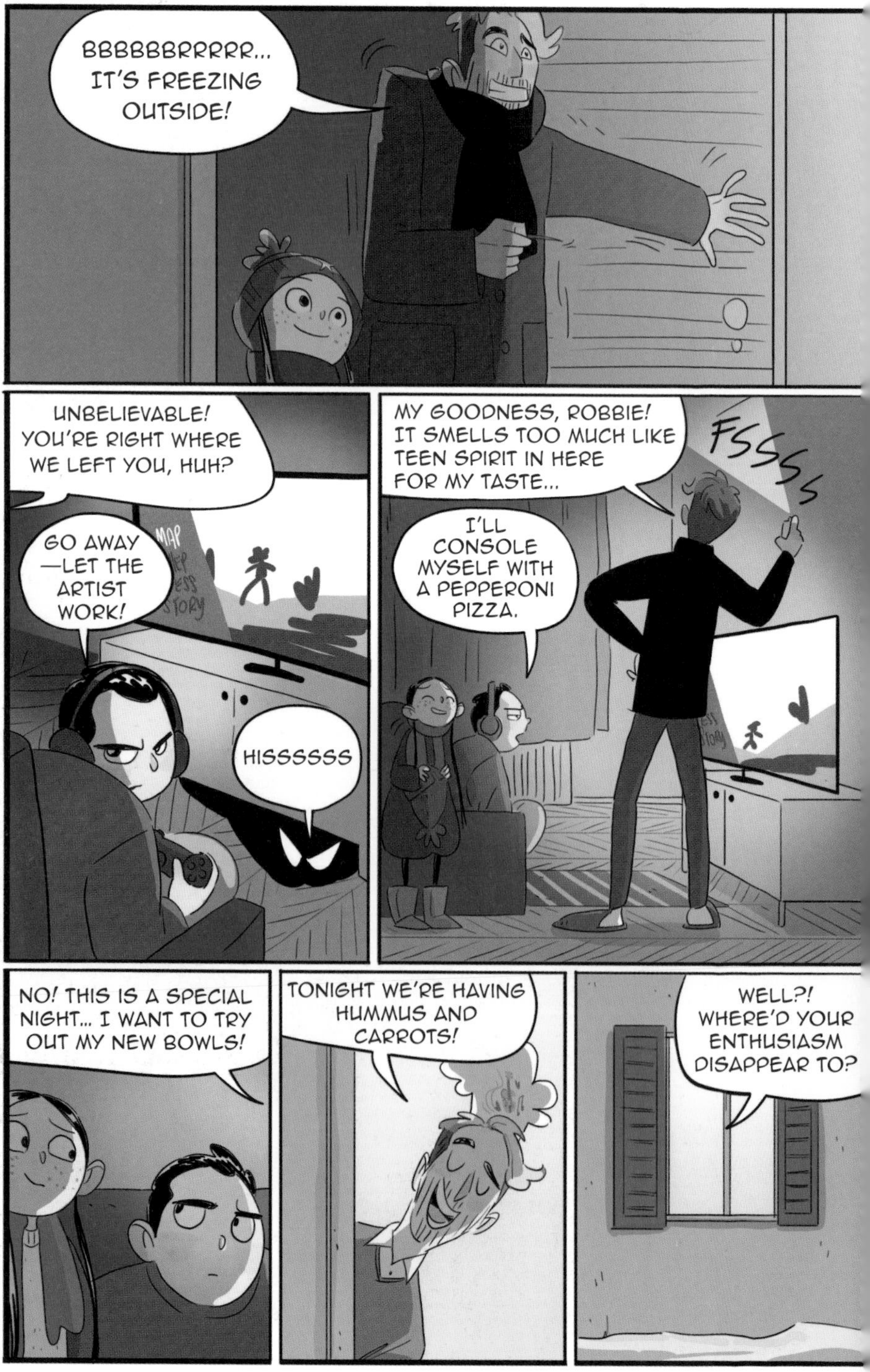
BBBBBBRRRRR...
IT'S FREEZING
OUTSIDE!
UNBELIEVABLE!
YOU'RE RIGHT WHERE
WE LEFT YOU, HUH?
GO AWAY
—LET THE
ARTIST
WORK!
HISSSSSS
MY GOODNESS, ROBBIE!
IT SMELLS TOO MUCH LIKE
TEEN SPIRIT IN HERE
FOR MY TASTE...
FSSSS
I'LL
CONSOLE
MYSELF WITH
A PEPPERONI
PIZZA.
NO! THIS IS A SPECIAL
NIGHT... I WANT TO TRY
OUT MY NEW BOWLS!
TONIGHT WE'RE HAVING
HUMMUS AND
CARROTS!
WELL?!
WHERE'D YOUR
ENTHUSIASM
DISAPPEAR TO?

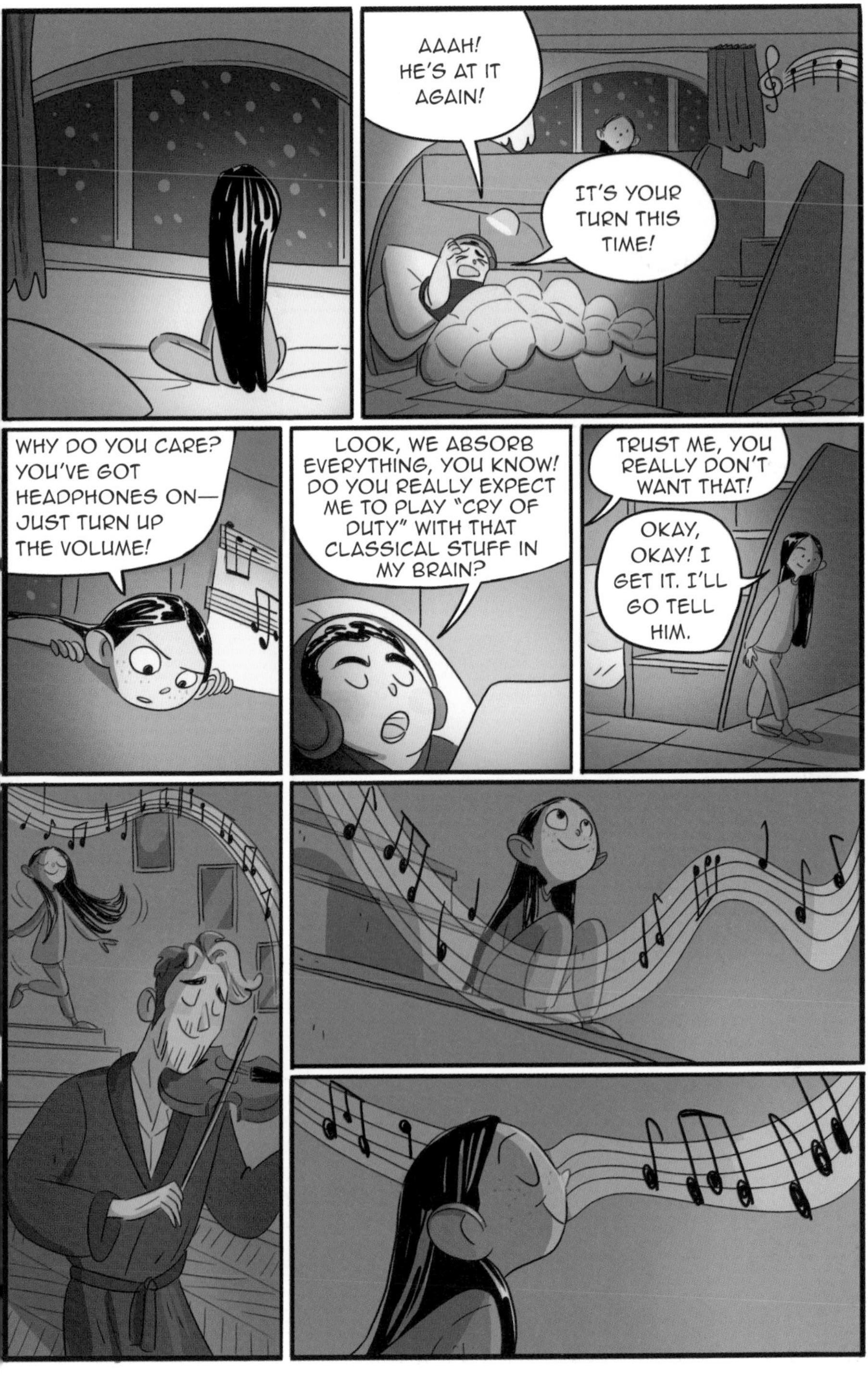
AAAH! HE'S AT IT AGAIN!
IT'S YOUR TURN THIS TIME!
WHY DO YOU CARE? YOU'VE GOT HEADPHONES ON—JUST TURN UP THE VOLUME!
LOOK, WE ABSORB EVERYTHING, YOU KNOW! DO YOU REALLY EXPECT ME TO PLAY "CRY OF DUTY" WITH THAT CLASSICAL STUFF IN MY BRAIN?
TRUST ME, YOU REALLY DON'T WANT THAT!
OKAY, OKAY! I GET IT. I'LL GO TELL HIM.

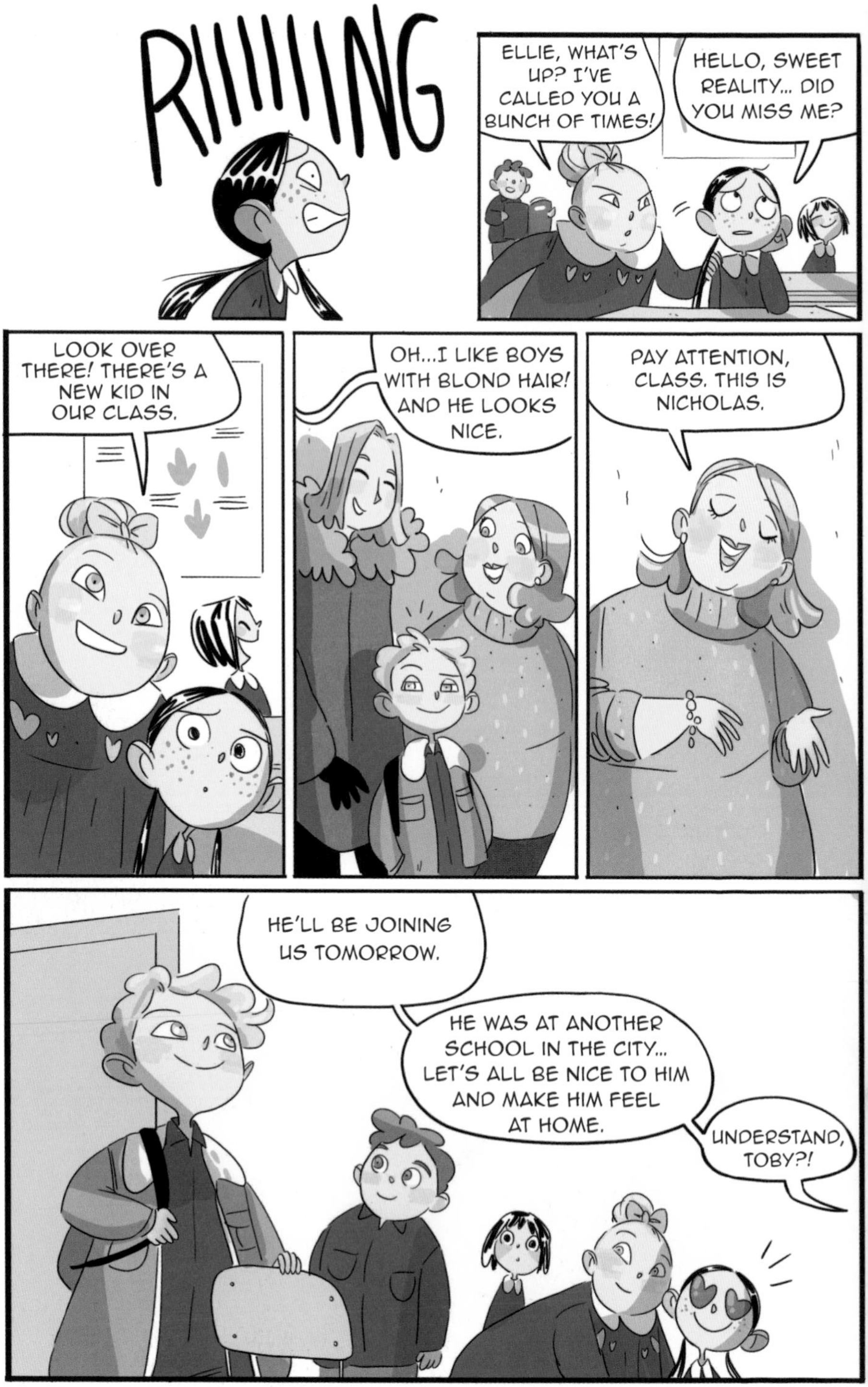
RIIIIIING
ELLIE, WHAT'S UP? I'VE CALLED YOU A BUNCH OF TIMES!
HELLO, SWEET REALITY... DID YOU MISS ME?
LOOK OVER THERE! THERE'S A NEW KID IN OUR CLASS.
OH...I LIKE BOYS WITH BLOND HAIR! AND HE LOOKS NICE.
PAY ATTENTION, CLASS. THIS IS NICHOLAS.
HE'LL BE JOINING US TOMORROW.
HE WAS AT ANOTHER SCHOOL IN THE CITY... LET'S ALL BE NICE TO HIM AND MAKE HIM FEEL AT HOME.
UNDERSTAND, TOBY?!

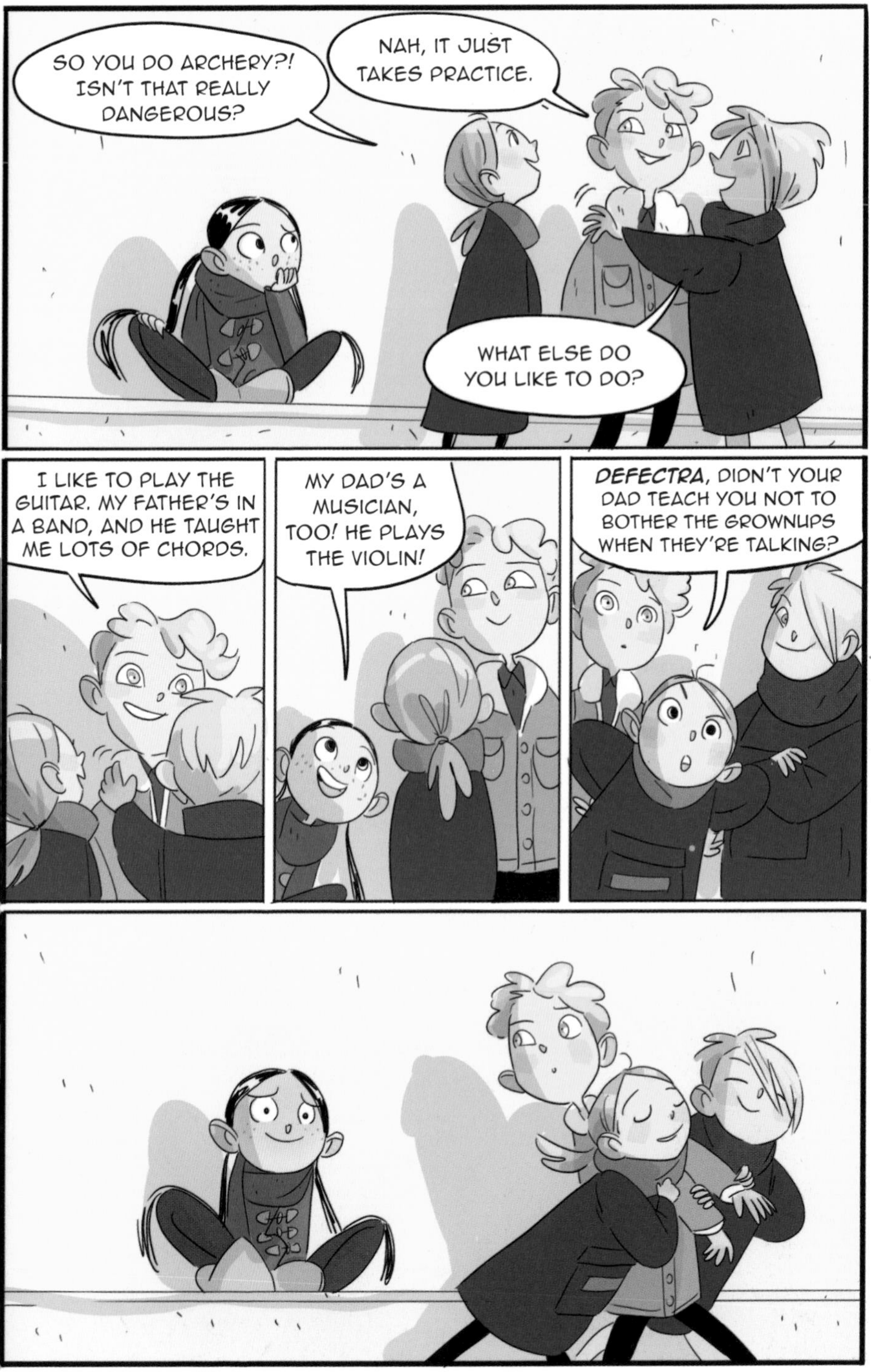
SO YOU DO ARCHERY?! ISN'T THAT REALLY DANGEROUS?
NAH, IT JUST TAKES PRACTICE.
WHAT ELSE DO YOU LIKE TO DO?
I LIKE TO PLAY THE GUITAR. MY FATHER'S IN A BAND, AND HE TAUGHT ME LOTS OF CHORDS.
MY DAD'S A MUSICIAN, TOO! HE PLAYS THE VIOLIN!
DEFECTRA, DIDN'T YOUR DAD TEACH YOU NOT TO BOTHER THE GROWNUPS WHEN THEY'RE TALKING?

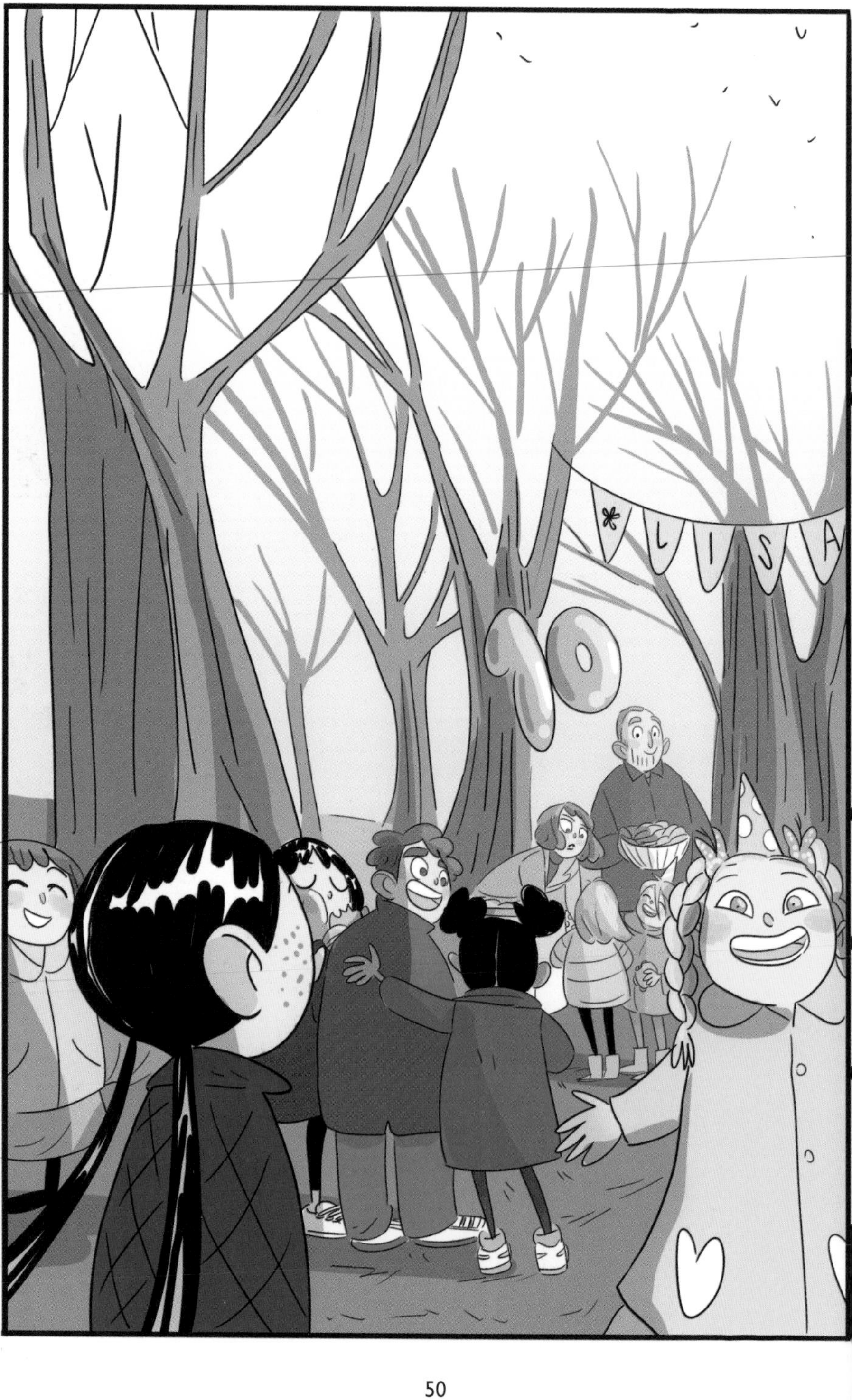
LISA
10

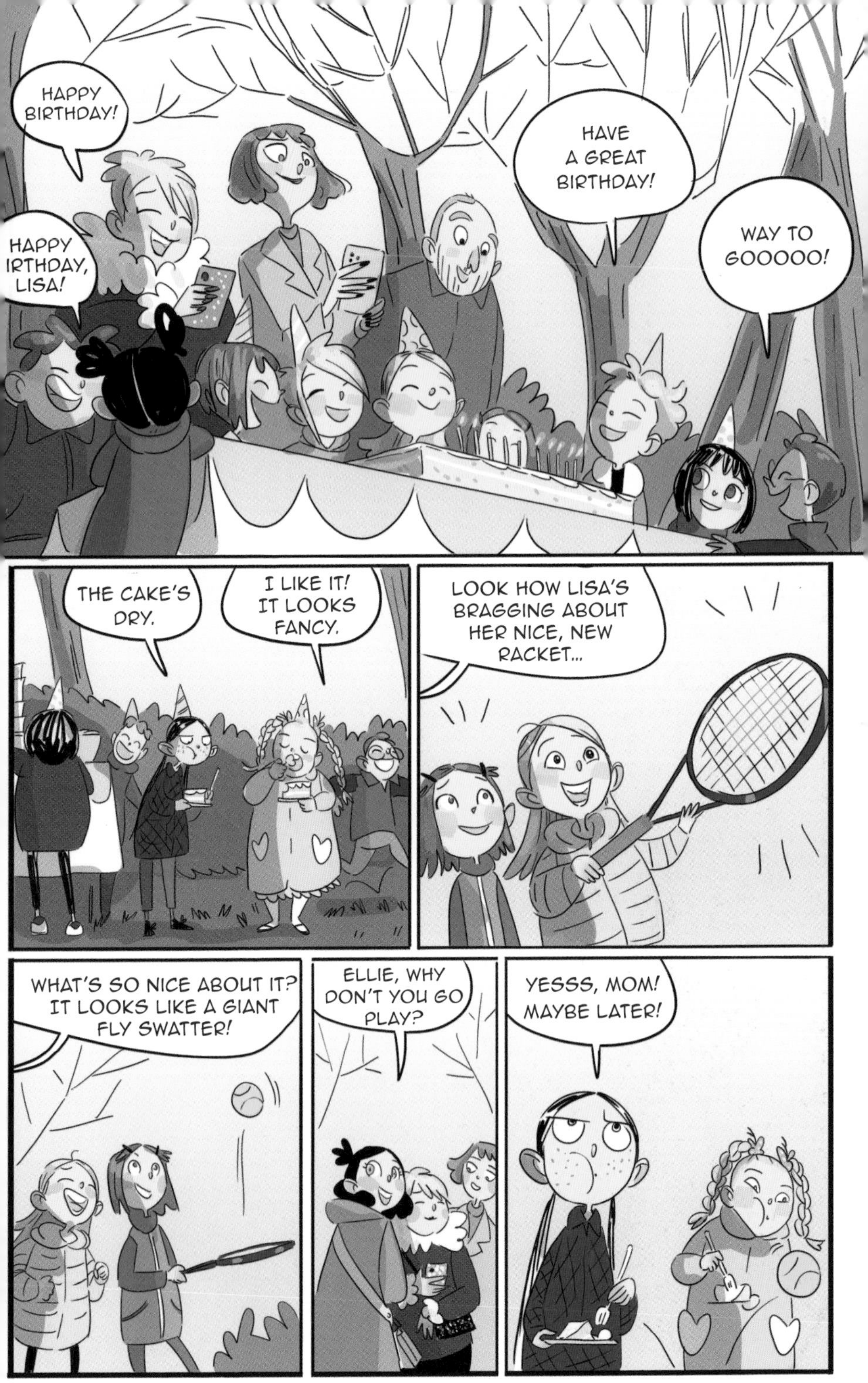
HAPPY BIRTHDAY!
HAPPY IRTHDAY, LISA!
HAVE A GREAT BIRTHDAY!
WAY TO GOOOOO!
THE CAKE'S DRY.
I LIKE IT! IT LOOKS FANCY.
LOOK HOW LISA'S BRAGGING ABOUT HER NICE, NEW RACKET...
WHAT'S SO NICE ABOUT IT? IT LOOKS LIKE A GIANT FLY SWATTER!
ELLIE, WHY DON'T YOU GO PLAY?
YESSS, MOM! MAYBE LATER!

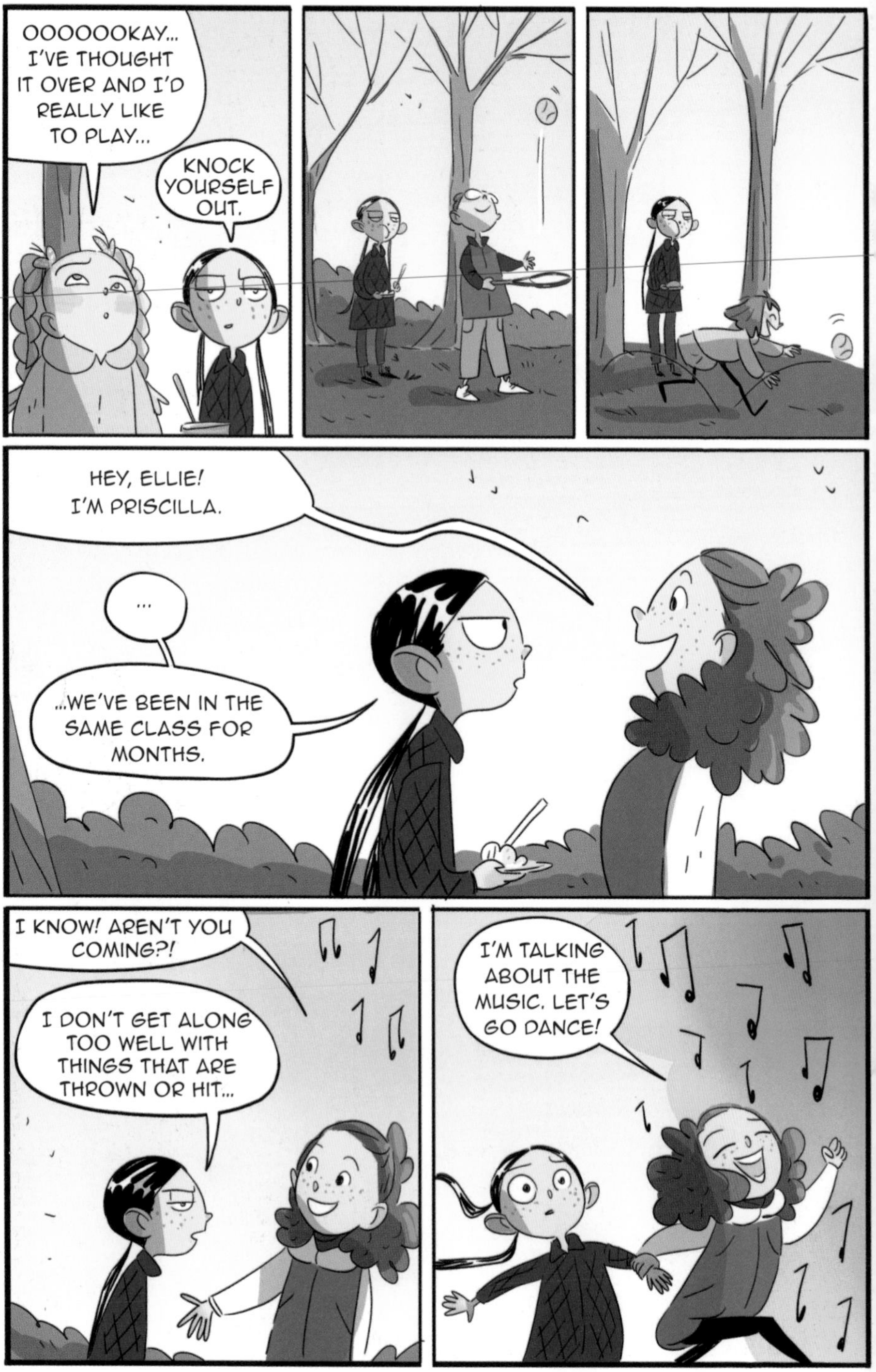

OOOOOOKAY... I'VE THOUGHT IT OVER AND I'D REALLY LIKE TO PLAY...
KNOCK YOURSELF OUT.
HEY, ELLIE! I'M PRISCILLA.
...
...WE'VE BEEN IN THE SAME CLASS FOR MONTHS.
I KNOW! AREN'T YOU COMING?!
I DON'T GET ALONG TOO WELL WITH THINGS THAT ARE THROWN OR HIT...
I'M TALKING ABOUT THE MUSIC. LET'S GO DANCE!

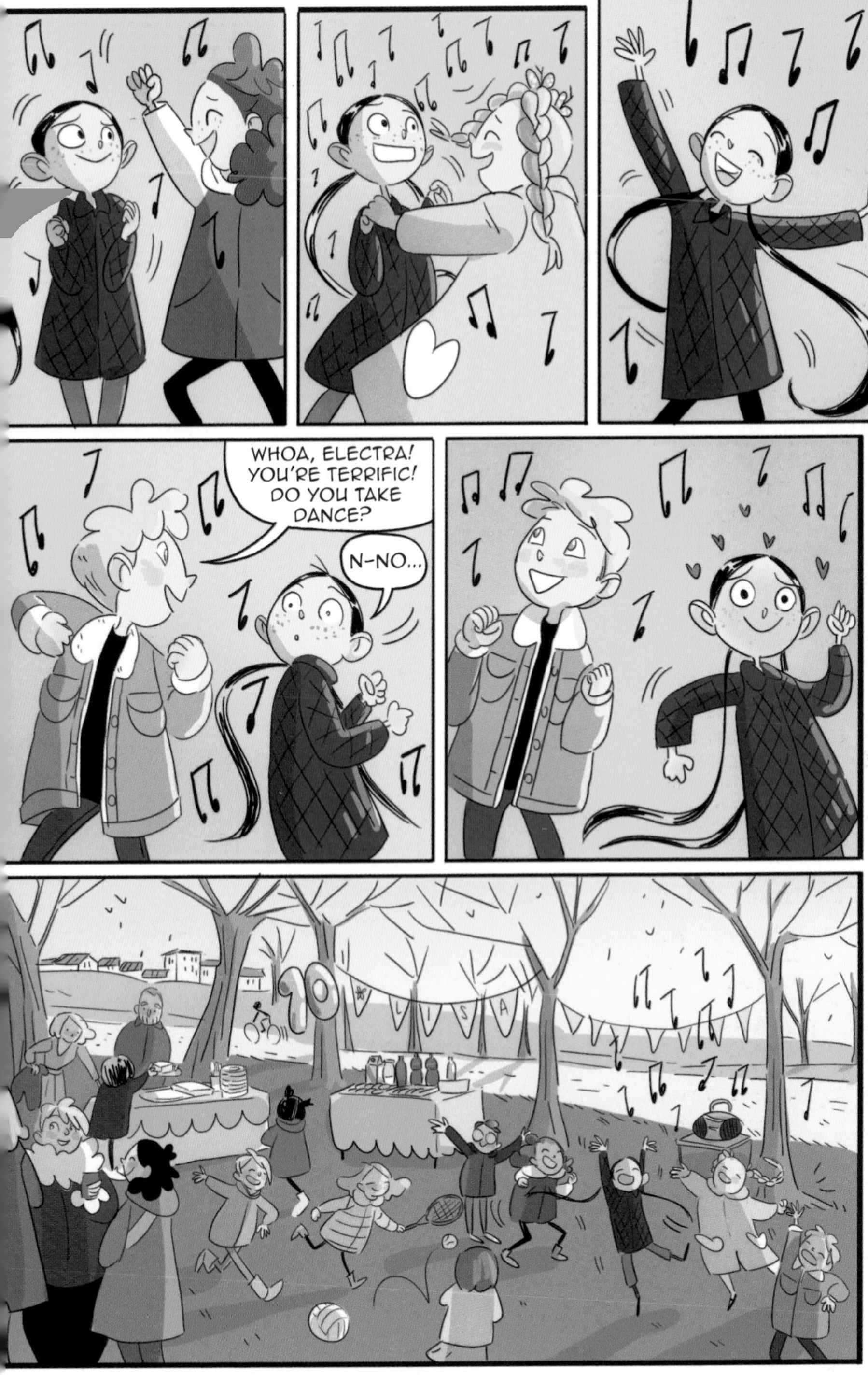
WHOA, ELECTRA! YOU'RE TERRIFIC! DO YOU TAKE DANCE?
N-NO...
L I S A

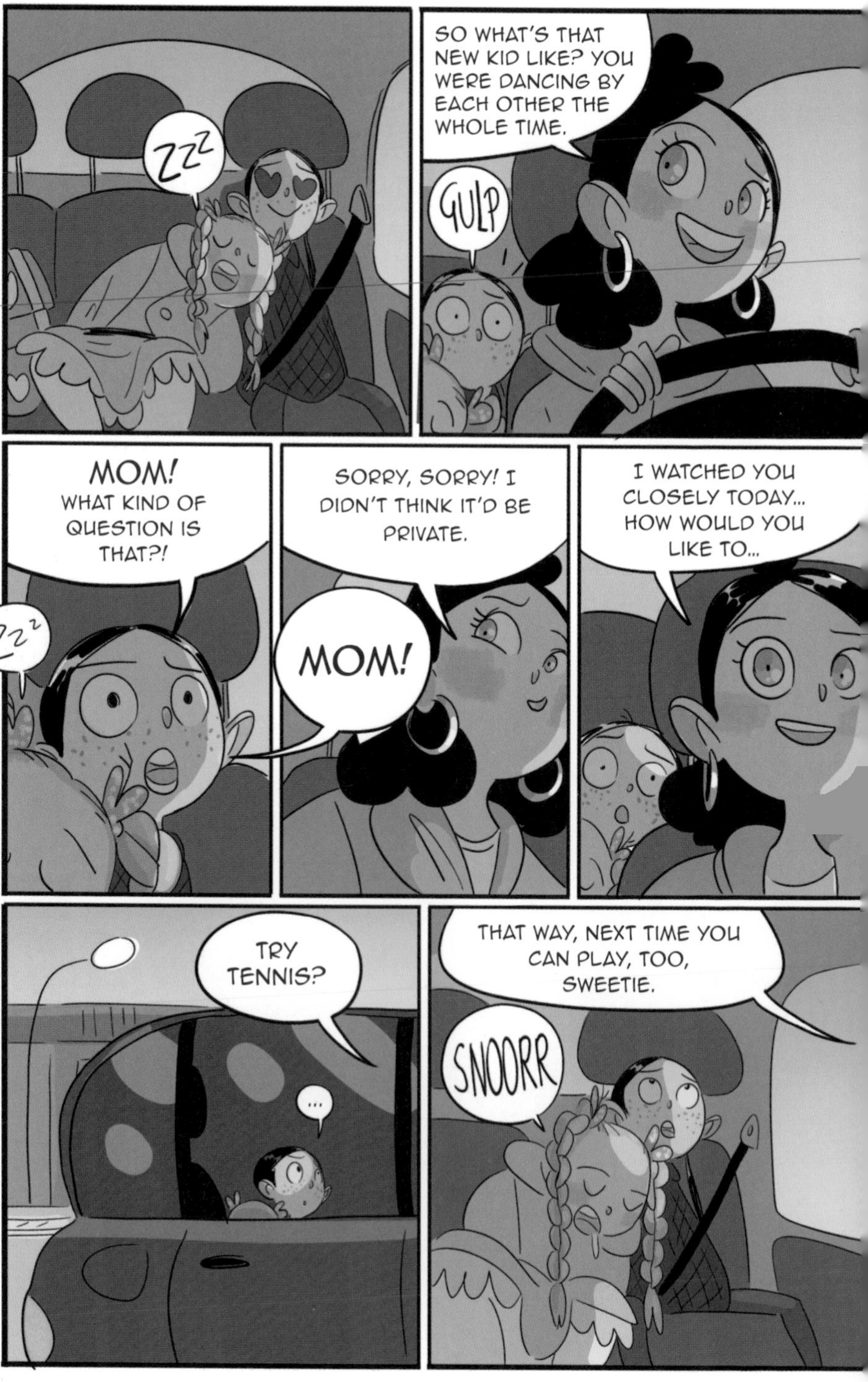
ZZZ
SO WHAT'S THAT NEW KID LIKE? YOU WERE DANCING BY EACH OTHER THE WHOLE TIME.
GULP
MOM! WHAT KIND OF QUESTION IS THAT?!
ZZZ
SORRY, SORRY! I DIDN'T THINK IT'D BE PRIVATE.
MOM!
I WATCHED YOU CLOSELY TODAY... HOW WOULD YOU LIKE TO...
TRY TENNIS?
...
THAT WAY, NEXT TIME YOU CAN PLAY, TOO, SWEETIE.
SNOORR

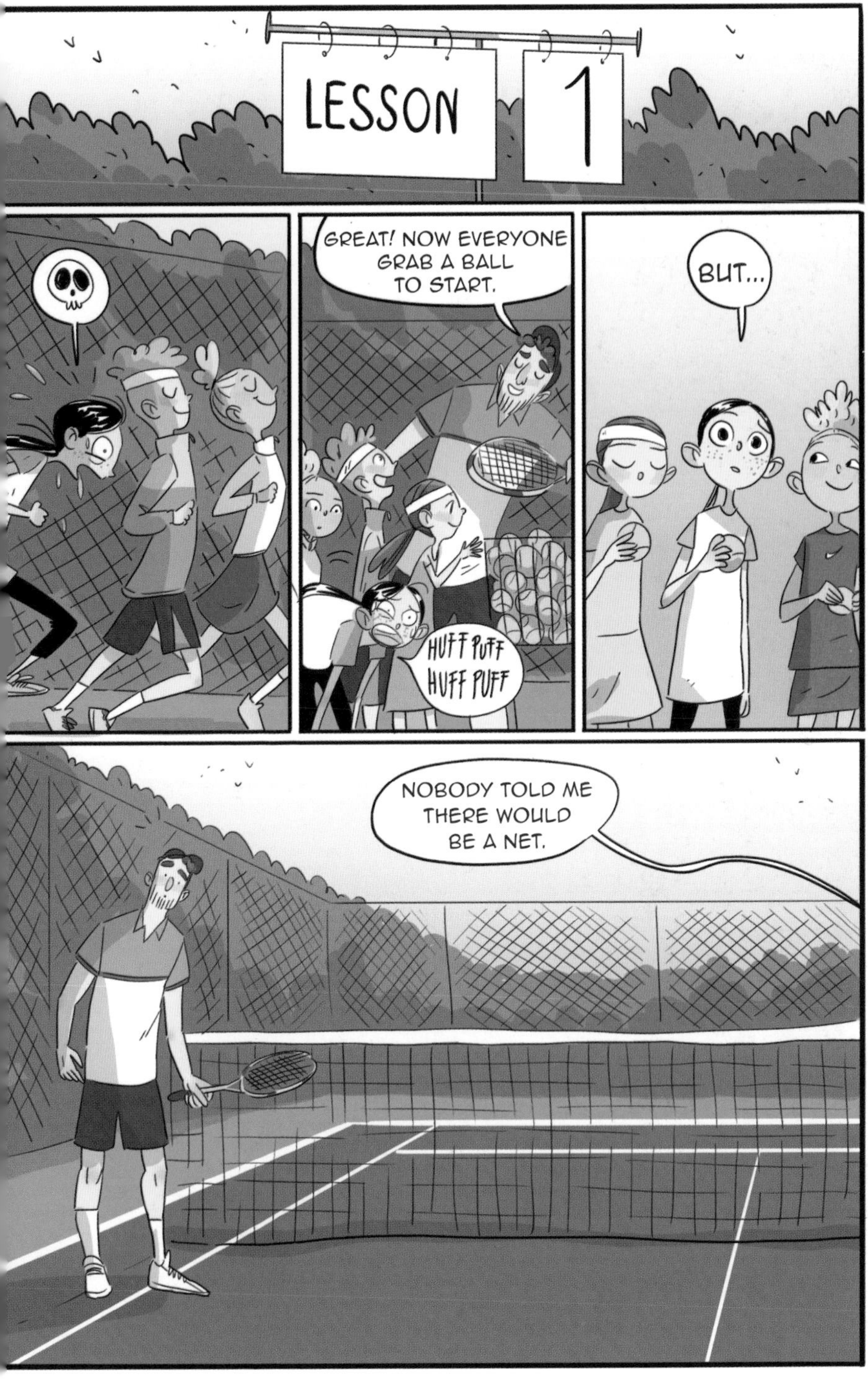
LESSON 1
GREAT! NOW EVERYONE GRAB A BALL TO START.
HUFF PUFF HUFF PUFF
BUT...
NOBODY TOLD ME THERE WOULD BE A NET.

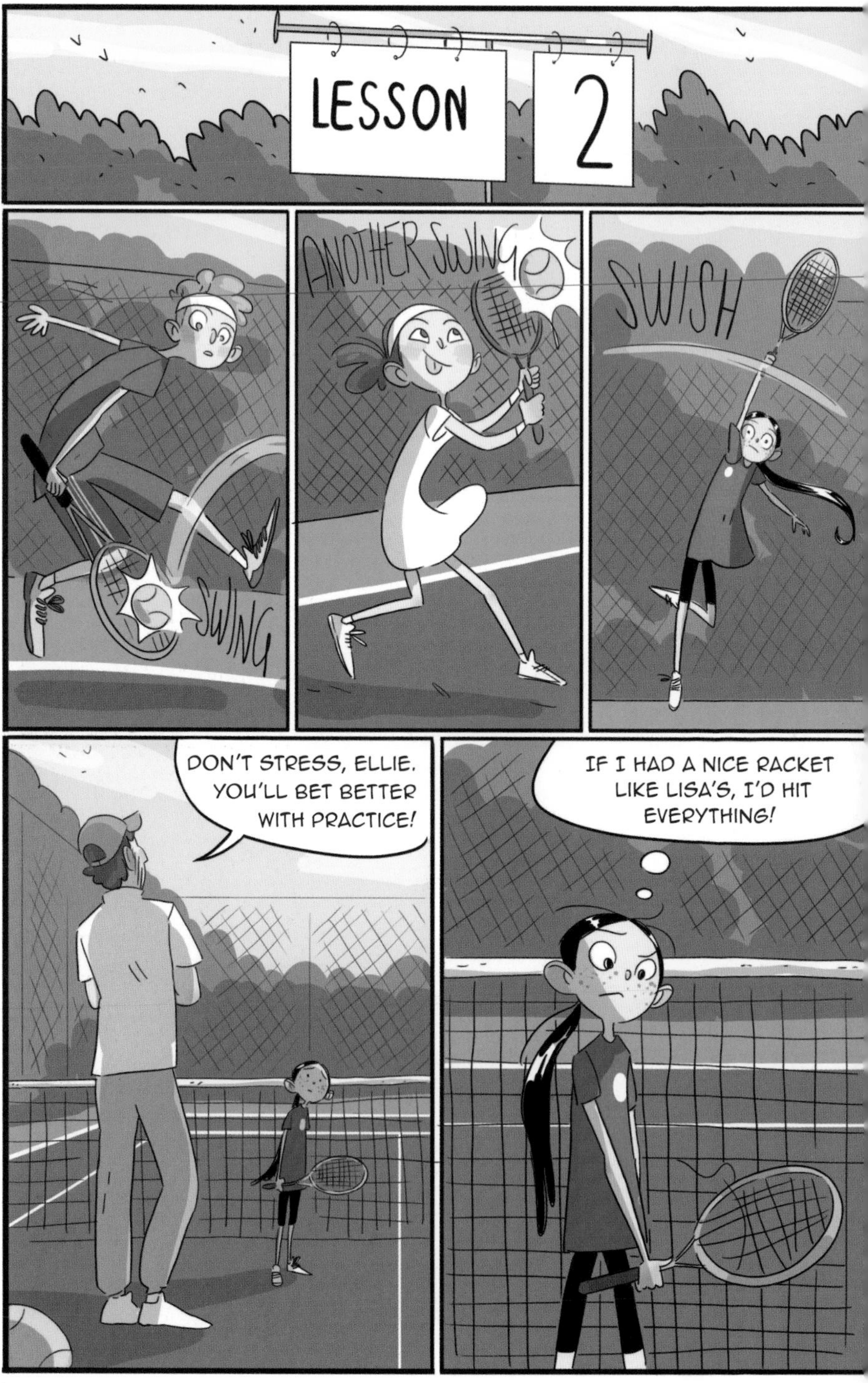
LESSON 2
SWING
ANOTHER SWING
SWISH
DON'T STRESS, ELLIE. YOU'LL BET BETTER WITH PRACTICE!
IF I HAD A NICE RACKET LIKE LISA'S, I'D HIT EVERYTHING!

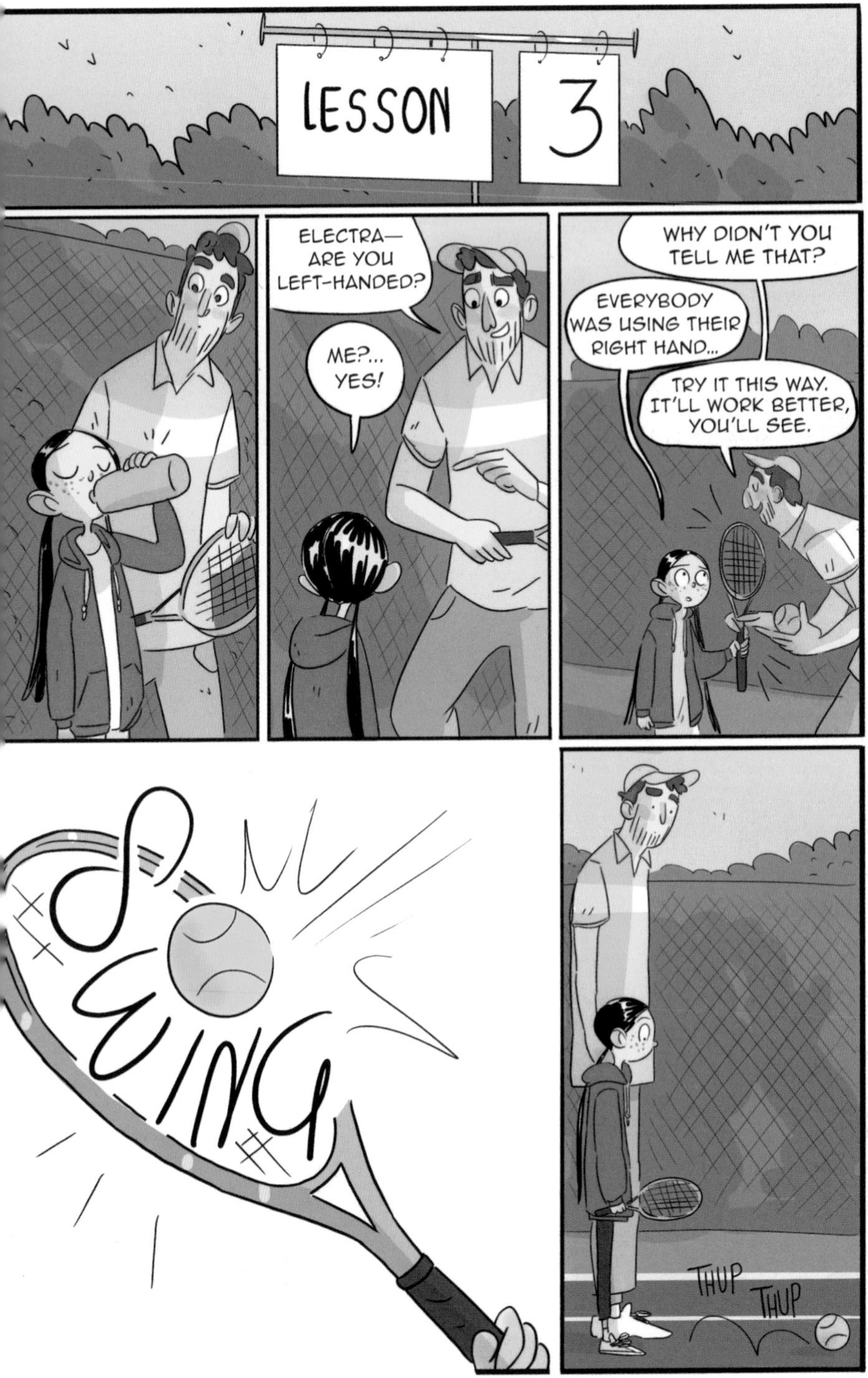
LESSON 3
ELECTRA—
ARE YOU
LEFT-HANDED?
ME?...
YES!
WHY DIDN'T YOU TELL ME THAT?
EVERYBODY WAS USING THEIR RIGHT HAND...
TRY IT THIS WAY. IT'LL WORK BETTER, YOU'LL SEE.
SWING
THUP THUP

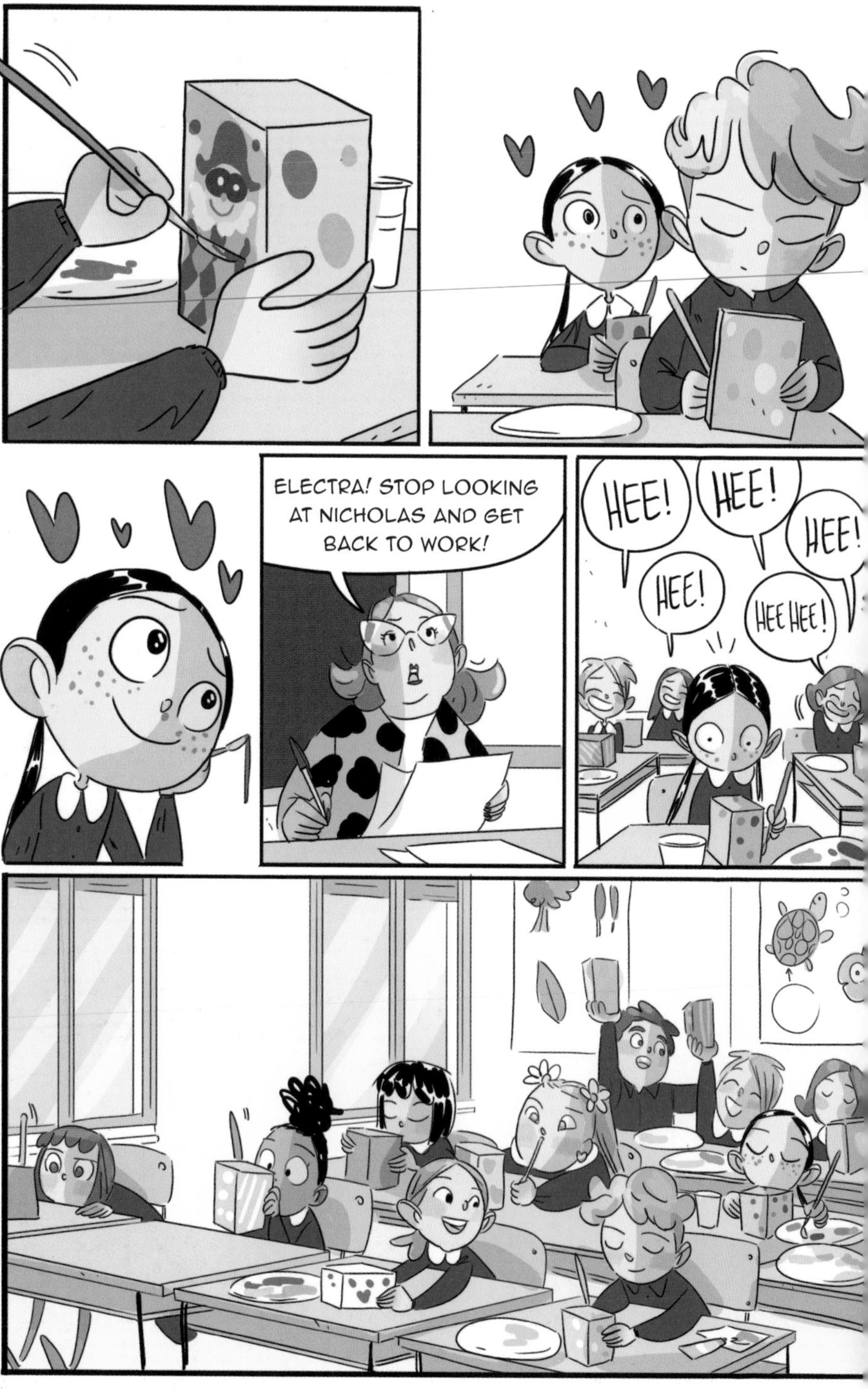

ELECTRA! STOP LOOKING AT NICHOLAS AND GET BACK TO WORK!
HEE!
HEE!
HEE!
HEE!
HEE HEE!

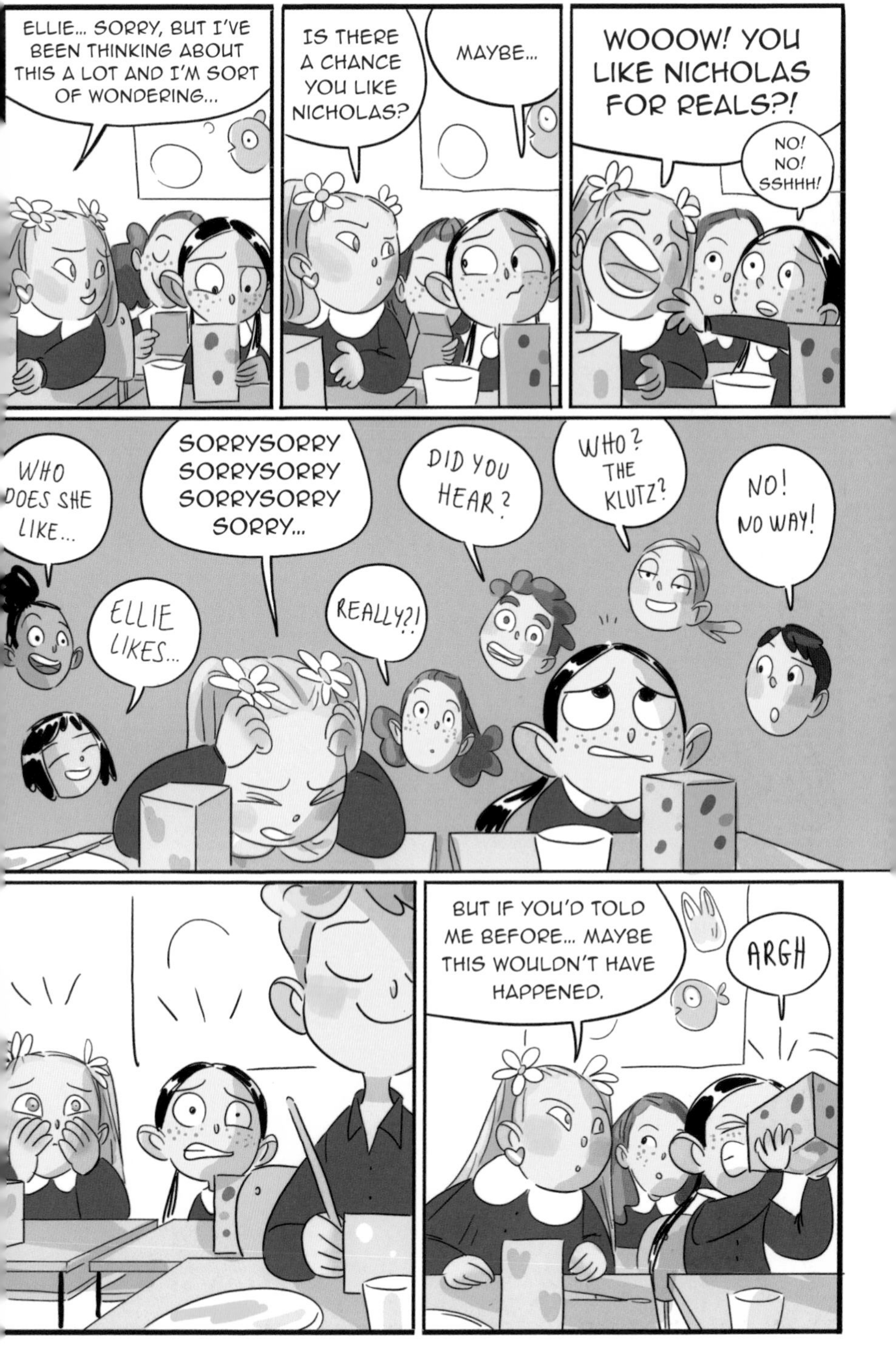
ELLIE... SORRY, BUT I'VE BEEN THINKING ABOUT THIS A LOT AND I'M SORT OF WONDERING...
IS THERE A CHANCE YOU LIKE NICHOLAS?
MAYBE...
WOOOW! YOU LIKE NICHOLAS FOR REALS?!
NO! NO! SSHHH!
WHO DOES SHE LIKE...
SORRYSORRY SORRYSORRY SORRYSORRY SORRY...
DID YOU HEAR?
WHO? THE KLUTZ?
NO! NO WAY!
ELLIE LIKES...
REALLY?!
BUT IF YOU'D TOLD ME BEFORE... MAYBE THIS WOULDN'T HAVE HAPPENED.
ARGH

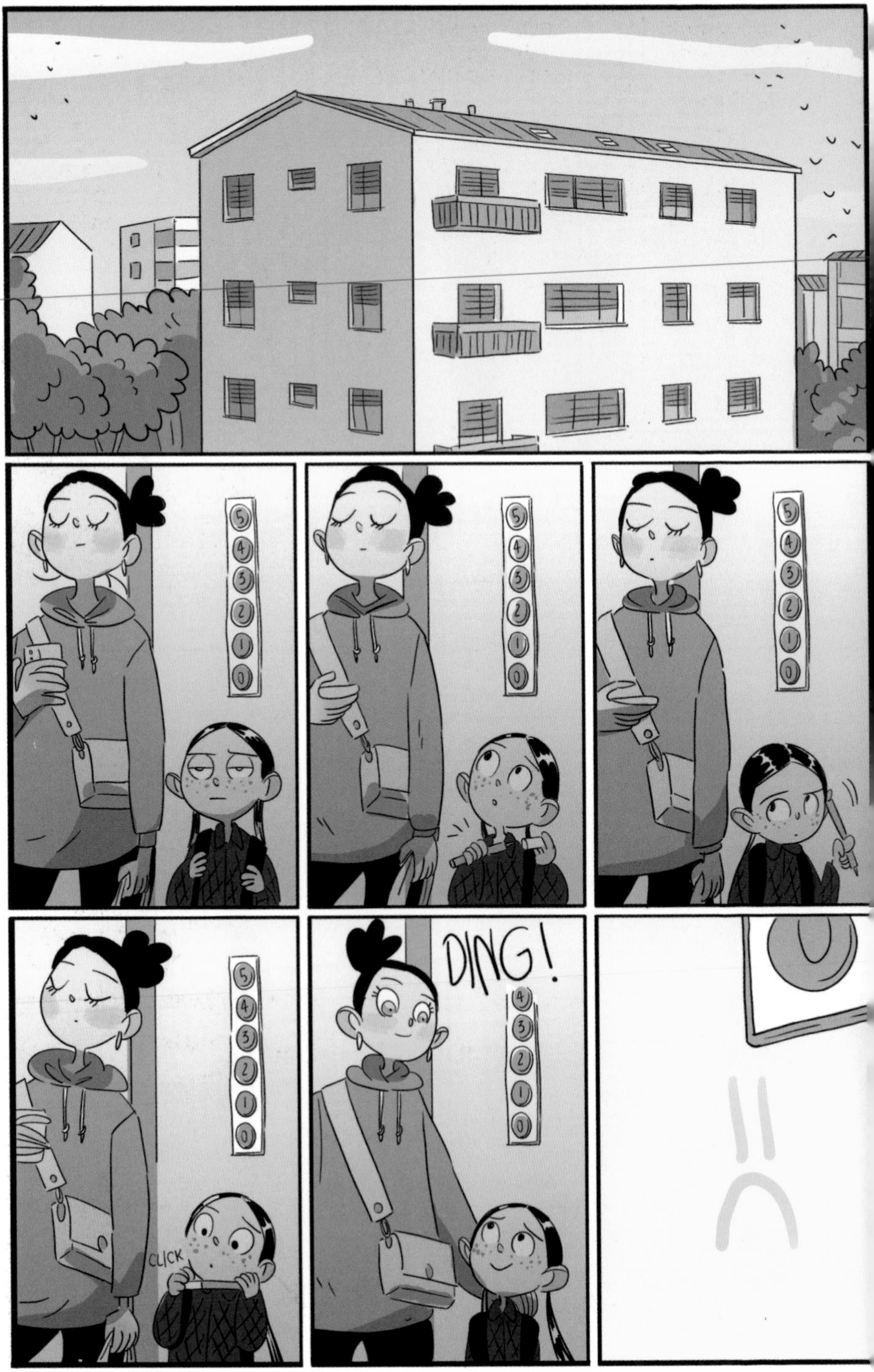
CLICK
DING!

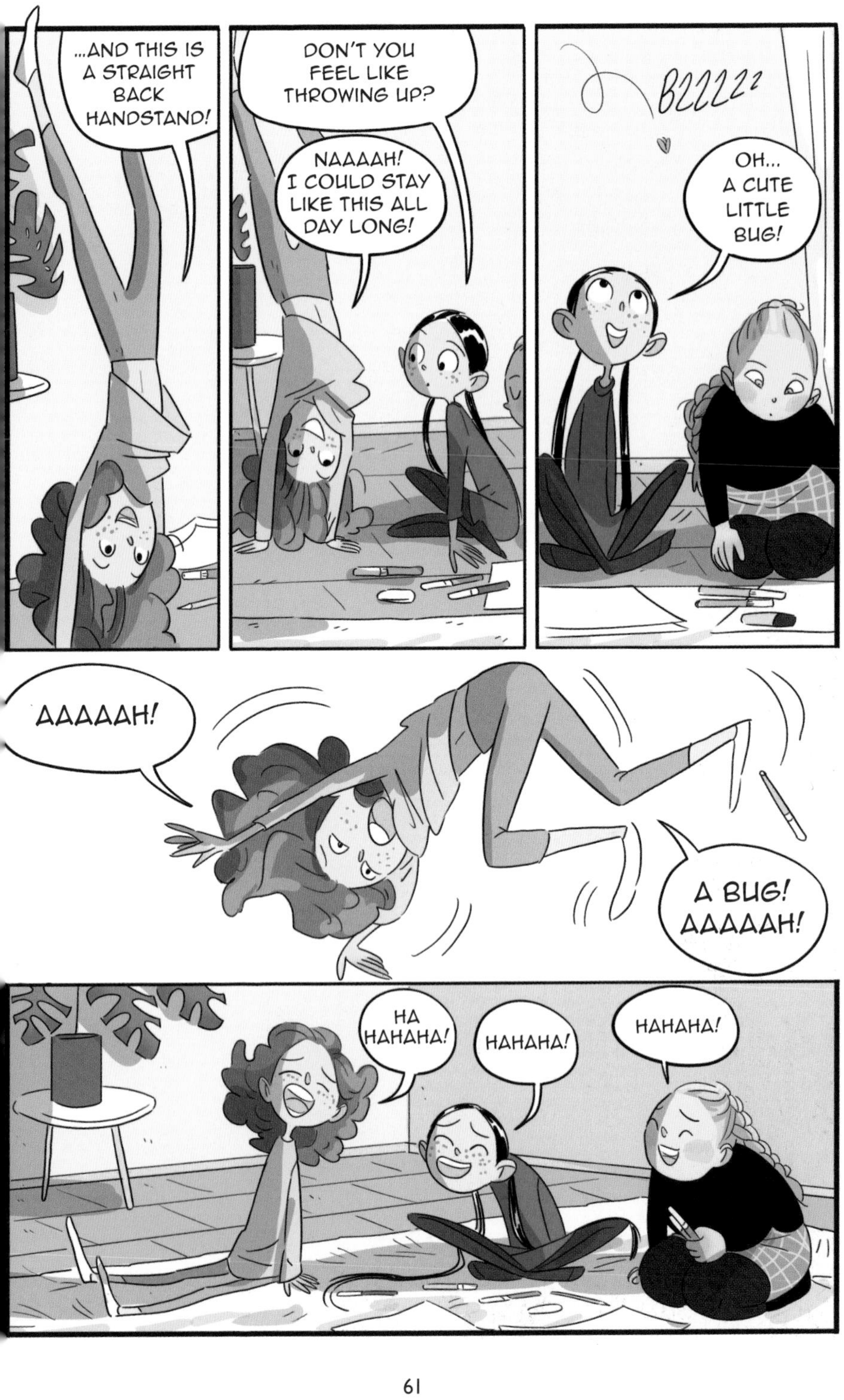
...AND THIS IS A STRAIGHT BACK HANDSTAND!
DON'T YOU FEEL LIKE THROWING UP?
NAAAAH! I COULD STAY LIKE THIS ALL DAY LONG!
BZZZZZ
OH... A CUTE LITTLE BUG!
AAAAAH!
A BUG! AAAAAH!
HA HAHAHA!
HAHAHA!
HAHAHA!

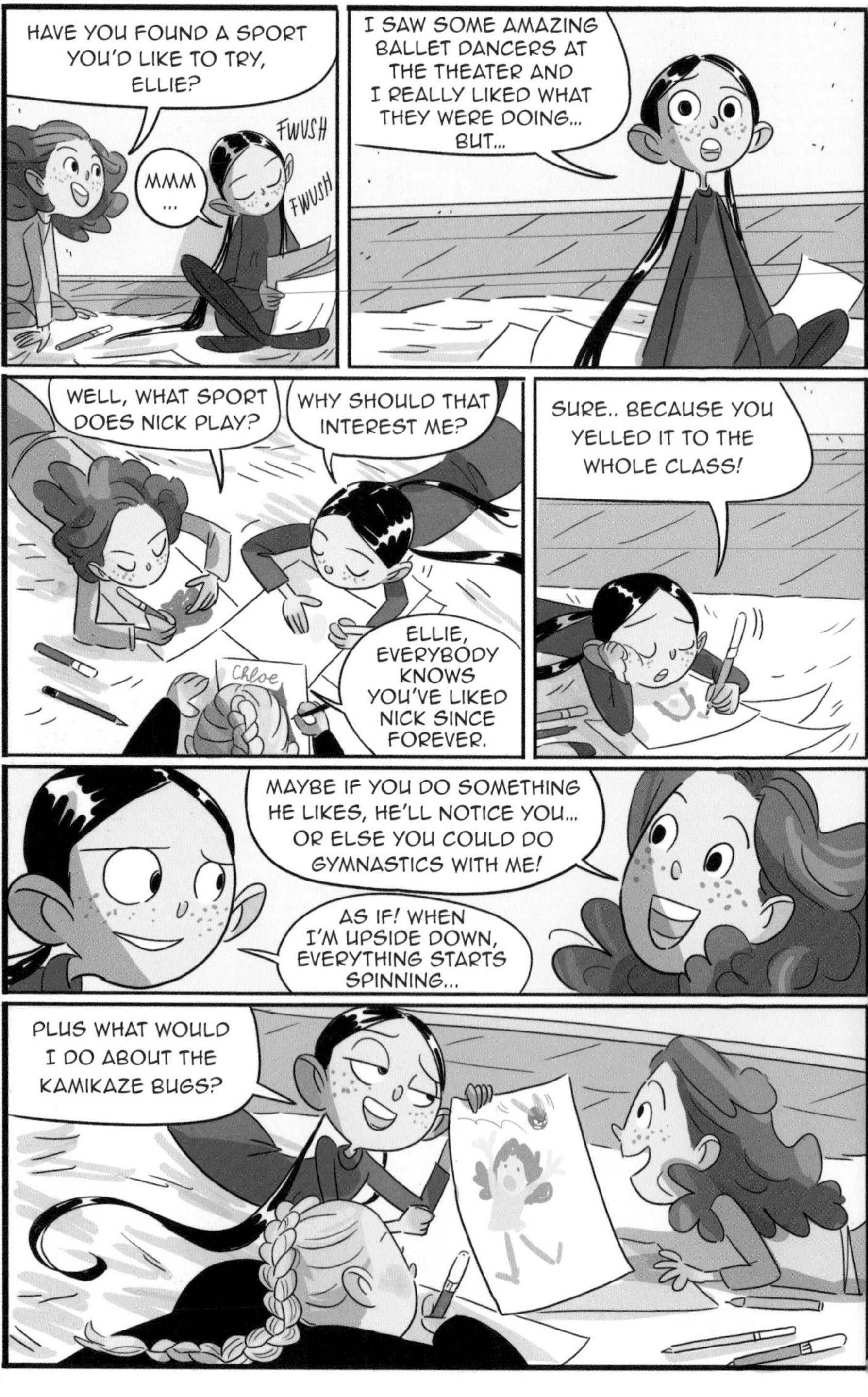
HAVE YOU FOUND A SPORT YOU'D LIKE TO TRY, ELLIE?
MMM ...
FWUSH
FWUSH
I SAW SOME AMAZING BALLET DANCERS AT THE THEATER AND I REALLY LIKED WHAT THEY WERE DOING... BUT...
WELL, WHAT SPORT DOES NICK PLAY?
WHY SHOULD THAT INTEREST ME?
Chloe
ELLIE, EVERYBODY KNOWS YOU'VE LIKED NICK SINCE FOREVER.
SURE.. BECAUSE YOU YELLED IT TO THE WHOLE CLASS!
MAYBE IF YOU DO SOMETHING HE LIKES, HE'LL NOTICE YOU... OR ELSE YOU COULD DO GYMNASTICS WITH ME!
AS IF! WHEN I'M UPSIDE DOWN, EVERYTHING STARTS SPINNING...
PLUS WHAT WOULD I DO ABOUT THE KAMIKAZE BUGS?

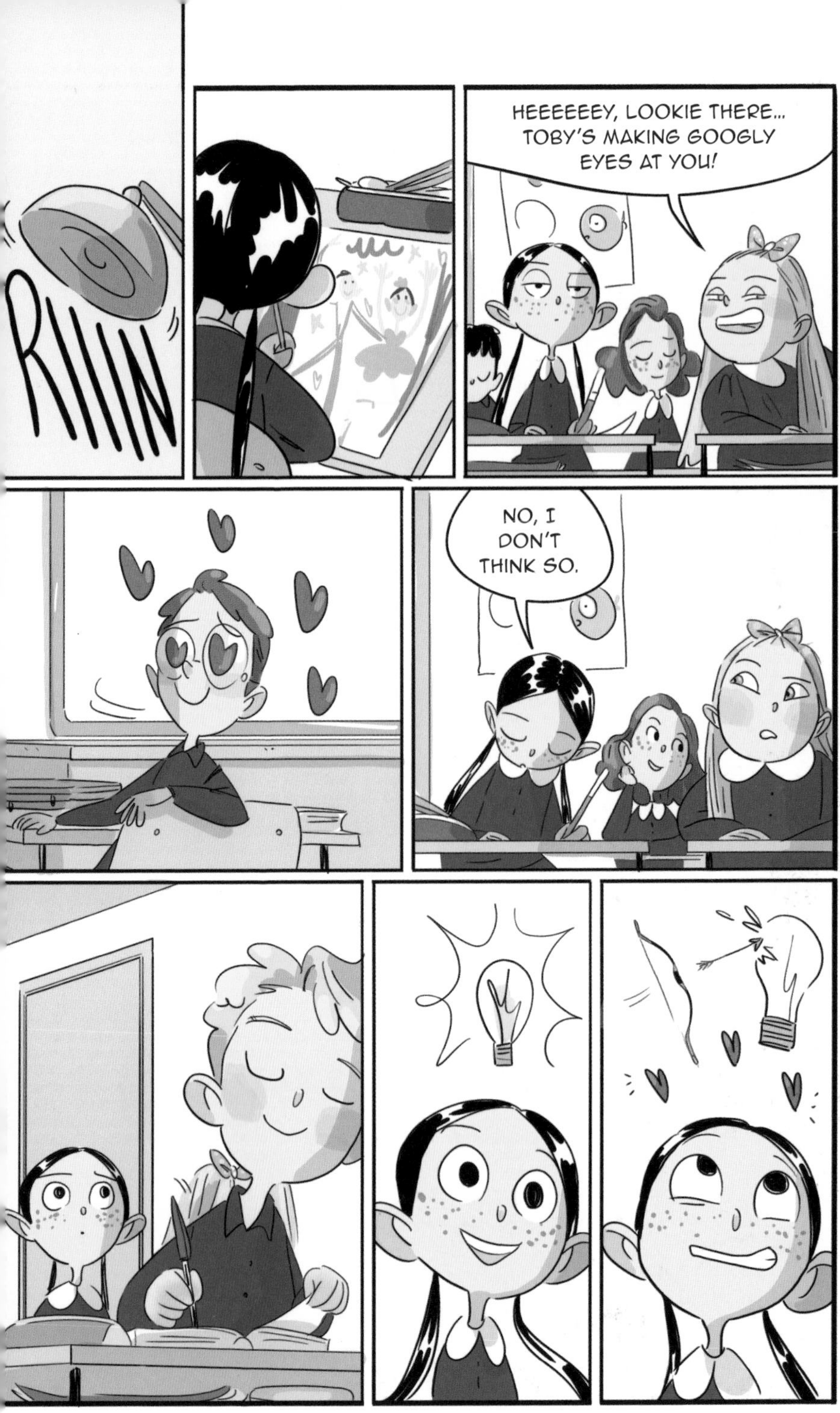
RIIIN
HEEEEEEY, LOOKIE THERE... TOBY'S MAKING GOOGLY EYES AT YOU!
NO, I DON'T THINK SO.

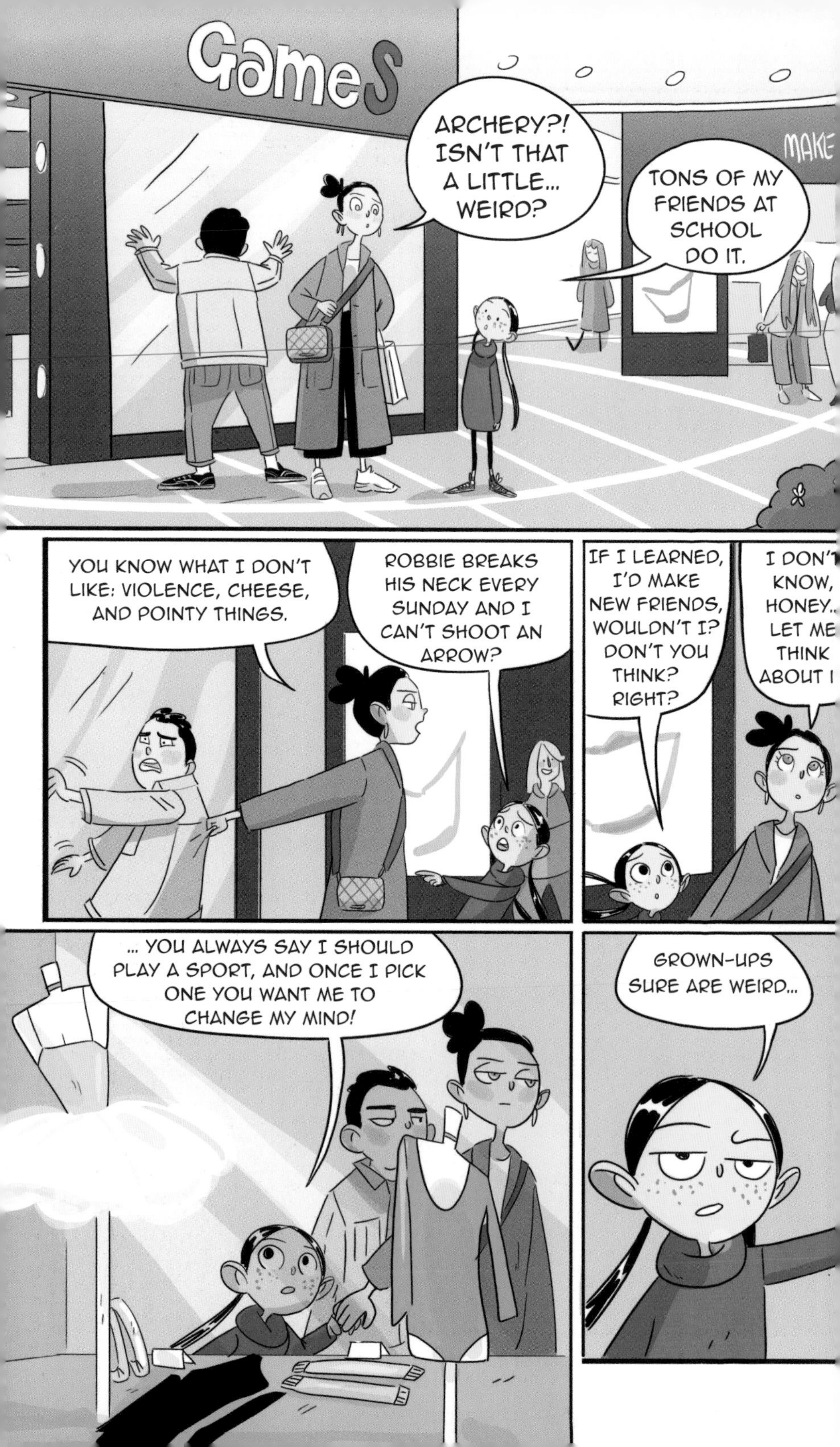
GameS
ARCHERY?! ISN'T THAT A LITTLE... WEIRD?
MAKE
TONS OF MY FRIENDS AT SCHOOL DO IT.
YOU KNOW WHAT I DON'T LIKE: VIOLENCE, CHEESE, AND POINTY THINGS.
ROBBIE BREAKS HIS NECK EVERY SUNDAY AND I CAN'T SHOOT AN ARROW?
IF I LEARNED, I'D MAKE NEW FRIENDS, WOULDN'T I? DON'T YOU THINK? RIGHT?
I DON'T KNOW, HONEY... LET ME THINK ABOUT I
... YOU ALWAYS SAY I SHOULD PLAY A SPORT, AND ONCE I PICK ONE YOU WANT ME TO CHANGE MY MIND!
GROWN-UPS SURE ARE WEIRD...

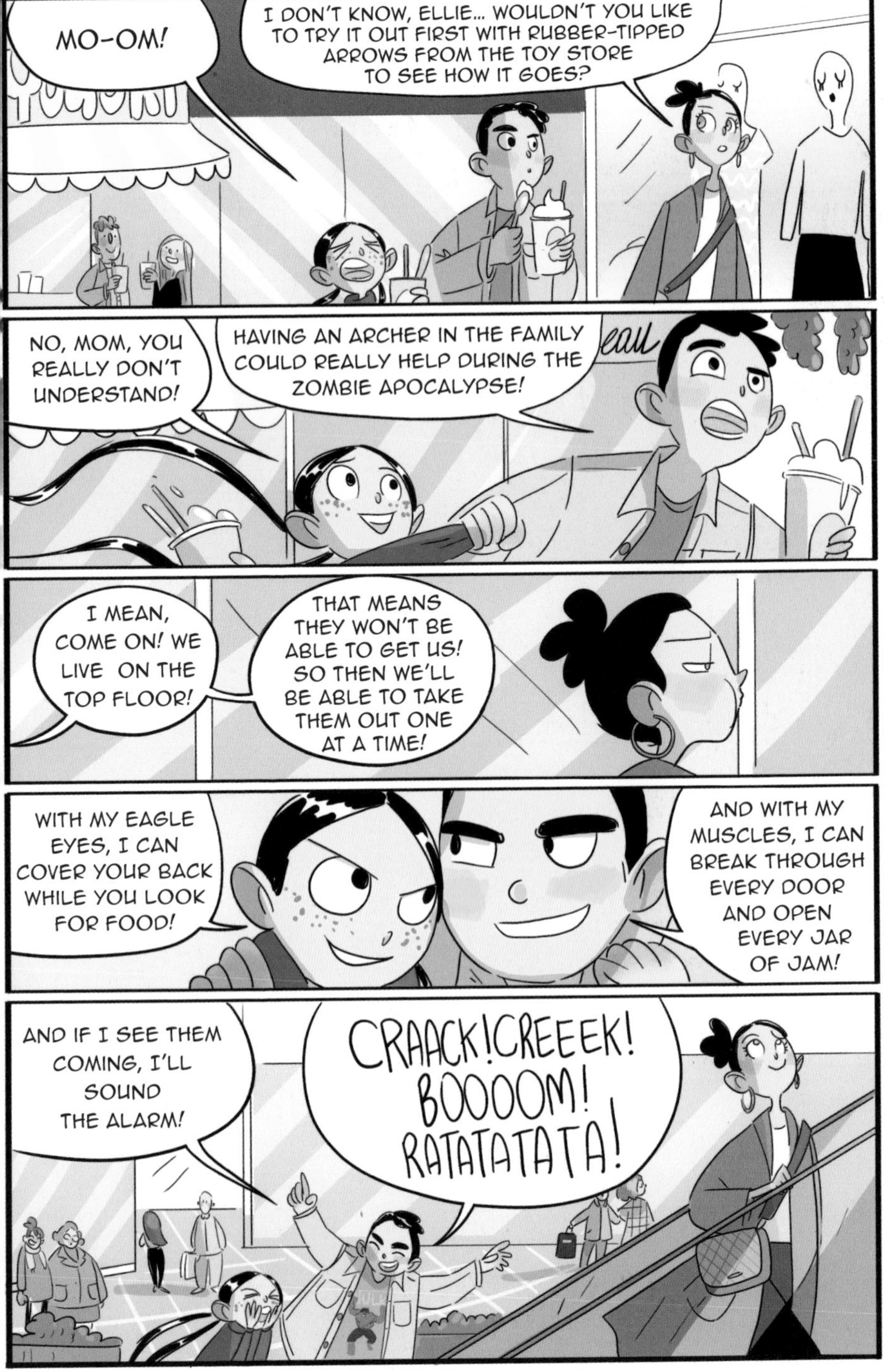
MO-OM!
I DON'T KNOW, ELLIE... WOULDN'T YOU LIKE TO TRY IT OUT FIRST WITH RUBBER-TIPPED ARROWS FROM THE TOY STORE TO SEE HOW IT GOES?
NO, MOM, YOU REALLY DON'T UNDERSTAND!
HAVING AN ARCHER IN THE FAMILY COULD REALLY HELP DURING THE ZOMBIE APOCALYPSE!
I MEAN, COME ON! WE LIVE ON THE TOP FLOOR!
THAT MEANS THEY WON'T BE ABLE TO GET US! SO THEN WE'LL BE ABLE TO TAKE THEM OUT ONE AT A TIME!
WITH MY EAGLE EYES, I CAN COVER YOUR BACK WHILE YOU LOOK FOR FOOD!
AND WITH MY MUSCLES, I CAN BREAK THROUGH EVERY DOOR AND OPEN EVERY JAR OF JAM!
AND IF I SEE THEM COMING, I'LL SOUND THE ALARM!
CRAACK! CREEEK! BOOOOM! RATATATATA!

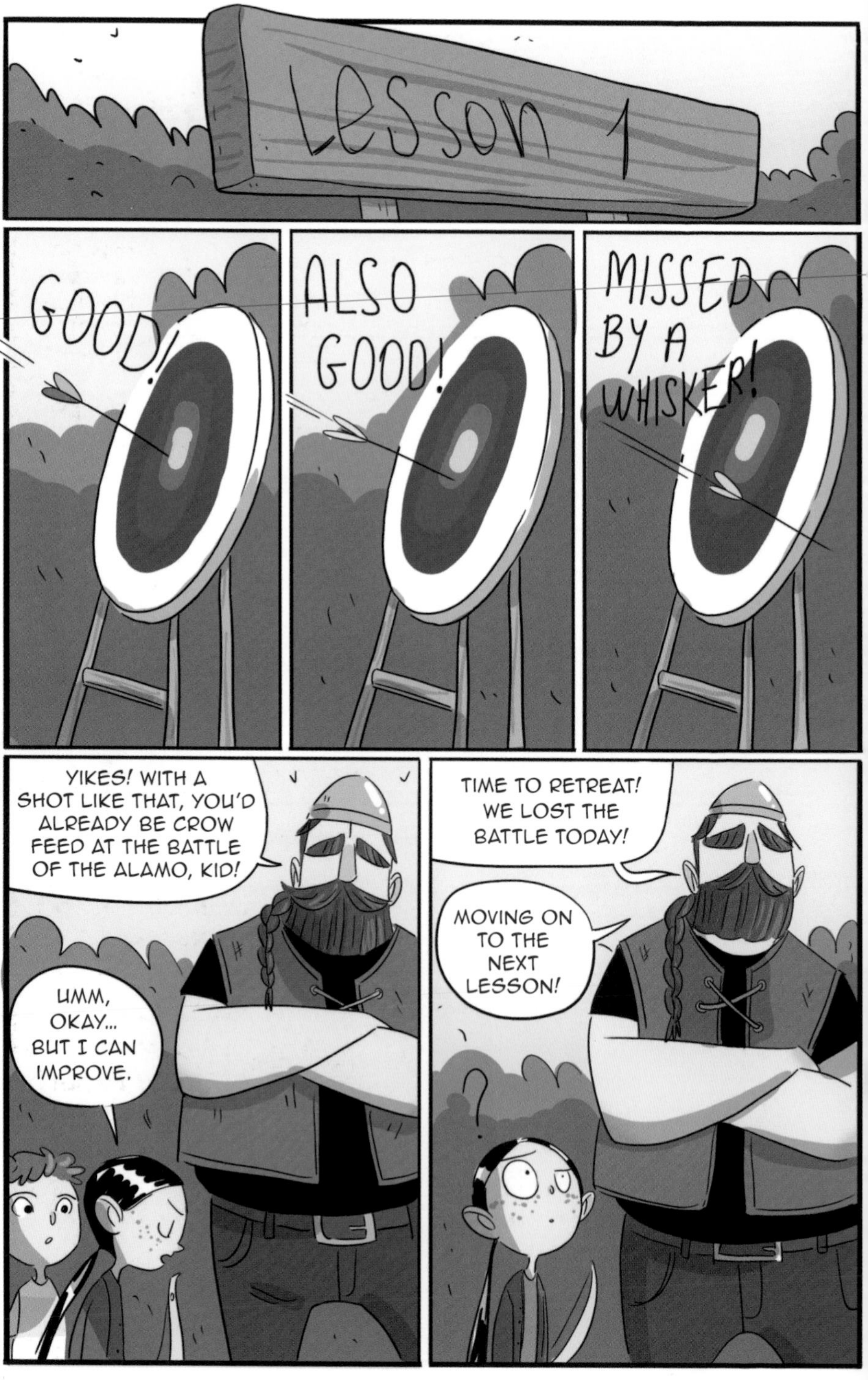

LESSON 1
GOOD!
ALSO GOOD!
MISSED BY A WHISKER!
YIKES! WITH A SHOT LIKE THAT, YOU'D ALREADY BE CROW FEED AT THE BATTLE OF THE ALAMO, KID!
UMM, OKAY... BUT I CAN IMPROVE.
TIME TO RETREAT! WE LOST THE BATTLE TODAY!
MOVING ON TO THE NEXT LESSON!
?

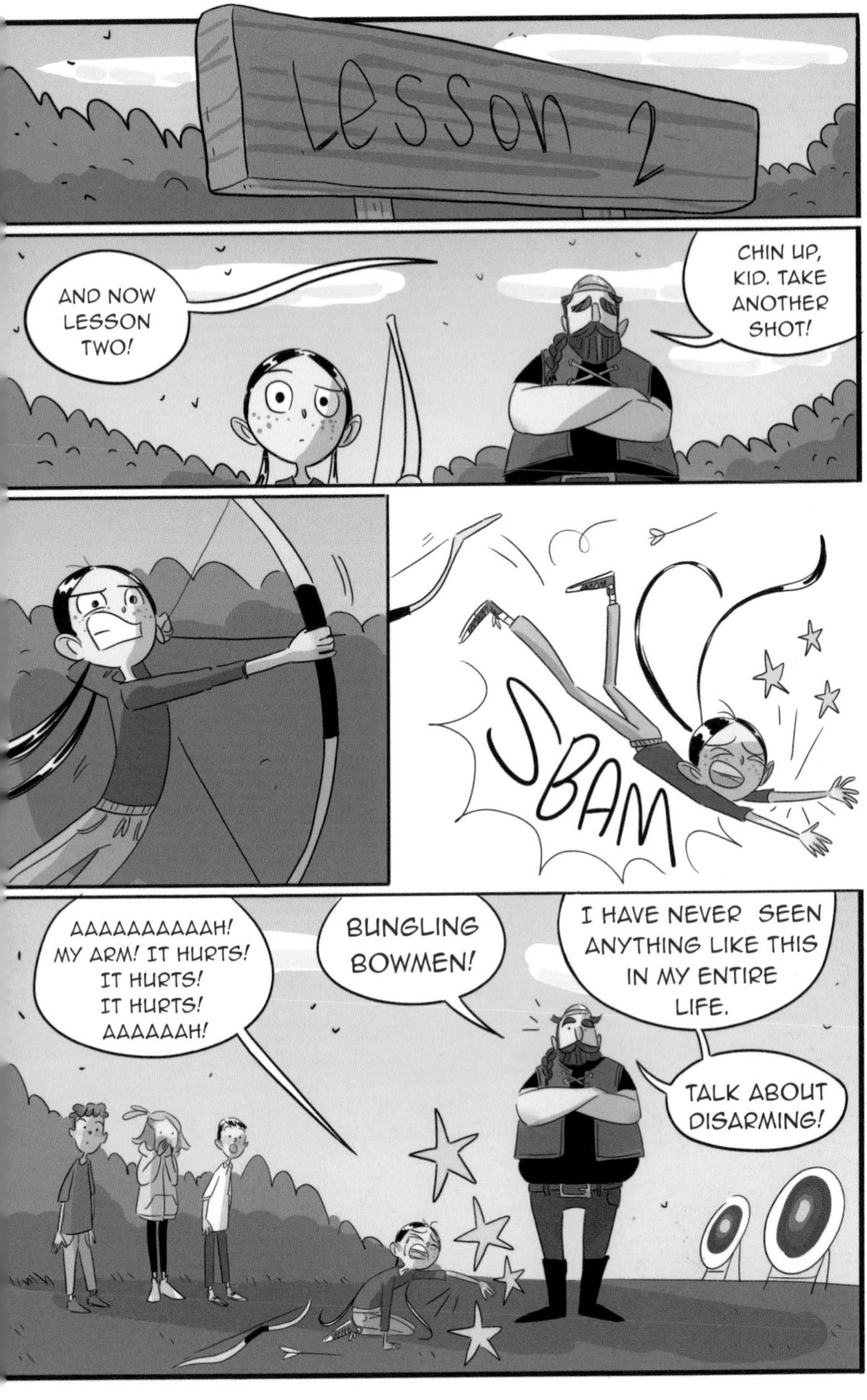
LESSON 2
AND NOW LESSON TWO!
CHIN UP, KID. TAKE ANOTHER SHOT!
SBAM
AAAAAAAAAAH! MY ARM! IT HURTS! IT HURTS! IT HURTS! AAAAAAH!
BUNGLING BOWMEN!
I HAVE NEVER SEEN ANYTHING LIKE THIS IN MY ENTIRE LIFE.
TALK ABOUT DISARMING!

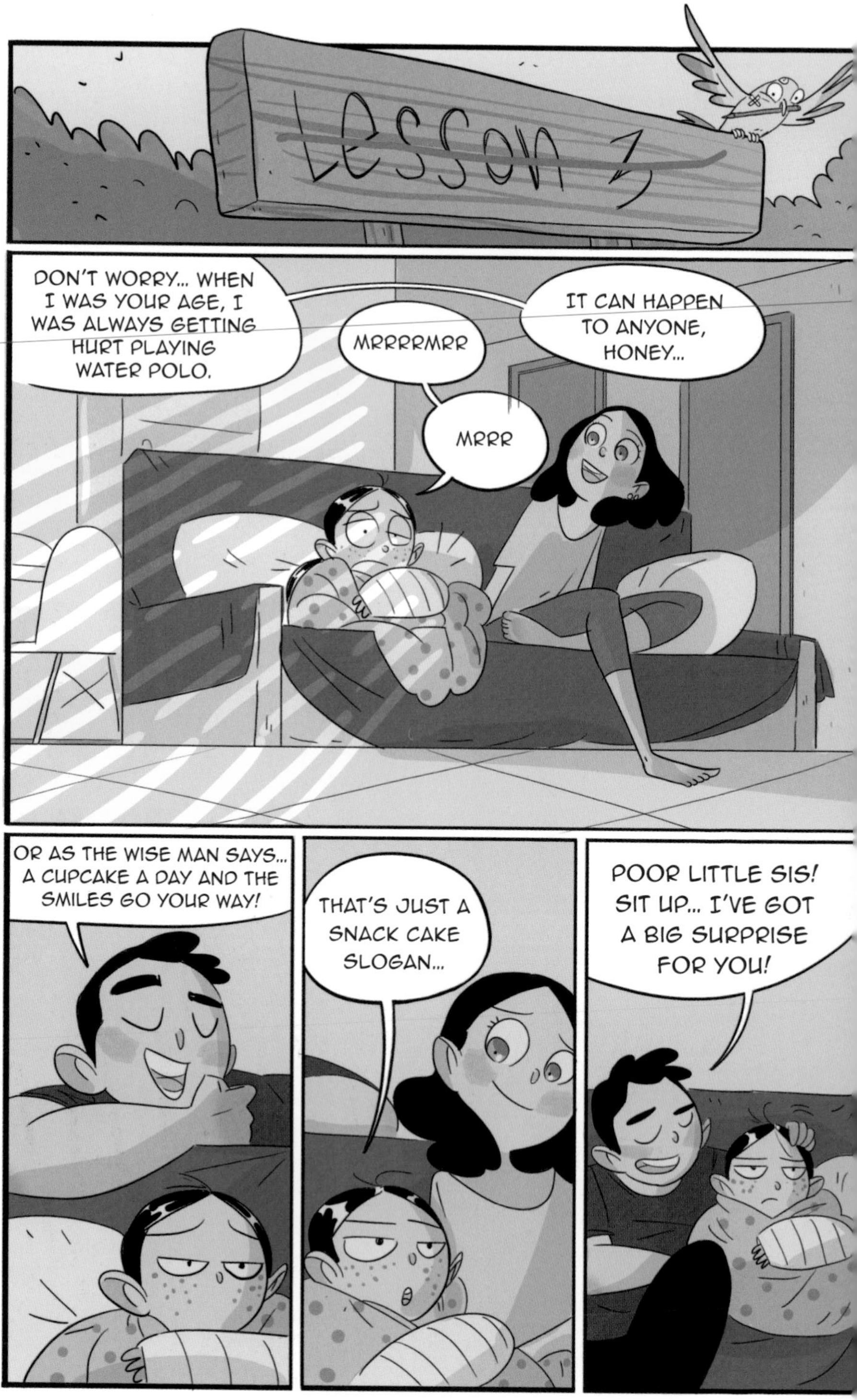
LESSON 1
DON'T WORRY... WHEN I WAS YOUR AGE, I WAS ALWAYS GETTING HURT PLAYING WATER POLO.
MRRRRMRR
IT CAN HAPPEN TO ANYONE, HONEY...
MRRR
OR AS THE WISE MAN SAYS... A CUPCAKE A DAY AND THE SMILES GO YOUR WAY!
THAT'S JUST A SNACK CAKE SLOGAN...
POOR LITTLE SIS! SIT UP... I'VE GOT A BIG SURPRISE FOR YOU!

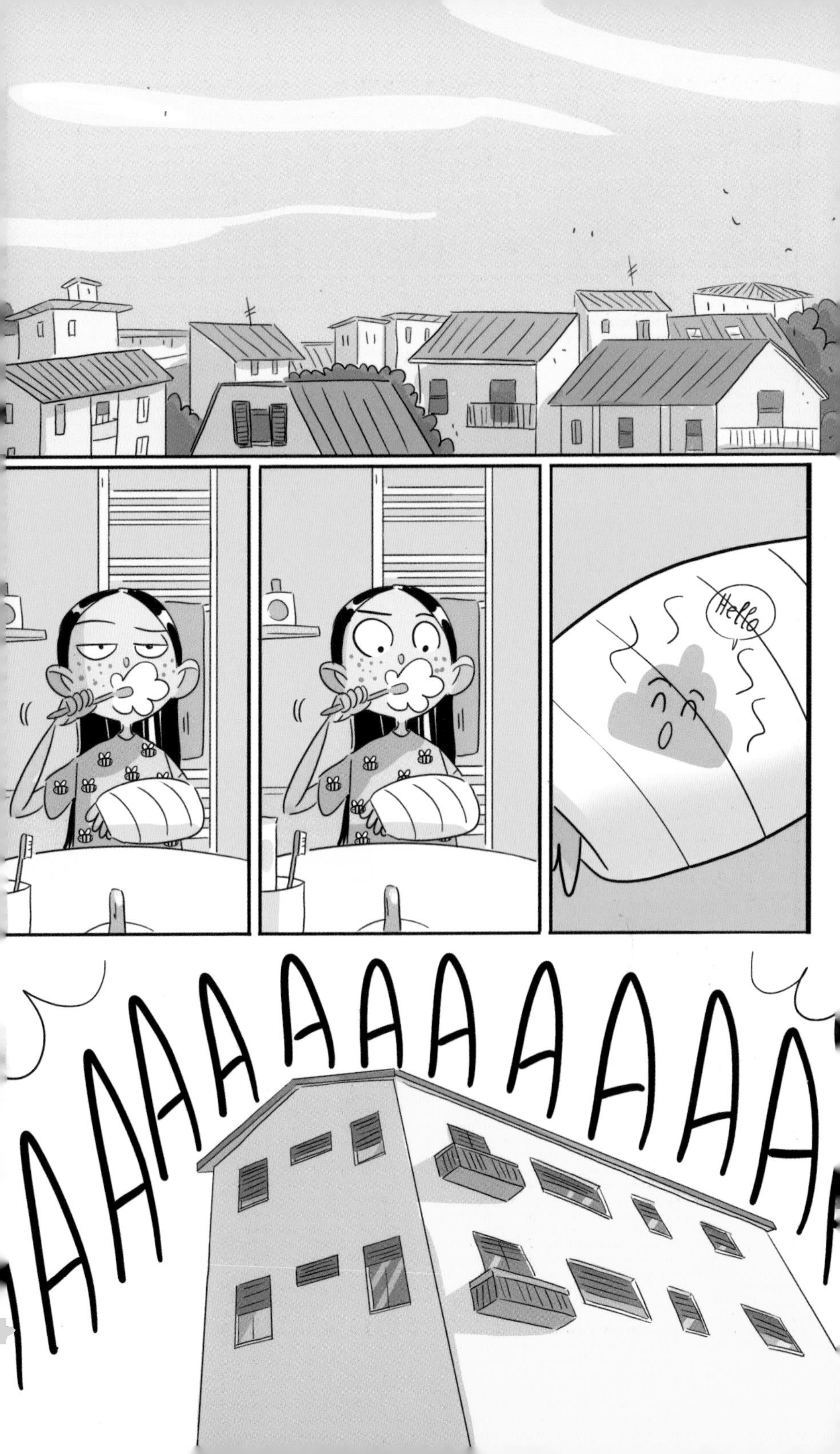
Hello
AAAAAAAAAAAAA

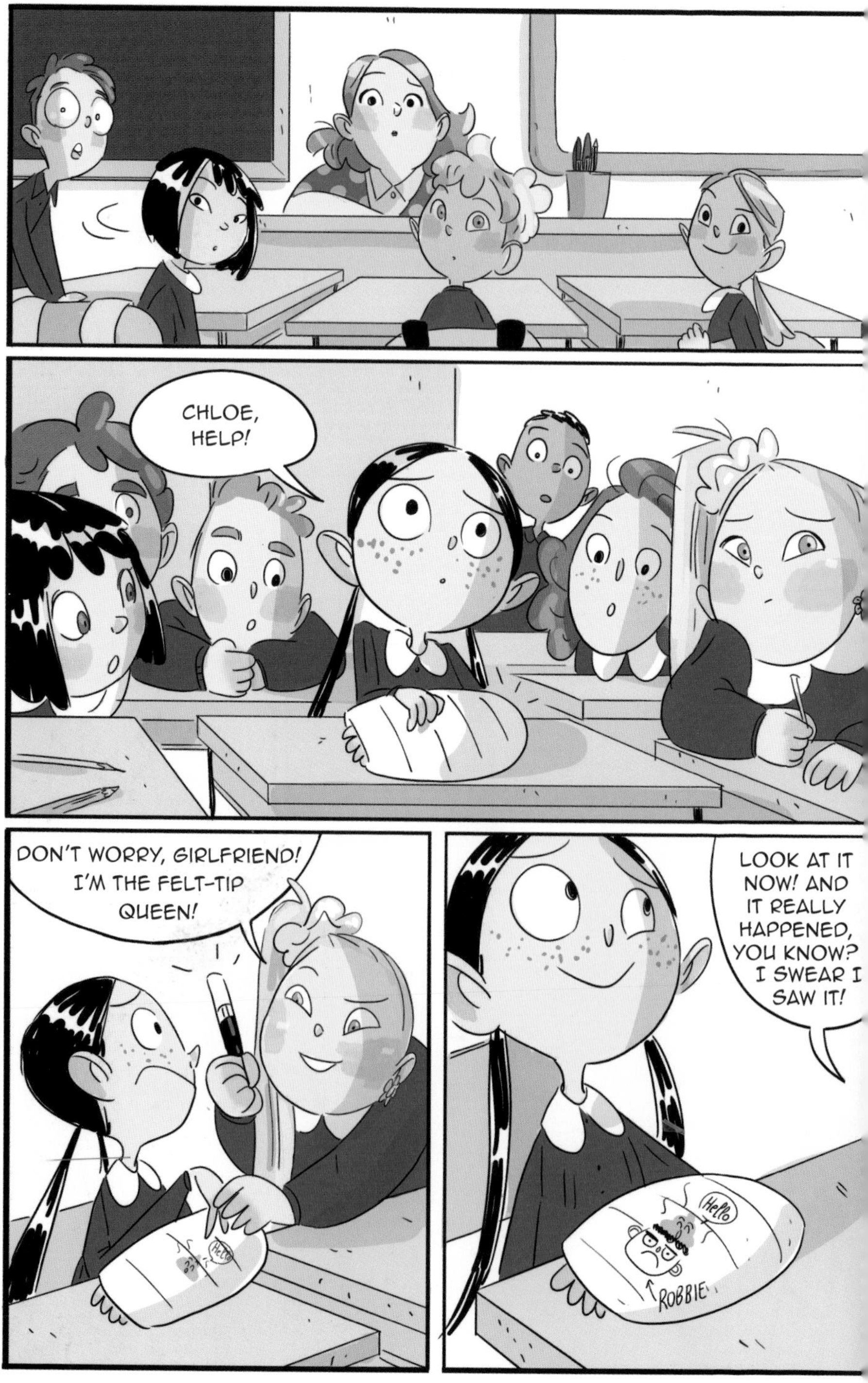
CHLOE, HELP!
DON'T WORRY, GIRLFRIEND! I'M THE FELT-TIP QUEEN!
LOOK AT IT NOW! AND IT REALLY HAPPENED, YOU KNOW? I SWEAR I SAW IT!
Hello
ROBBIE

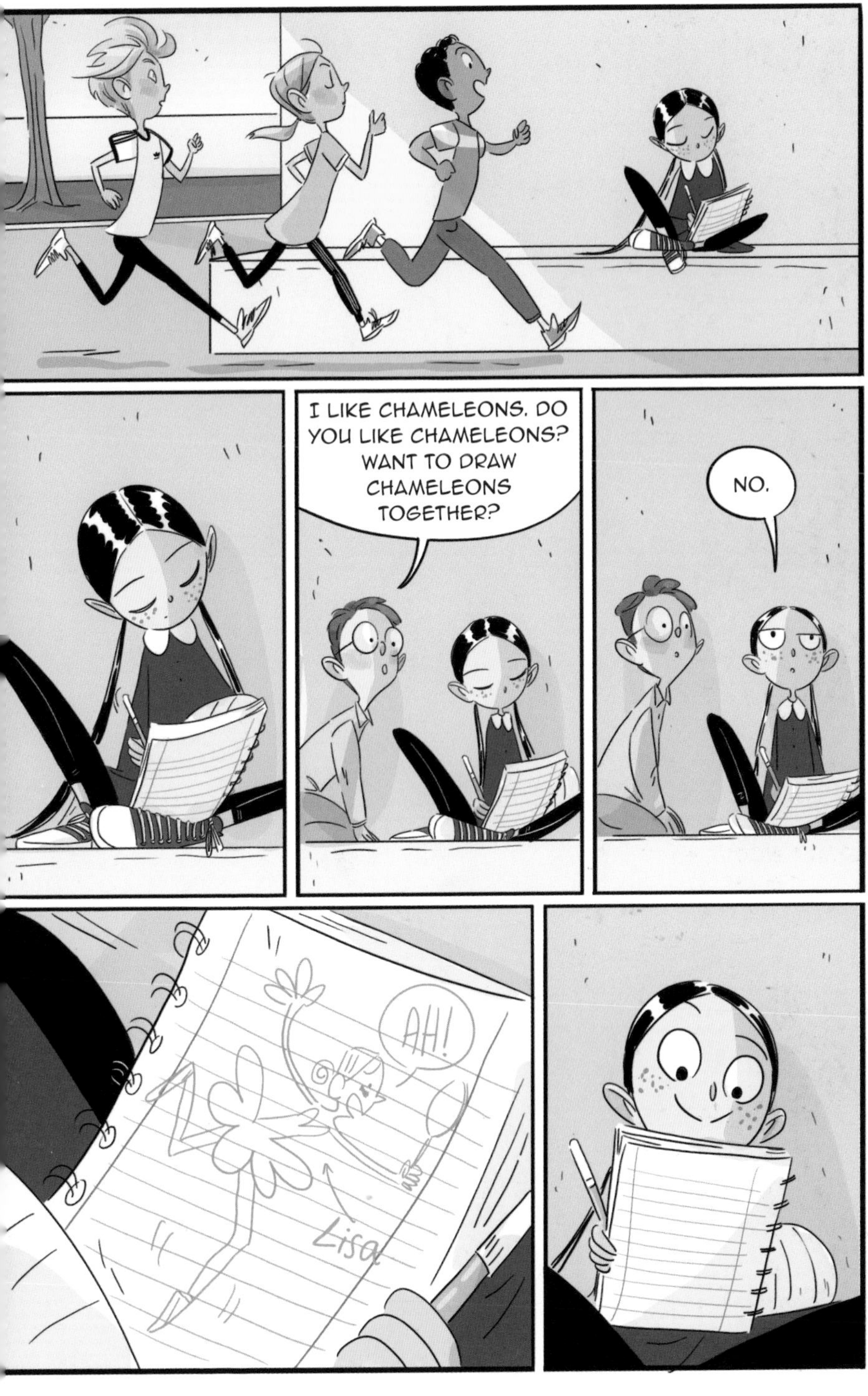
I LIKE CHAMELEONS. DO YOU LIKE CHAMELEONS? WANT TO DRAW CHAMELEONS TOGETHER?
NO.
AH!
Lisa

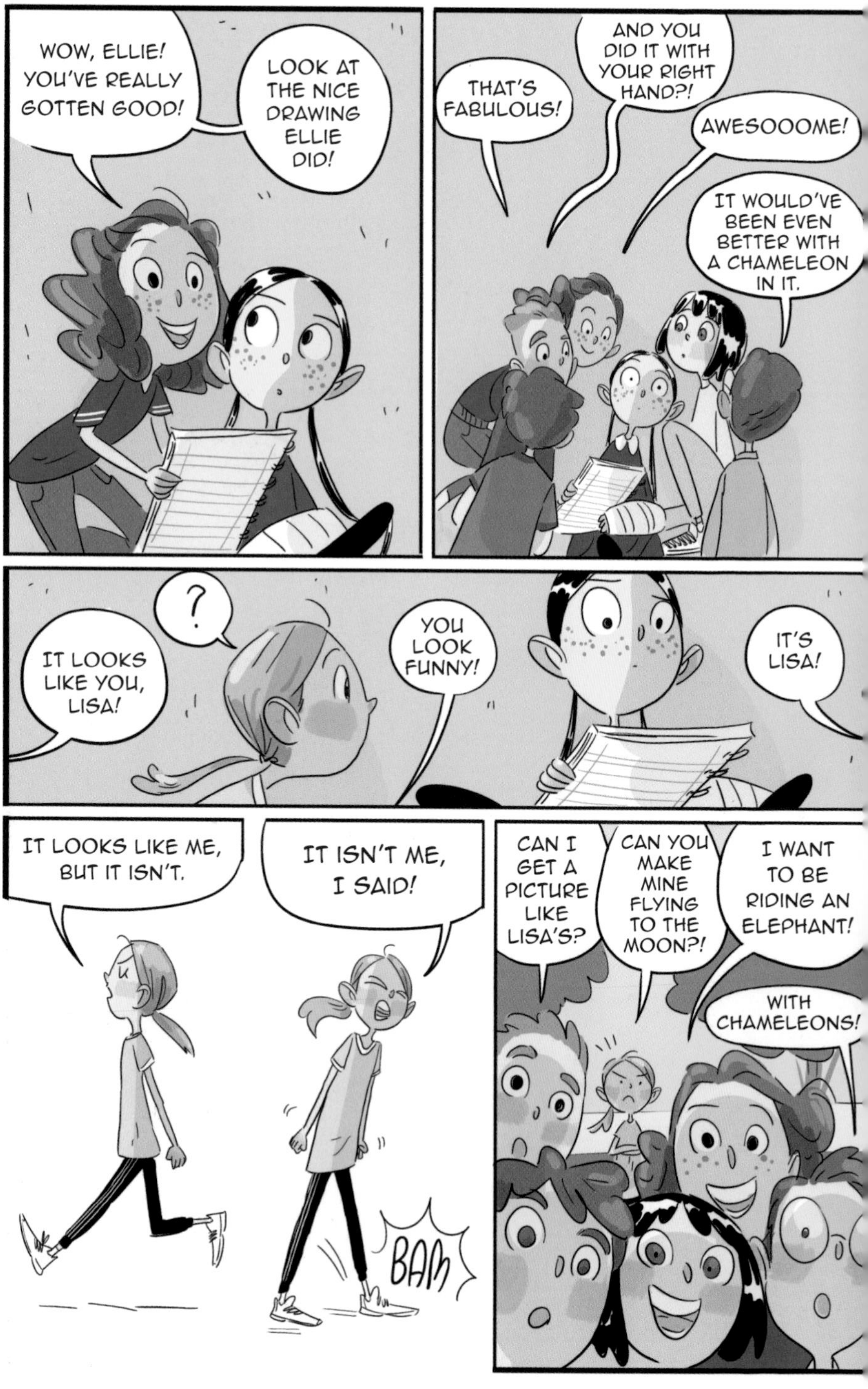
WOW, ELLIE! YOU'VE REALLY GOTTEN GOOD!
LOOK AT THE NICE DRAWING ELLIE DID!
THAT'S FABULOUS!
AND YOU DID IT WITH YOUR RIGHT HAND?!
AWESOOOME!
IT WOULD'VE BEEN EVEN BETTER WITH A CHAMELEON IN IT.
IT LOOKS LIKE YOU, LISA!
?
YOU LOOK FUNNY!
IT'S LISA!
IT LOOKS LIKE ME, BUT IT ISN'T.
IT ISN'T ME, I SAID!
BAM
CAN I GET A PICTURE LIKE LISA'S?
CAN YOU MAKE MINE FLYING TO THE MOON?!
I WANT TO BE RIDING AN ELEPHANT!
WITH CHAMELEONS!

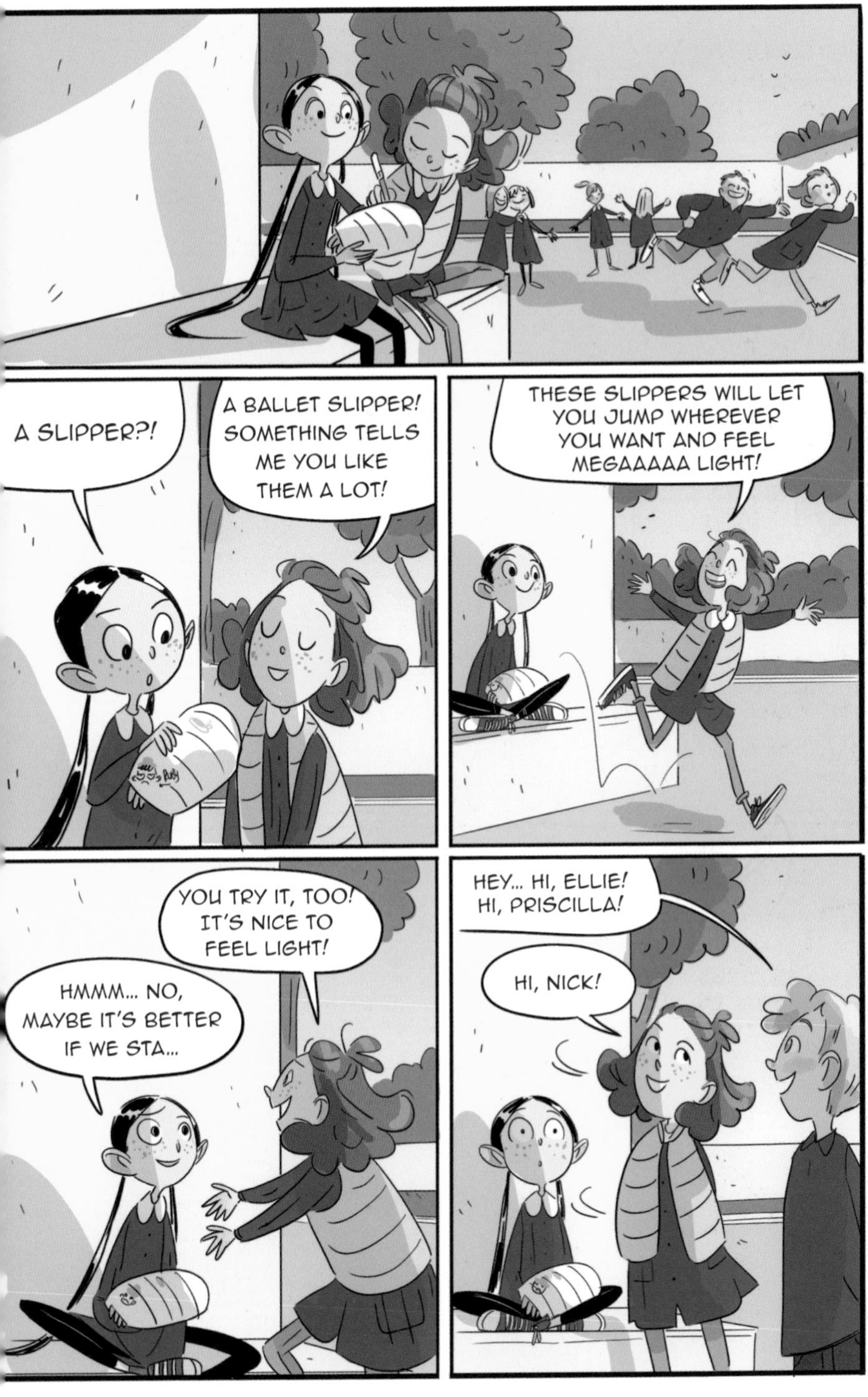
A SLIPPER?!
A BALLET SLIPPER! SOMETHING TELLS ME YOU LIKE THEM A LOT!
THESE SLIPPERS WILL LET YOU JUMP WHEREVER YOU WANT AND FEEL MEGAAAAA LIGHT!
YOU TRY IT, TOO! IT'S NICE TO FEEL LIGHT!
HMMM... NO, MAYBE IT'S BETTER IF WE STA...
HEY... HI, ELLIE! HI, PRISCILLA!
HI, NICK!

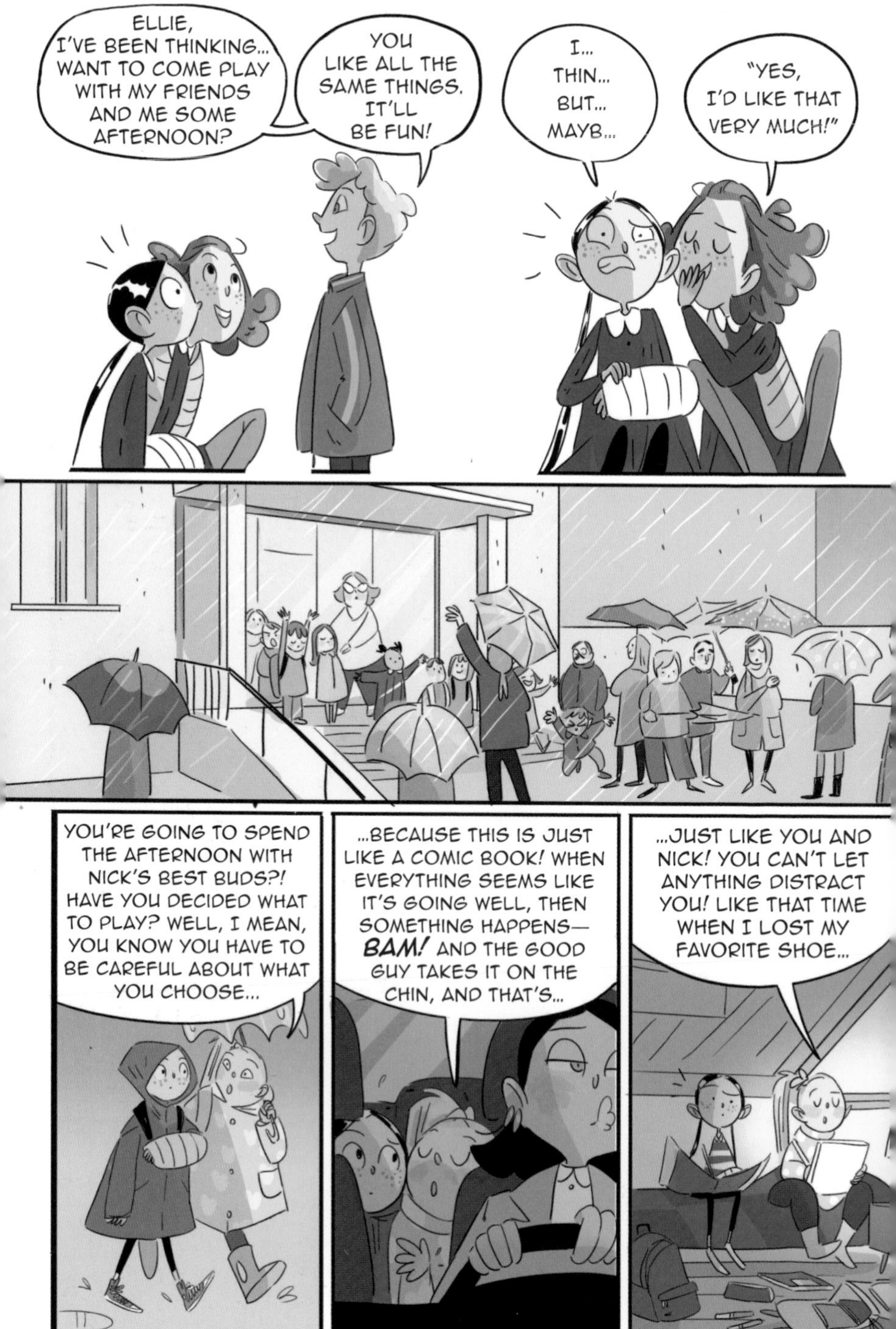
ELLIE, I'VE BEEN THINKING... WANT TO COME PLAY WITH MY FRIENDS AND ME SOME AFTERNOON?
YOU LIKE ALL THE SAME THINGS. IT'LL BE FUN!
I... THIN... BUT... MAYB...
"YES, I'D LIKE THAT VERY MUCH!"
YOU'RE GOING TO SPEND THE AFTERNOON WITH NICK'S BEST BUDS?! HAVE YOU DECIDED WHAT TO PLAY? WELL, I MEAN, YOU KNOW YOU HAVE TO BE CAREFUL ABOUT WHAT YOU CHOOSE...
...BECAUSE THIS IS JUST LIKE A COMIC BOOK! WHEN EVERYTHING SEEMS LIKE IT'S GOING WELL, THEN SOMETHING HAPPENS—*BAM!* AND THE GOOD GUY TAKES IT ON THE CHIN, AND THAT'S...
...JUST LIKE YOU AND NICK! YOU CAN'T LET ANYTHING DISTRACT YOU! LIKE THAT TIME WHEN I LOST MY FAVORITE SHOE...

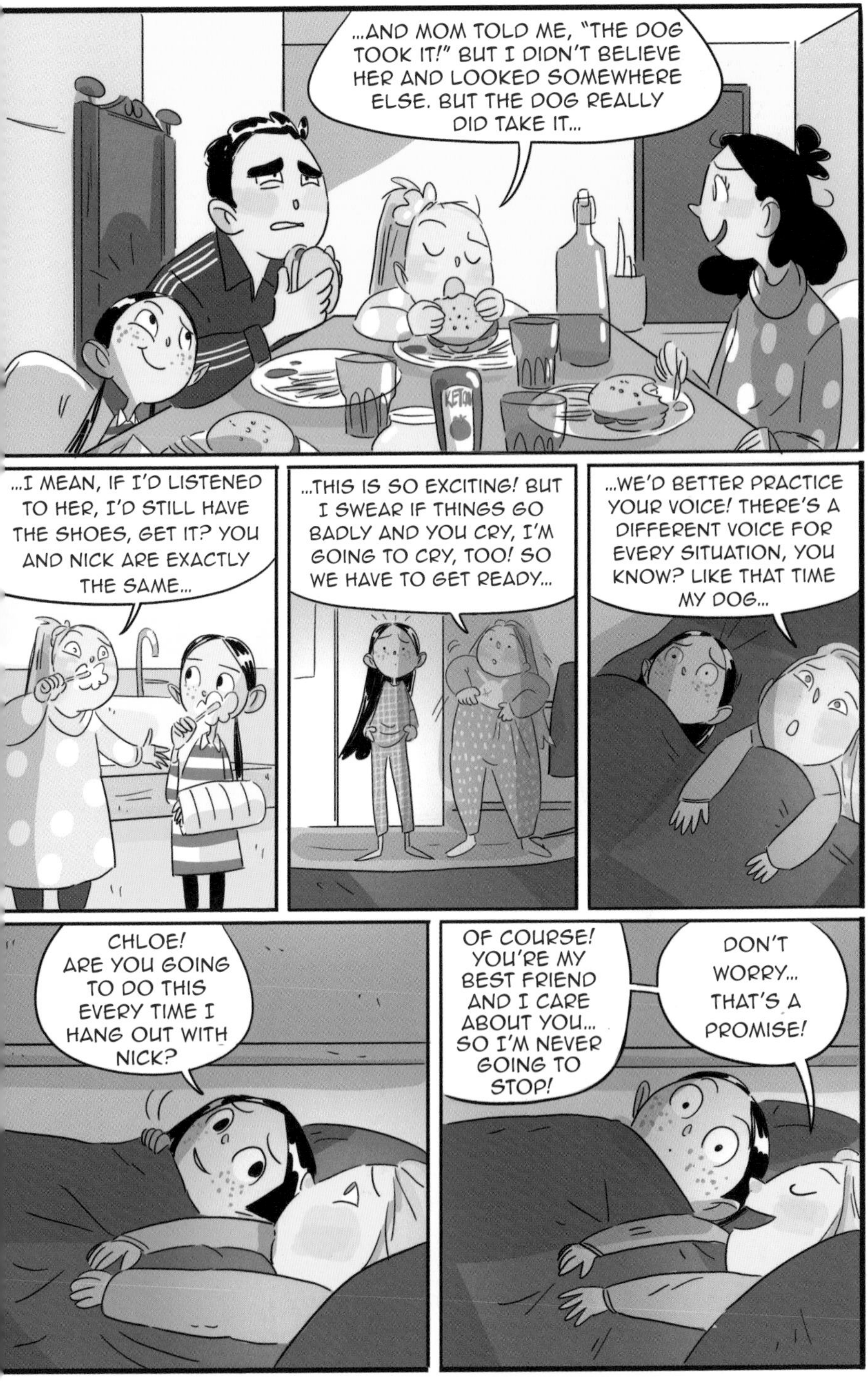
...AND MOM TOLD ME, "THE DOG TOOK IT!" BUT I DIDN'T BELIEVE HER AND LOOKED SOMEWHERE ELSE. BUT THE DOG REALLY DID TAKE IT...
...I MEAN, IF I'D LISTENED TO HER, I'D STILL HAVE THE SHOES, GET IT? YOU AND NICK ARE EXACTLY THE SAME...
...THIS IS SO EXCITING! BUT I SWEAR IF THINGS GO BADLY AND YOU CRY, I'M GOING TO CRY, TOO! SO WE HAVE TO GET READY...
...WE'D BETTER PRACTICE YOUR VOICE! THERE'S A DIFFERENT VOICE FOR EVERY SITUATION, YOU KNOW? LIKE THAT TIME MY DOG...
CHLOE! ARE YOU GOING TO DO THIS EVERY TIME I HANG OUT WITH NICK?
OF COURSE! YOU'RE MY BEST FRIEND AND I CARE ABOUT YOU... SO I'M NEVER GOING TO STOP!
DON'T WORRY... THAT'S A PROMISE!

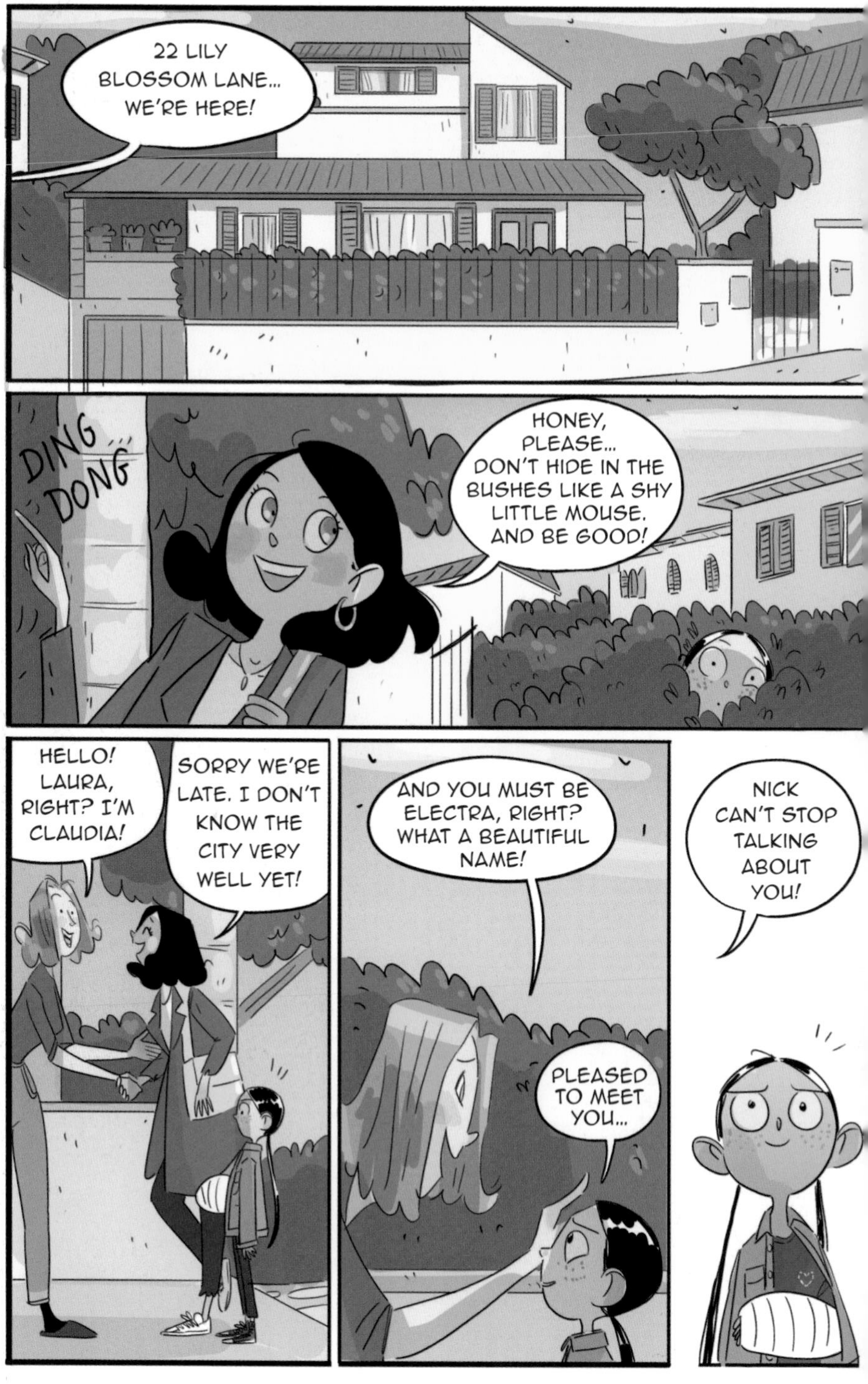

22 LILY BLOSSOM LANE... WE'RE HERE!
DING DONG
HONEY, PLEASE... DON'T HIDE IN THE BUSHES LIKE A SHY LITTLE MOUSE. AND BE GOOD!
HELLO! LAURA, RIGHT? I'M CLAUDIA!
SORRY WE'RE LATE. I DON'T KNOW THE CITY VERY WELL YET!
AND YOU MUST BE ELECTRA, RIGHT? WHAT A BEAUTIFUL NAME!
PLEASED TO MEET YOU...
NICK CAN'T STOP TALKING ABOUT YOU!

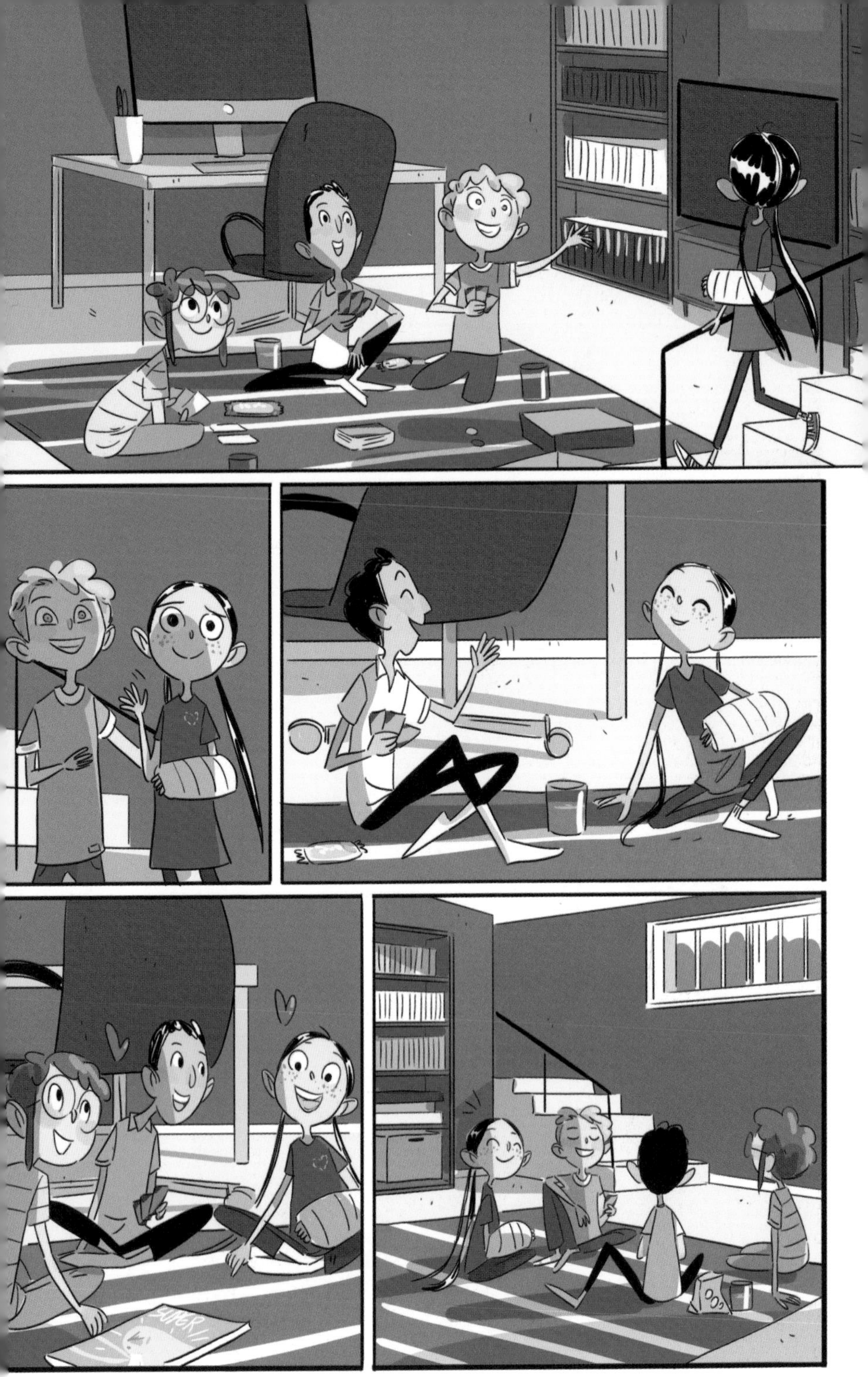
SUPER

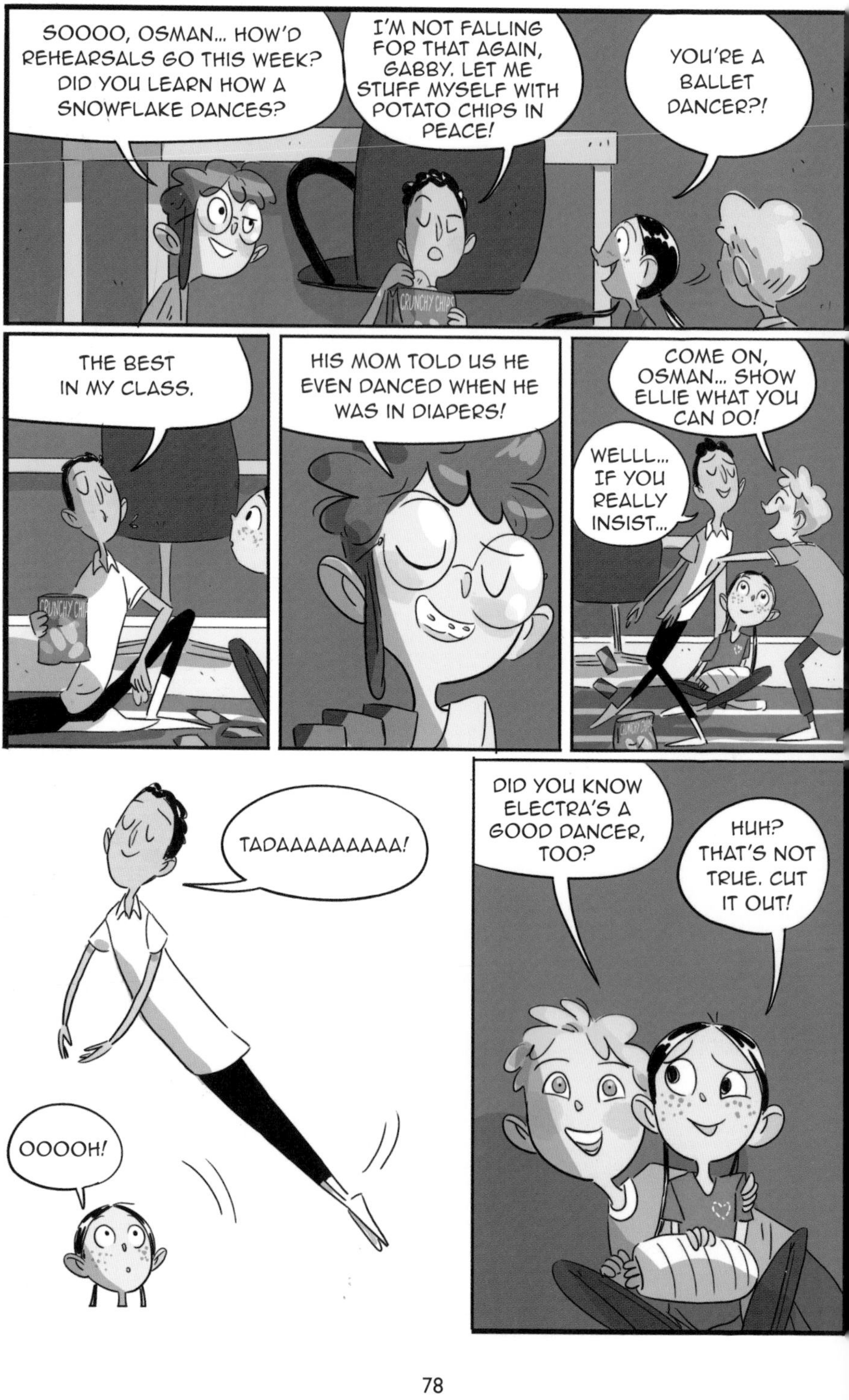
SOOOO, OSMAN... HOW'D REHEARSALS GO THIS WEEK? DID YOU LEARN HOW A SNOWFLAKE DANCES?
I'M NOT FALLING FOR THAT AGAIN, GABBY. LET ME STUFF MYSELF WITH POTATO CHIPS IN PEACE!
YOU'RE A BALLET DANCER?!
CRUNCHY CHIPS
THE BEST IN MY CLASS.
HIS MOM TOLD US HE EVEN DANCED WHEN HE WAS IN DIAPERS!
COME ON, OSMAN... SHOW ELLIE WHAT YOU CAN DO!
WELLL... IF YOU REALLY INSIST...
TADAAAAAAAAAA!
OOOOH!
DID YOU KNOW ELECTRA'S A GOOD DANCER, TOO?
HUH? THAT'S NOT TRUE. CUT IT OUT!

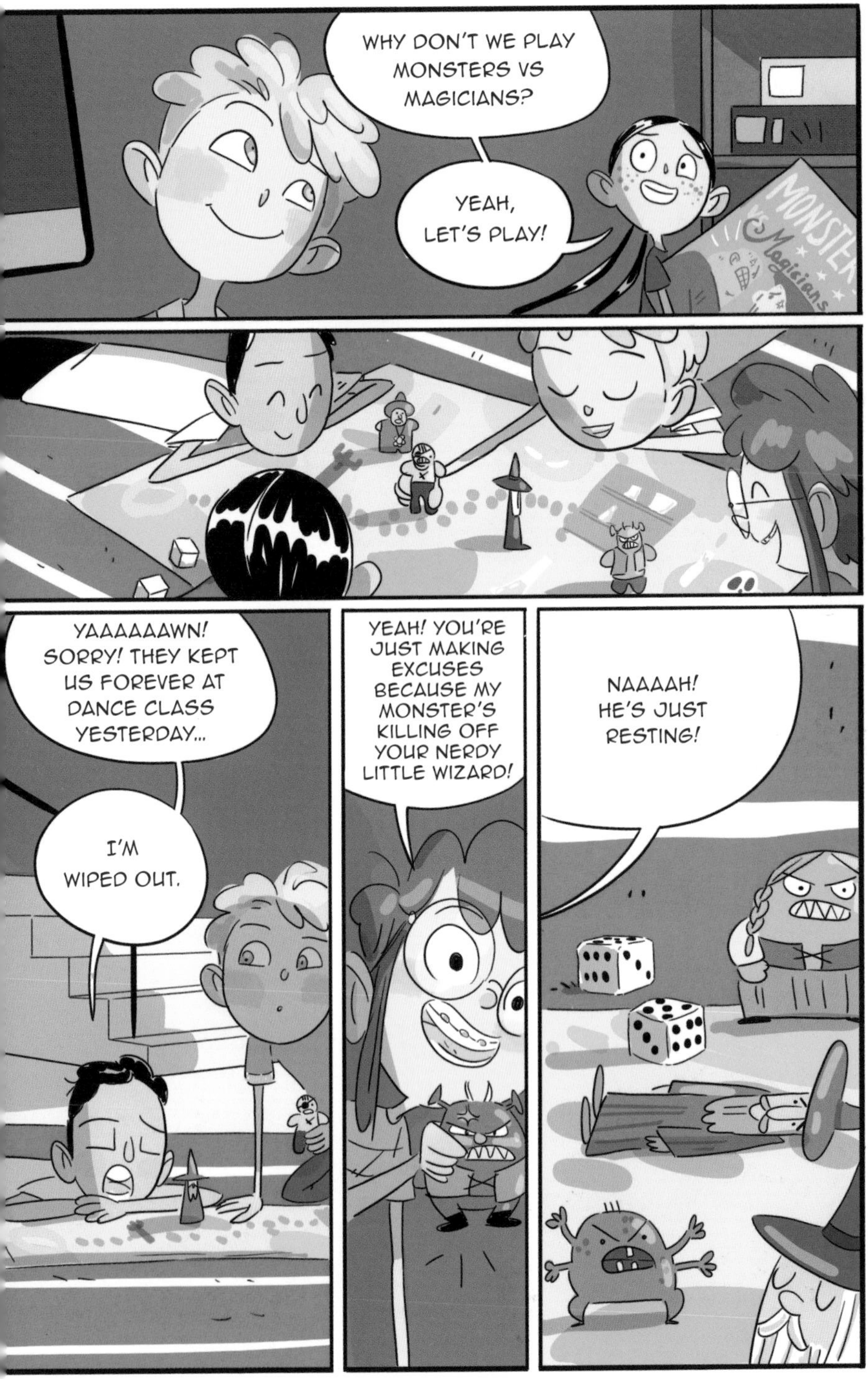

WHY DON'T WE PLAY MONSTERS VS MAGICIANS?
YEAH, LET'S PLAY!
MONSTERS VS Magicians
YAAAAAAWN! SORRY! THEY KEPT US FOREVER AT DANCE CLASS YESTERDAY...
I'M WIPED OUT.
YEAH! YOU'RE JUST MAKING EXCUSES BECAUSE MY MONSTER'S KILLING OFF YOUR NERDY LITTLE WIZARD!
NAAAAH! HE'S JUST RESTING!

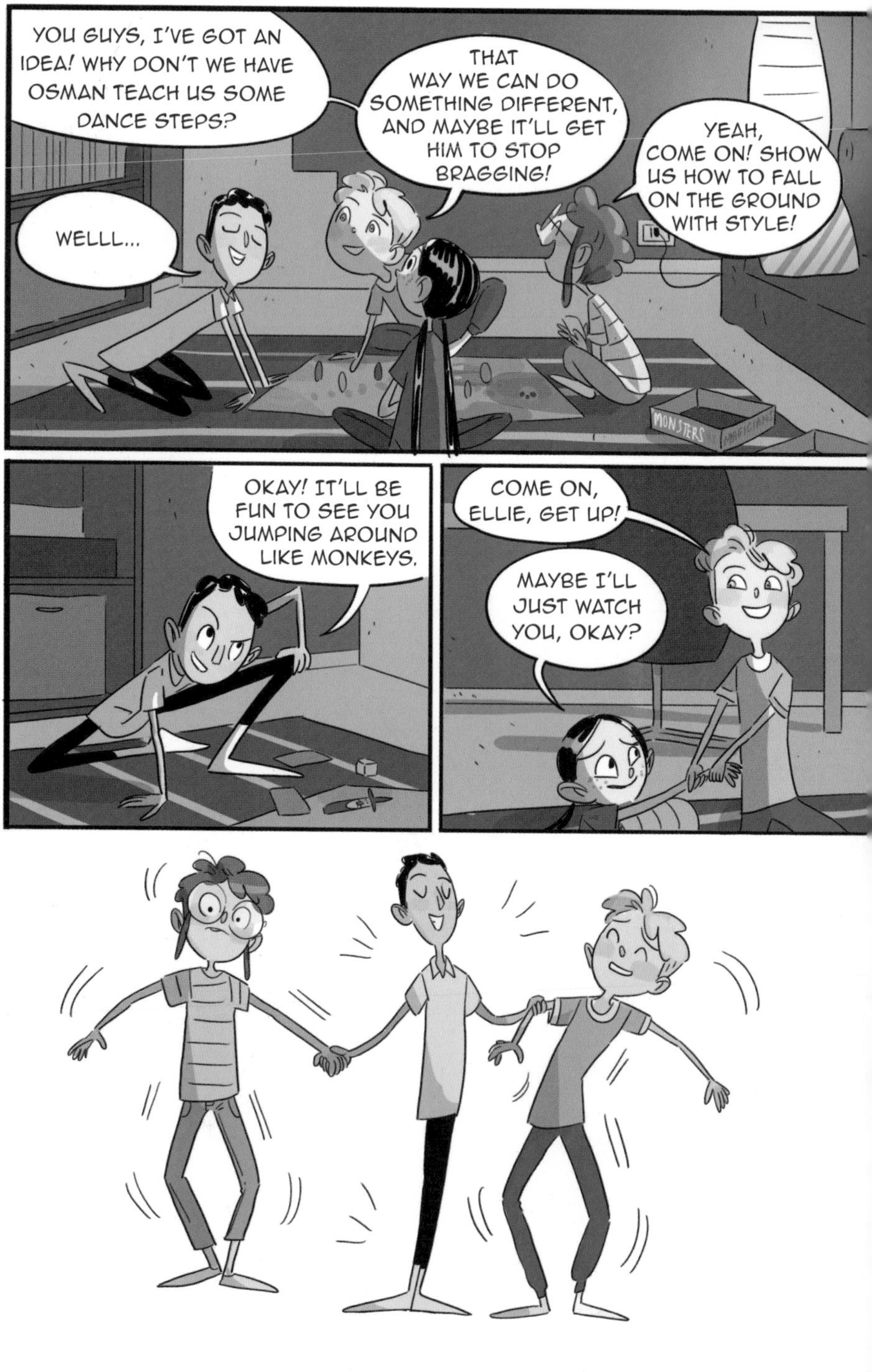
YOU GUYS, I'VE GOT AN IDEA! WHY DON'T WE HAVE OSMAN TEACH US SOME DANCE STEPS?
THAT WAY WE CAN DO SOMETHING DIFFERENT, AND MAYBE IT'LL GET HIM TO STOP BRAGGING!
WELLL...
YEAH, COME ON! SHOW US HOW TO FALL ON THE GROUND WITH STYLE!
MONSTERS
OKAY! IT'LL BE FUN TO SEE YOU JUMPING AROUND LIKE MONKEYS.
COME ON, ELLIE, GET UP!
MAYBE I'LL JUST WATCH YOU, OKAY?

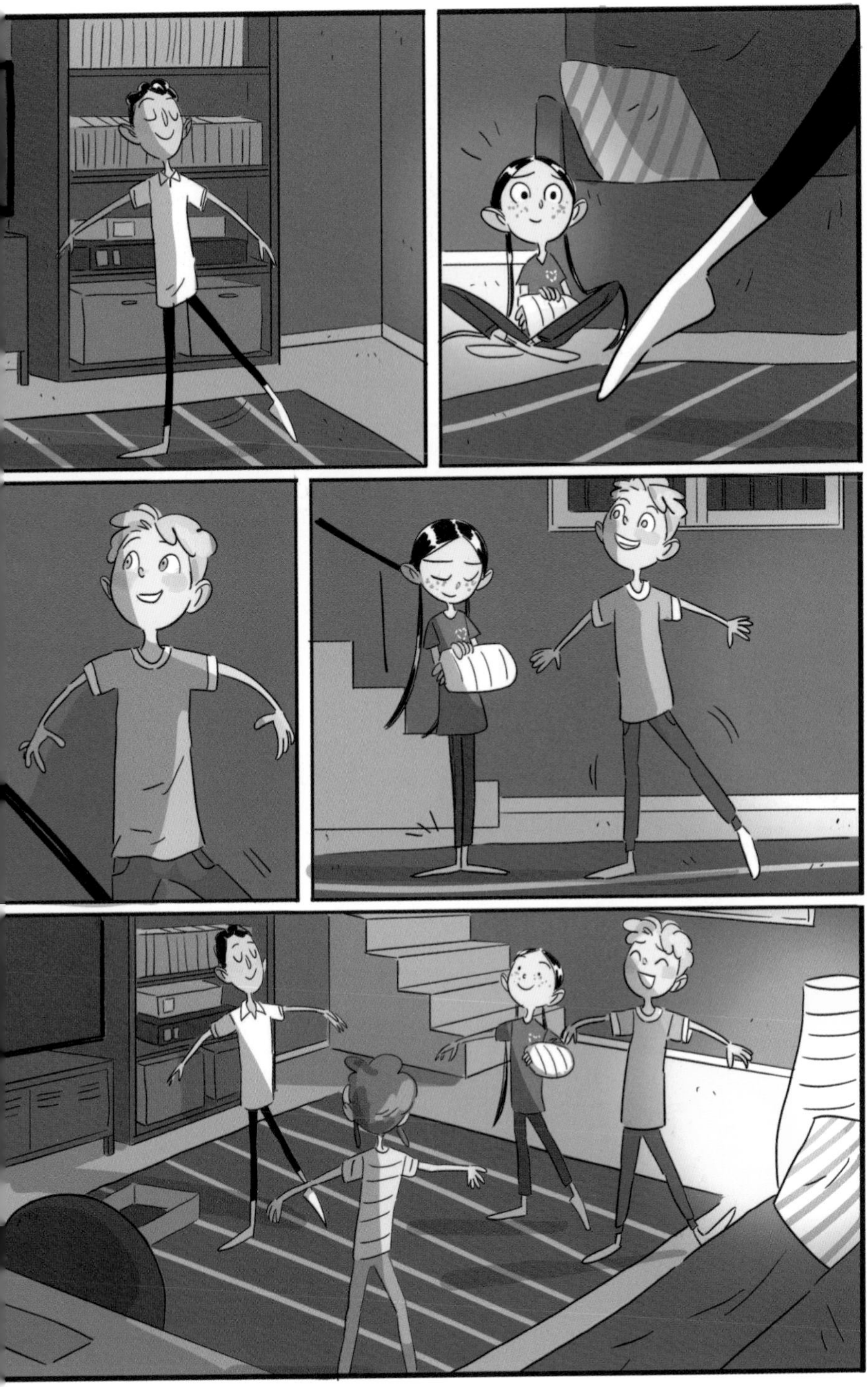

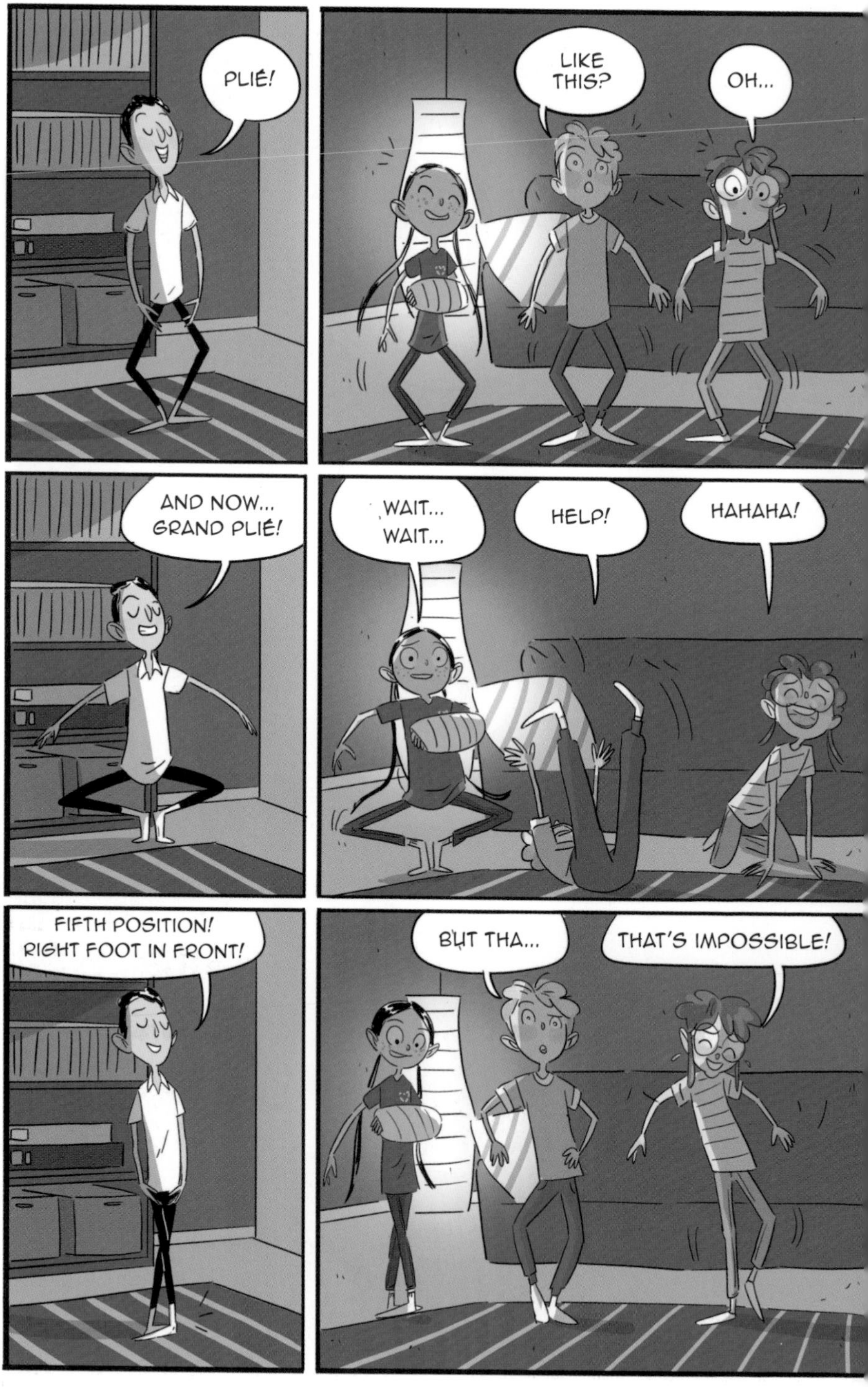
PLIÉ!
LIKE THIS?
OH...
AND NOW... GRAND PLIÉ!
WAIT... WAIT...
HELP!
HAHAHA!
FIFTH POSITION! RIGHT FOOT IN FRONT!
BUT THA...
THAT'S IMPOSSIBLE!

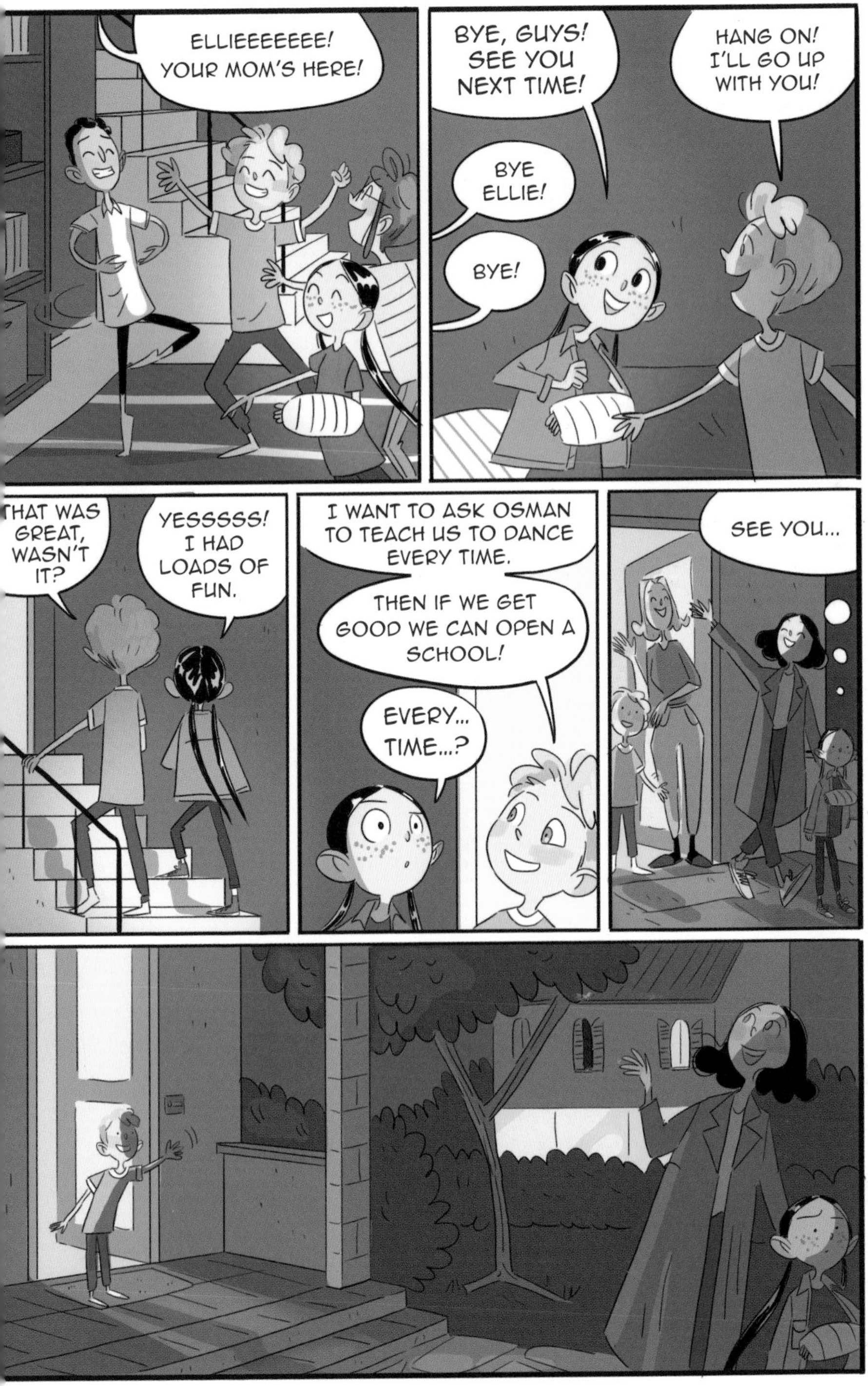
ELLIEEEEEEE!
YOUR MOM'S HERE!
BYE, GUYS! SEE YOU NEXT TIME!
HANG ON! I'LL GO UP WITH YOU!
BYE ELLIE!
BYE!
THAT WAS GREAT, WASN'T IT?
YESSSSS! I HAD LOADS OF FUN.
I WANT TO ASK OSMAN TO TEACH US TO DANCE EVERY TIME.
THEN IF WE GET GOOD WE CAN OPEN A SCHOOL!
EVERY... TIME...?
SEE YOU...

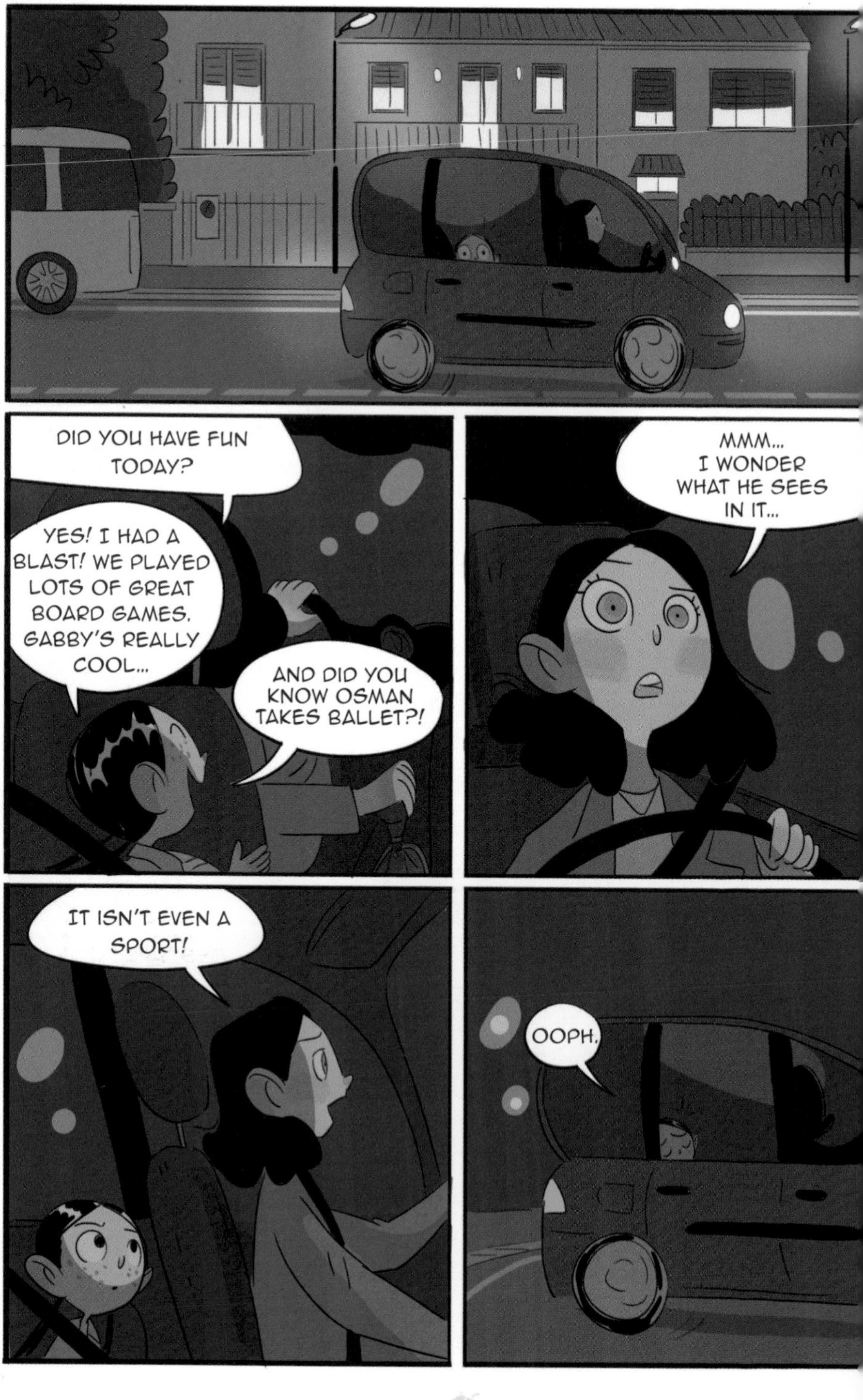
DID YOU HAVE FUN TODAY?
YES! I HAD A BLAST! WE PLAYED LOTS OF GREAT BOARD GAMES. GABBY'S REALLY COOL...
AND DID YOU KNOW OSMAN TAKES BALLET?!
MMM... I WONDER WHAT HE SEES IN IT...
IT ISN'T EVEN A SPORT!
OOPH.

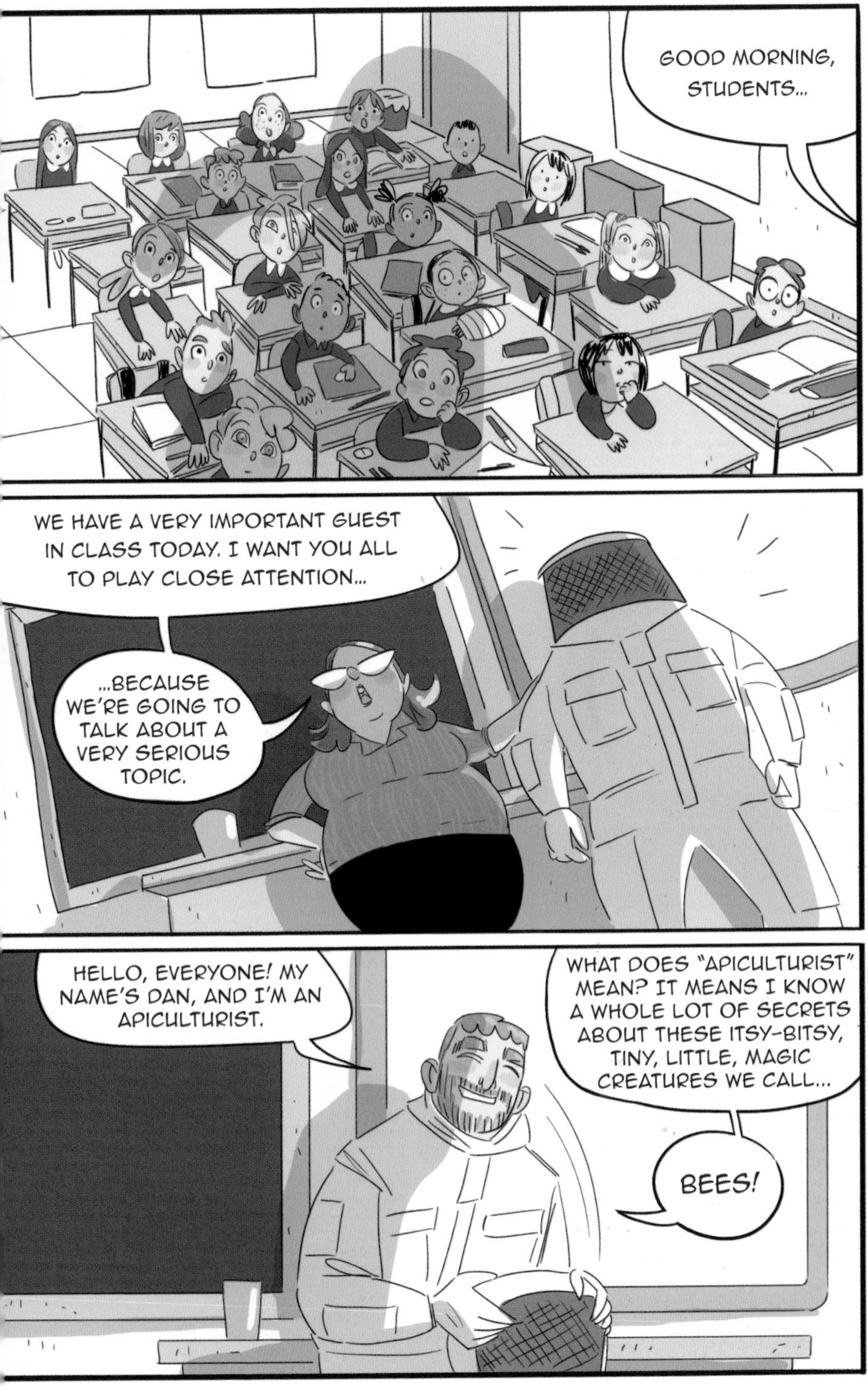
GOOD MORNING, STUDENTS...
WE HAVE A VERY IMPORTANT GUEST IN CLASS TODAY. I WANT YOU ALL TO PLAY CLOSE ATTENTION...
...BECAUSE WE'RE GOING TO TALK ABOUT A VERY SERIOUS TOPIC.
HELLO, EVERYONE! MY NAME'S DAN, AND I'M AN APICULTURIST.
WHAT DOES "APICULTURIST" MEAN? IT MEANS I KNOW A WHOLE LOT OF SECRETS ABOUT THESE ITSY-BITSY, TINY, LITTLE, MAGIC CREATURES WE CALL...
BEES!

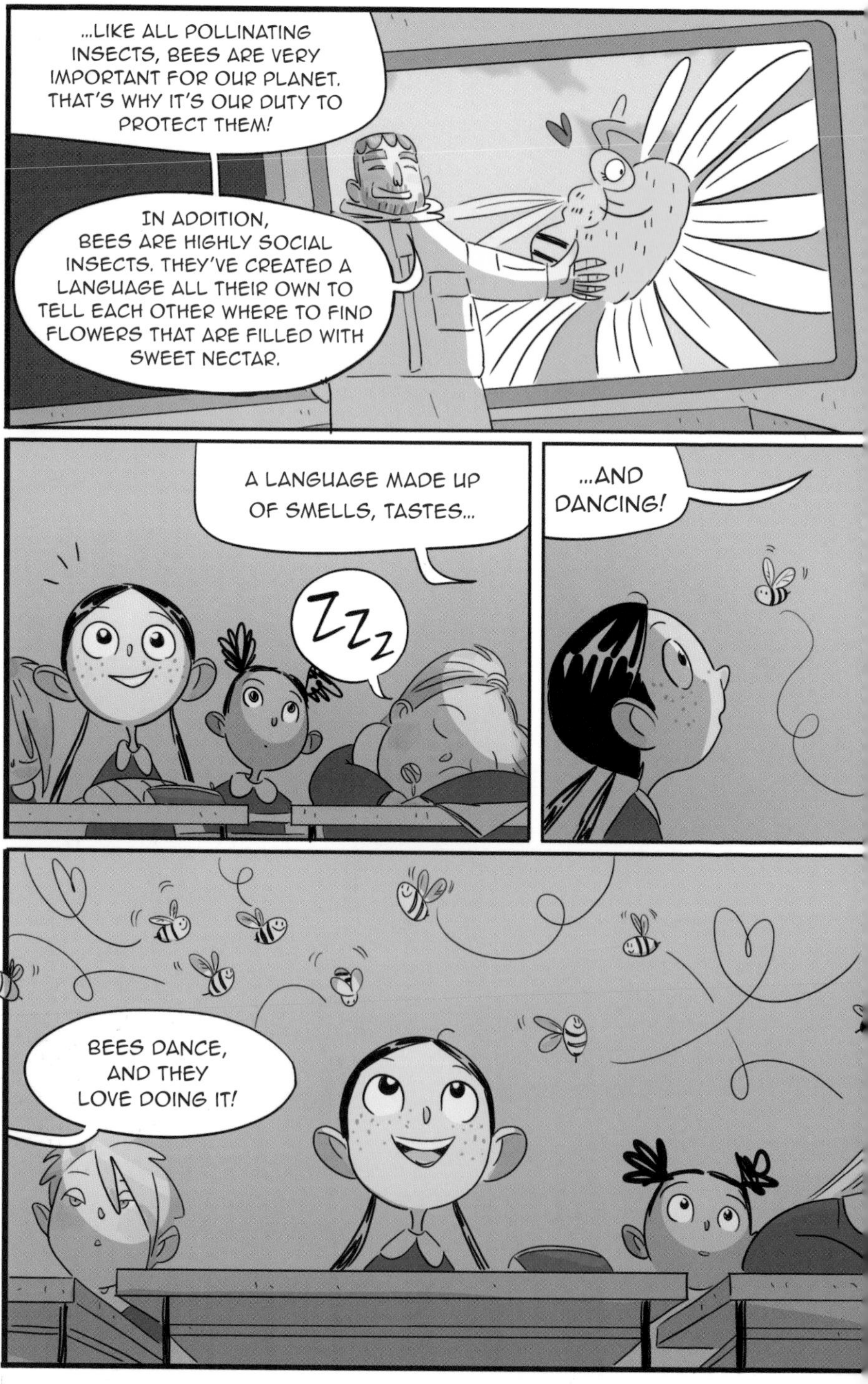
...LIKE ALL POLLINATING INSECTS, BEES ARE VERY IMPORTANT FOR OUR PLANET. THAT'S WHY IT'S OUR DUTY TO PROTECT THEM!
IN ADDITION, BEES ARE HIGHLY SOCIAL INSECTS. THEY'VE CREATED A LANGUAGE ALL THEIR OWN TO TELL EACH OTHER WHERE TO FIND FLOWERS THAT ARE FILLED WITH SWEET NECTAR.
A LANGUAGE MADE UP OF SMELLS, TASTES...
ZZZ
...AND DANCING!
BEES DANCE, AND THEY LOVE DOING IT!

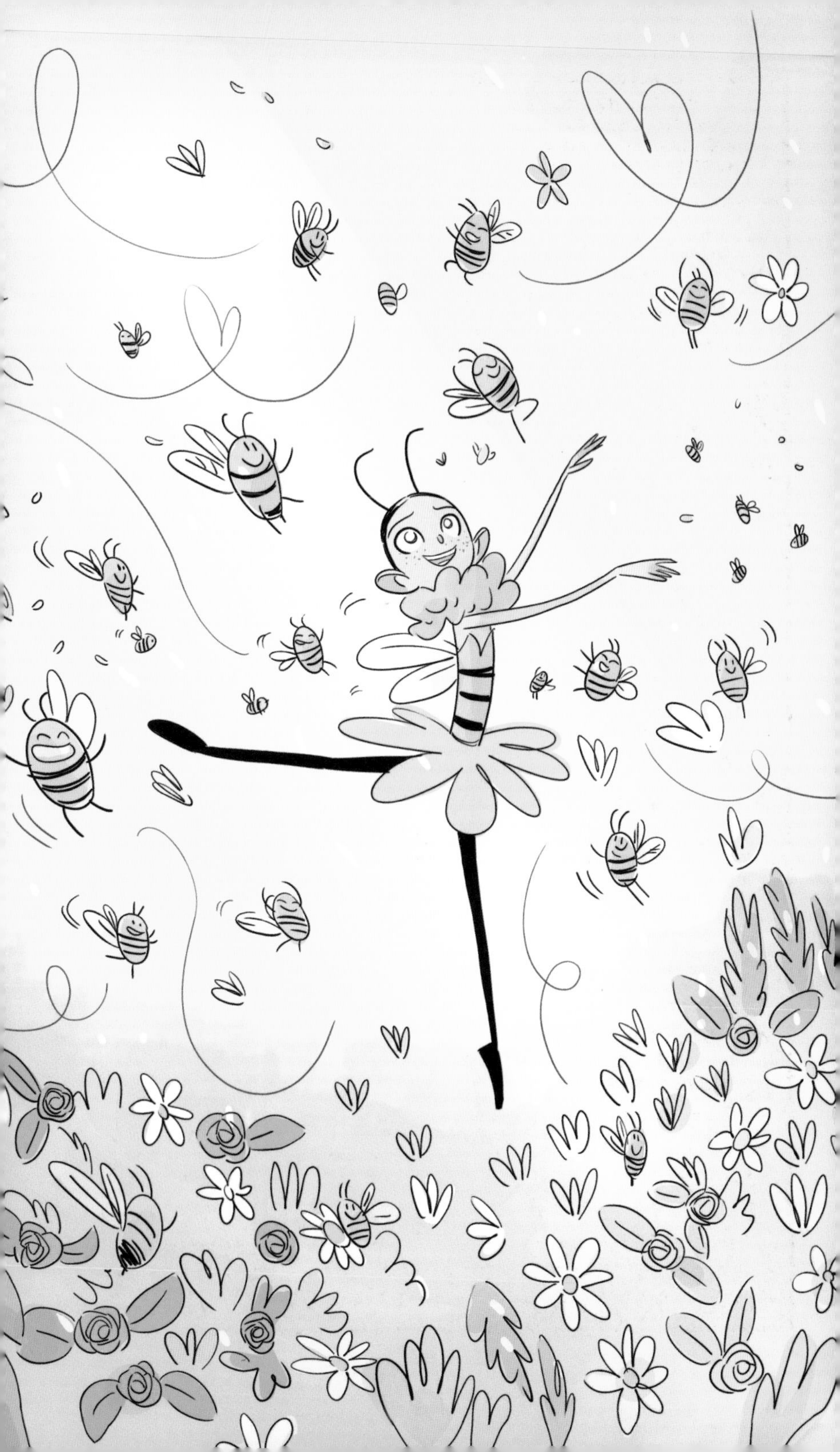

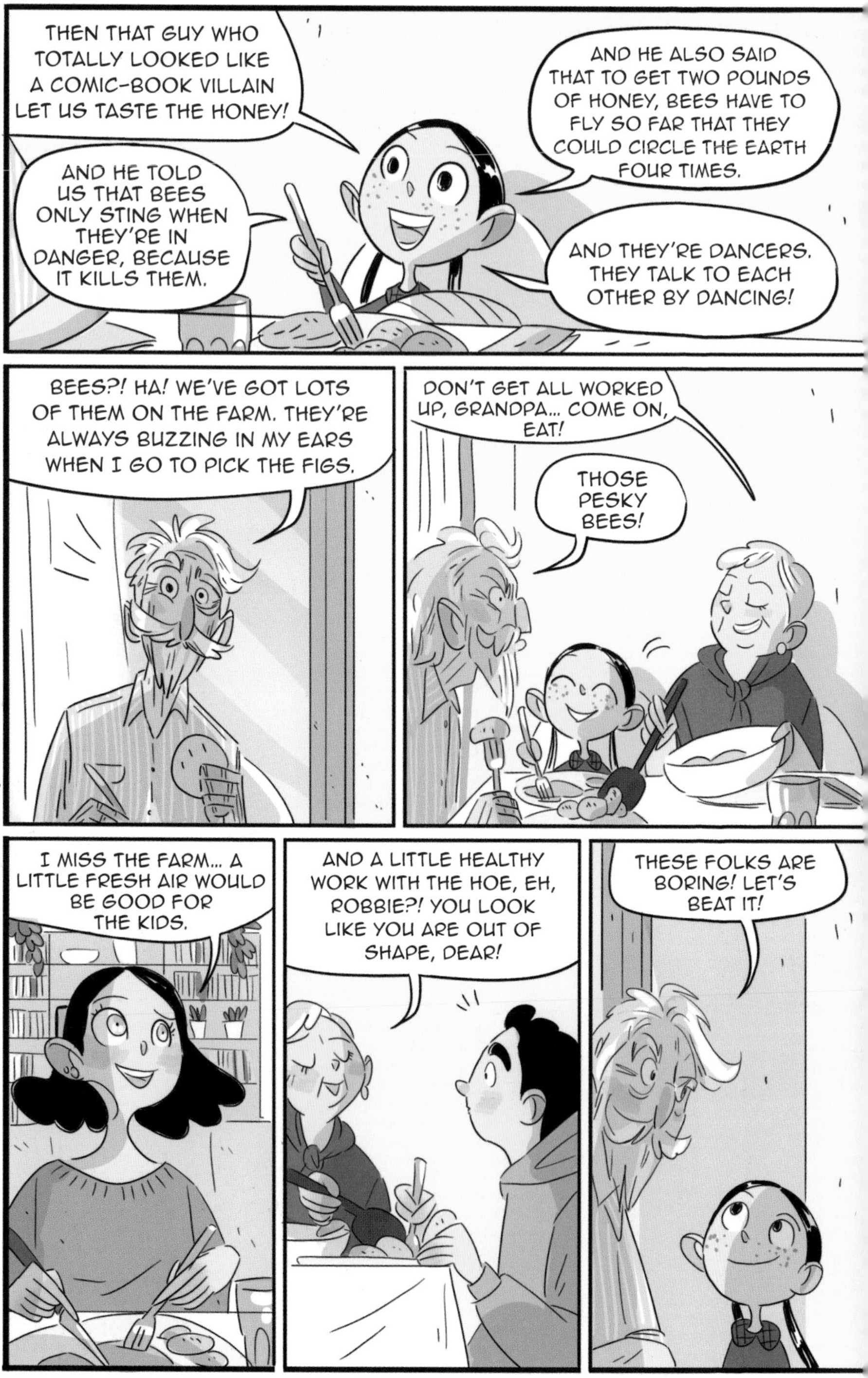
THEN THAT GUY WHO TOTALLY LOOKED LIKE A COMIC-BOOK VILLAIN LET US TASTE THE HONEY!
AND HE TOLD US THAT BEES ONLY STING WHEN THEY'RE IN DANGER, BECAUSE IT KILLS THEM.
AND HE ALSO SAID THAT TO GET TWO POUNDS OF HONEY, BEES HAVE TO FLY SO FAR THAT THEY COULD CIRCLE THE EARTH FOUR TIMES.
AND THEY'RE DANCERS. THEY TALK TO EACH OTHER BY DANCING!
BEES?! HA! WE'VE GOT LOTS OF THEM ON THE FARM. THEY'RE ALWAYS BUZZING IN MY EARS WHEN I GO TO PICK THE FIGS.
DON'T GET ALL WORKED UP, GRANDPA... COME ON, EAT!
THOSE PESKY BEES!
I MISS THE FARM... A LITTLE FRESH AIR WOULD BE GOOD FOR THE KIDS.
AND A LITTLE HEALTHY WORK WITH THE HOE, EH, ROBBIE?! YOU LOOK LIKE YOU ARE OUT OF SHAPE, DEAR!
THESE FOLKS ARE BORING! LET'S BEAT IT!

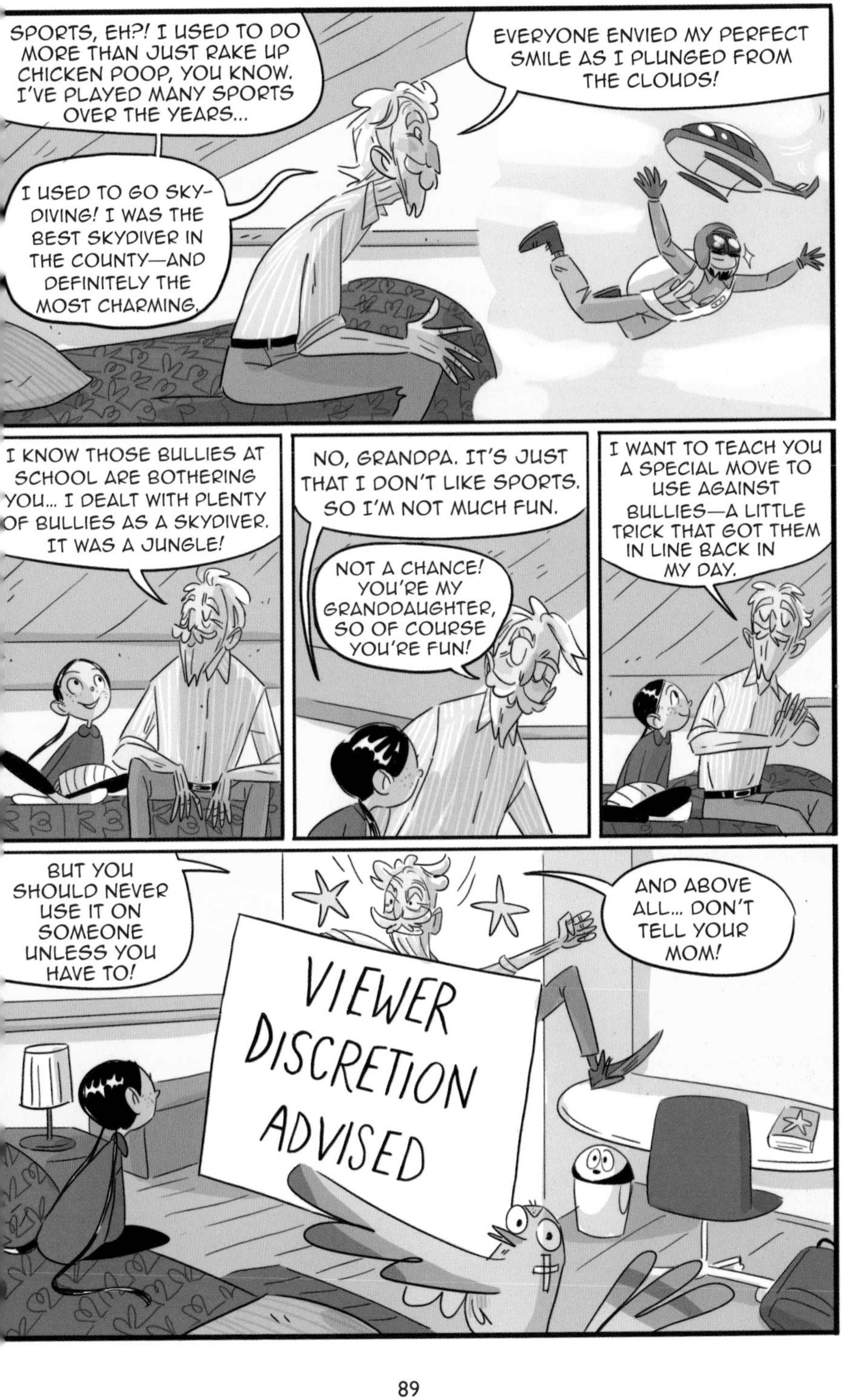
SPORTS, EH?! I USED TO DO MORE THAN JUST RAKE UP CHICKEN POOP, YOU KNOW. I'VE PLAYED MANY SPORTS OVER THE YEARS...
I USED TO GO SKY-DIVING! I WAS THE BEST SKYDIVER IN THE COUNTY—AND DEFINITELY THE MOST CHARMING.
EVERYONE ENVIED MY PERFECT SMILE AS I PLUNGED FROM THE CLOUDS!
I KNOW THOSE BULLIES AT SCHOOL ARE BOTHERING YOU... I DEALT WITH PLENTY OF BULLIES AS A SKYDIVER. IT WAS A JUNGLE!
NO, GRANDPA. IT'S JUST THAT I DON'T LIKE SPORTS. SO I'M NOT MUCH FUN.
NOT A CHANCE! YOU'RE MY GRANDDAUGHTER, SO OF COURSE YOU'RE FUN!
I WANT TO TEACH YOU A SPECIAL MOVE TO USE AGAINST BULLIES—A LITTLE TRICK THAT GOT THEM IN LINE BACK IN MY DAY.
BUT YOU SHOULD NEVER USE IT ON SOMEONE UNLESS YOU HAVE TO!
AND ABOVE ALL... DON'T TELL YOUR MOM!
VIEWER DISCRETION ADVISED

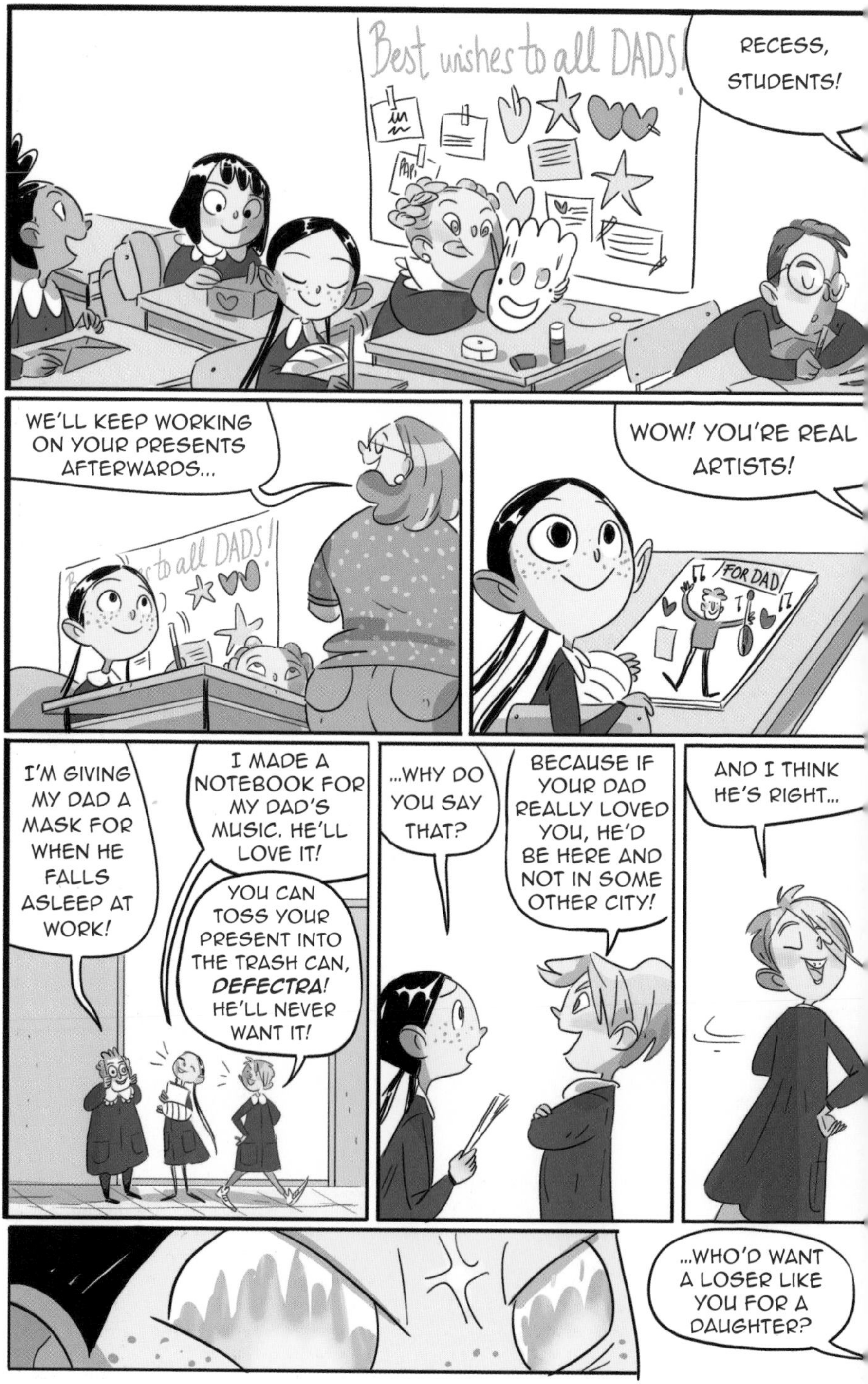
Best wishes to all DADS!
RECESS, STUDENTS!
WE'LL KEEP WORKING ON YOUR PRESENTS AFTERWARDS...
WOW! YOU'RE REAL ARTISTS!
FOR DAD
I'M GIVING MY DAD A MASK FOR WHEN HE FALLS ASLEEP AT WORK!
I MADE A NOTEBOOK FOR MY DAD'S MUSIC. HE'LL LOVE IT!
YOU CAN TOSS YOUR PRESENT INTO THE TRASH CAN, ***DEFECTRA!*** HE'LL NEVER WANT IT!
...WHY DO YOU SAY THAT?
BECAUSE IF YOUR DAD REALLY LOVED YOU, HE'D BE HERE AND NOT IN SOME OTHER CITY!
AND I THINK HE'S RIGHT...
...WHO'D WANT A LOSER LIKE YOU FOR A DAUGHTER?

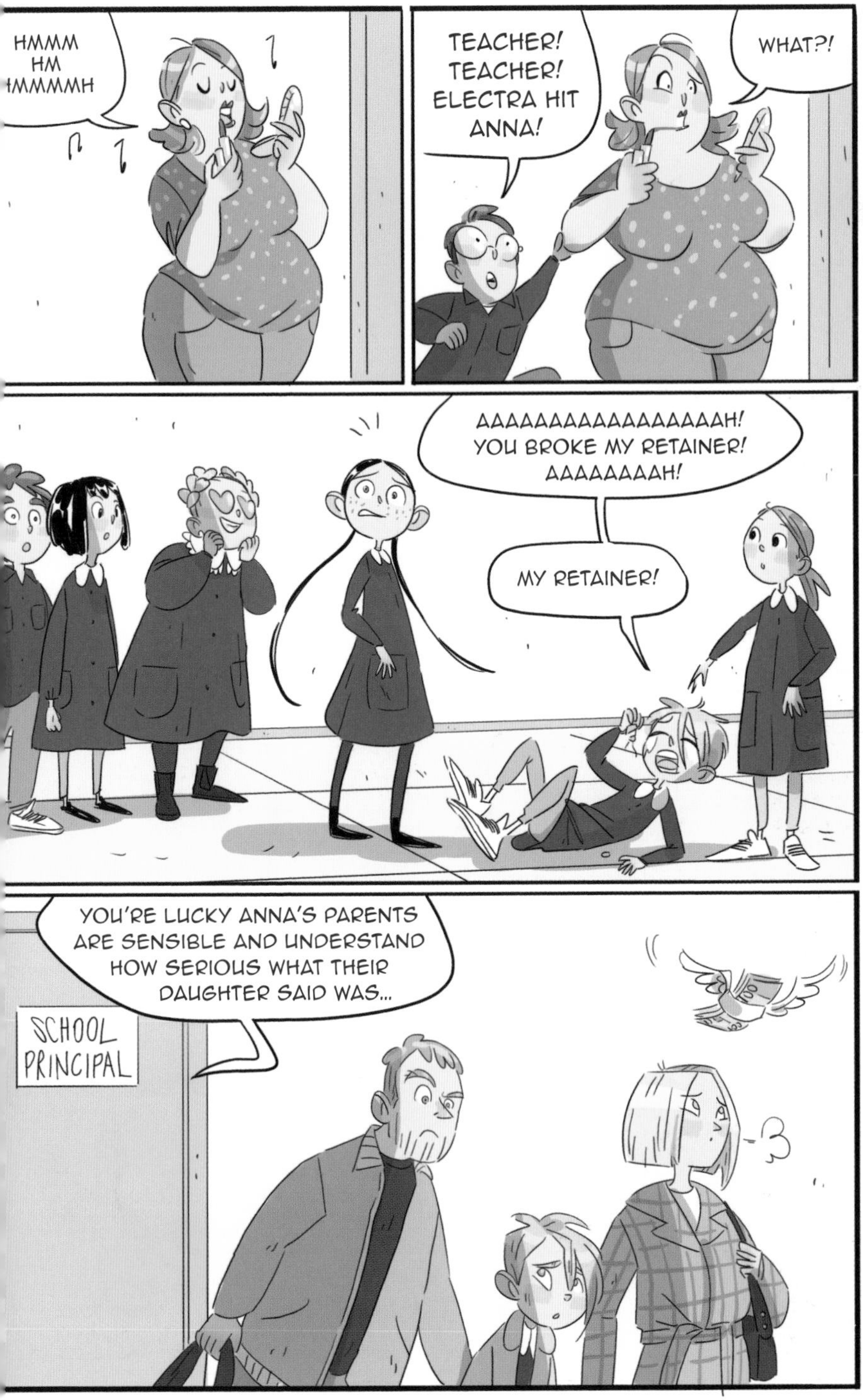
HMMM
HM
HMMMMH
TEACHER! TEACHER! ELECTRA HIT ANNA!
WHAT?!
AAAAAAAAAAAAAAAAAH! YOU BROKE MY RETAINER! AAAAAAAAH!
MY RETAINER!
YOU'RE LUCKY ANNA'S PARENTS ARE SENSIBLE AND UNDERSTAND HOW SERIOUS WHAT THEIR DAUGHTER SAID WAS...
SCHOOL PRINCIPAL

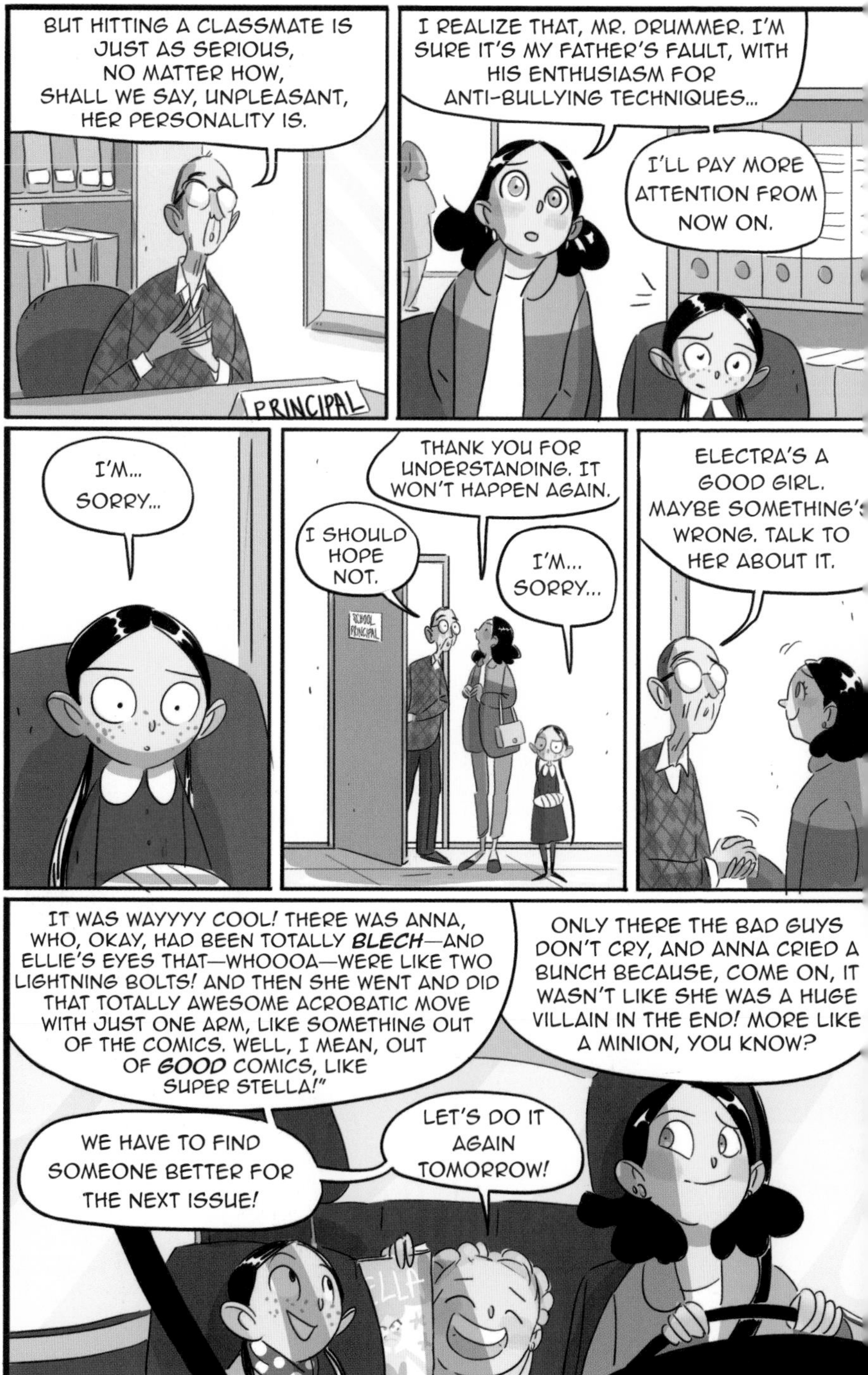
BUT HITTING A CLASSMATE IS JUST AS SERIOUS, NO MATTER HOW, SHALL WE SAY, UNPLEASANT, HER PERSONALITY IS.
PRINCIPAL
I REALIZE THAT, MR. DRUMMER. I'M SURE IT'S MY FATHER'S FAULT, WITH HIS ENTHUSIASM FOR ANTI-BULLYING TECHNIQUES...
I'LL PAY MORE ATTENTION FROM NOW ON.
I'M... SORRY...
THANK YOU FOR UNDERSTANDING. IT WON'T HAPPEN AGAIN.
I SHOULD HOPE NOT.
SCHOOL PRINCIPAL
I'M... SORRY...
ELECTRA'S A GOOD GIRL. MAYBE SOMETHING'S WRONG. TALK TO HER ABOUT IT.
IT WAS WAYYYY COOL! THERE WAS ANNA, WHO, OKAY, HAD BEEN TOTALLY BLECH—AND ELLIE'S EYES THAT—WHOOOA—WERE LIKE TWO LIGHTNING BOLTS! AND THEN SHE WENT AND DID THAT TOTALLY AWESOME ACROBATIC MOVE WITH JUST ONE ARM, LIKE SOMETHING OUT OF THE COMICS. WELL, I MEAN, OUT OF GOOD COMICS, LIKE SUPER STELLA!"
ONLY THERE THE BAD GUYS DON'T CRY, AND ANNA CRIED A BUNCH BECAUSE, COME ON, IT WASN'T LIKE SHE WAS A HUGE VILLAIN IN THE END! MORE LIKE A MINION, YOU KNOW?
WE HAVE TO FIND SOMEONE BETTER FOR THE NEXT ISSUE!
LET'S DO IT AGAIN TOMORROW!

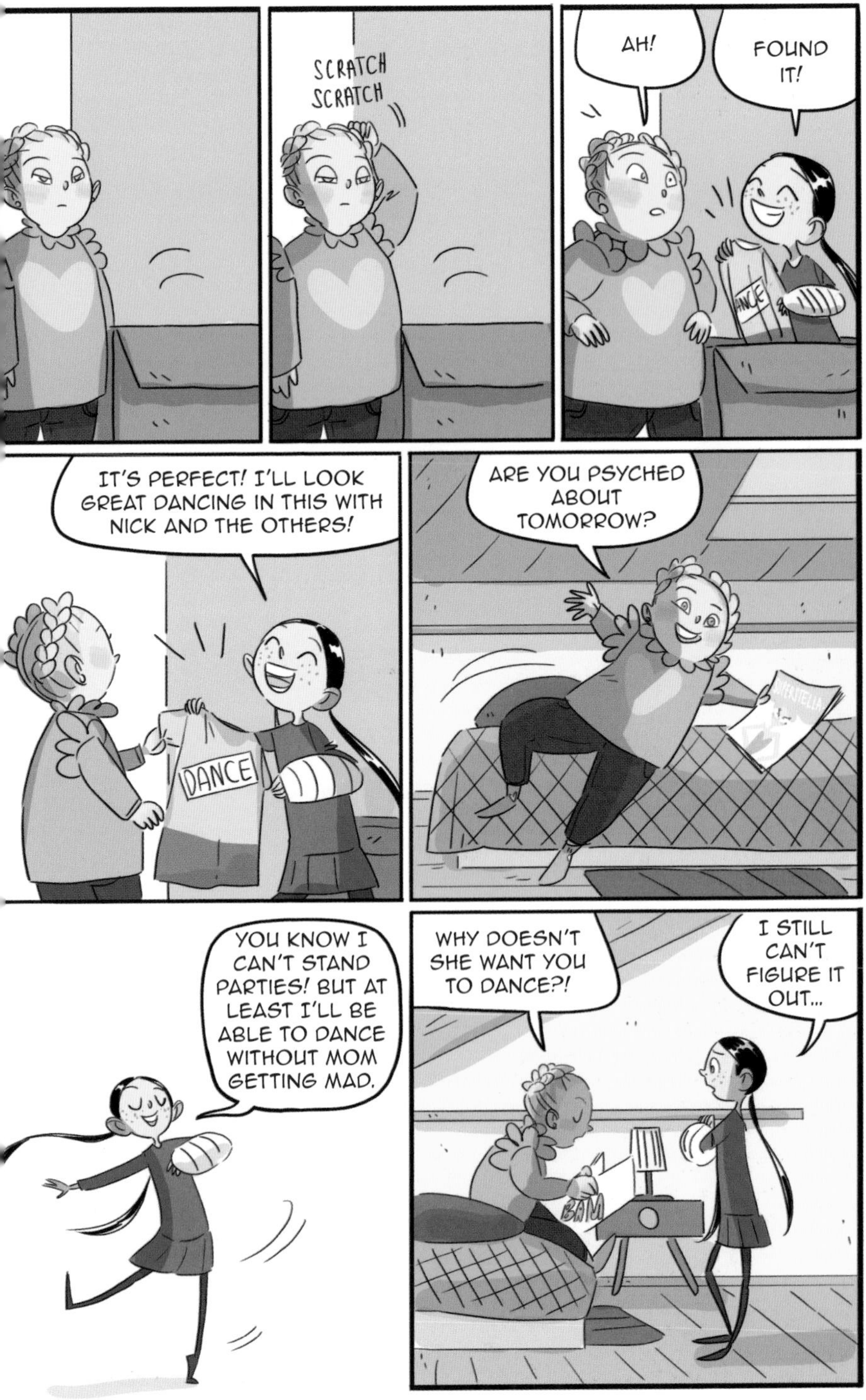
SCRATCH SCRATCH
AH!
FOUND IT!
IT'S PERFECT! I'LL LOOK GREAT DANCING IN THIS WITH NICK AND THE OTHERS!
DANCE
ARE YOU PSYCHED ABOUT TOMORROW?
YOU KNOW I CAN'T STAND PARTIES! BUT AT LEAST I'LL BE ABLE TO DANCE WITHOUT MOM GETTING MAD.
WHY DOESN'T SHE WANT YOU TO DANCE?!
I STILL CAN'T FIGURE IT OUT...
BAM

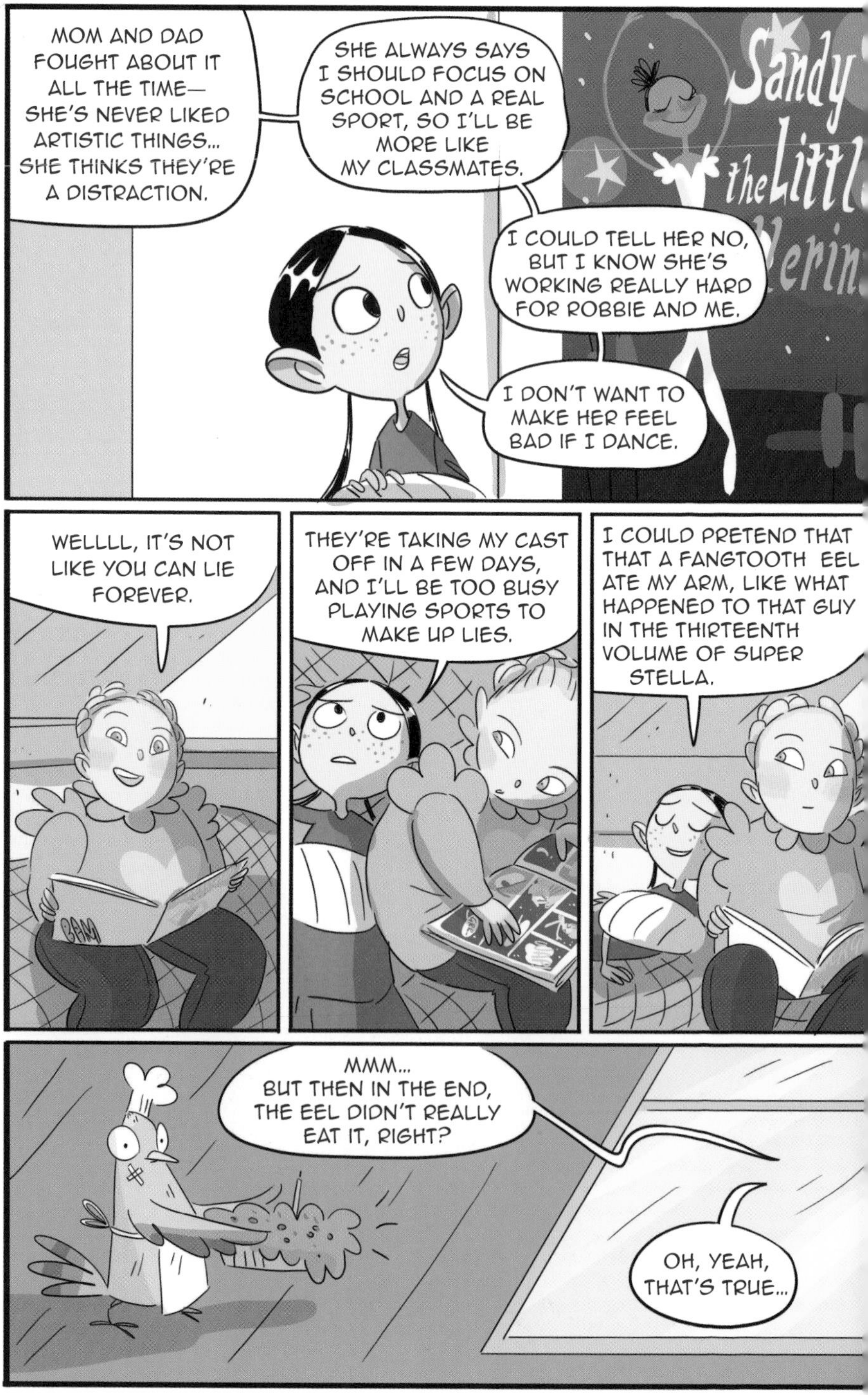

MOM AND DAD FOUGHT ABOUT IT ALL THE TIME— SHE'S NEVER LIKED ARTISTIC THINGS... SHE THINKS THEY'RE A DISTRACTION.
SHE ALWAYS SAYS I SHOULD FOCUS ON SCHOOL AND A REAL SPORT, SO I'LL BE MORE LIKE MY CLASSMATES.
I COULD TELL HER NO, BUT I KNOW SHE'S WORKING REALLY HARD FOR ROBBIE AND ME.
I DON'T WANT TO MAKE HER FEEL BAD IF I DANCE.
WELLLL, IT'S NOT LIKE YOU CAN LIE FOREVER.
THEY'RE TAKING MY CAST OFF IN A FEW DAYS, AND I'LL BE TOO BUSY PLAYING SPORTS TO MAKE UP LIES.
I COULD PRETEND THAT THAT A FANGTOOTH EEL ATE MY ARM, LIKE WHAT HAPPENED TO THAT GUY IN THE THIRTEENTH VOLUME OF SUPER STELLA.
MMM... BUT THEN IN THE END, THE EEL DIDN'T REALLY EAT IT, RIGHT?
OH, YEAH, THAT'S TRUE...

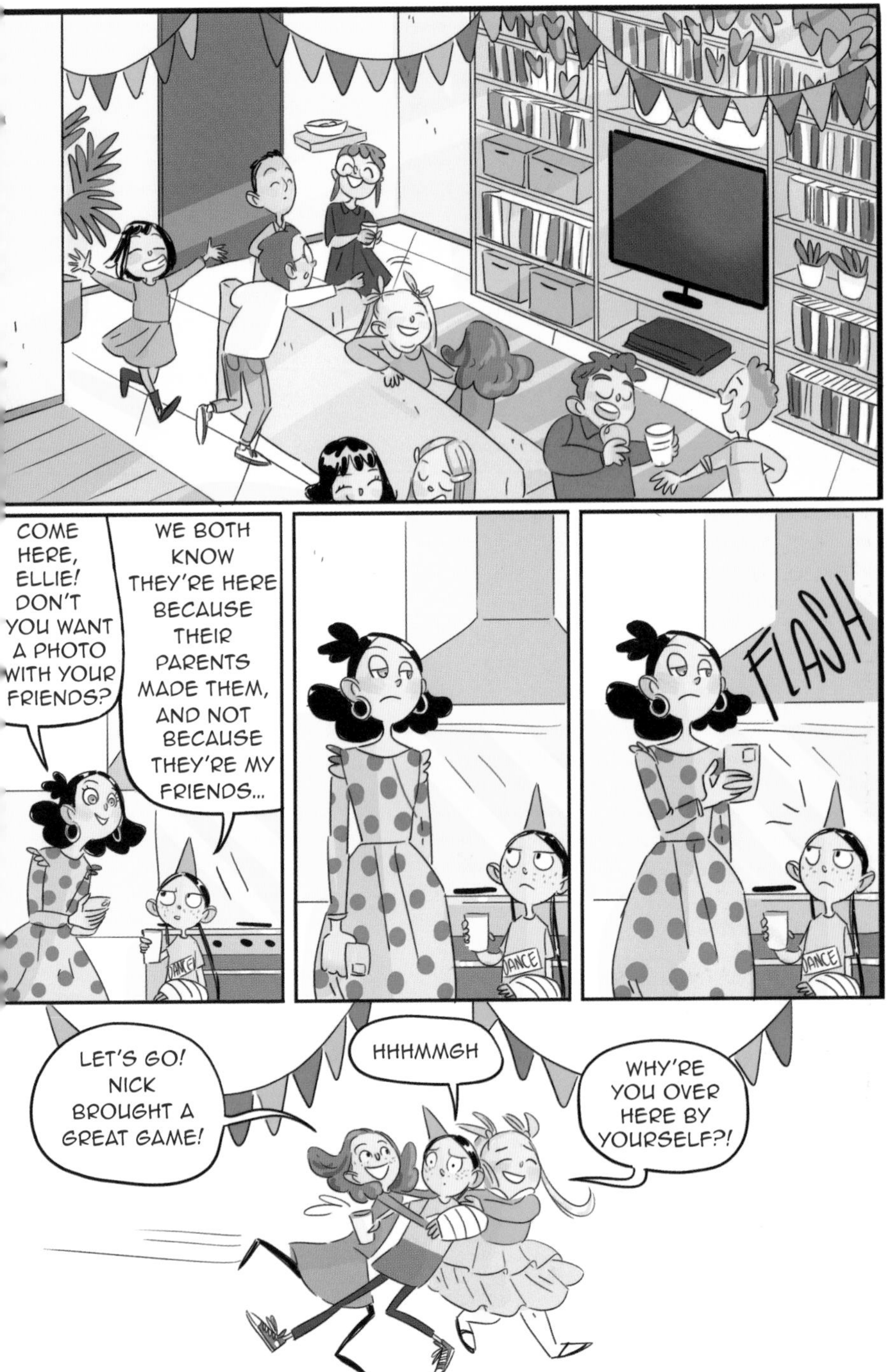
COME HERE, ELLIE! DON'T YOU WANT A PHOTO WITH YOUR FRIENDS?
WE BOTH KNOW THEY'RE HERE BECAUSE THEIR PARENTS MADE THEM, AND NOT BECAUSE THEY'RE MY FRIENDS...
DANCE
DANCE
FLASH
DANCE
LET'S GO! NICK BROUGHT A GREAT GAME!
HHHMMGH
WHY'RE YOU OVER HERE BY YOURSELF?!

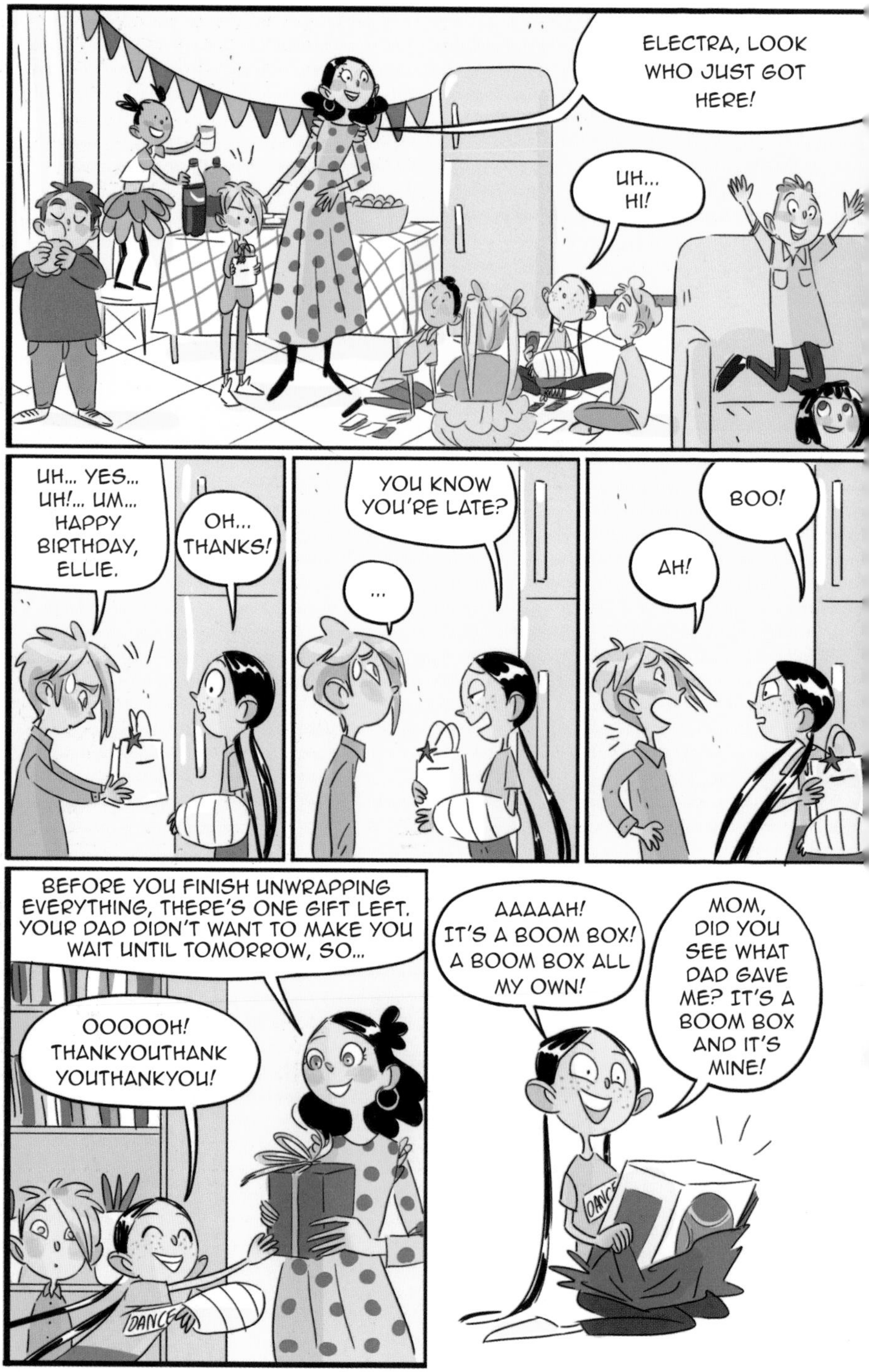
ELECTRA, LOOK WHO JUST GOT HERE!
UH... HI!
UH... YES... UH!... UM... HAPPY BIRTHDAY, ELLIE.
OH... THANKS!
YOU KNOW YOU'RE LATE?
...
BOO!
AH!
BEFORE YOU FINISH UNWRAPPING EVERYTHING, THERE'S ONE GIFT LEFT. YOUR DAD DIDN'T WANT TO MAKE YOU WAIT UNTIL TOMORROW, SO...
OOOOOH! THANKYOUTHANK YOUTHANKYOU!
AAAAAH! IT'S A BOOM BOX! A BOOM BOX ALL MY OWN!
MOM, DID YOU SEE WHAT DAD GAVE ME? IT'S A BOOM BOX AND IT'S MINE!
DANCE
DANCE

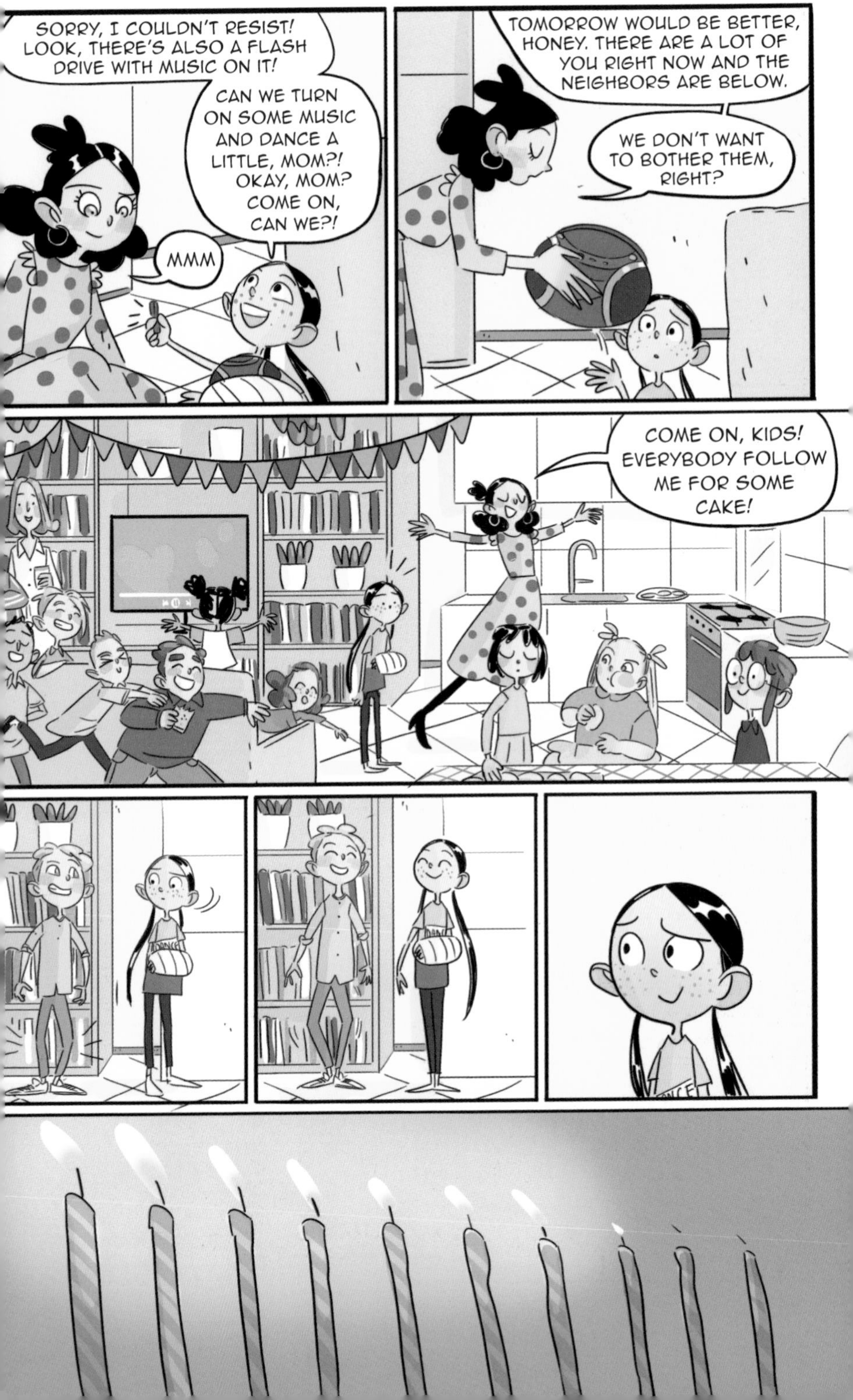
SORRY, I COULDN'T RESIST! LOOK, THERE'S ALSO A FLASH DRIVE WITH MUSIC ON IT!
MMM
CAN WE TURN ON SOME MUSIC AND DANCE A LITTLE, MOM?! OKAY, MOM? COME ON, CAN WE?!
TOMORROW WOULD BE BETTER, HONEY. THERE ARE A LOT OF YOU RIGHT NOW AND THE NEIGHBORS ARE BELOW.
WE DON'T WANT TO BOTHER THEM, RIGHT?
COME ON, KIDS! EVERYBODY FOLLOW ME FOR SOME CAKE!

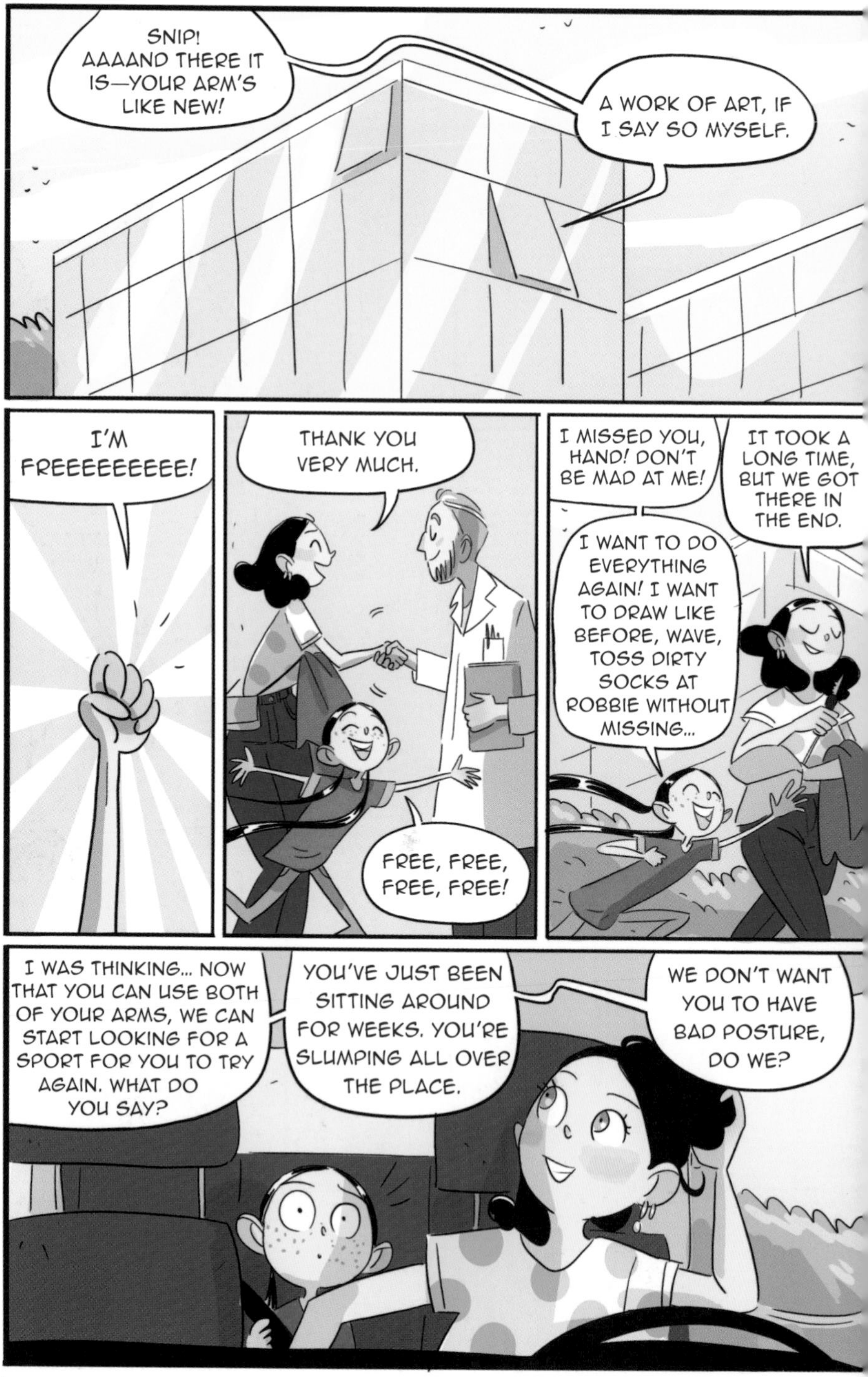
SNIP! AAAAND THERE IT IS—YOUR ARM'S LIKE NEW!
A WORK OF ART, IF I SAY SO MYSELF.
I'M FREEEEEEEEE!
THANK YOU VERY MUCH.
FREE, FREE, FREE, FREE!
I MISSED YOU, HAND! DON'T BE MAD AT ME!
I WANT TO DO EVERYTHING AGAIN! I WANT TO DRAW LIKE BEFORE, WAVE, TOSS DIRTY SOCKS AT ROBBIE WITHOUT MISSING...
IT TOOK A LONG TIME, BUT WE GOT THERE IN THE END.
I WAS THINKING... NOW THAT YOU CAN USE BOTH OF YOUR ARMS, WE CAN START LOOKING FOR A SPORT FOR YOU TO TRY AGAIN. WHAT DO YOU SAY?
YOU'VE JUST BEEN SITTING AROUND FOR WEEKS. YOU'RE SLUMPING ALL OVER THE PLACE.
WE DON'T WANT YOU TO HAVE BAD POSTURE, DO WE?

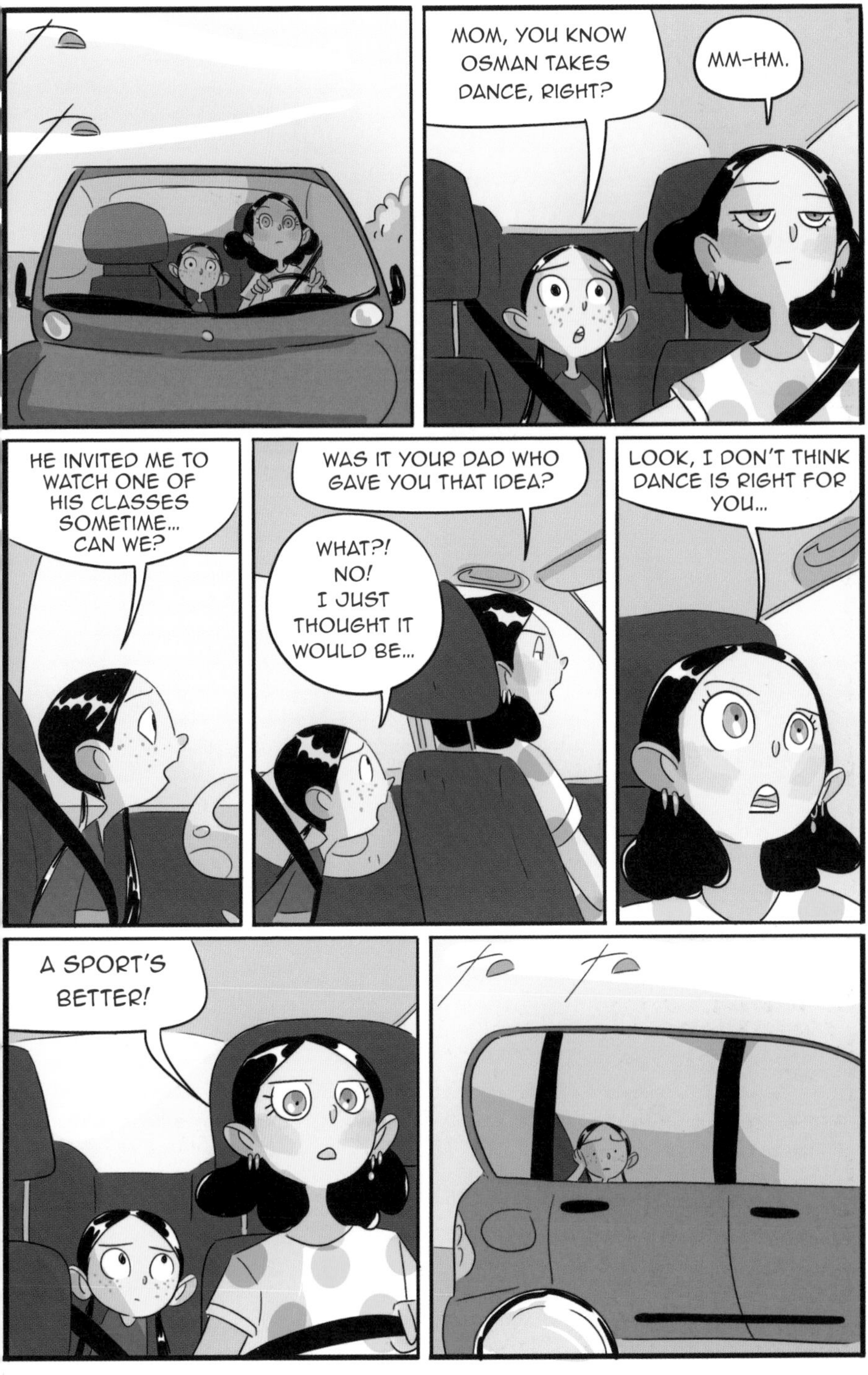
MOM, YOU KNOW OSMAN TAKES DANCE, RIGHT?
MM-HM.
HE INVITED ME TO WATCH ONE OF HIS CLASSES SOMETIME... CAN WE?
WAS IT YOUR DAD WHO GAVE YOU THAT IDEA?
WHAT?! NO! I JUST THOUGHT IT WOULD BE...
LOOK, I DON'T THINK DANCE IS RIGHT FOR YOU...
A SPORT'S BETTER!

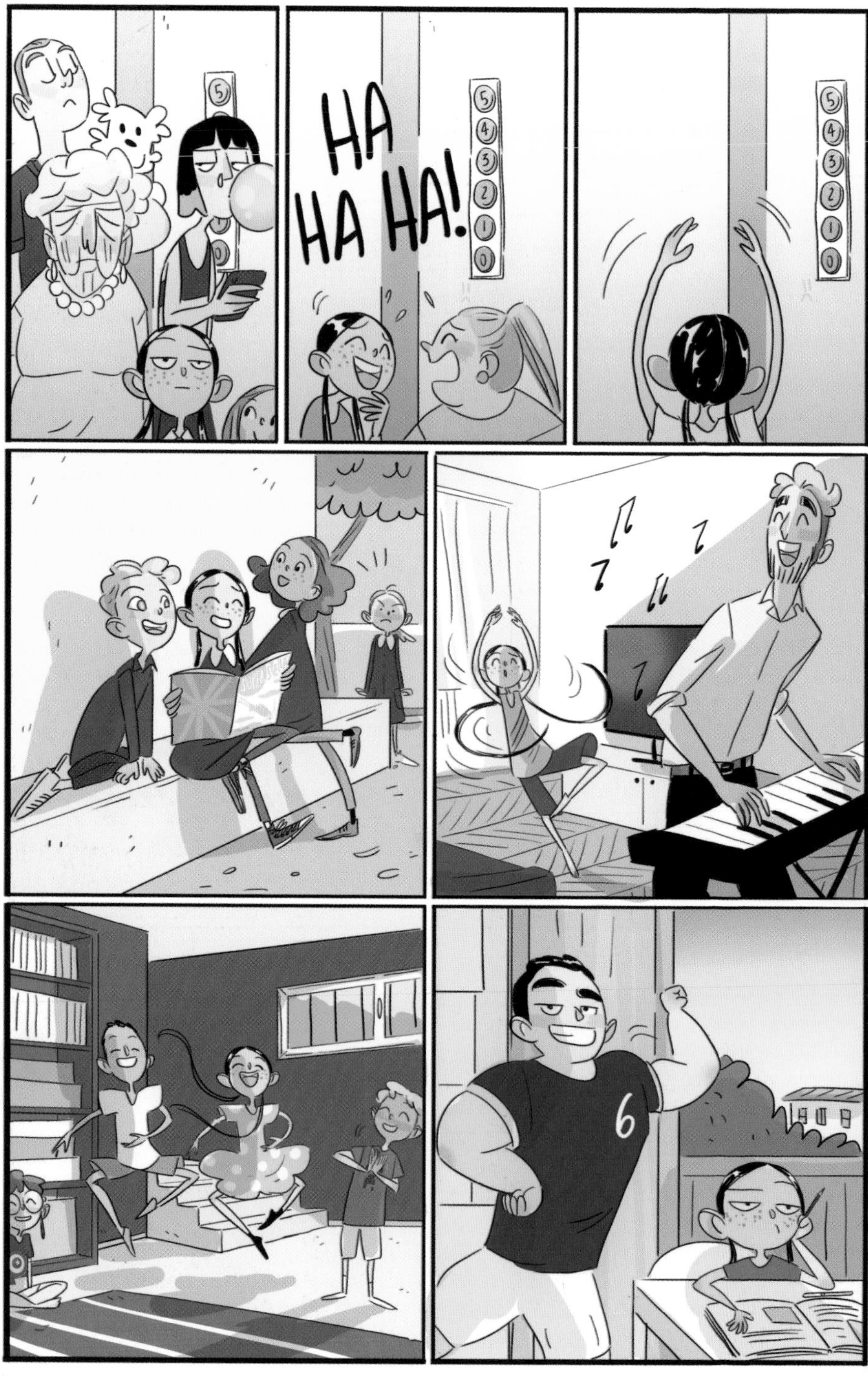
HA HA HA!

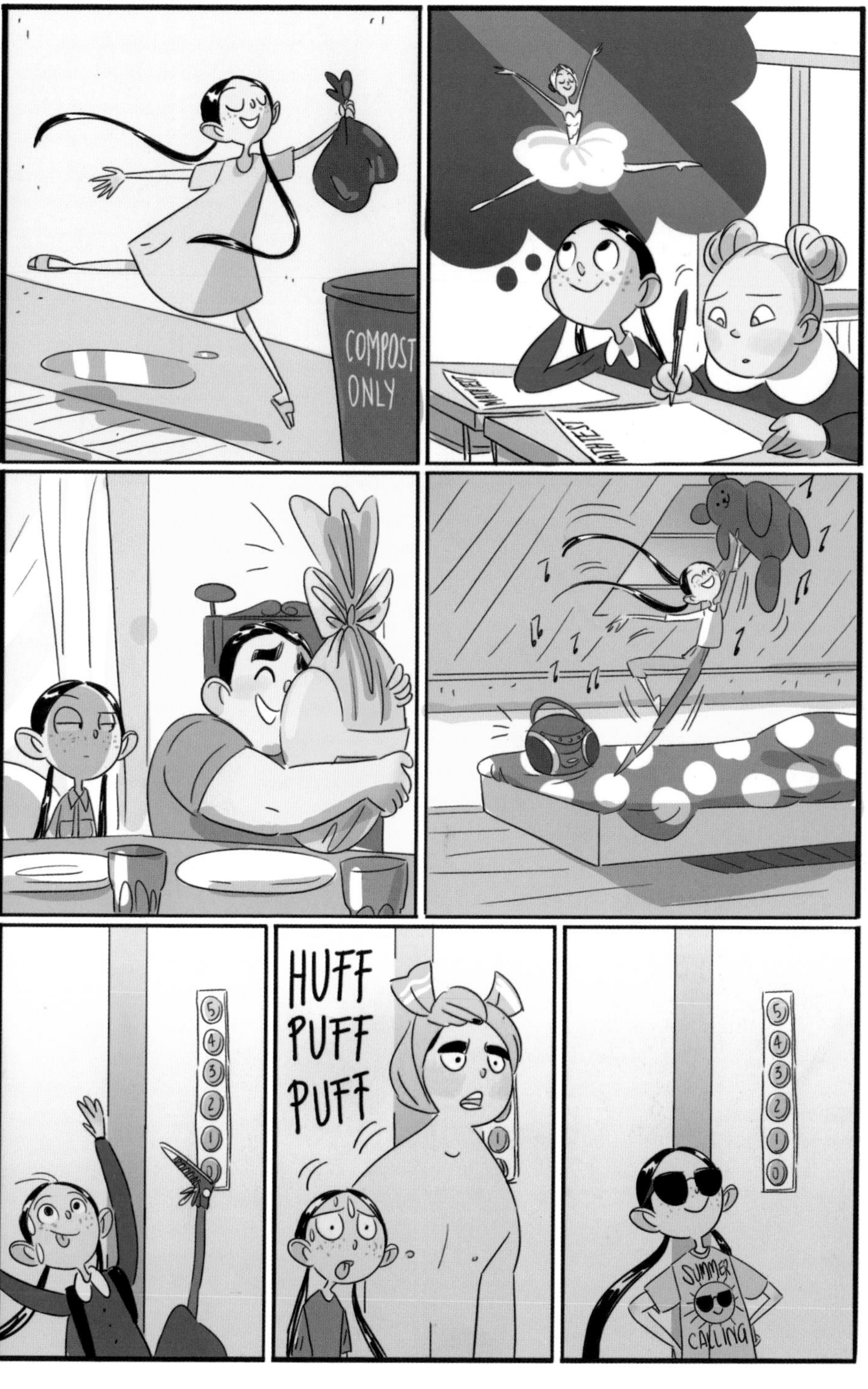
COMPOST ONLY
HUFF
PUFF
PUFF
SUMMER CALLING

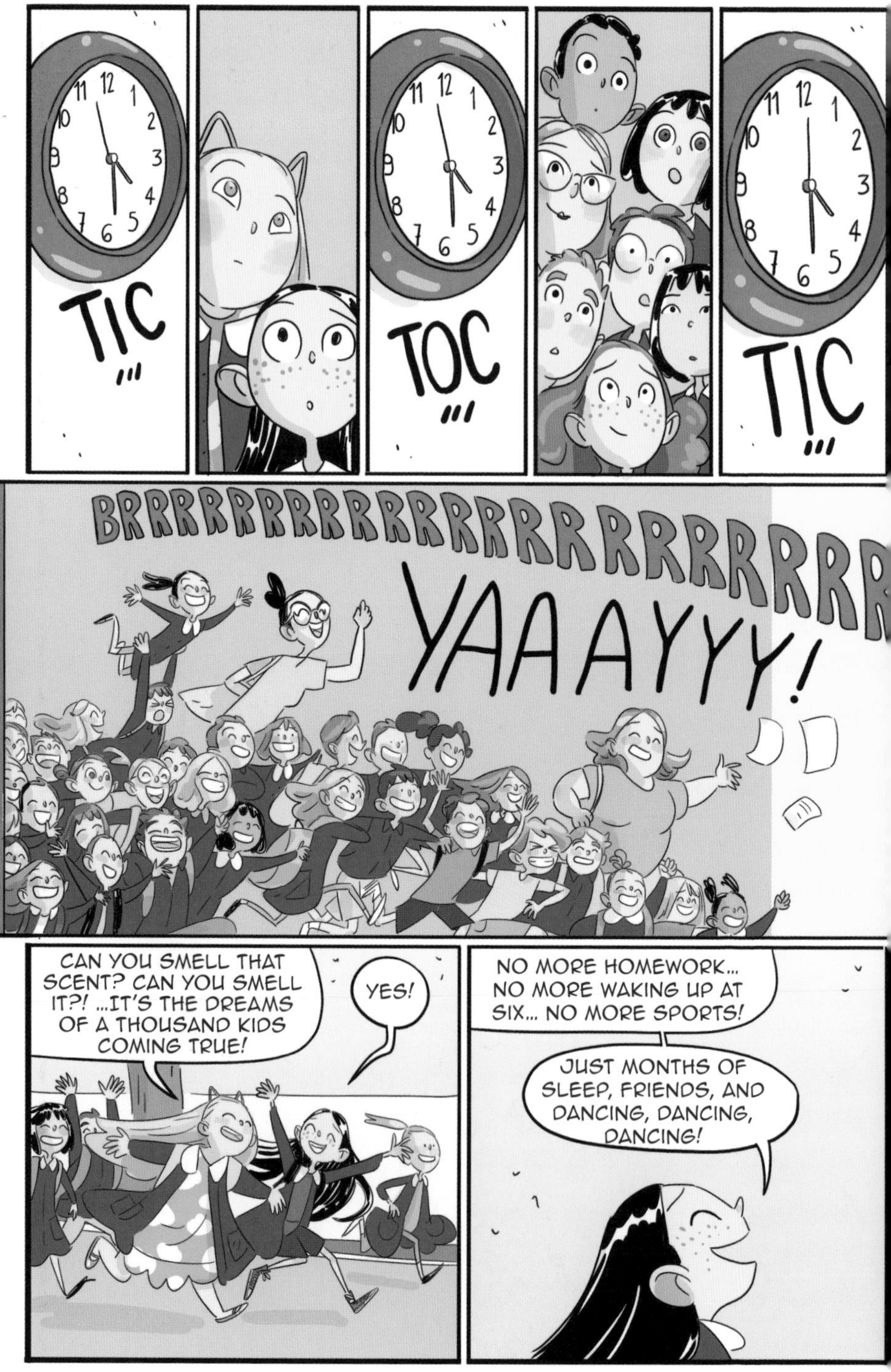
TIC
TOC
TIC
BRRRRRRRRRRRRRRRRRRRRR
YAAAYYY!
CAN YOU SMELL THAT SCENT? CAN YOU SMELL IT?! ...IT'S THE DREAMS OF A THOUSAND KIDS COMING TRUE!
YES!
NO MORE HOMEWORK... NO MORE WAKING UP AT SIX... NO MORE SPORTS!
JUST MONTHS OF SLEEP, FRIENDS, AND DANCING, DANCING, DANCING!

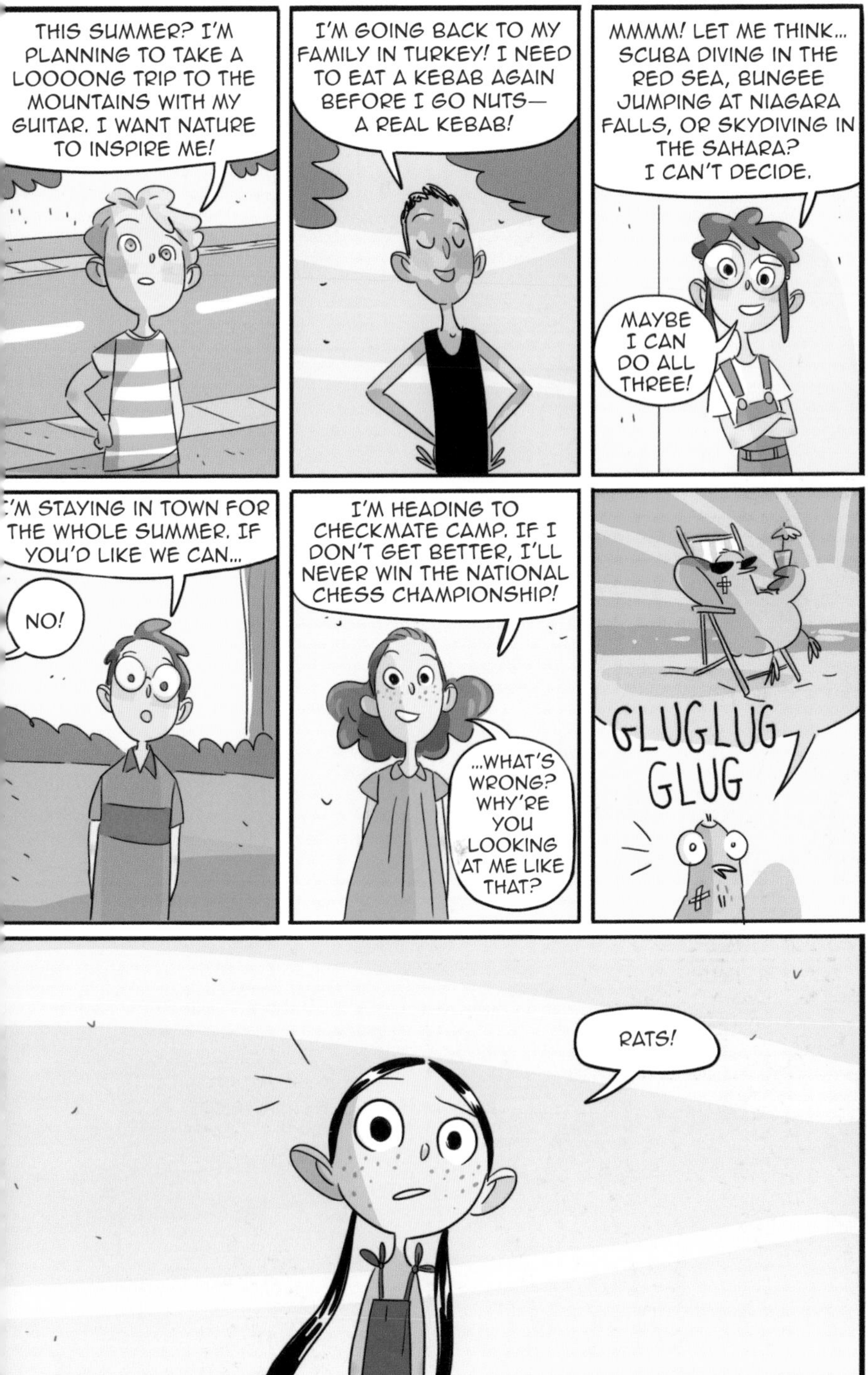
THIS SUMMER? I'M PLANNING TO TAKE A LOOOONG TRIP TO THE MOUNTAINS WITH MY GUITAR. I WANT NATURE TO INSPIRE ME!
I'M GOING BACK TO MY FAMILY IN TURKEY! I NEED TO EAT A KEBAB AGAIN BEFORE I GO NUTS— A REAL KEBAB!
MMMM! LET ME THINK... SCUBA DIVING IN THE RED SEA, BUNGEE JUMPING AT NIAGARA FALLS, OR SKYDIVING IN THE SAHARA? I CAN'T DECIDE.
MAYBE I CAN DO ALL THREE!
I'M STAYING IN TOWN FOR THE WHOLE SUMMER. IF YOU'D LIKE WE CAN...
NO!
I'M HEADING TO CHECKMATE CAMP. IF I DON'T GET BETTER, I'LL NEVER WIN THE NATIONAL CHESS CHAMPIONSHIP!
...WHAT'S WRONG? WHY'RE YOU LOOKING AT ME LIKE THAT?
GLUGLUG GLUG
RATS!

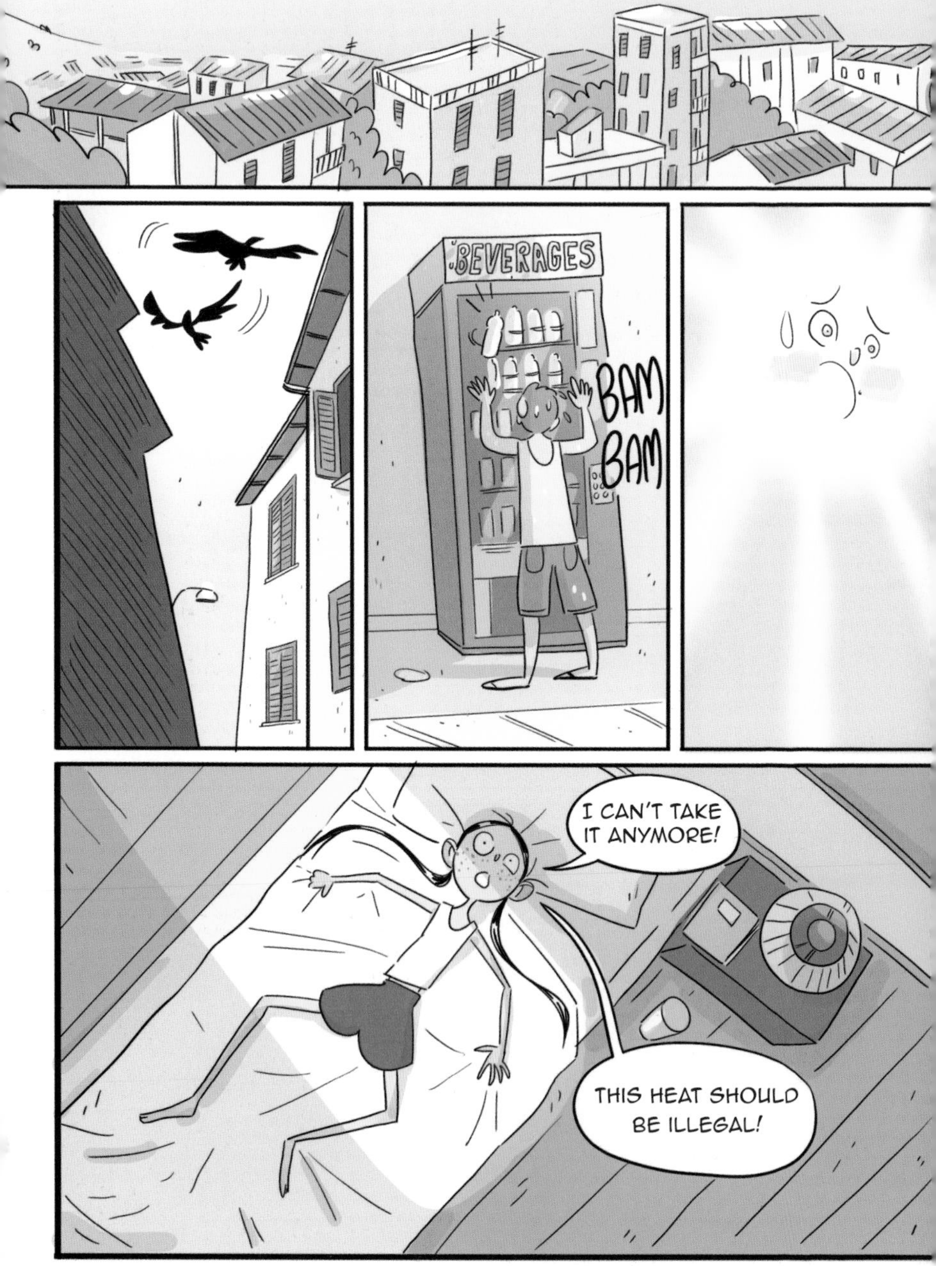
BEVERAGES
BAM BAM
I CAN'T TAKE IT ANYMORE!
THIS HEAT SHOULD BE ILLEGAL!

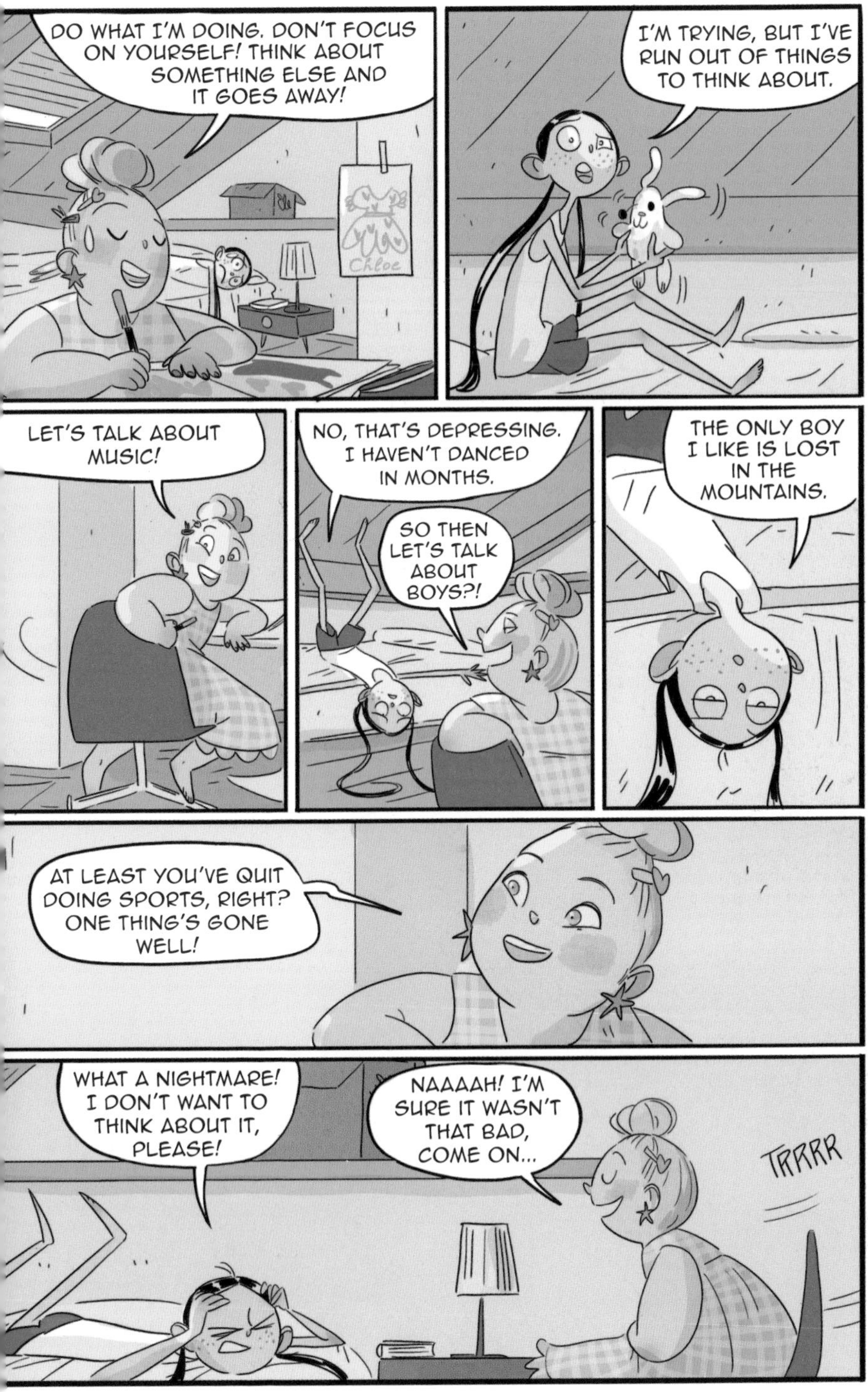
DO WHAT I'M DOING. DON'T FOCUS ON YOURSELF! THINK ABOUT SOMETHING ELSE AND IT GOES AWAY!
Chloe
I'M TRYING, BUT I'VE RUN OUT OF THINGS TO THINK ABOUT.
LET'S TALK ABOUT MUSIC!
NO, THAT'S DEPRESSING. I HAVEN'T DANCED IN MONTHS.
SO THEN LET'S TALK ABOUT BOYS?!
THE ONLY BOY I LIKE IS LOST IN THE MOUNTAINS.
AT LEAST YOU'VE QUIT DOING SPORTS, RIGHT? ONE THING'S GONE WELL!
WHAT A NIGHTMARE! I DON'T WANT TO THINK ABOUT IT, PLEASE!
NAAAAH! I'M SURE IT WASN'T THAT BAD, COME ON...
TRRRR

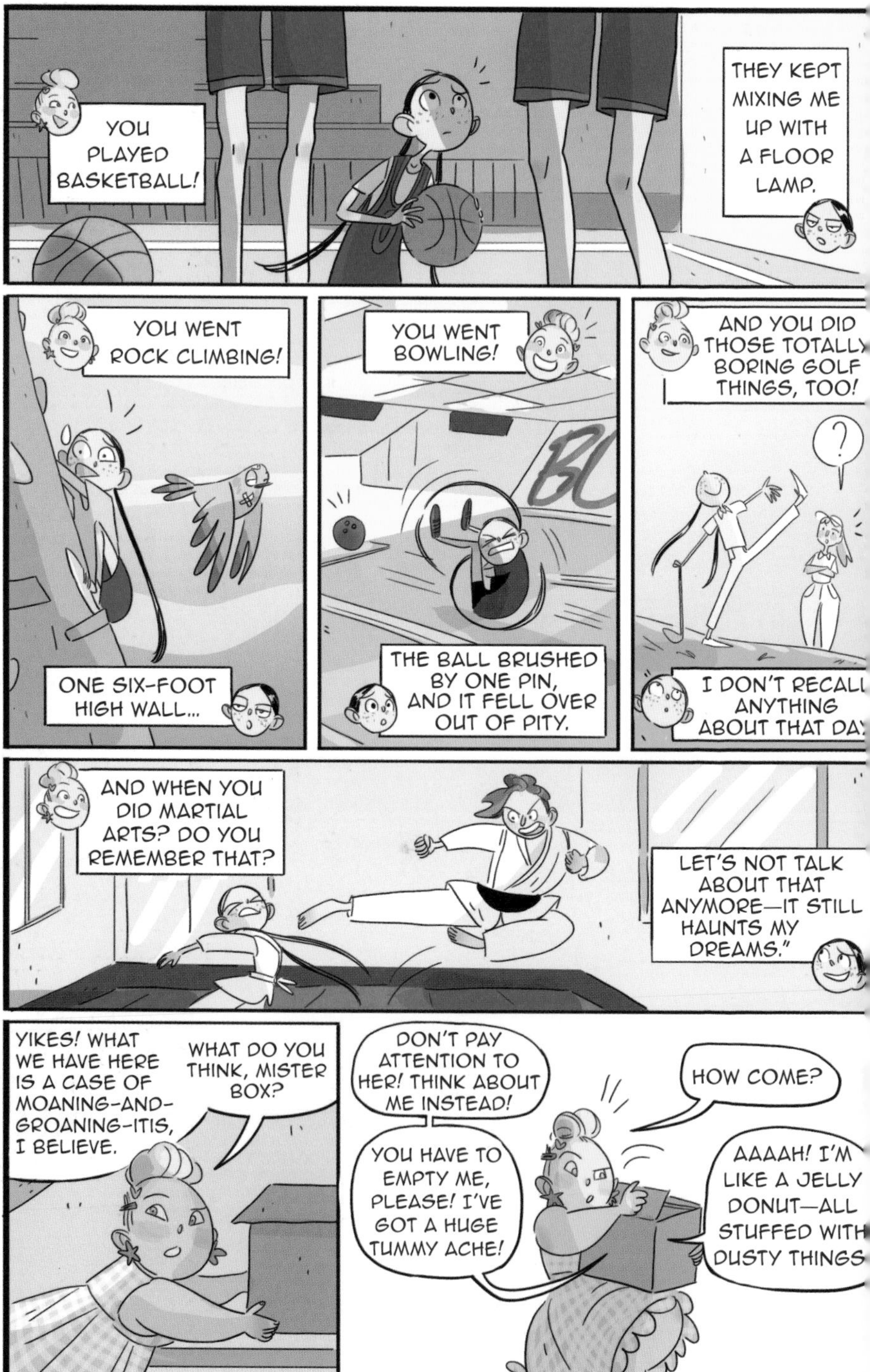
YOU PLAYED BASKETBALL!
THEY KEPT MIXING ME UP WITH A FLOOR LAMP.
YOU WENT ROCK CLIMBING!
ONE SIX-FOOT HIGH WALL...
YOU WENT BOWLING!
THE BALL BRUSHED BY ONE PIN, AND IT FELL OVER OUT OF PITY.
AND YOU DID THOSE TOTALLY BORING GOLF THINGS, TOO!
?
I DON'T RECALL ANYTHING ABOUT THAT DAY
AND WHEN YOU DID MARTIAL ARTS? DO YOU REMEMBER THAT?
LET'S NOT TALK ABOUT THAT ANYMORE—IT STILL HAUNTS MY DREAMS."
YIKES! WHAT WE HAVE HERE IS A CASE OF MOANING-AND-GROANING-ITIS, I BELIEVE.
WHAT DO YOU THINK, MISTER BOX?
DON'T PAY ATTENTION TO HER! THINK ABOUT ME INSTEAD!
YOU HAVE TO EMPTY ME, PLEASE! I'VE GOT A HUGE TUMMY ACHE!
HOW COME?
AAAAH! I'M LIKE A JELLY DONUT—ALL STUFFED WITH DUSTY THINGS

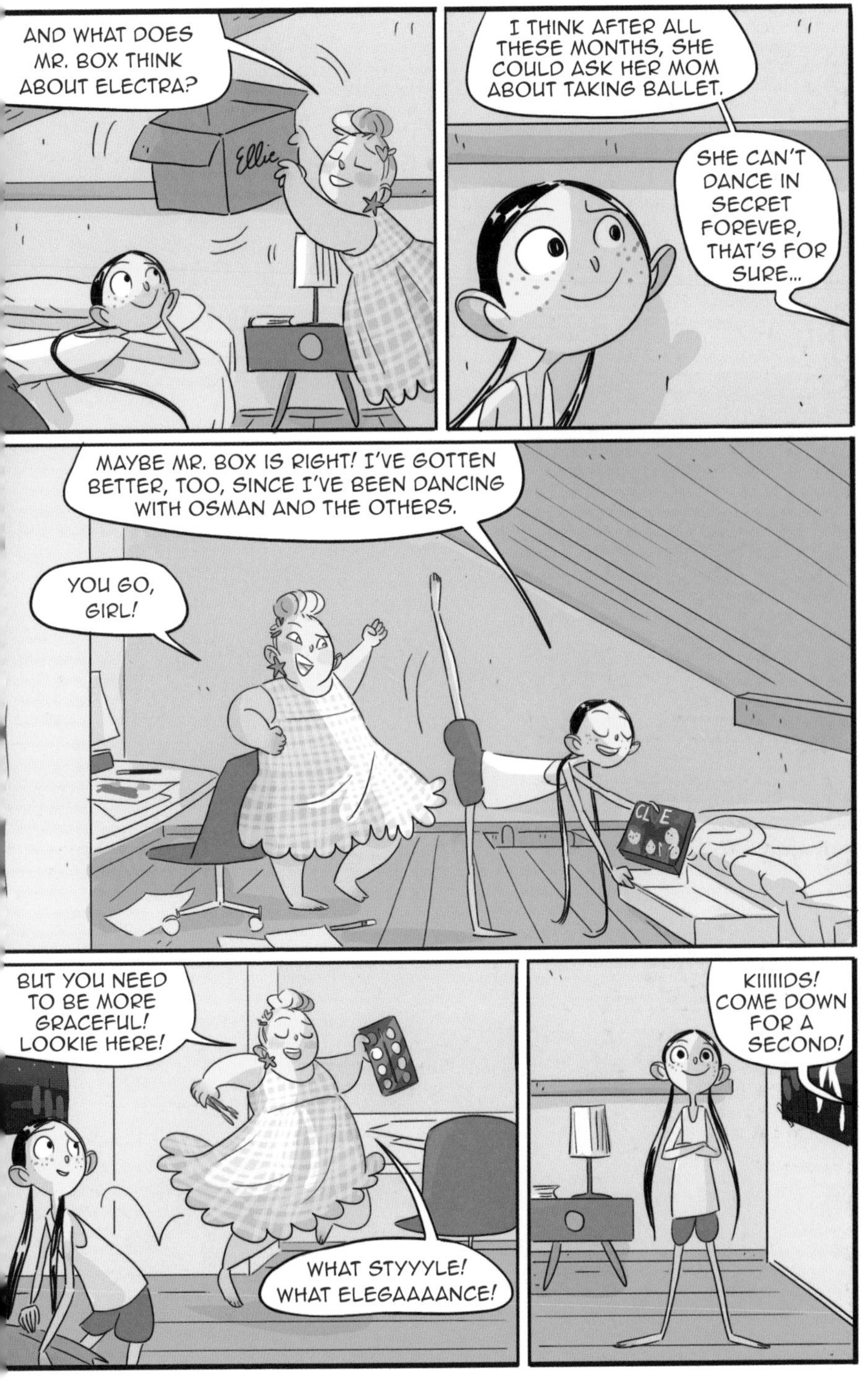
AND WHAT DOES MR. BOX THINK ABOUT ELECTRA?
Ellie
I THINK AFTER ALL THESE MONTHS, SHE COULD ASK HER MOM ABOUT TAKING BALLET.
SHE CAN'T DANCE IN SECRET FOREVER, THAT'S FOR SURE...
MAYBE MR. BOX IS RIGHT! I'VE GOTTEN BETTER, TOO, SINCE I'VE BEEN DANCING WITH OSMAN AND THE OTHERS.
YOU GO, GIRL!
BUT YOU NEED TO BE MORE GRACEFUL! LOOKIE HERE!
WHAT STYYYLE! WHAT ELEGAAAAANCE!
KIIIIIDS! COME DOWN FOR A SECOND!

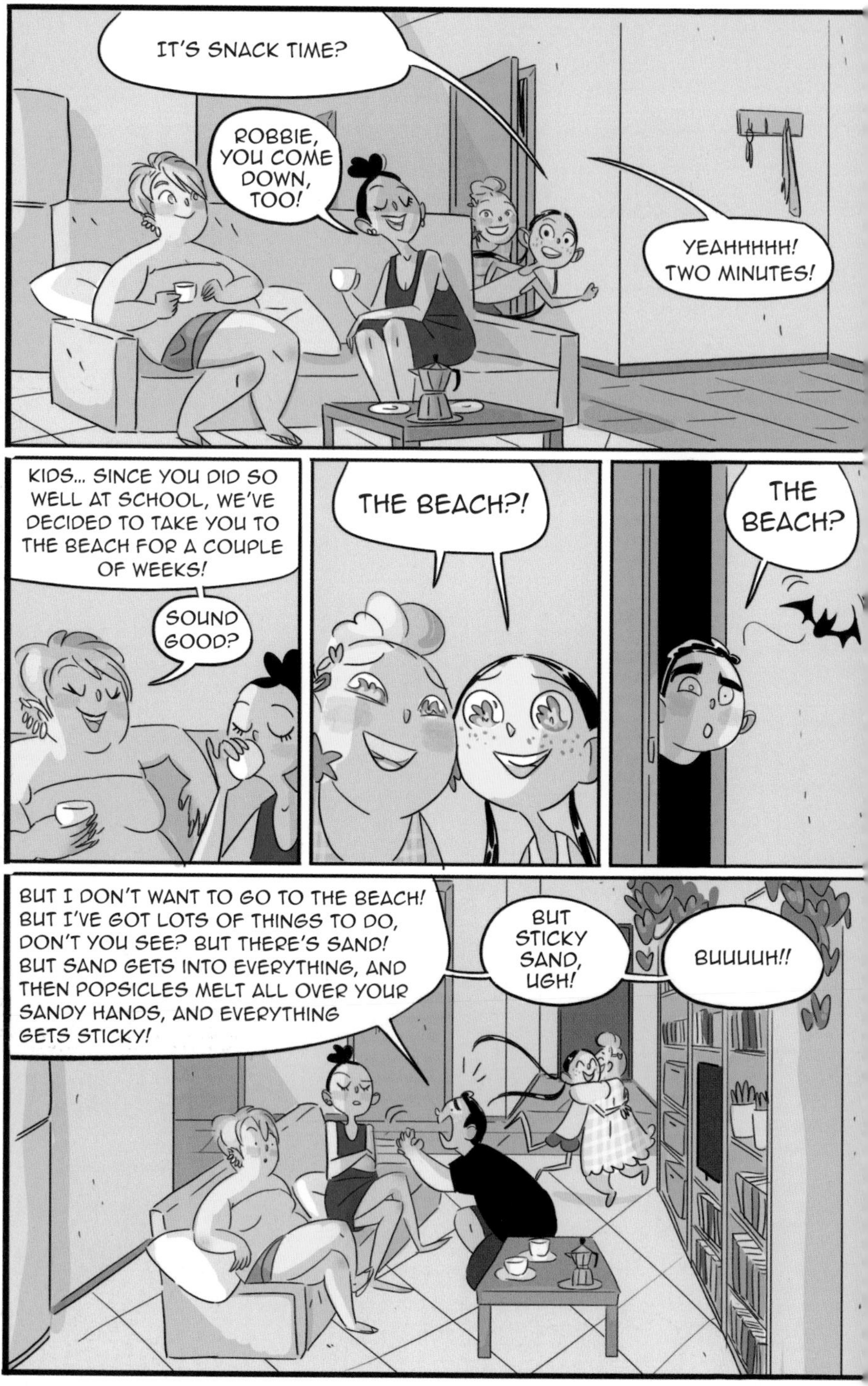
IT'S SNACK TIME?
ROBBIE, YOU COME DOWN, TOO!
YEAHHHHH! TWO MINUTES!
KIDS... SINCE YOU DID SO WELL AT SCHOOL, WE'VE DECIDED TO TAKE YOU TO THE BEACH FOR A COUPLE OF WEEKS!
SOUND GOOD?
THE BEACH?!
THE BEACH?
BUT I DON'T WANT TO GO TO THE BEACH! BUT I'VE GOT LOTS OF THINGS TO DO, DON'T YOU SEE? BUT THERE'S SAND! BUT SAND GETS INTO EVERYTHING, AND THEN POPSICLES MELT ALL OVER YOUR SANDY HANDS, AND EVERYTHING GETS STICKY!
BUT STICKY SAND, UGH!
BUUUUH!!

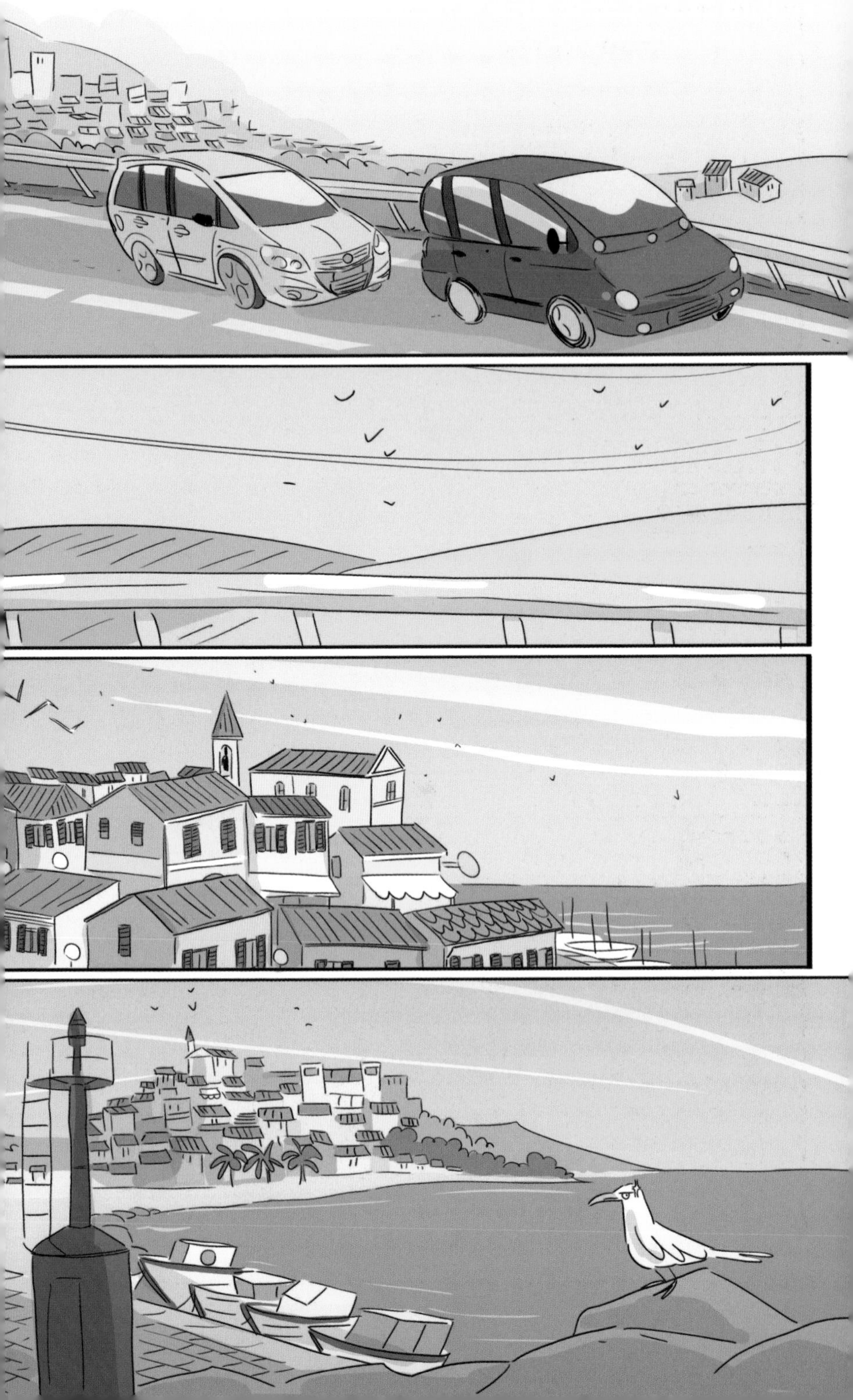

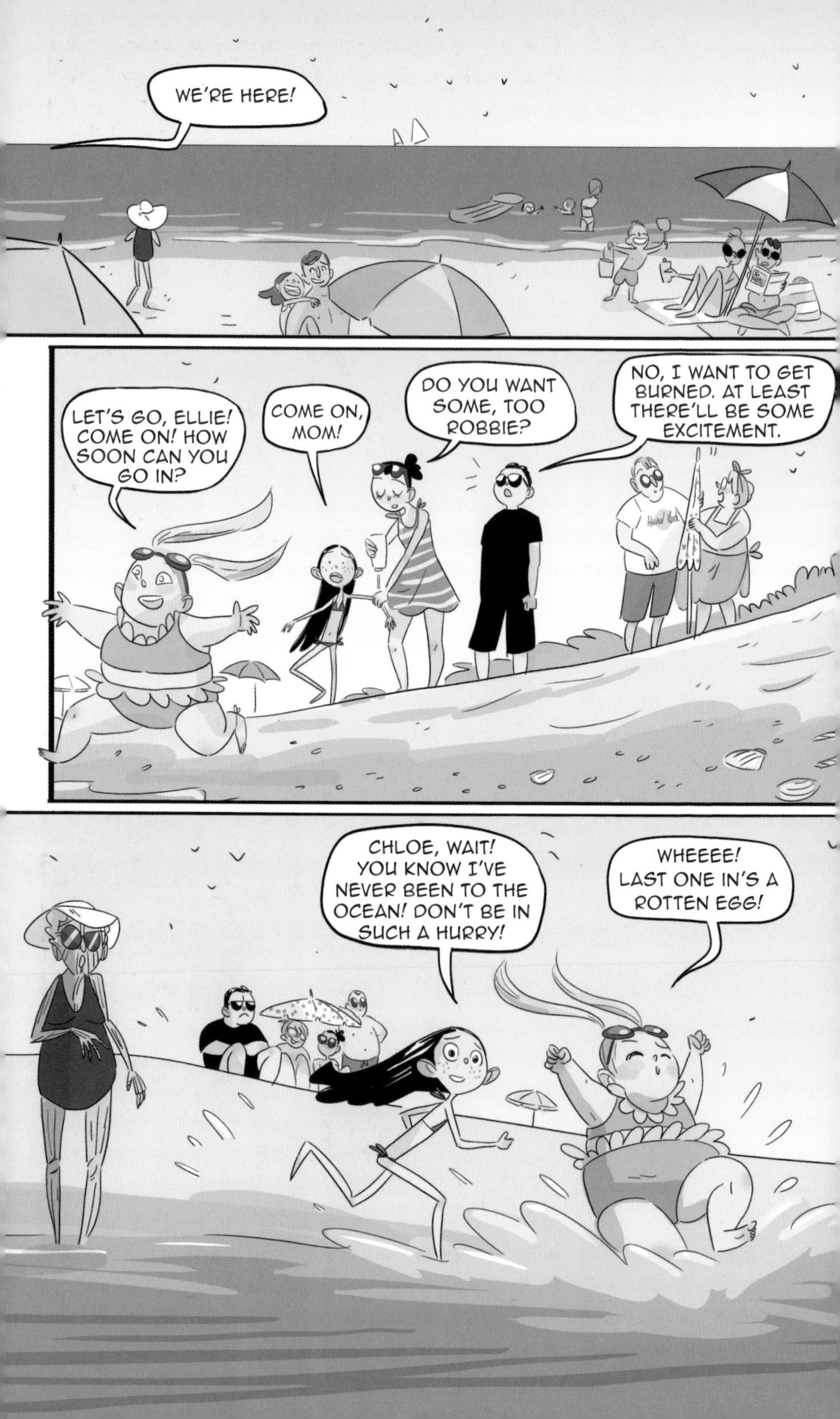
WE'RE HERE!
LET'S GO, ELLIE! COME ON! HOW SOON CAN YOU GO IN?
COME ON, MOM!
DO YOU WANT SOME, TOO ROBBIE?
NO, I WANT TO GET BURNED. AT LEAST THERE'LL BE SOME EXCITEMENT.
CHLOE, WAIT! YOU KNOW I'VE NEVER BEEN TO THE OCEAN! DON'T BE IN SUCH A HURRY!
WHEEEE! LAST ONE IN'S A ROTTEN EGG!

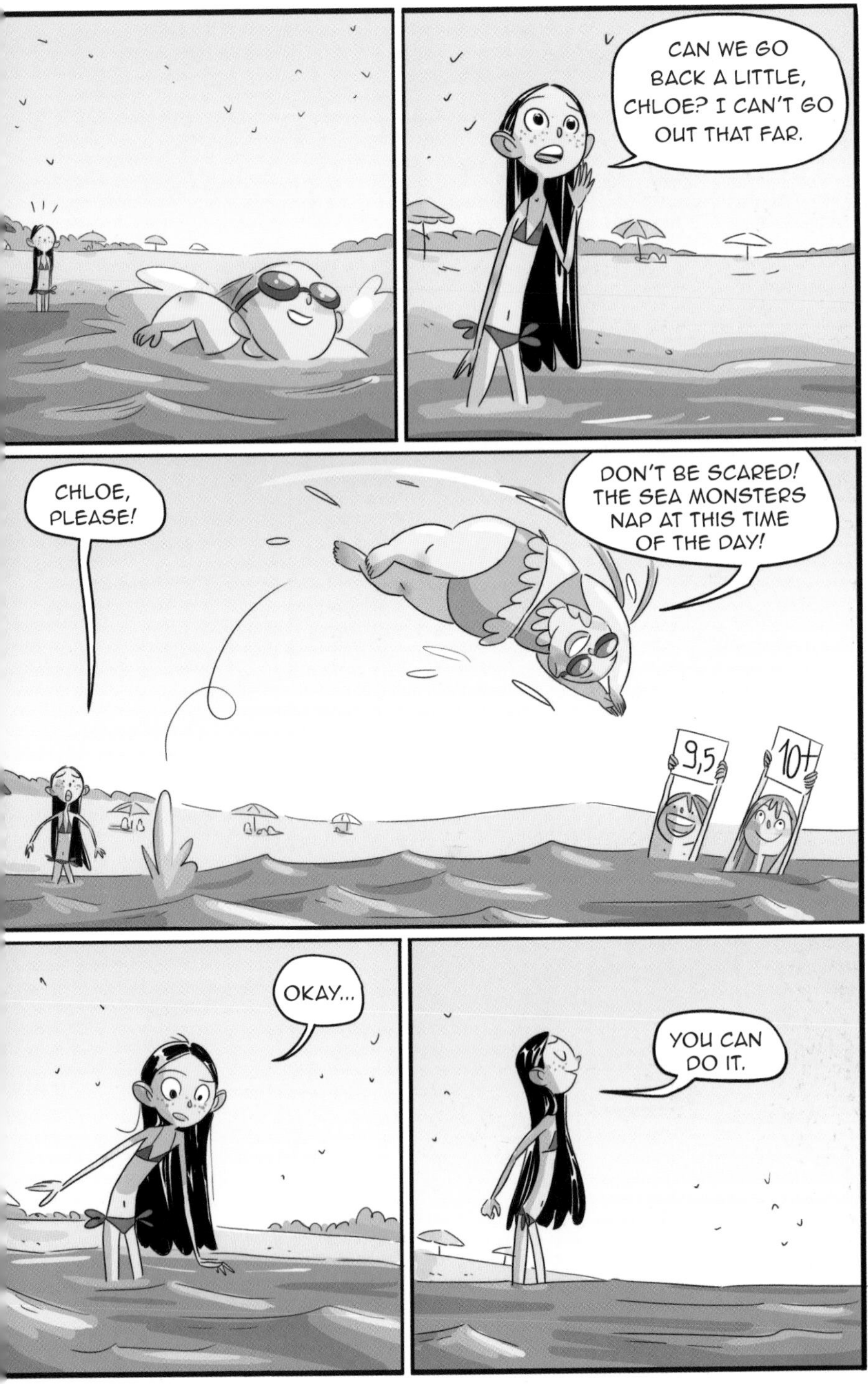
CAN WE GO BACK A LITTLE, CHLOE? I CAN'T GO OUT THAT FAR.
CHLOE, PLEASE!
DON'T BE SCARED! THE SEA MONSTERS NAP AT THIS TIME OF THE DAY!
9,5
10+
OKAY...
YOU CAN DO IT.

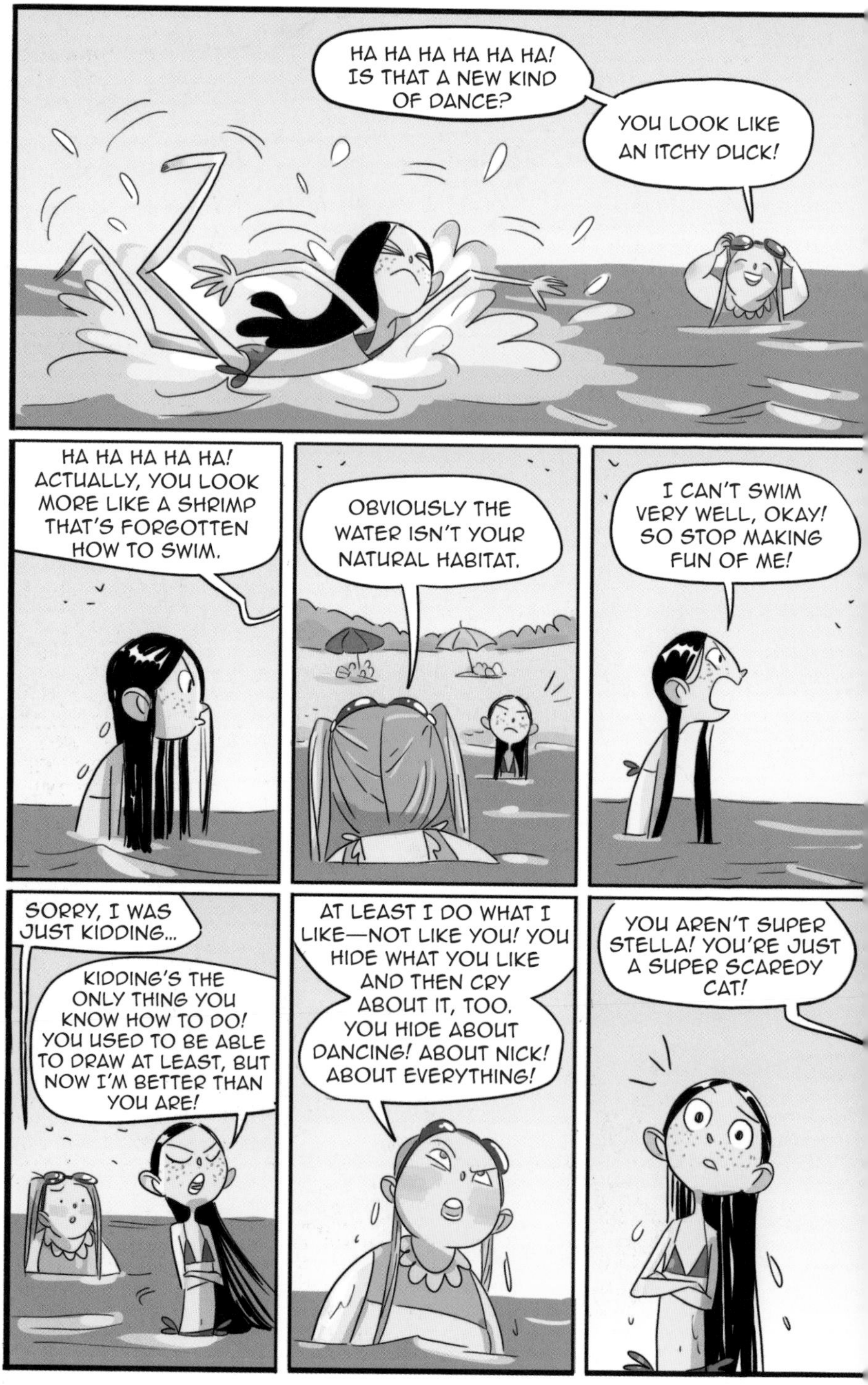
HA HA HA HA HA HA! IS THAT A NEW KIND OF DANCE?
YOU LOOK LIKE AN ITCHY DUCK!
HA HA HA HA HA! ACTUALLY, YOU LOOK MORE LIKE A SHRIMP THAT'S FORGOTTEN HOW TO SWIM.
OBVIOUSLY THE WATER ISN'T YOUR NATURAL HABITAT.
I CAN'T SWIM VERY WELL, OKAY! SO STOP MAKING FUN OF ME!
SORRY, I WAS JUST KIDDING...
KIDDING'S THE ONLY THING YOU KNOW HOW TO DO! YOU USED TO BE ABLE TO DRAW AT LEAST, BUT NOW I'M BETTER THAN YOU ARE!
AT LEAST I DO WHAT I LIKE—NOT LIKE YOU! YOU HIDE WHAT YOU LIKE AND THEN CRY ABOUT IT, TOO. YOU HIDE ABOUT DANCING! ABOUT NICK! ABOUT EVERYTHING!
YOU AREN'T SUPER STELLA! YOU'RE JUST A SUPER SCAREDY CAT!

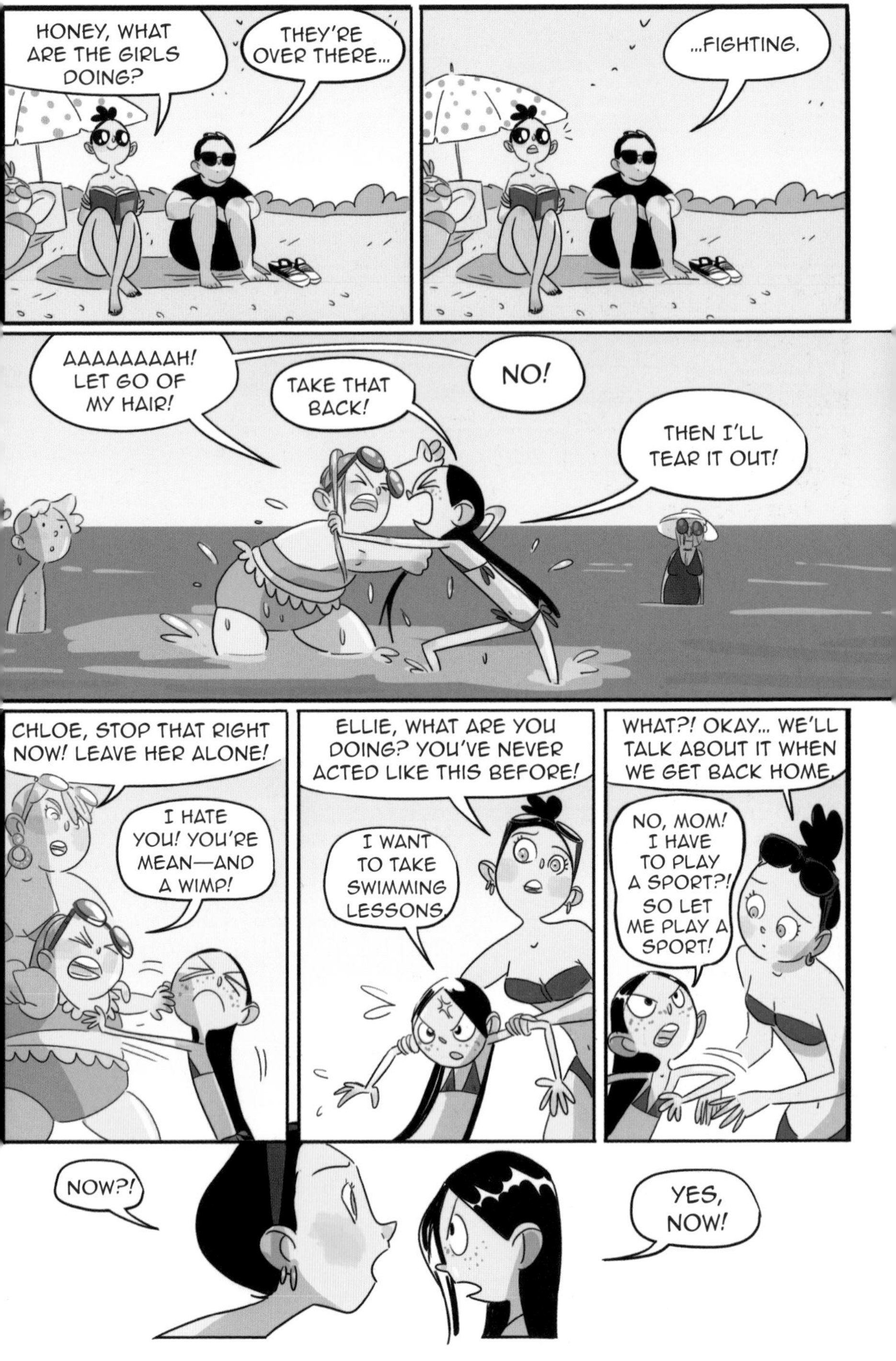
HONEY, WHAT ARE THE GIRLS DOING?
THEY'RE OVER THERE...
...FIGHTING.
AAAAAAAAH! LET GO OF MY HAIR!
TAKE THAT BACK!
NO!
THEN I'LL TEAR IT OUT!
CHLOE, STOP THAT RIGHT NOW! LEAVE HER ALONE!
I HATE YOU! YOU'RE MEAN—AND A WIMP!
ELLIE, WHAT ARE YOU DOING? YOU'VE NEVER ACTED LIKE THIS BEFORE!
I WANT TO TAKE SWIMMING LESSONS.
WHAT?! OKAY... WE'LL TALK ABOUT IT WHEN WE GET BACK HOME.
NO, MOM! I HAVE TO PLAY A SPORT?! SO LET ME PLAY A SPORT!
NOW?!
YES, NOW!

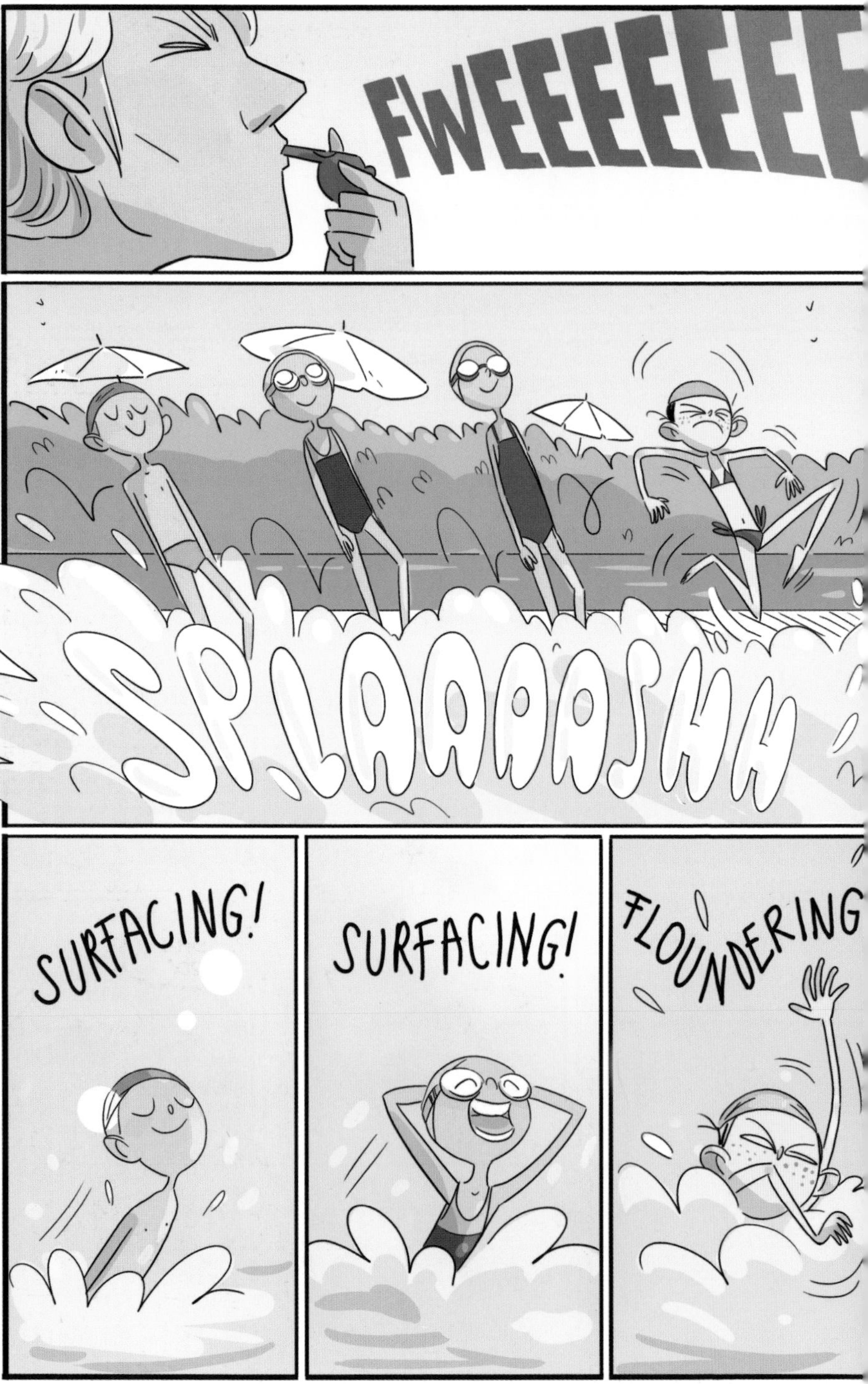
FWEEEEEEEE
SPLAAAASHH
SURFACING!
SURFACING!
FLOUNDERING

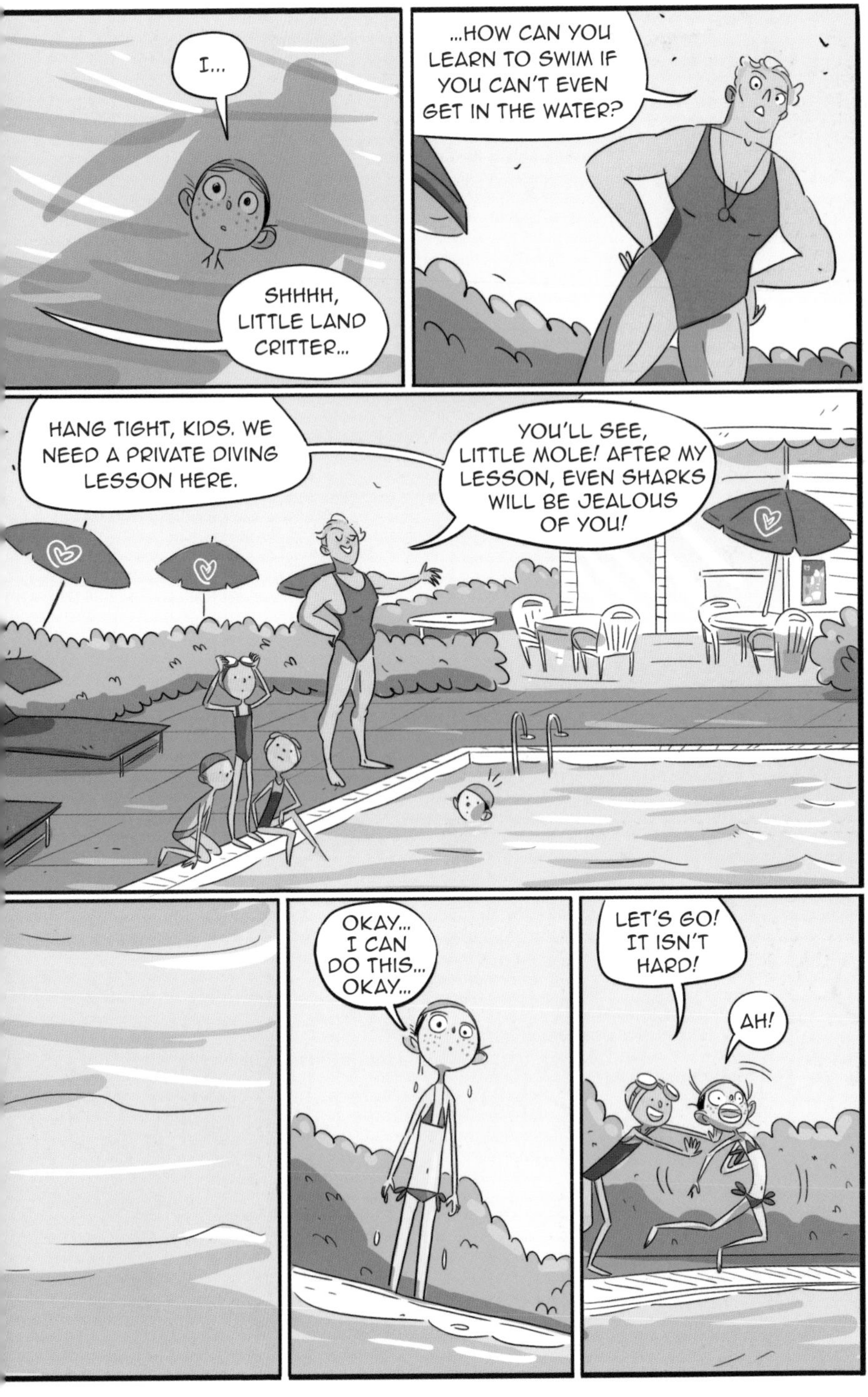
I...
SHHHH, LITTLE LAND CRITTER...
...HOW CAN YOU LEARN TO SWIM IF YOU CAN'T EVEN GET IN THE WATER?
HANG TIGHT, KIDS. WE NEED A PRIVATE DIVING LESSON HERE.
YOU'LL SEE, LITTLE MOLE! AFTER MY LESSON, EVEN SHARKS WILL BE JEALOUS OF YOU!
OKAY... I CAN DO THIS... OKAY...
LET'S GO! IT ISN'T HARD!
AH!

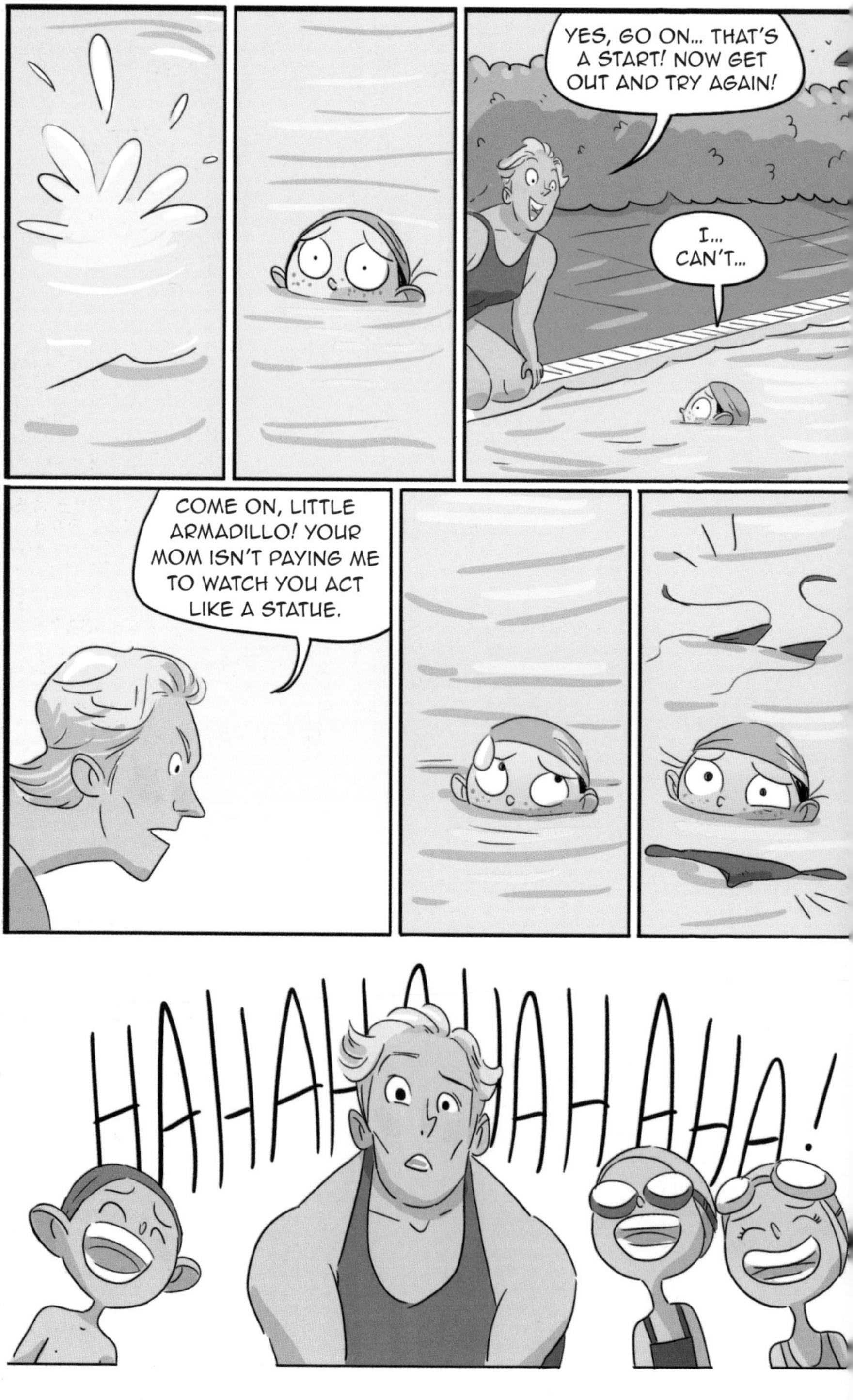
YES, GO ON... THAT'S A START! NOW GET OUT AND TRY AGAIN!
I... CAN'T...
COME ON, LITTLE ARMADILLO! YOUR MOM ISN'T PAYING ME TO WATCH YOU ACT LIKE A STATUE.
HAHAHAHAHAHAHA!

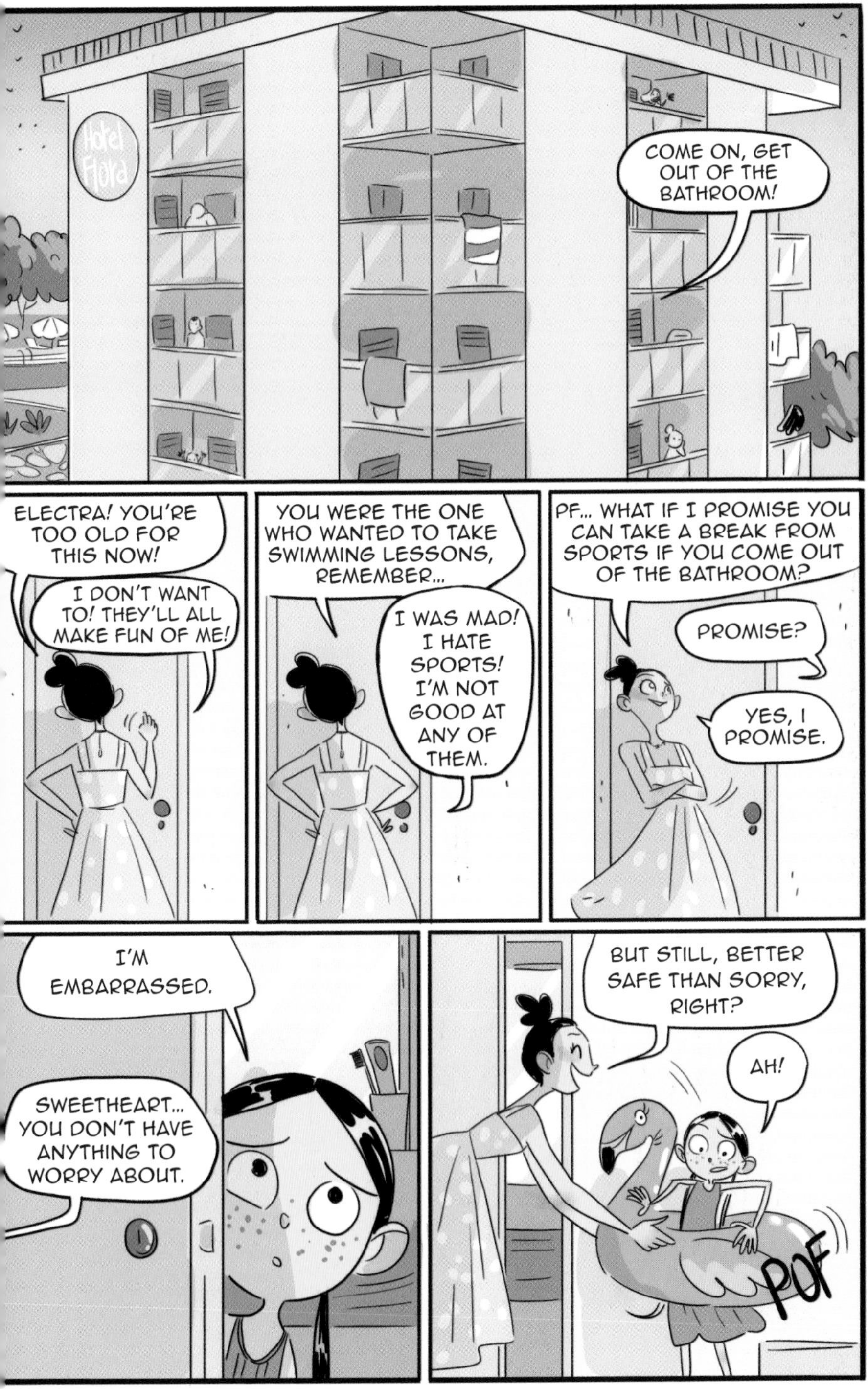
Hotel Flora
COME ON, GET OUT OF THE BATHROOM!
ELECTRA! YOU'RE TOO OLD FOR THIS NOW!
I DON'T WANT TO! THEY'LL ALL MAKE FUN OF ME!
YOU WERE THE ONE WHO WANTED TO TAKE SWIMMING LESSONS, REMEMBER...
I WAS MAD! I HATE SPORTS! I'M NOT GOOD AT ANY OF THEM.
PF... WHAT IF I PROMISE YOU CAN TAKE A BREAK FROM SPORTS IF YOU COME OUT OF THE BATHROOM?
PROMISE?
YES, I PROMISE.
I'M EMBARRASSED.
SWEETHEART... YOU DON'T HAVE ANYTHING TO WORRY ABOUT.
BUT STILL, BETTER SAFE THAN SORRY, RIGHT?
AH!
POF

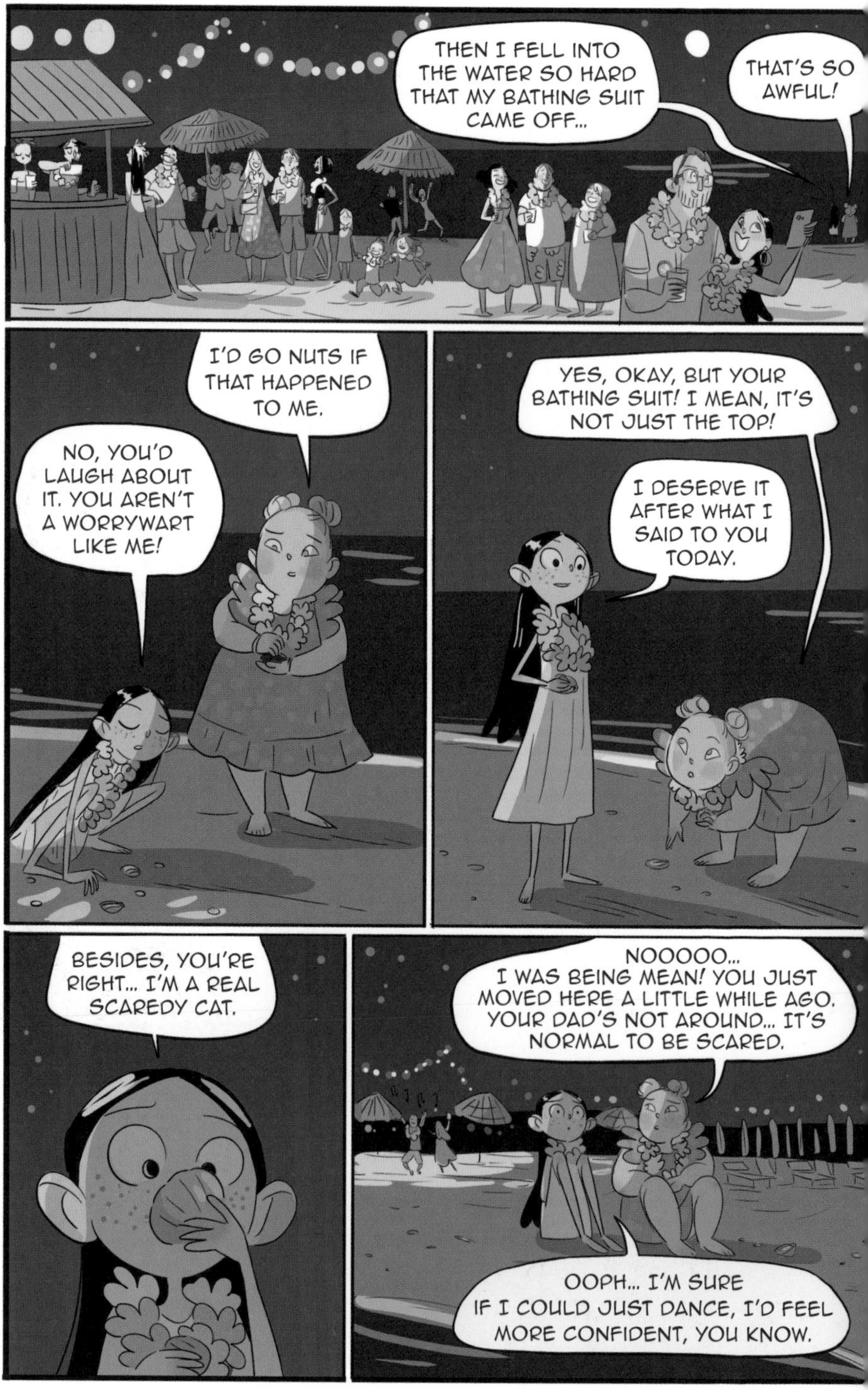
THEN I FELL INTO THE WATER SO HARD THAT MY BATHING SUIT CAME OFF...
THAT'S SO AWFUL!
I'D GO NUTS IF THAT HAPPENED TO ME.
NO, YOU'D LAUGH ABOUT IT. YOU AREN'T A WORRYWART LIKE ME!
YES, OKAY, BUT YOUR BATHING SUIT! I MEAN, IT'S NOT JUST THE TOP!
I DESERVE IT AFTER WHAT I SAID TO YOU TODAY.
BESIDES, YOU'RE RIGHT... I'M A REAL SCAREDY CAT.
NOOOOO... I WAS BEING MEAN! YOU JUST MOVED HERE A LITTLE WHILE AGO. YOUR DAD'S NOT AROUND... IT'S NORMAL TO BE SCARED.
OOPH... I'M SURE IF I COULD JUST DANCE, I'D FEEL MORE CONFIDENT, YOU KNOW.

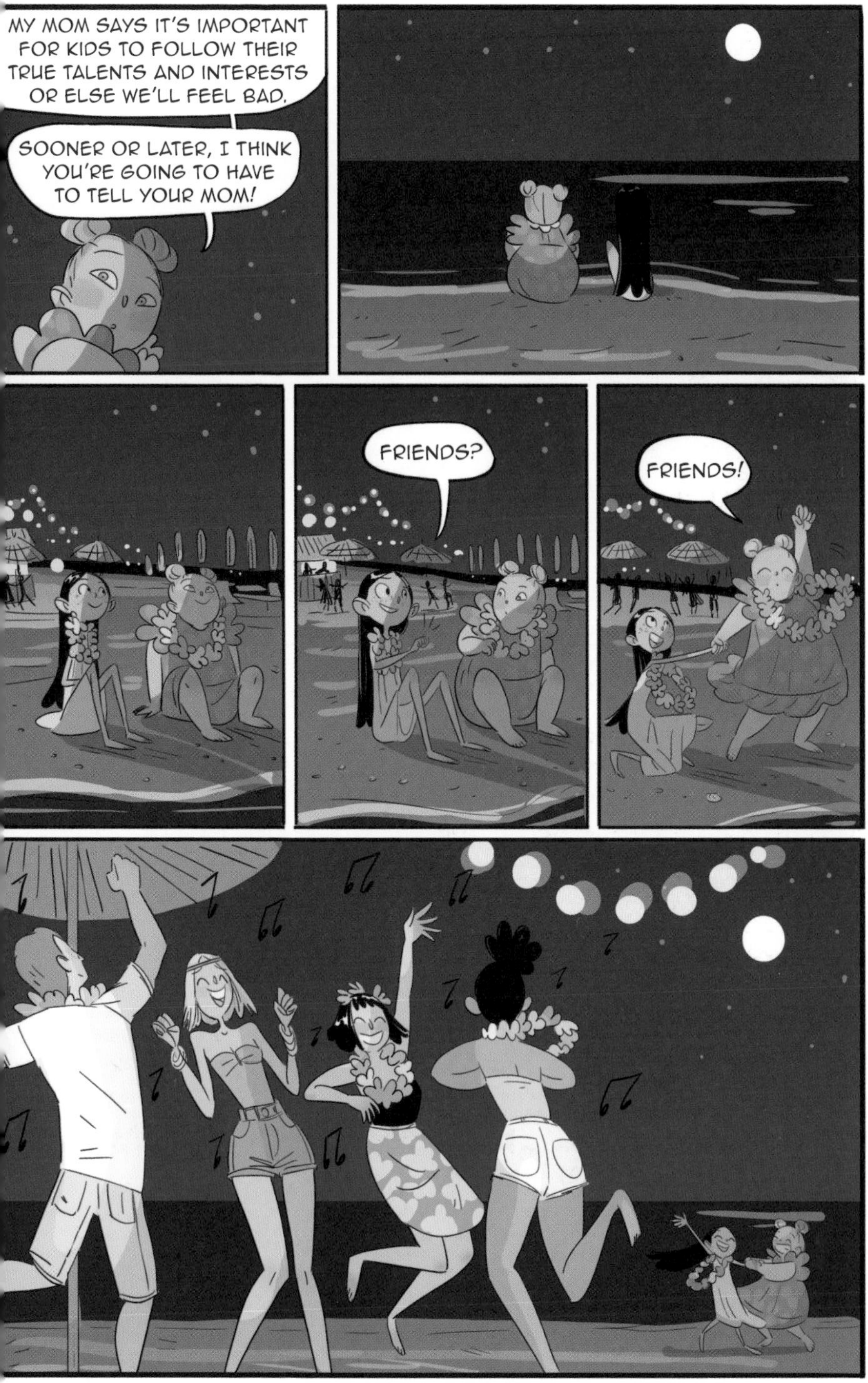
MY MOM SAYS IT'S IMPORTANT FOR KIDS TO FOLLOW THEIR TRUE TALENTS AND INTERESTS OR ELSE WE'LL FEEL BAD.
SOONER OR LATER, I THINK YOU'RE GOING TO HAVE TO TELL YOUR MOM!
FRIENDS?
FRIENDS!

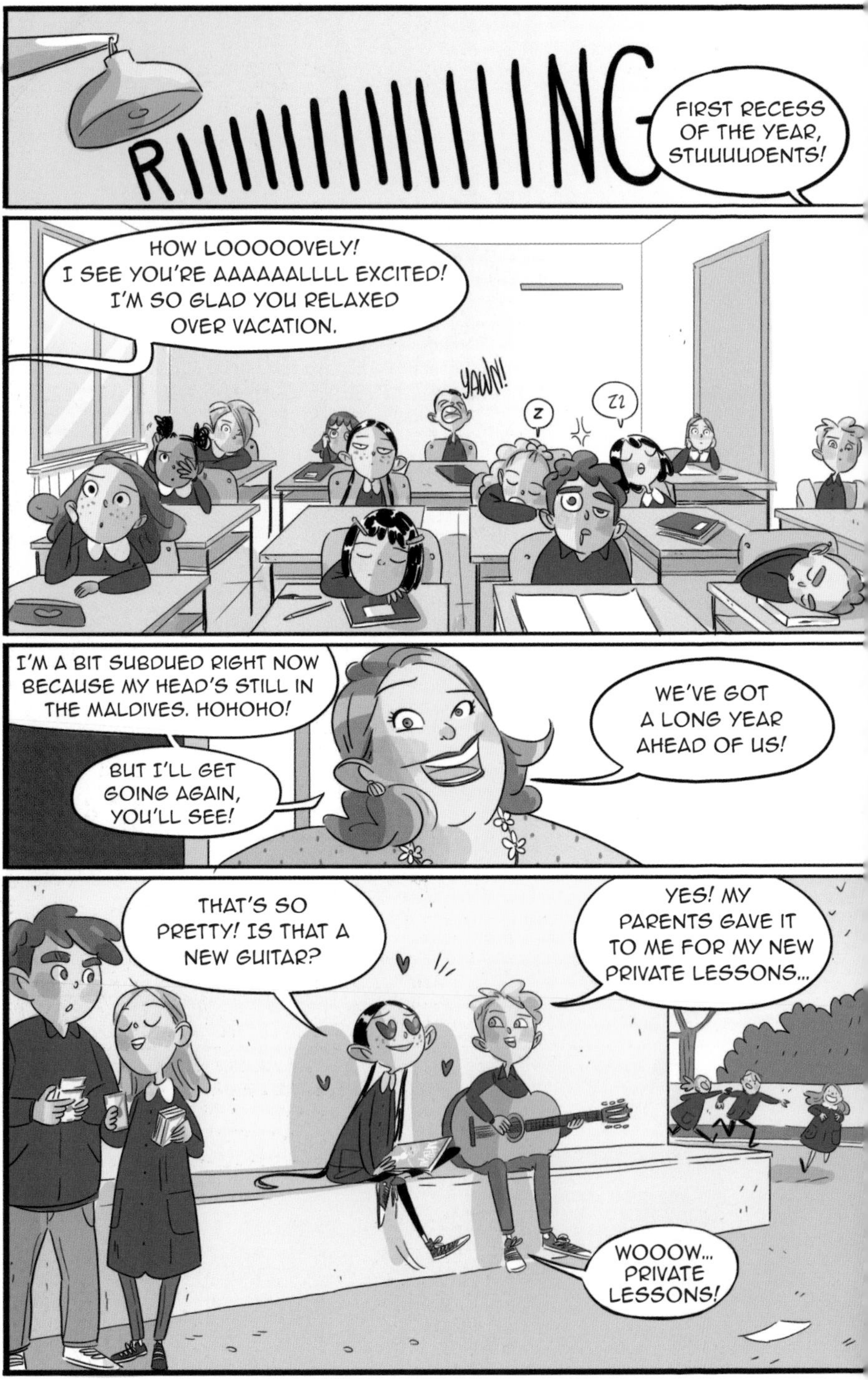
RIIIIIIIIIIIIING
FIRST RECESS OF THE YEAR, STUUUUDENTS!
HOW LOOOOOVELY! I SEE YOU'RE AAAAAALLLL EXCITED! I'M SO GLAD YOU RELAXED OVER VACATION.
YAWN!
Z
ZZ
I'M A BIT SUBDUED RIGHT NOW BECAUSE MY HEAD'S STILL IN THE MALDIVES. HOHOHO!
BUT I'LL GET GOING AGAIN, YOU'LL SEE!
WE'VE GOT A LONG YEAR AHEAD OF US!
THAT'S SO PRETTY! IS THAT A NEW GUITAR?
YES! MY PARENTS GAVE IT TO ME FOR MY NEW PRIVATE LESSONS...
WOOOW... PRIVATE LESSONS!

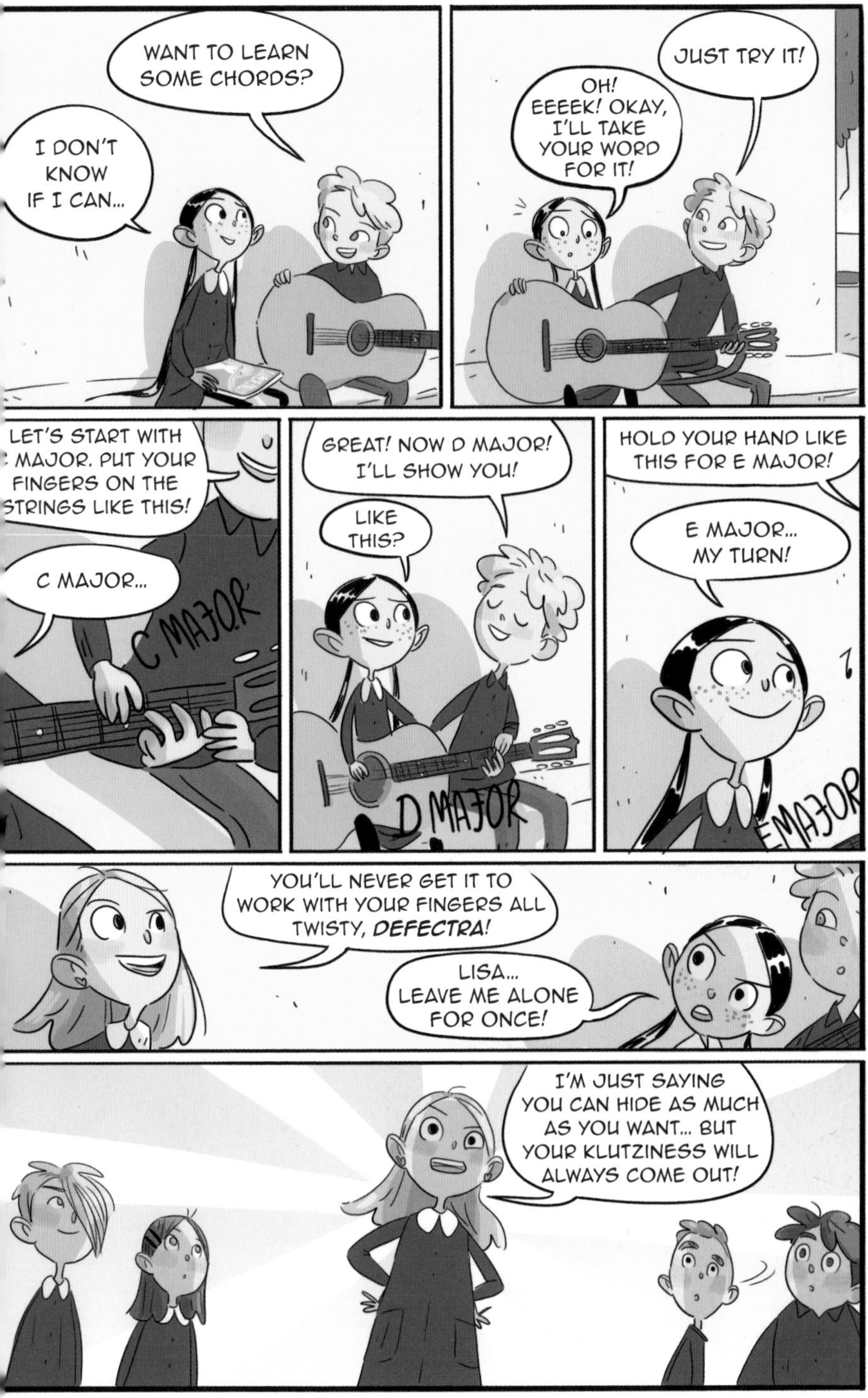
WANT TO LEARN SOME CHORDS?
I DON'T KNOW IF I CAN...
JUST TRY IT!
OH! EEEEK! OKAY, I'LL TAKE YOUR WORD FOR IT!
LET'S START WITH C MAJOR. PUT YOUR FINGERS ON THE STRINGS LIKE THIS!
C MAJOR...
C MAJOR
GREAT! NOW D MAJOR! I'LL SHOW YOU!
LIKE THIS?
D MAJOR
HOLD YOUR HAND LIKE THIS FOR E MAJOR!
E MAJOR... MY TURN!
E MAJOR
YOU'LL NEVER GET IT TO WORK WITH YOUR FINGERS ALL TWISTY, *DEFECTRA*!
LISA... LEAVE ME ALONE FOR ONCE!
I'M JUST SAYING YOU CAN HIDE AS MUCH AS YOU WANT... BUT YOUR KLUTZINESS WILL ALWAYS COME OUT!

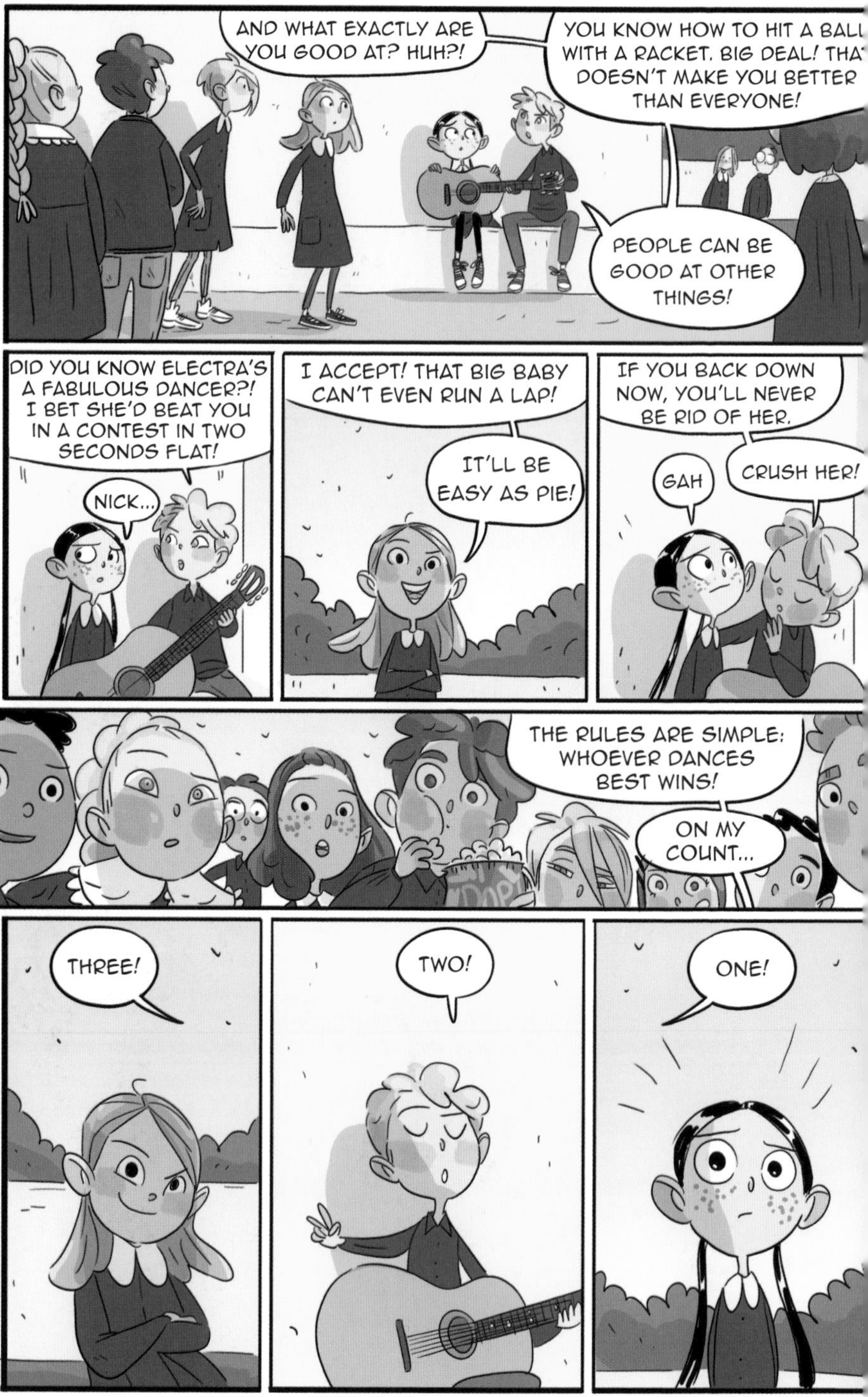
AND WHAT EXACTLY ARE YOU GOOD AT? HUH?!
YOU KNOW HOW TO HIT A BALL WITH A RACKET. BIG DEAL! THAT DOESN'T MAKE YOU BETTER THAN EVERYONE!
PEOPLE CAN BE GOOD AT OTHER THINGS!
DID YOU KNOW ELECTRA'S A FABULOUS DANCER?! I BET SHE'D BEAT YOU IN A CONTEST IN TWO SECONDS FLAT!
NICK...
I ACCEPT! THAT BIG BABY CAN'T EVEN RUN A LAP!
IT'LL BE EASY AS PIE!
IF YOU BACK DOWN NOW, YOU'LL NEVER BE RID OF HER.
GAH
CRUSH HER!
THE RULES ARE SIMPLE: WHOEVER DANCES BEST WINS!
ON MY COUNT...
THREE!
TWO!
ONE!

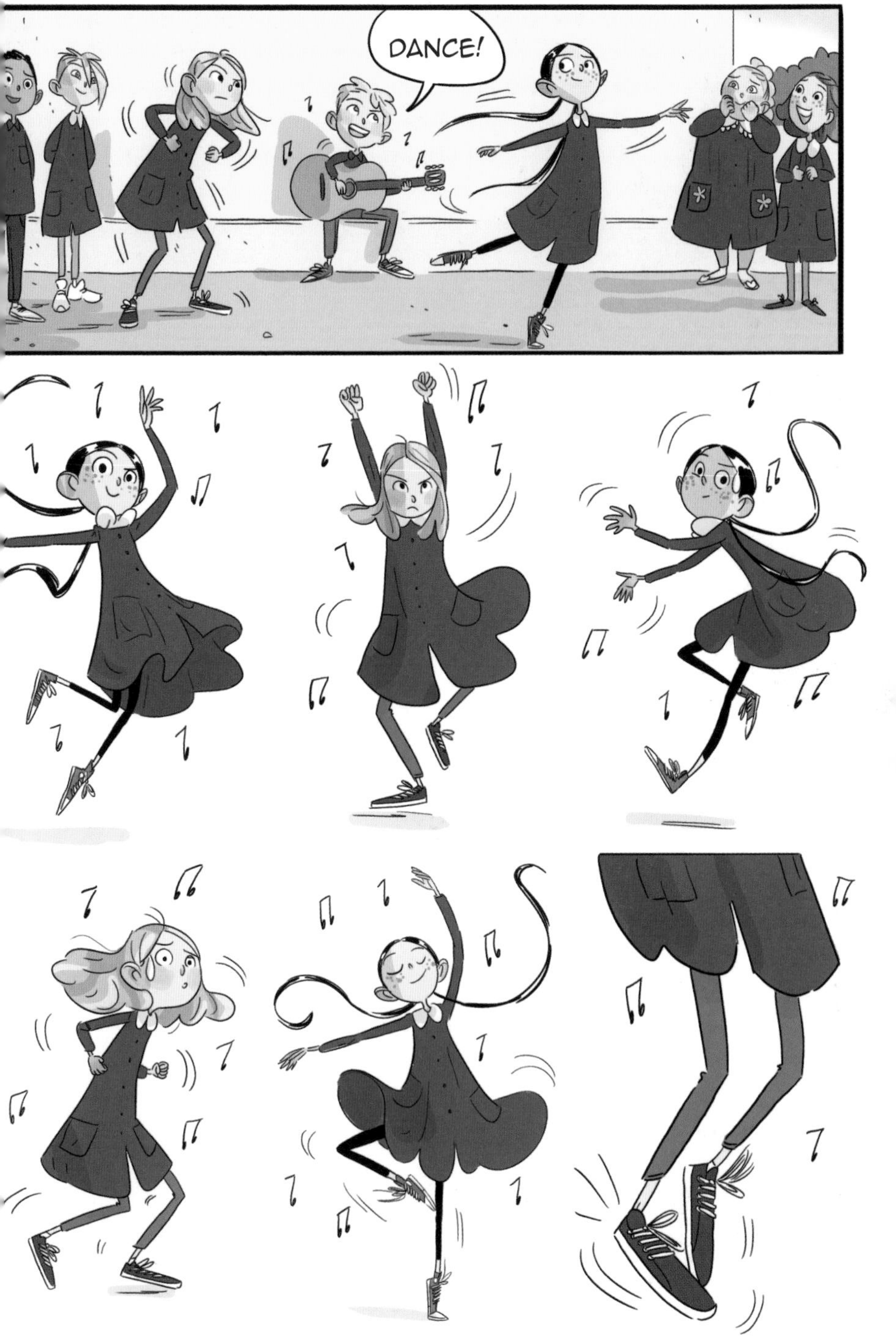
DANCE!

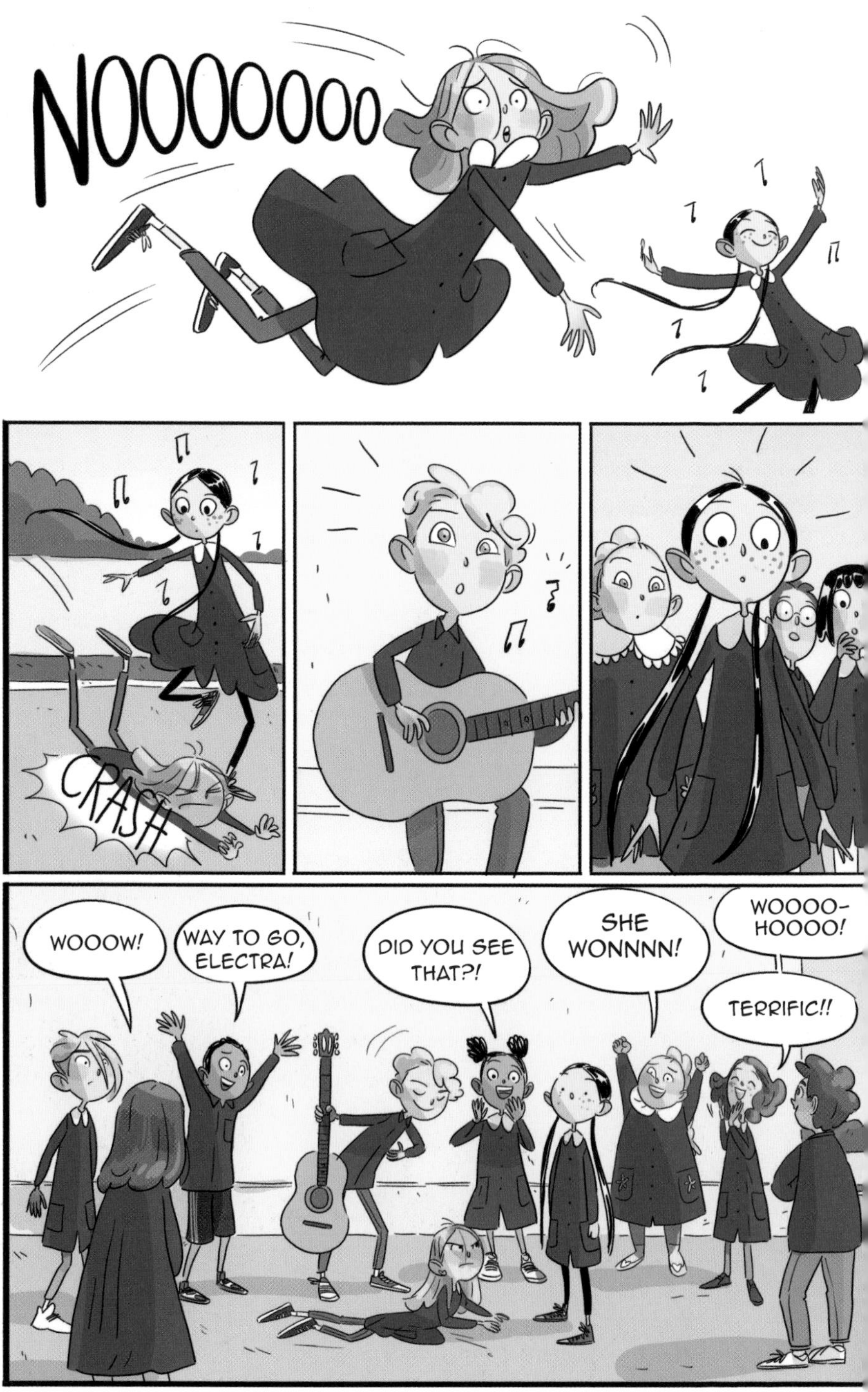
NOOOOOOO
CRASH
WOOOW!
WAY TO GO, ELECTRA!
DID YOU SEE THAT?!
SHE WONNNN!
WOOOO-HOOOOO!
TERRIFIC!!

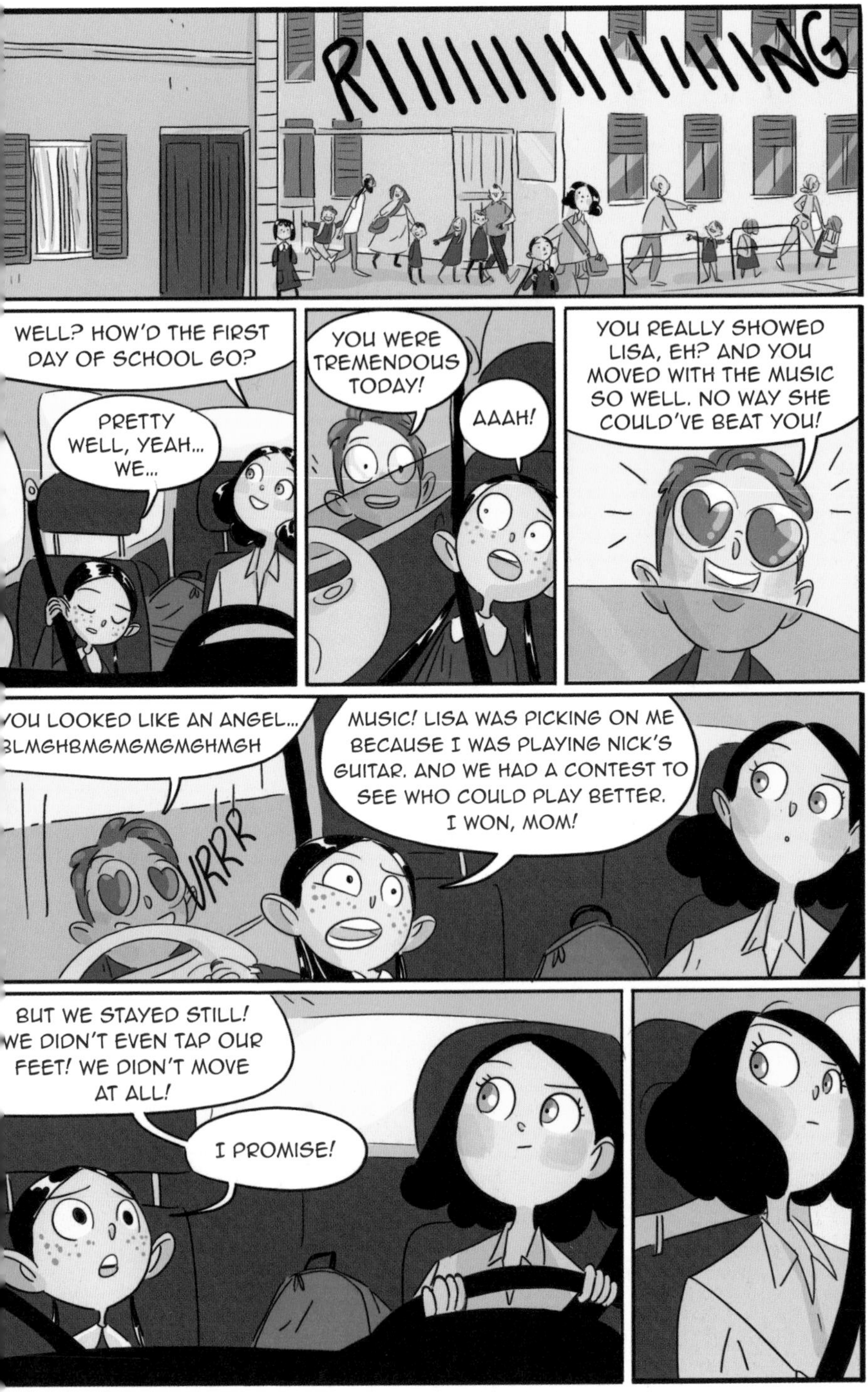
RIIIIIIIIIIIIING
WELL? HOW'D THE FIRST DAY OF SCHOOL GO?
PRETTY WELL, YEAH... WE...
YOU WERE TREMENDOUS TODAY!
AAAH!
YOU REALLY SHOWED LISA, EH? AND YOU MOVED WITH THE MUSIC SO WELL. NO WAY SHE COULD'VE BEAT YOU!
YOU LOOKED LIKE AN ANGEL... BLMGHBMGMGMGMGHMGH
VRRR
MUSIC! LISA WAS PICKING ON ME BECAUSE I WAS PLAYING NICK'S GUITAR. AND WE HAD A CONTEST TO SEE WHO COULD PLAY BETTER. I WON, MOM!
BUT WE STAYED STILL! WE DIDN'T EVEN TAP OUR FEET! WE DIDN'T MOVE AT ALL!
I PROMISE!

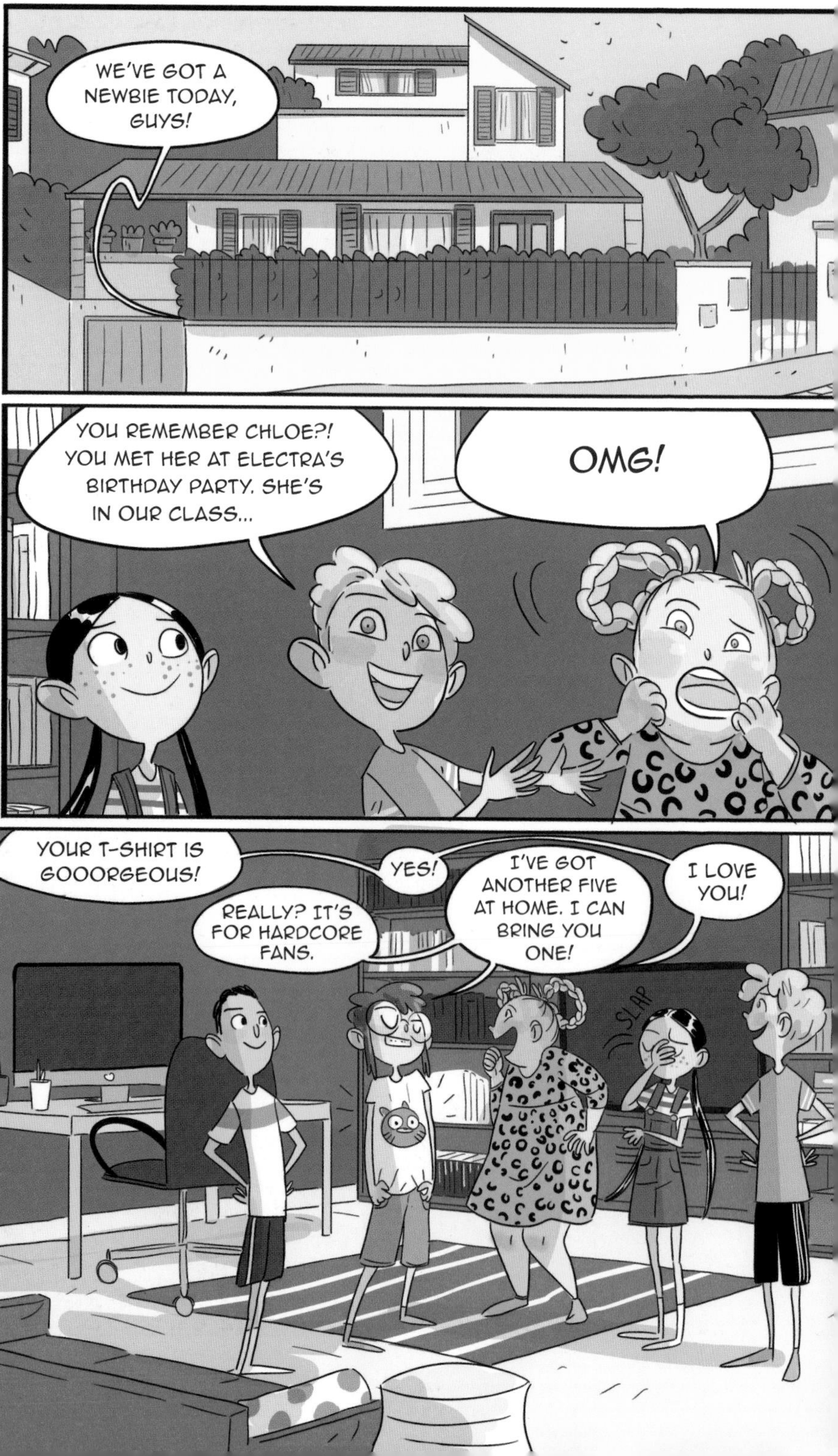
WE'VE GOT A NEWBIE TODAY, GUYS!
YOU REMEMBER CHLOE?! YOU MET HER AT ELECTRA'S BIRTHDAY PARTY. SHE'S IN OUR CLASS...
OMG!
YOUR T-SHIRT IS GOOORGEOUS!
REALLY? IT'S FOR HARDCORE FANS.
YES!
I'VE GOT ANOTHER FIVE AT HOME. I CAN BRING YOU ONE!
I LOVE YOU!
SLAP

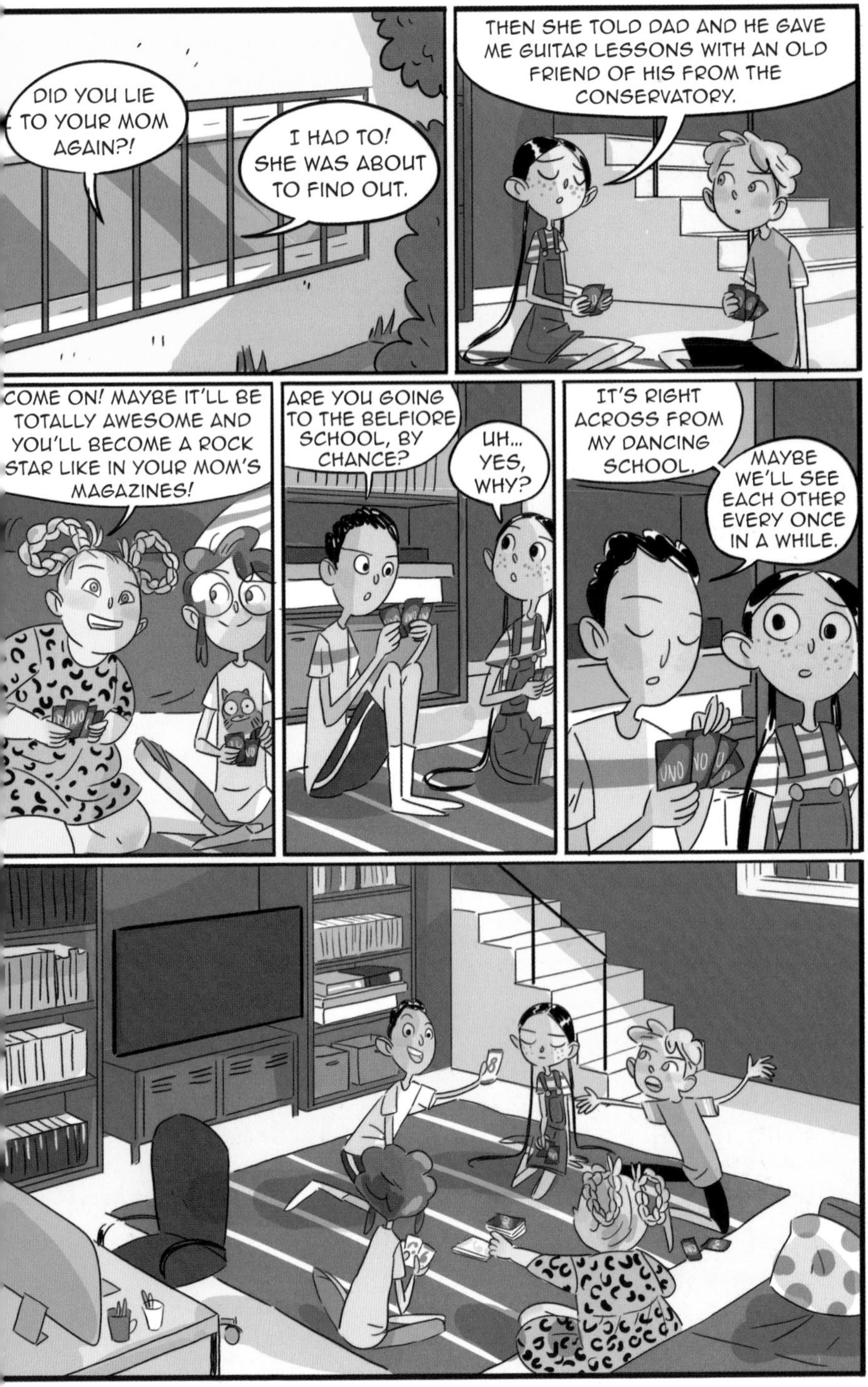
DID YOU LIE TO YOUR MOM AGAIN?!
I HAD TO! SHE WAS ABOUT TO FIND OUT.
THEN SHE TOLD DAD AND HE GAVE ME GUITAR LESSONS WITH AN OLD FRIEND OF HIS FROM THE CONSERVATORY.
COME ON! MAYBE IT'LL BE TOTALLY AWESOME AND YOU'LL BECOME A ROCK STAR LIKE IN YOUR MOM'S MAGAZINES!
ARE YOU GOING TO THE BELFIORE SCHOOL, BY CHANCE?
UH... YES, WHY?
IT'S RIGHT ACROSS FROM MY DANCING SCHOOL.
MAYBE WE'LL SEE EACH OTHER EVERY ONCE IN A WHILE.

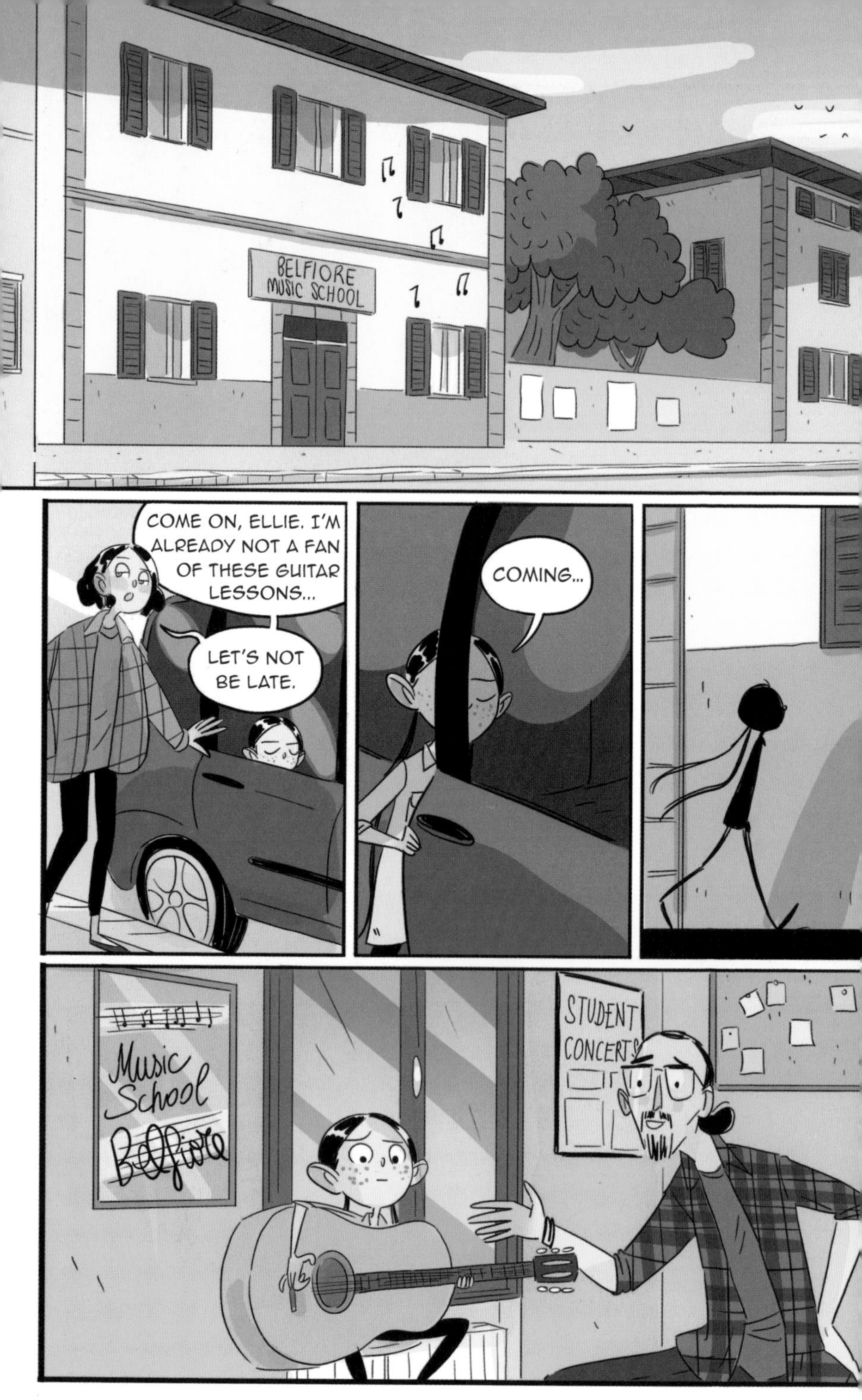

BELFIORE MUSIC SCHOOL
COME ON, ELLIE. I'M ALREADY NOT A FAN OF THESE GUITAR LESSONS...
LET'S NOT BE LATE.
COMING...
Music School
Belfiore
STUDENT CONCERTS

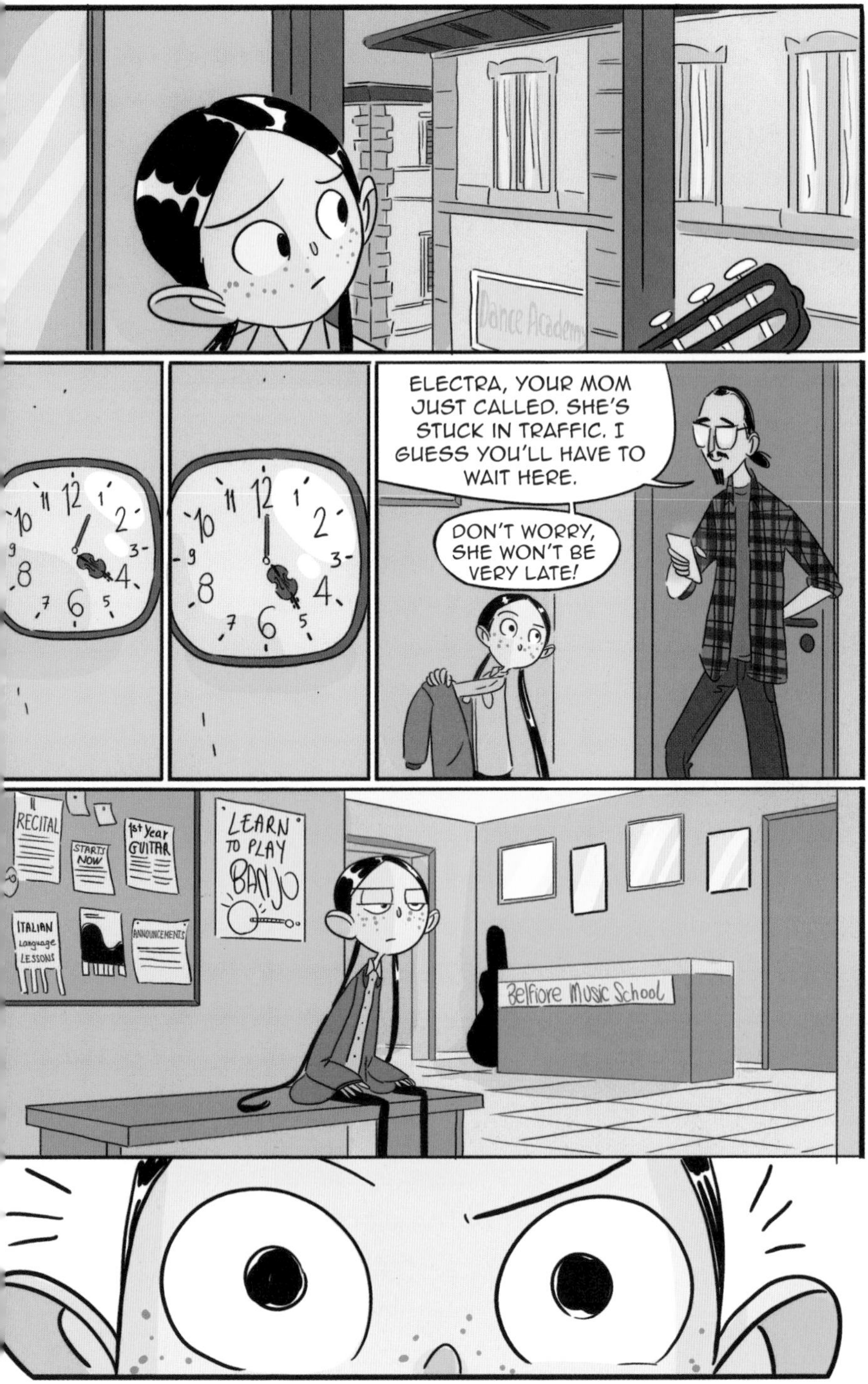
Dance Academy
ELECTRA, YOUR MOM JUST CALLED. SHE'S STUCK IN TRAFFIC. I GUESS YOU'LL HAVE TO WAIT HERE.
DON'T WORRY, SHE WON'T BE VERY LATE!
RECITAL
STARTS NOW
1st Year GUITAR
ITALIAN Language LESSONS
ANNOUNCEMENTS
LEARN TO PLAY BANJO
Belfiore Music School

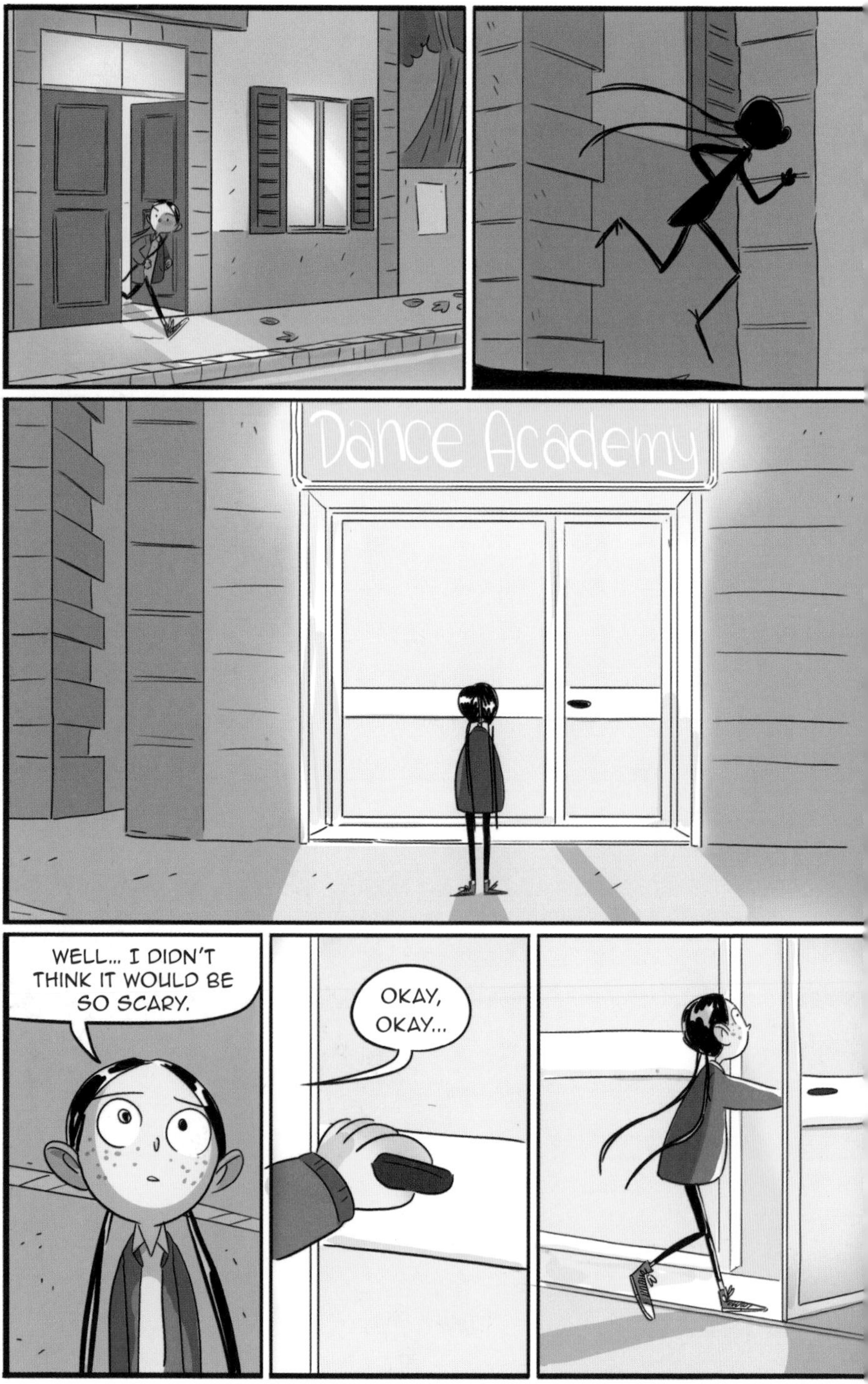
Dance Academy
WELL... I DIDN'T THINK IT WOULD BE SO SCARY.
OKAY, OKAY...

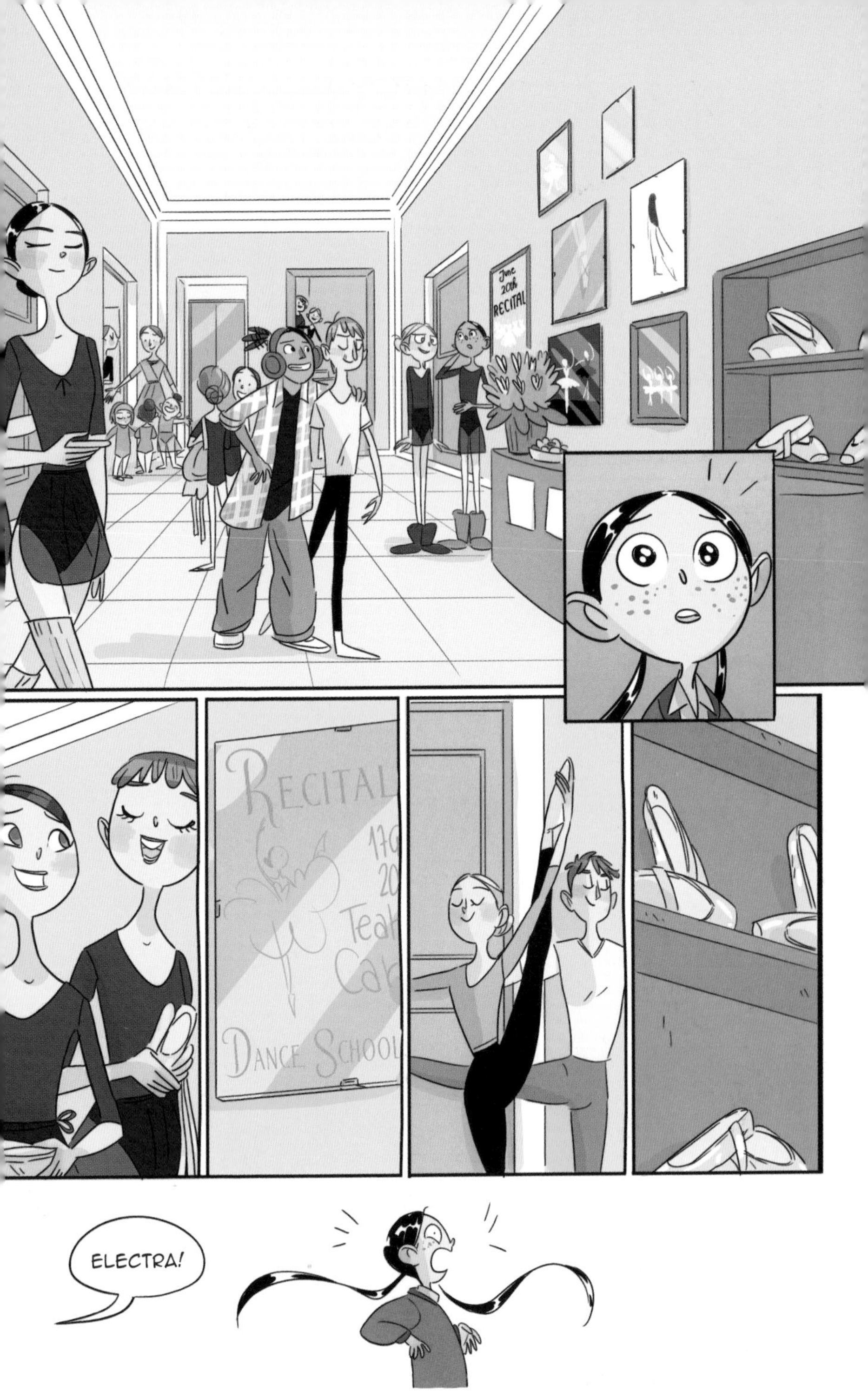
June 20th RECITAL
RECITAL
DANCE SCHOOL
ELECTRA!

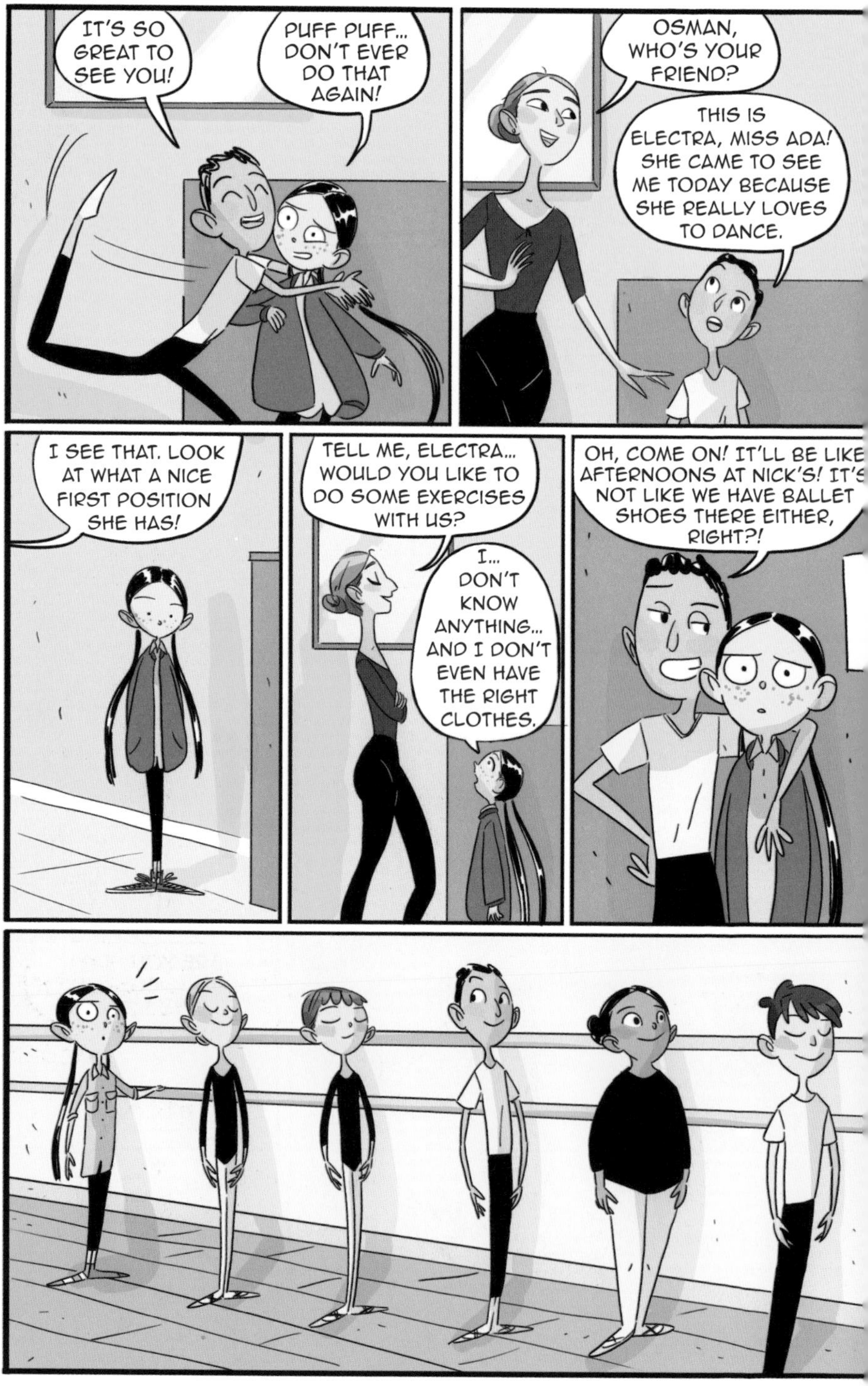
IT'S SO GREAT TO SEE YOU!
PUFF PUFF... DON'T EVER DO THAT AGAIN!
OSMAN, WHO'S YOUR FRIEND?
THIS IS ELECTRA, MISS ADA! SHE CAME TO SEE ME TODAY BECAUSE SHE REALLY LOVES TO DANCE.
I SEE THAT. LOOK AT WHAT A NICE FIRST POSITION SHE HAS!
TELL ME, ELECTRA... WOULD YOU LIKE TO DO SOME EXERCISES WITH US?
I... DON'T KNOW ANYTHING... AND I DON'T EVEN HAVE THE RIGHT CLOTHES.
OH, COME ON! IT'LL BE LIKE AFTERNOONS AT NICK'S! IT'S NOT LIKE WE HAVE BALLET SHOES THERE EITHER, RIGHT?!

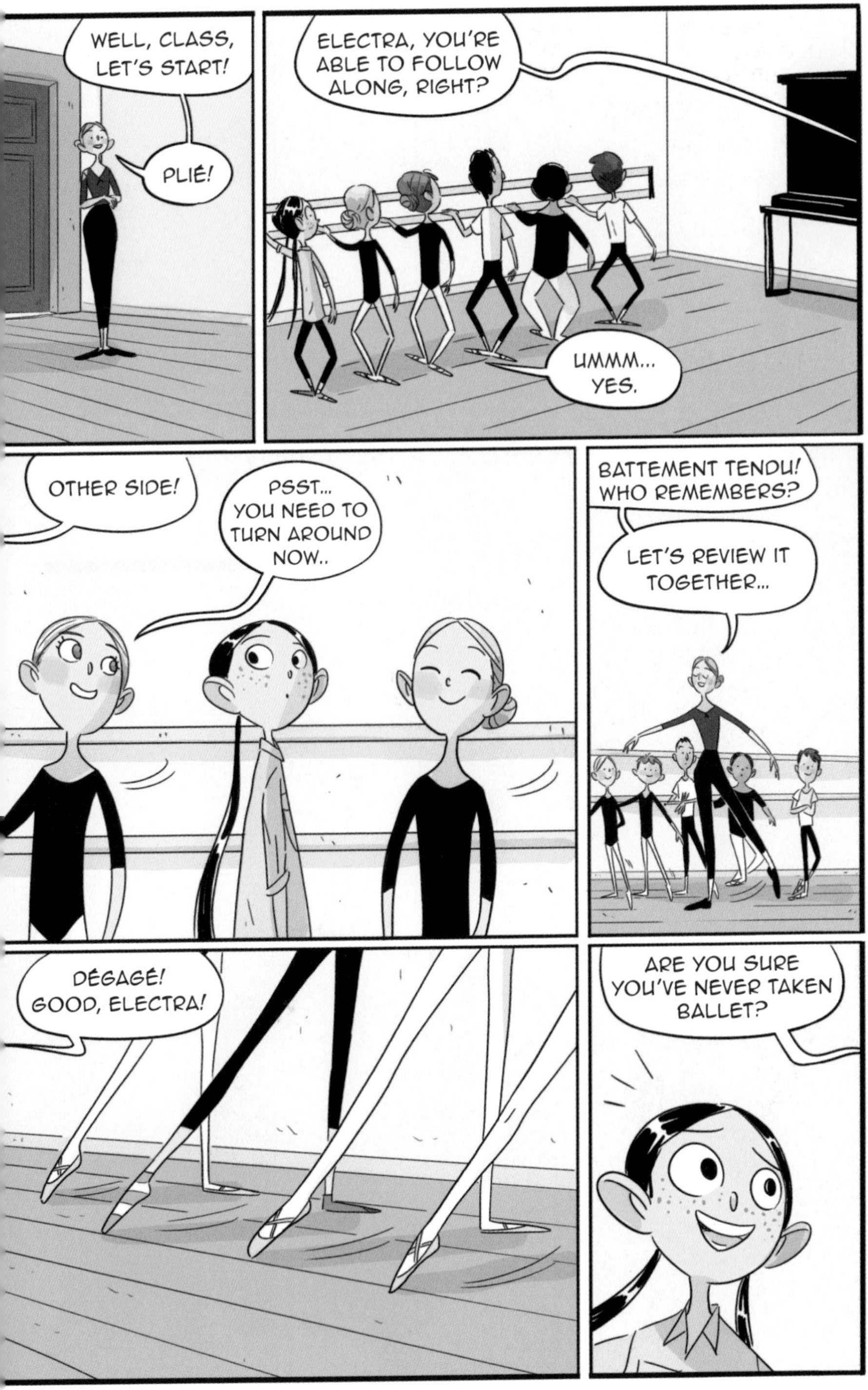
WELL, CLASS, LET'S START!
PLIÉ!
ELECTRA, YOU'RE ABLE TO FOLLOW ALONG, RIGHT?
UMMM... YES.
OTHER SIDE!
PSST... YOU NEED TO TURN AROUND NOW..
BATTEMENT TENDU! WHO REMEMBERS?
LET'S REVIEW IT TOGETHER...
DÉGAGÉ! GOOD, ELECTRA!
ARE YOU SURE YOU'VE NEVER TAKEN BALLET?

ELLIE, ISN'T THAT YOUR MOM'S CAR?

WHAT?!

AAH! SHE'S HERE!

PHEW... ROTTEN CITY!

IHAVETOGOIMLATEITWASGREATBYYYE!

ELECTRA!... WHERE ARE YOU?

I'M HERE, MOM!

Belfiore

UUUUH! WHAT A LESSON, MOM! IT WAS REALLY HARD WORK.

DAD NEVER TOLD ME THAT MAKIN MUSIC GOT YOU SO SWEATY... UUUH! SUCI HARD WORK

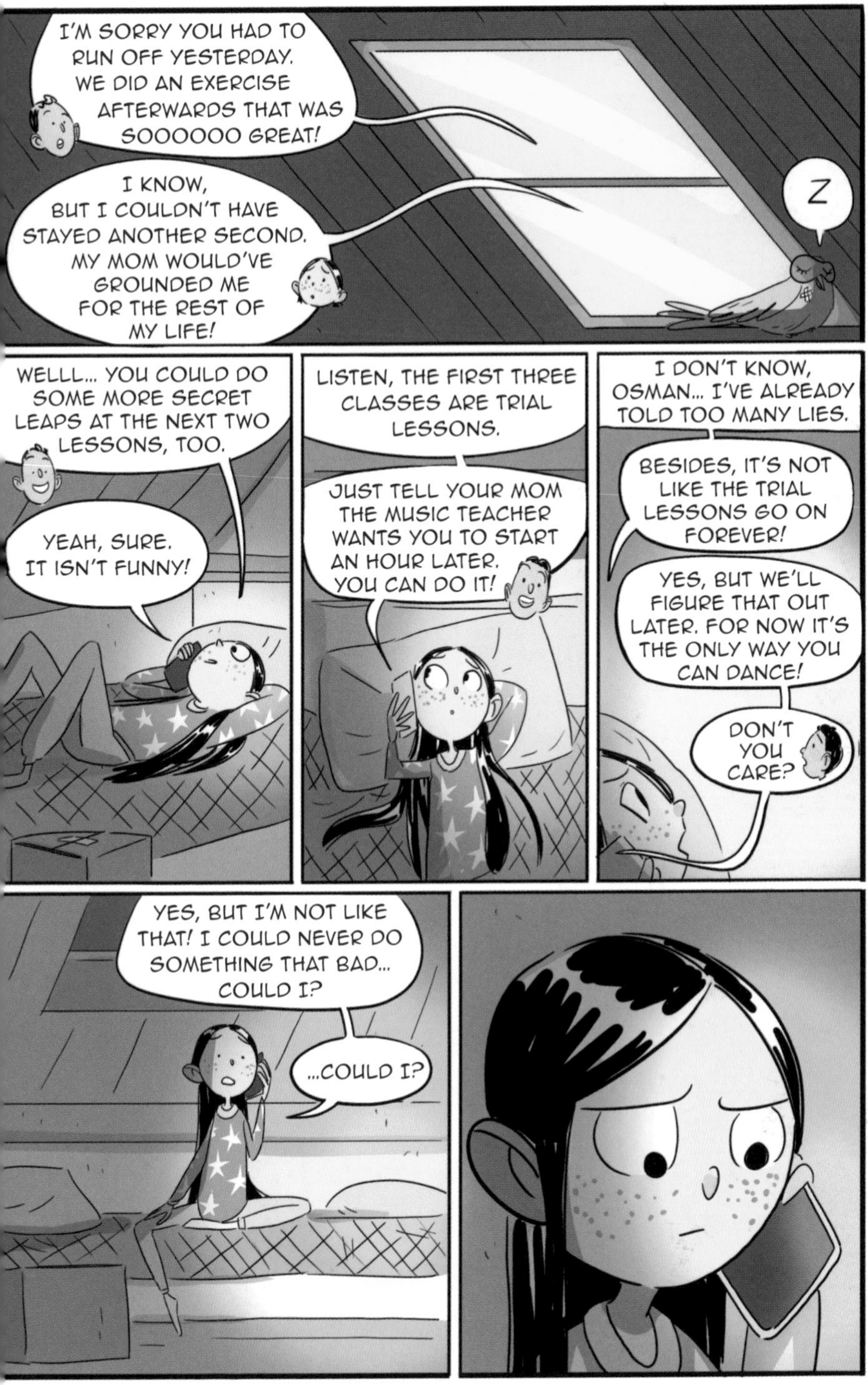
I'M SORRY YOU HAD TO RUN OFF YESTERDAY. WE DID AN EXERCISE AFTERWARDS THAT WAS SOOOOOO GREAT!
I KNOW, BUT I COULDN'T HAVE STAYED ANOTHER SECOND. MY MOM WOULD'VE GROUNDED ME FOR THE REST OF MY LIFE!
Z
WELLL... YOU COULD DO SOME MORE SECRET LEAPS AT THE NEXT TWO LESSONS, TOO.
YEAH, SURE. IT ISN'T FUNNY!
LISTEN, THE FIRST THREE CLASSES ARE TRIAL LESSONS.
JUST TELL YOUR MOM THE MUSIC TEACHER WANTS YOU TO START AN HOUR LATER. YOU CAN DO IT!
I DON'T KNOW, OSMAN... I'VE ALREADY TOLD TOO MANY LIES.
BESIDES, IT'S NOT LIKE THE TRIAL LESSONS GO ON FOREVER!
YES, BUT WE'LL FIGURE THAT OUT LATER. FOR NOW IT'S THE ONLY WAY YOU CAN DANCE!
DON'T YOU CARE?
YES, BUT I'M NOT LIKE THAT! I COULD NEVER DO SOMETHING THAT BAD... COULD I?
...COULD I?

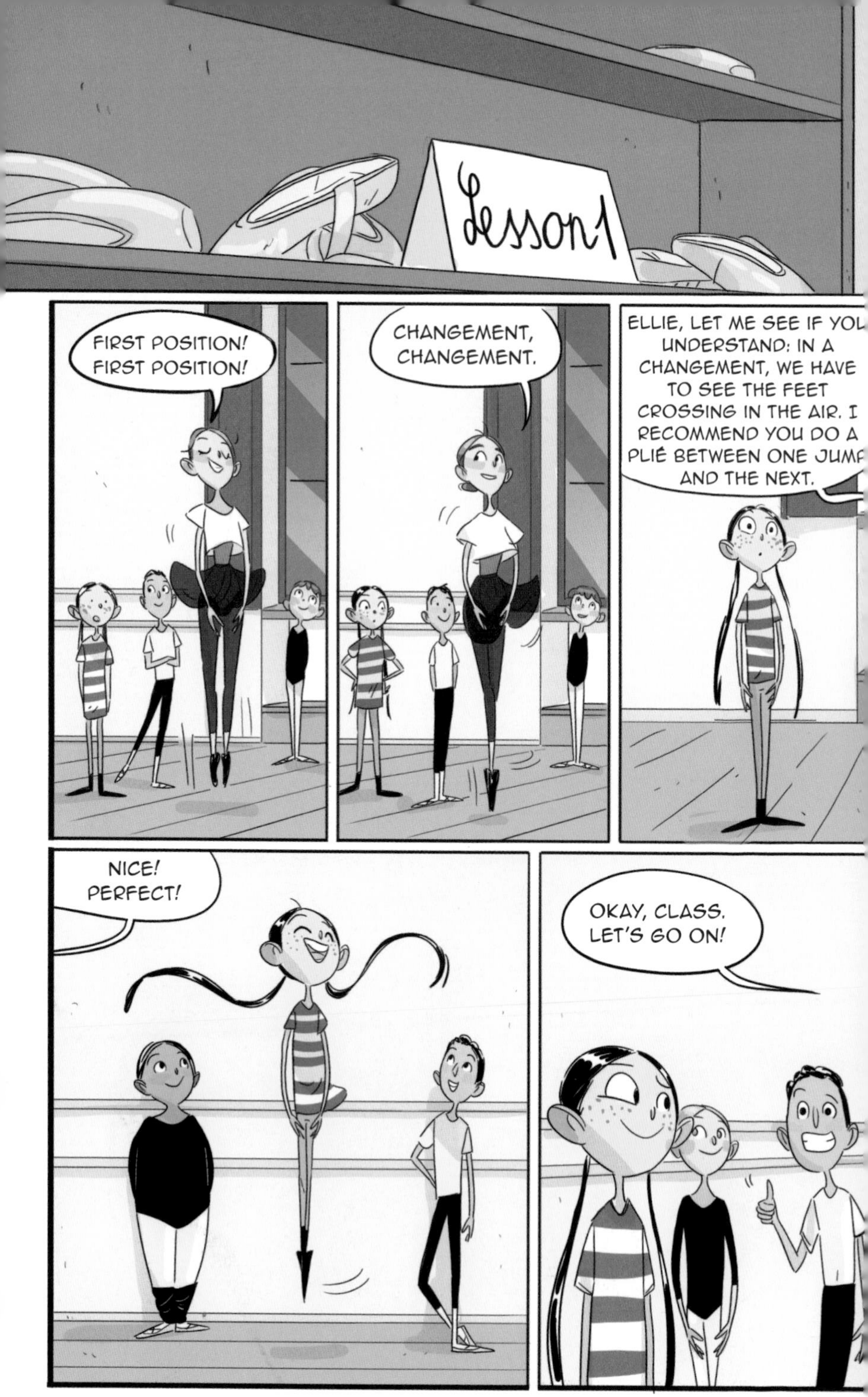

Lesson 1
FIRST POSITION! FIRST POSITION!
CHANGEMENT, CHANGEMENT.
ELLIE, LET ME SEE IF YOU UNDERSTAND: IN A CHANGEMENT, WE HAVE TO SEE THE FEET CROSSING IN THE AIR. I RECOMMEND YOU DO A PLIÉ BETWEEN ONE JUMP AND THE NEXT.
NICE! PERFECT!
OKAY, CLASS. LET'S GO ON!

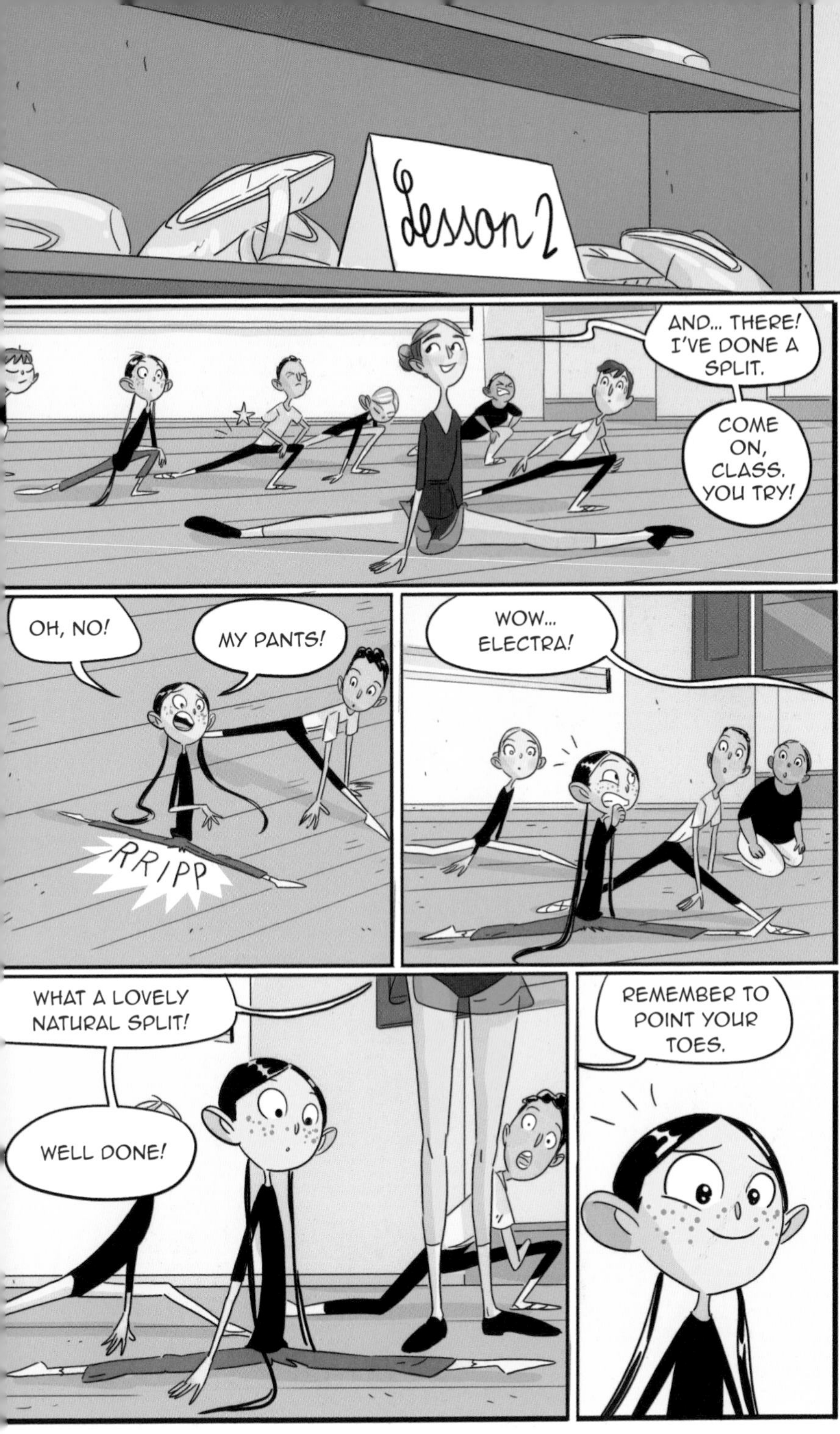
Lesson 2
AND... THERE! I'VE DONE A SPLIT.
COME ON, CLASS. YOU TRY!
OH, NO!
MY PANTS!
RRIPP
WOW... ELECTRA!
WHAT A LOVELY NATURAL SPLIT!
WELL DONE!
REMEMBER TO POINT YOUR TOES.

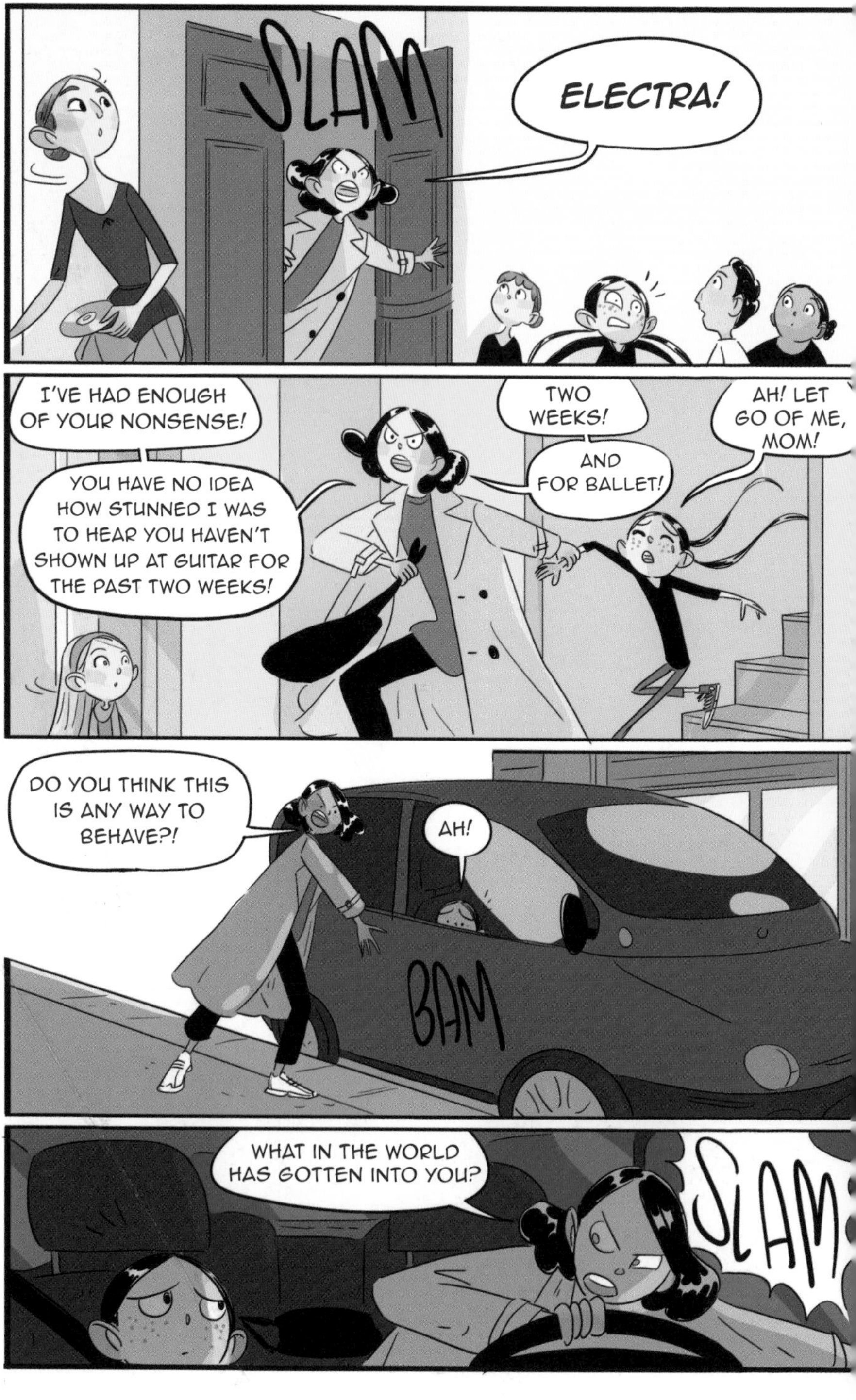
SLAM
ELECTRA!
I'VE HAD ENOUGH OF YOUR NONSENSE!
YOU HAVE NO IDEA HOW STUNNED I WAS TO HEAR YOU HAVEN'T SHOWN UP AT GUITAR FOR THE PAST TWO WEEKS!
TWO WEEKS!
AND FOR BALLET!
AH! LET GO OF ME, MOM!
DO YOU THINK THIS IS ANY WAY TO BEHAVE?!
AH!
BAM
WHAT IN THE WORLD HAS GOTTEN INTO YOU?
SLAM

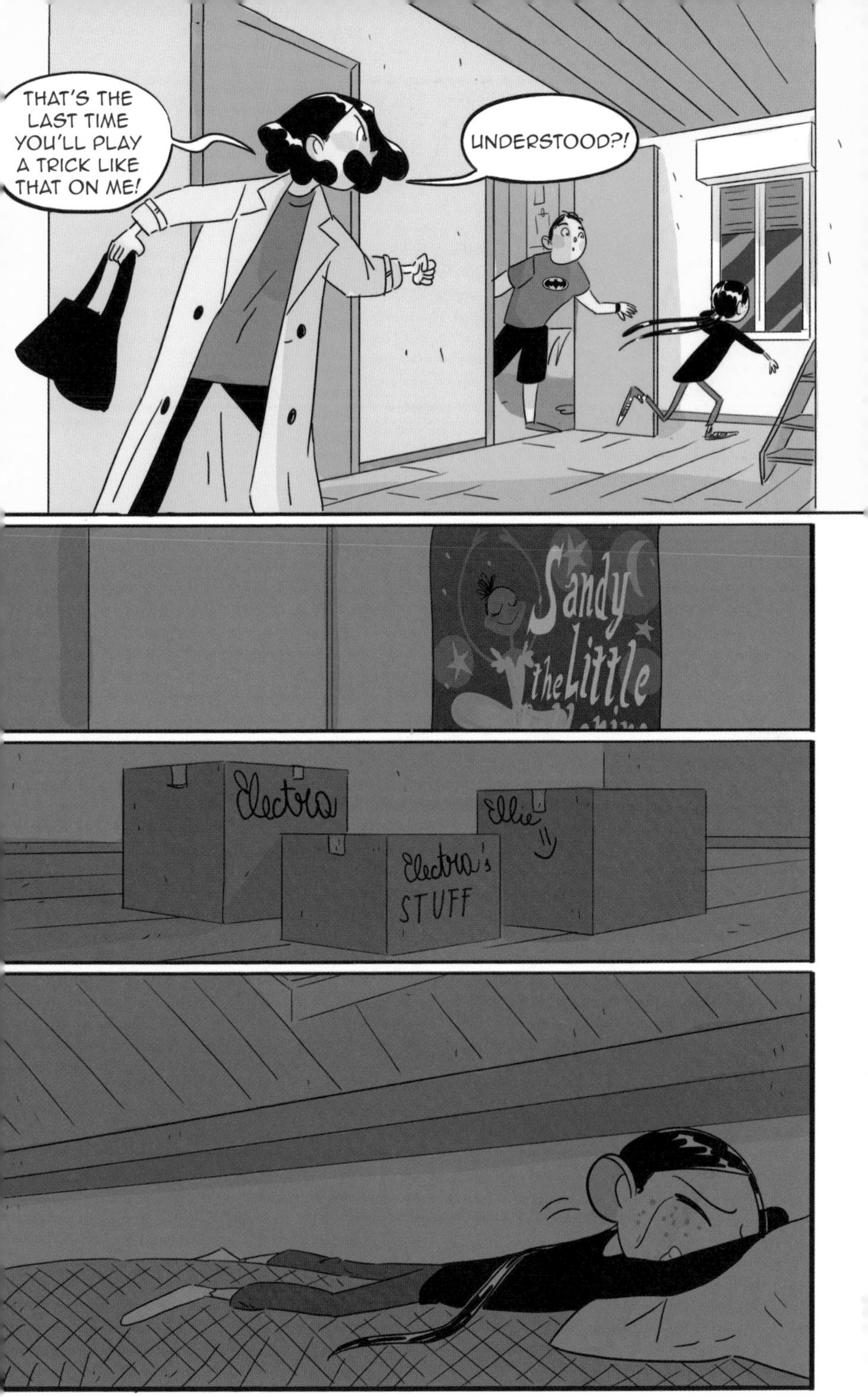

THAT'S THE LAST TIME YOU'LL PLAY A TRICK LIKE THAT ON ME!
UNDERSTOOD?!
Sandy the Little
Electra
Ellie
Electra's STUFF

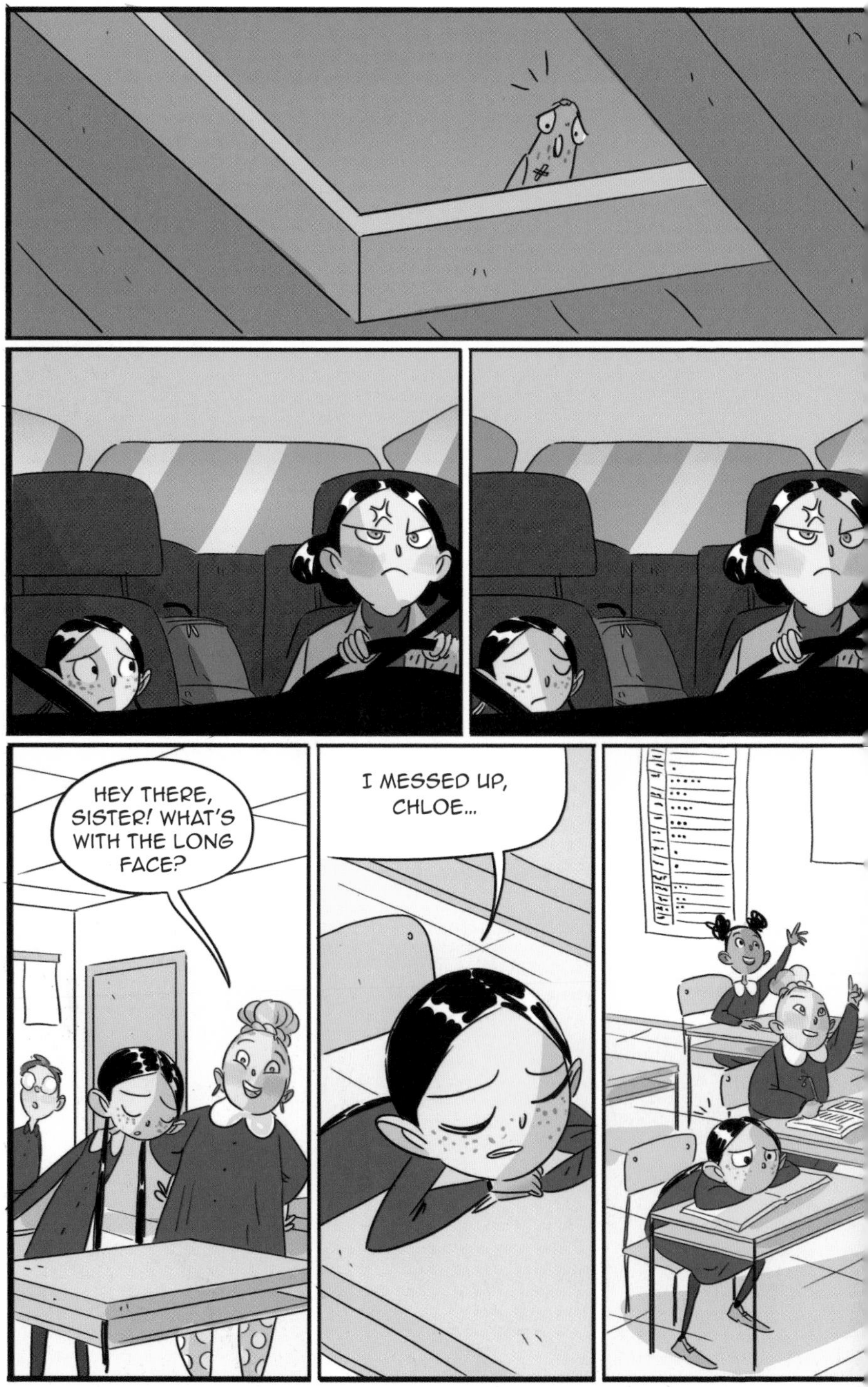
HEY THERE, SISTER! WHAT'S WITH THE LONG FACE?
I MESSED UP, CHLOE...

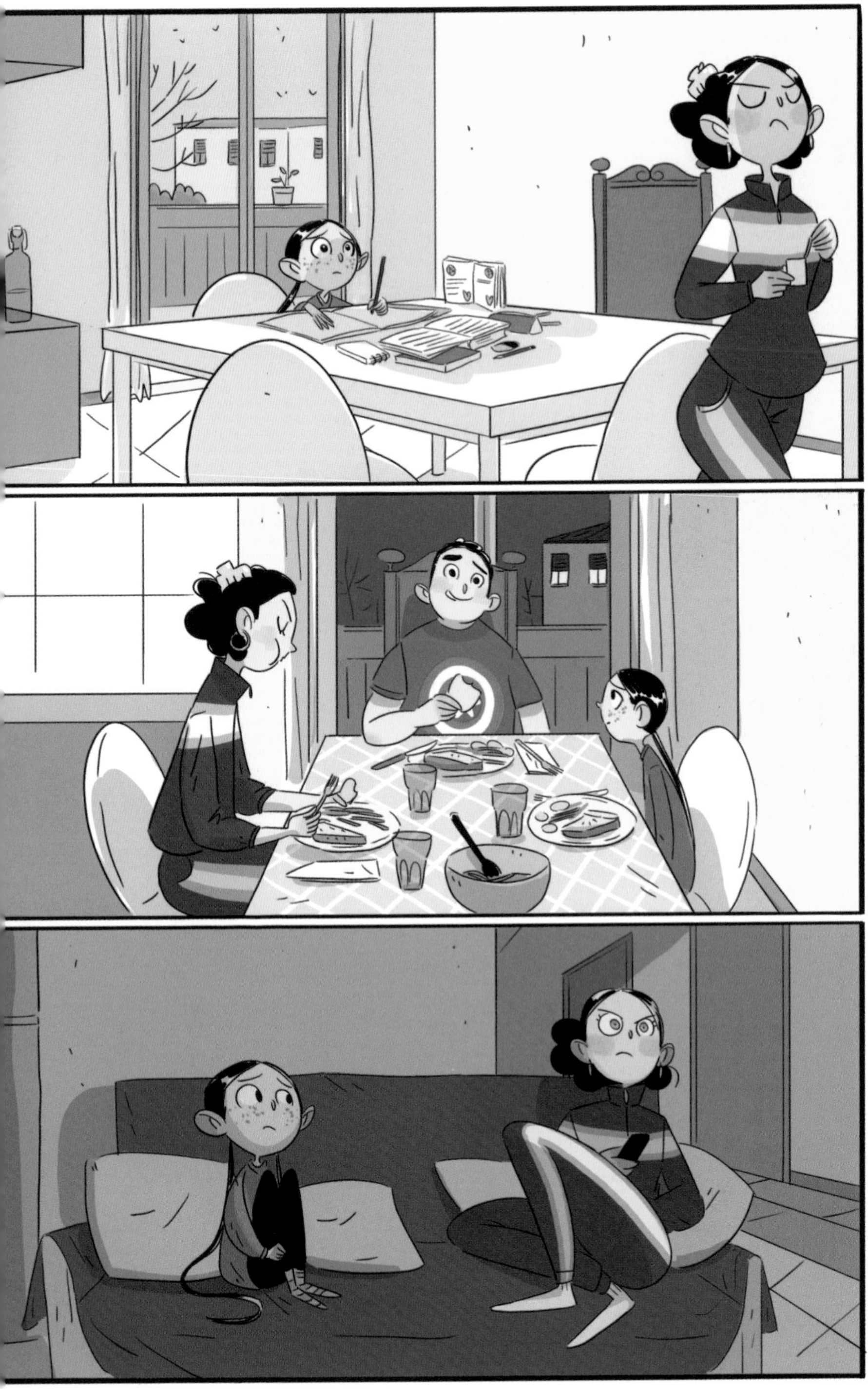

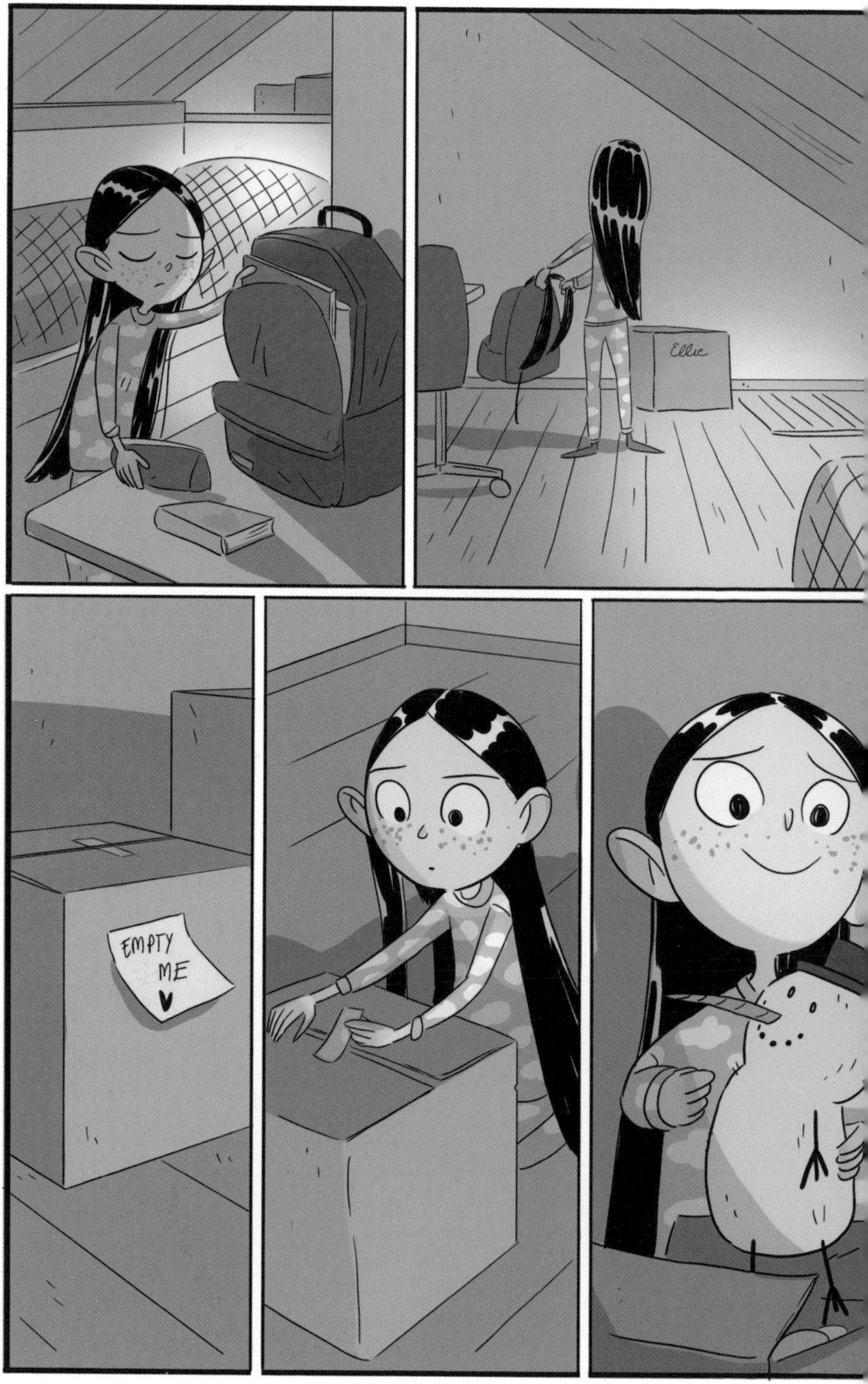
Ellie
EMPTY ME

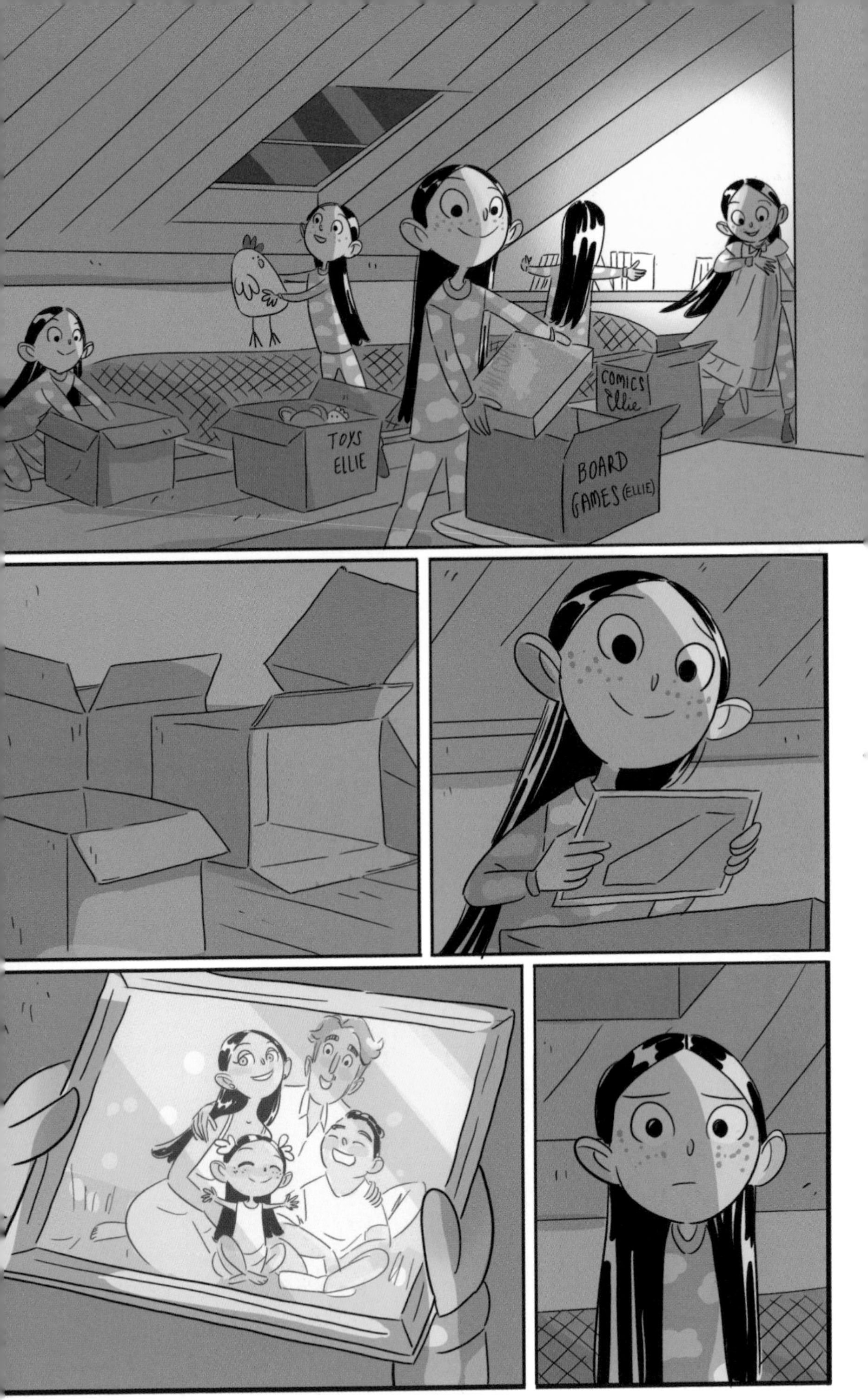
TOYS
ELLIE
COMICS
Ellie
BOARD
GAMES (ELLIE)

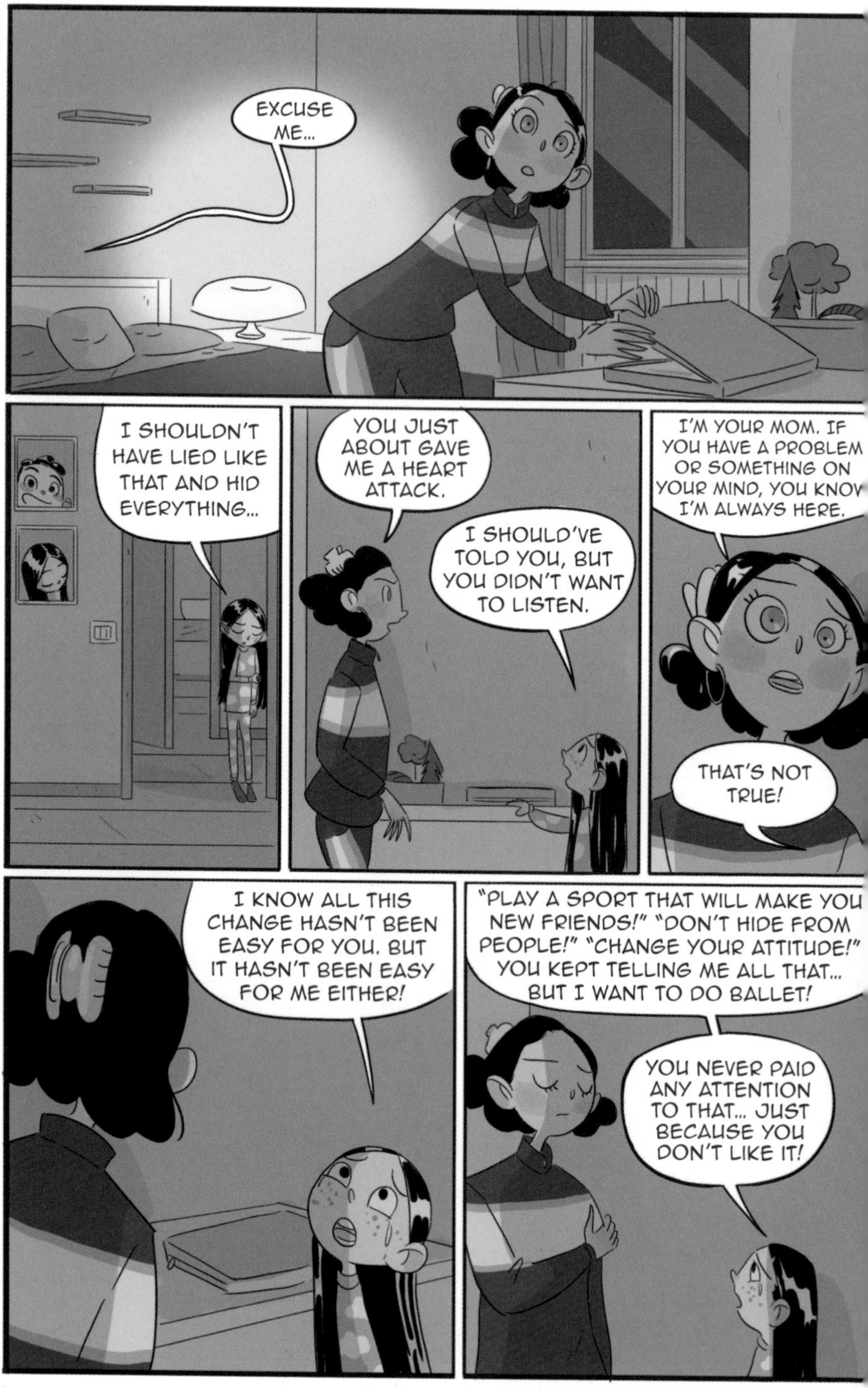

EXCUSE ME...
I SHOULDN'T HAVE LIED LIKE THAT AND HID EVERYTHING...
YOU JUST ABOUT GAVE ME A HEART ATTACK.
I SHOULD'VE TOLD YOU, BUT YOU DIDN'T WANT TO LISTEN.
I'M YOUR MOM. IF YOU HAVE A PROBLEM OR SOMETHING ON YOUR MIND, YOU KNOW I'M ALWAYS HERE.
THAT'S NOT TRUE!
I KNOW ALL THIS CHANGE HASN'T BEEN EASY FOR YOU. BUT IT HASN'T BEEN EASY FOR ME EITHER!
"PLAY A SPORT THAT WILL MAKE YOU NEW FRIENDS!" "DON'T HIDE FROM PEOPLE!" "CHANGE YOUR ATTITUDE!" YOU KEPT TELLING ME ALL THAT... BUT I WANT TO DO BALLET!
YOU NEVER PAID ANY ATTENTION TO THAT... JUST BECAUSE YOU DON'T LIKE IT!

YOU'RE RIGHT...

YOUR DAD AND I WERE ALWAYS FIGHTING ABOUT THAT...

I SHOULD'VE FIGURED IT OUT, ELLIE... AS SOON AS MUSIC STARTS, YOU CAN'T STAY STILL!

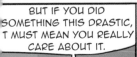

BUT IF YOU DID SOMETHING THIS DRASTIC, T MUST MEAN YOU REALLY CARE ABOUT IT.

I GUESS YOUR DAD WAS RIGHT ABOUT THIS ONE.

IT'S OKAY...

YOU CAN TAKE BALLET IF THAT'S WHAT YOU WANT.

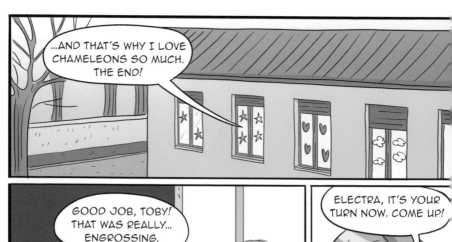

...AND THAT'S WHY I LOVE CHAMELEONS SO MUCH. THE END!

GOOD JOB, TOBY! THAT WAS REALLY... ENGROSSING.

ELECTRA, IT'S YOUR TURN NOW. COME UP!

Recycling

GO ON, DEAR, TELL US WHAT YOU'RE PASSIONATE ABOUT!

MY PASSION...

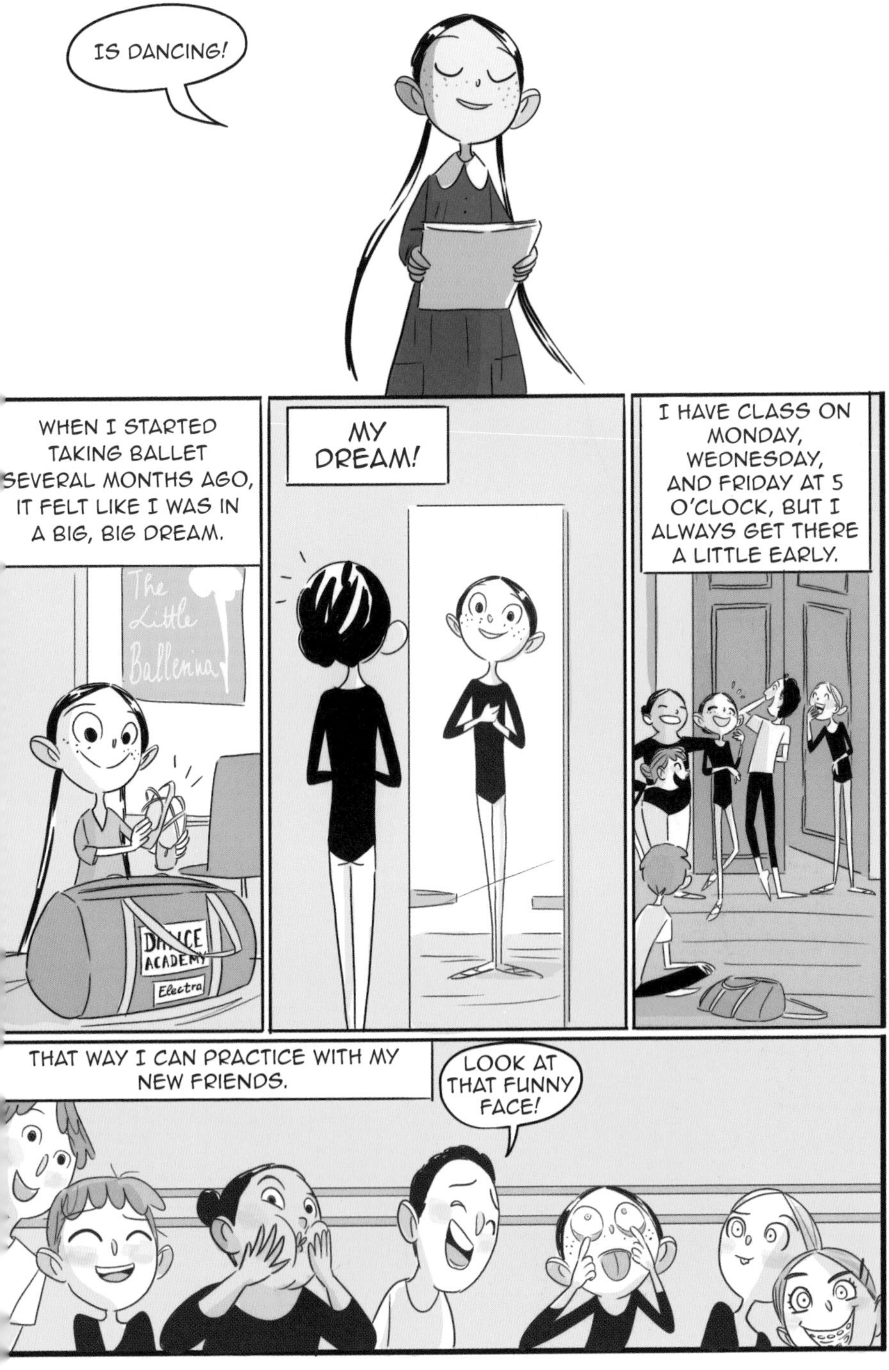

IS DANCING!
WHEN I STARTED TAKING BALLET SEVERAL MONTHS AGO, IT FELT LIKE I WAS IN A BIG, BIG DREAM.
The Little Ballerina
DANCE ACADEMY
Electra
MY DREAM!
I HAVE CLASS ON MONDAY, WEDNESDAY, AND FRIDAY AT 5 O'CLOCK, BUT I ALWAYS GET THERE A LITTLE EARLY.
THAT WAY I CAN PRACTICE WITH MY NEW FRIENDS.
LOOK AT THAT FUNNY FACE!

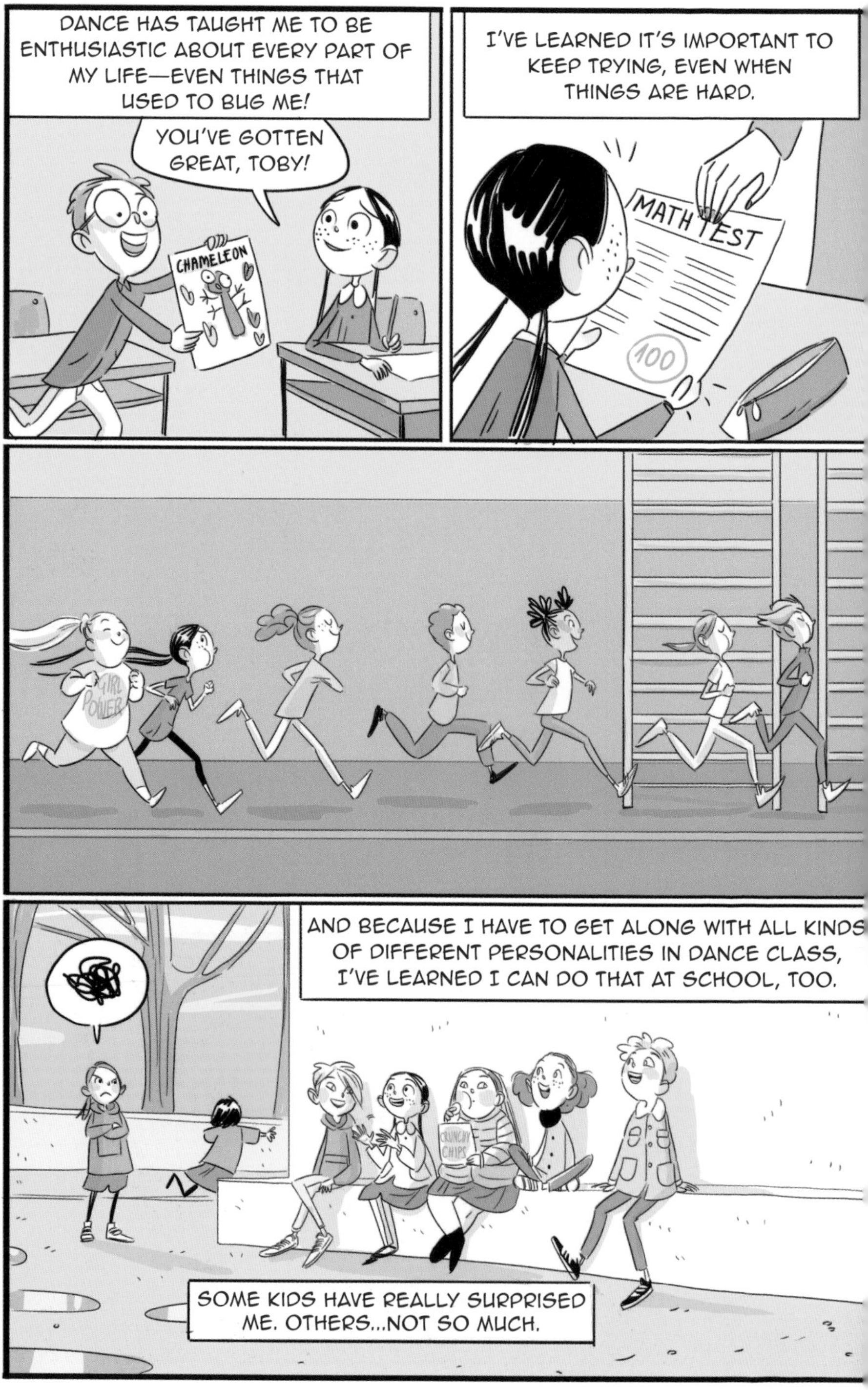
DANCE HAS TAUGHT ME TO BE ENTHUSIASTIC ABOUT EVERY PART OF MY LIFE—EVEN THINGS THAT USED TO BUG ME!
YOU'VE GOTTEN GREAT, TOBY!
CHAMELEON
I'VE LEARNED IT'S IMPORTANT TO KEEP TRYING, EVEN WHEN THINGS ARE HARD.
MATH TEST
100
GIRL POWER
AND BECAUSE I HAVE TO GET ALONG WITH ALL KINDS OF DIFFERENT PERSONALITIES IN DANCE CLASS, I'VE LEARNED I CAN DO THAT AT SCHOOL, TOO.
CRUNCHY CHIPS
SOME KIDS HAVE REALLY SURPRISED ME. OTHERS...NOT SO MUCH.

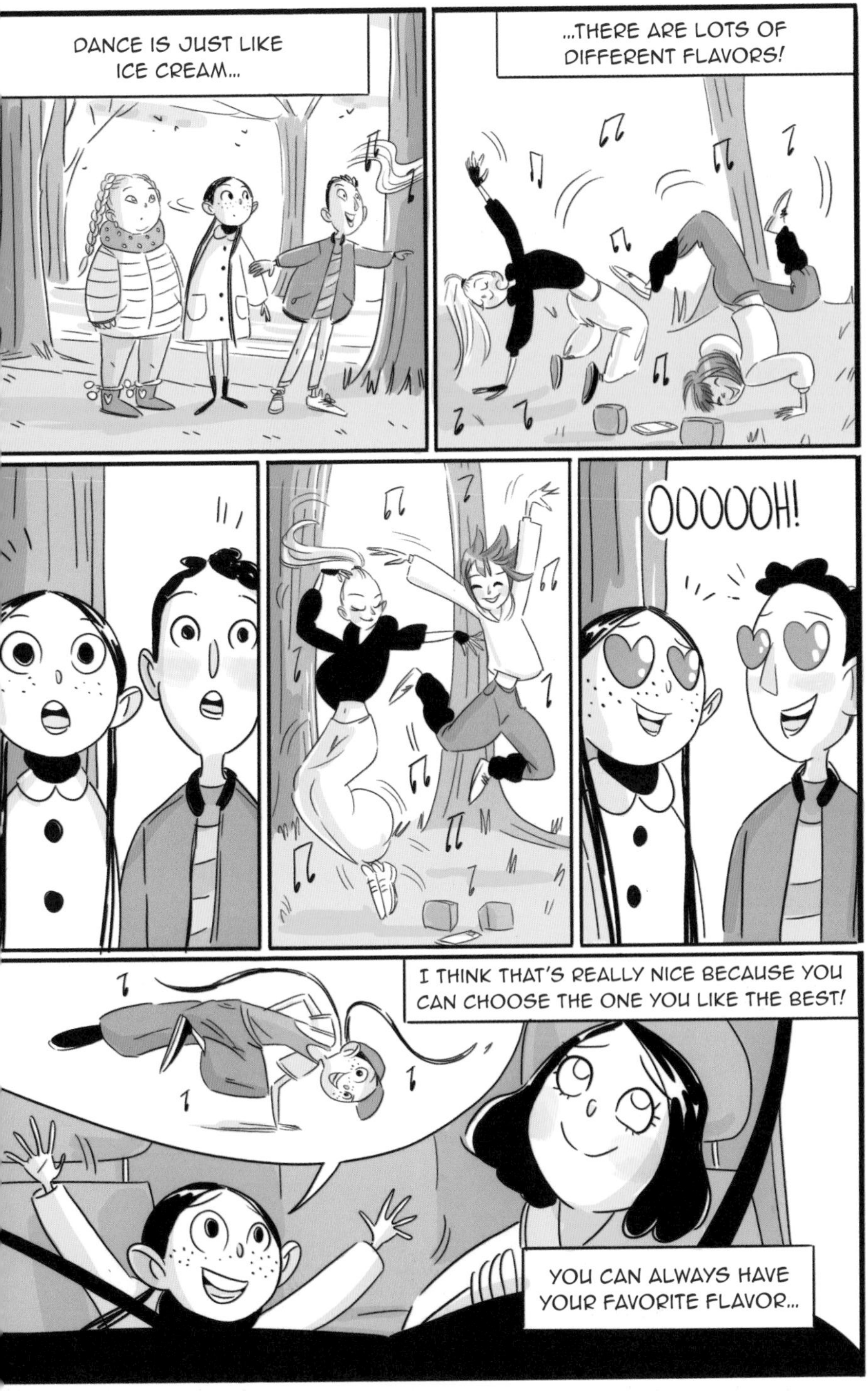
DANCE IS JUST LIKE ICE CREAM...
...THERE ARE LOTS OF DIFFERENT FLAVORS!
OOOOOH!
I THINK THAT'S REALLY NICE BECAUSE YOU CAN CHOOSE THE ONE YOU LIKE THE BEST!
YOU CAN ALWAYS HAVE YOUR FAVORITE FLAVOR...

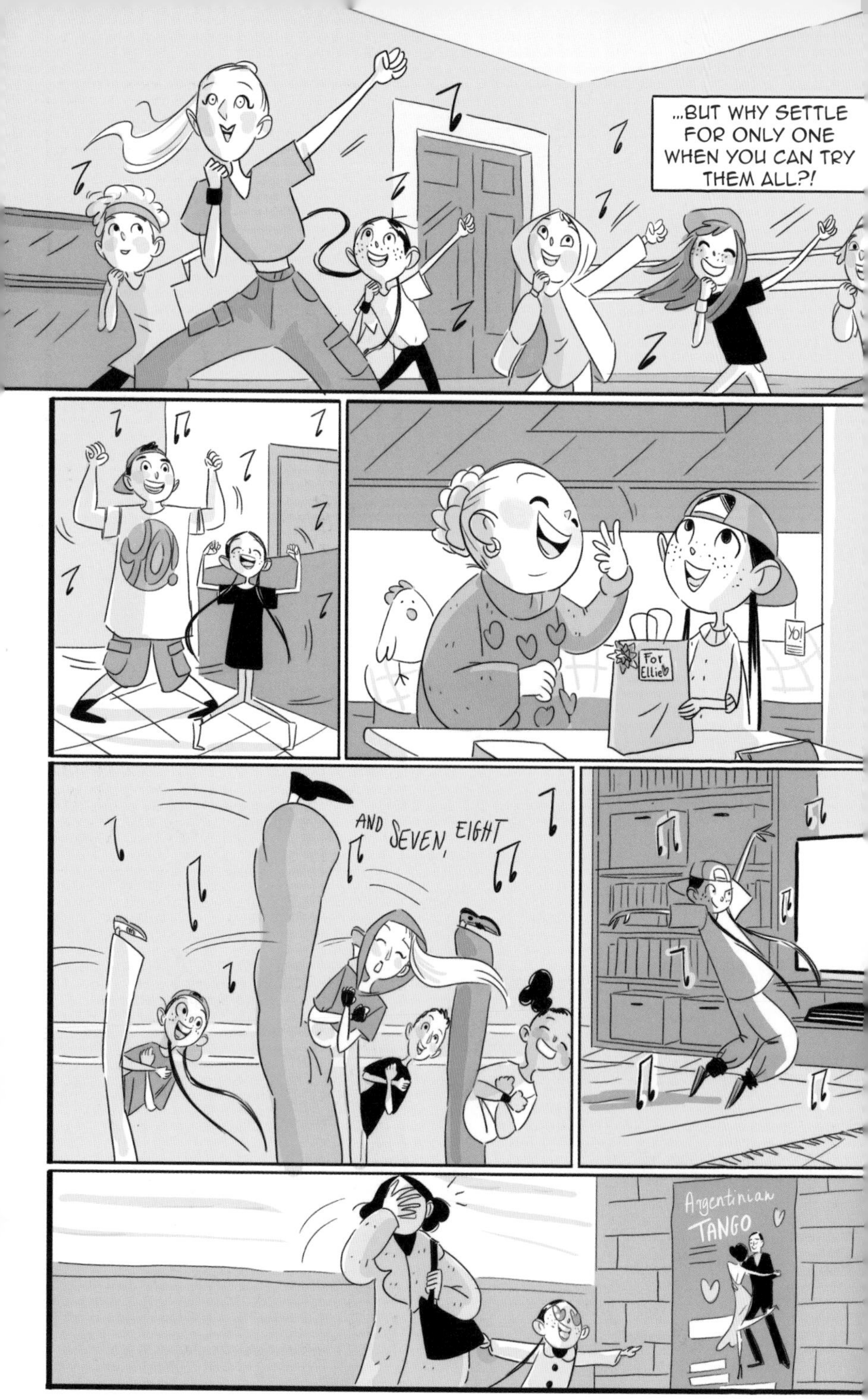
...BUT WHY SETTLE FOR ONLY ONE WHEN YOU CAN TRY THEM ALL?!
YO!
For Ellie
YO!
AND SEVEN, EIGHT
Argentinian TANGO

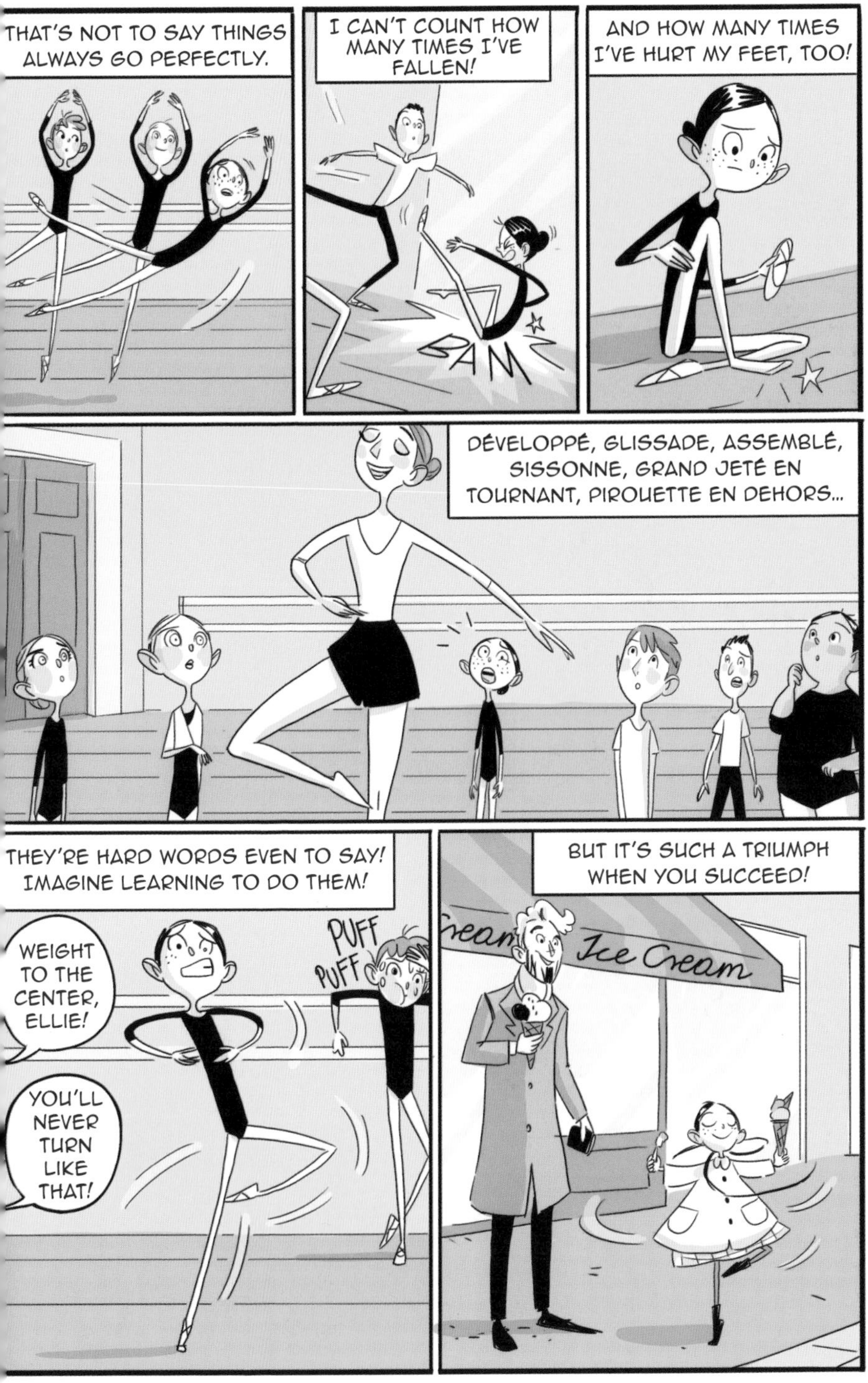
THAT'S NOT TO SAY THINGS ALWAYS GO PERFECTLY.
I CAN'T COUNT HOW MANY TIMES I'VE FALLEN!
BAM
AND HOW MANY TIMES I'VE HURT MY FEET, TOO!
DÉVELOPPÉ, GLISSADE, ASSEMBLÉ, SISSONNE, GRAND JETÉ EN TOURNANT, PIROUETTE EN DEHORS...
THEY'RE HARD WORDS EVEN TO SAY! IMAGINE LEARNING TO DO THEM!
WEIGHT TO THE CENTER, ELLIE!
YOU'LL NEVER TURN LIKE THAT!
PUFF PUFF
BUT IT'S SUCH A TRIUMPH WHEN YOU SUCCEED!
Ice Cream

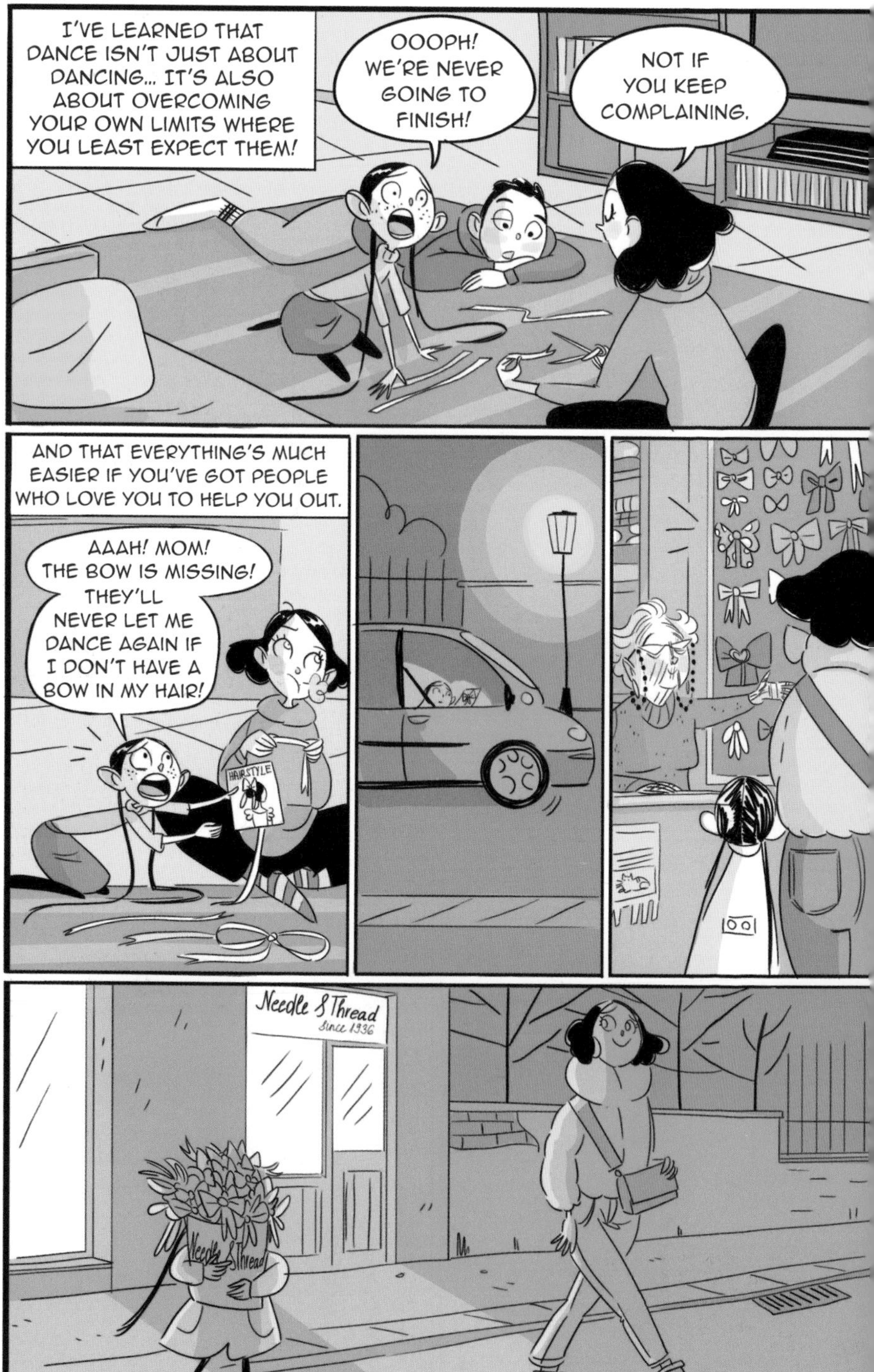

I'VE LEARNED THAT DANCE ISN'T JUST ABOUT DANCING... IT'S ALSO ABOUT OVERCOMING YOUR OWN LIMITS WHERE YOU LEAST EXPECT THEM!
OOOPH! WE'RE NEVER GOING TO FINISH!
NOT IF YOU KEEP COMPLAINING.
AND THAT EVERYTHING'S MUCH EASIER IF YOU'VE GOT PEOPLE WHO LOVE YOU TO HELP YOU OUT.
AAAH! MOM! THE BOW IS MISSING! THEY'LL NEVER LET ME DANCE AGAIN IF I DON'T HAVE A BOW IN MY HAIR!
HAIRSTYLE
Needle & Thread
Since 1936
Needle & Thread

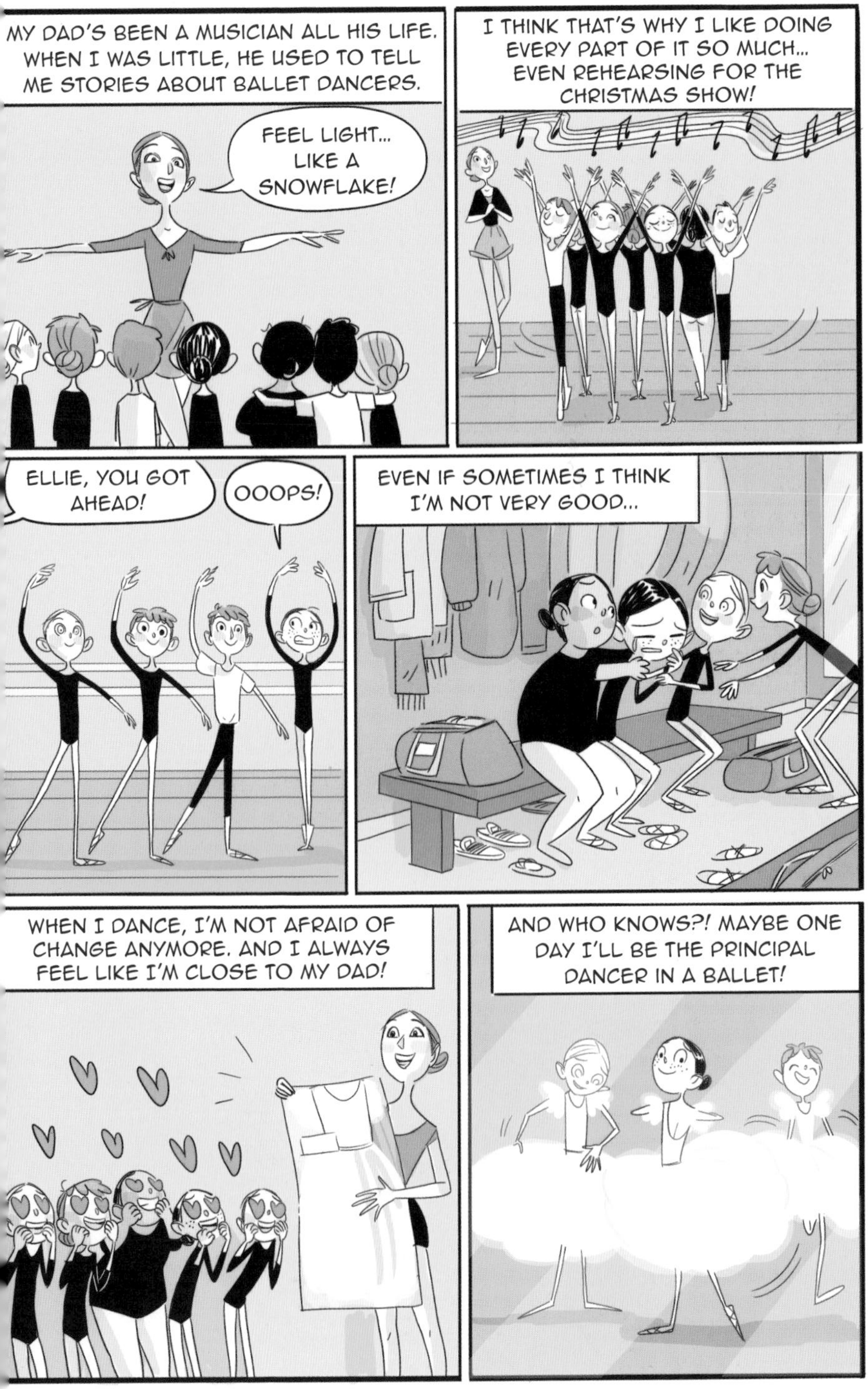
MY DAD'S BEEN A MUSICIAN ALL HIS LIFE. WHEN I WAS LITTLE, HE USED TO TELL ME STORIES ABOUT BALLET DANCERS.
FEEL LIGHT... LIKE A SNOWFLAKE!
I THINK THAT'S WHY I LIKE DOING EVERY PART OF IT SO MUCH... EVEN REHEARSING FOR THE CHRISTMAS SHOW!
ELLIE, YOU GOT AHEAD!
OOOPS!
EVEN IF SOMETIMES I THINK I'M NOT VERY GOOD...
WHEN I DANCE, I'M NOT AFRAID OF CHANGE ANYMORE. AND I ALWAYS FEEL LIKE I'M CLOSE TO MY DAD!
AND WHO KNOWS?! MAYBE ONE DAY I'LL BE THE PRINCIPAL DANCER IN A BALLET!

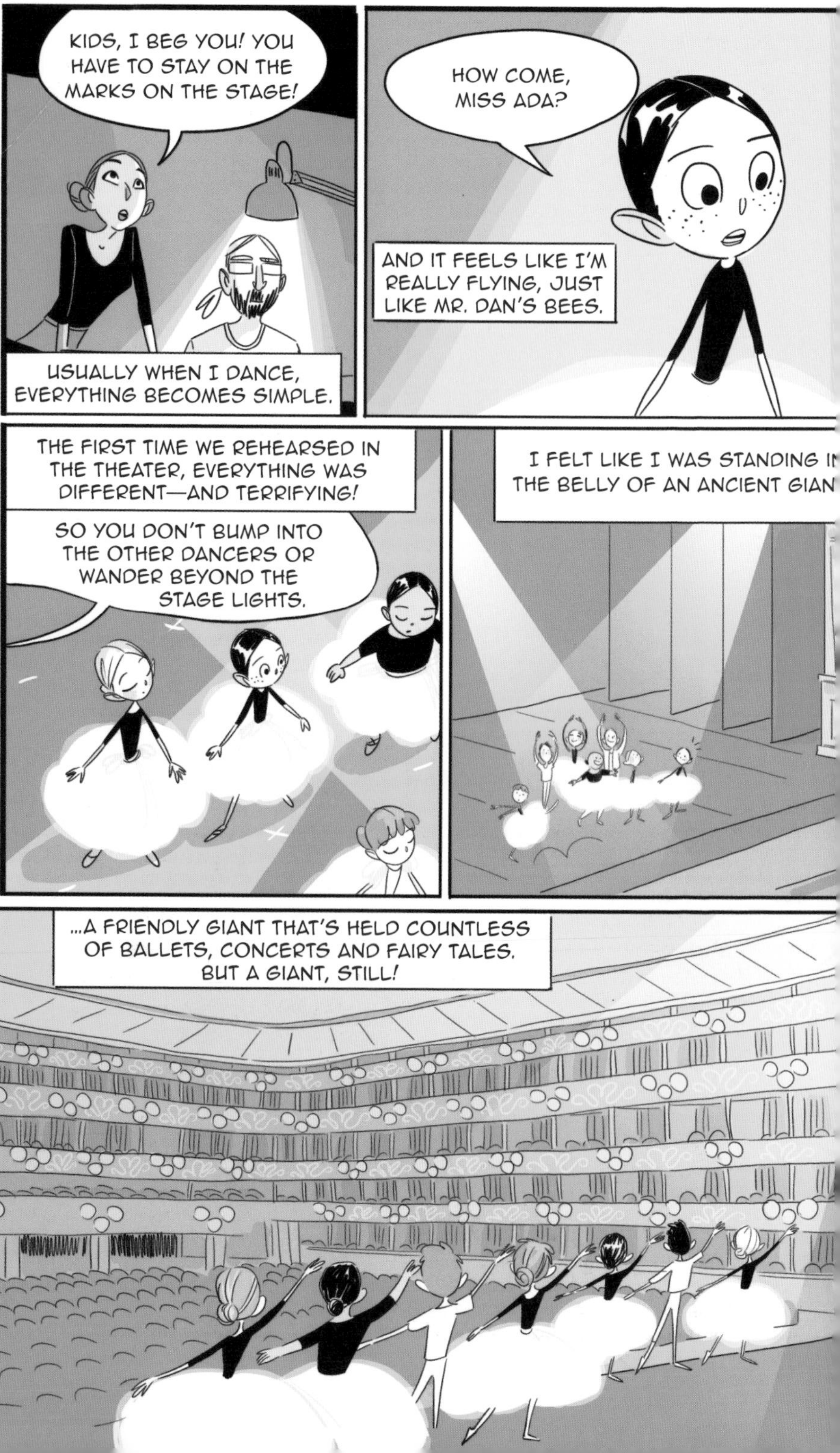
USUALLY WHEN I DANCE, EVERYTHING BECOMES SIMPLE.
KIDS, I BEG YOU! YOU HAVE TO STAY ON THE MARKS ON THE STAGE!
AND IT FEELS LIKE I'M REALLY FLYING, JUST LIKE MR. DAN'S BEES.
HOW COME, MISS ADA?
THE FIRST TIME WE REHEARSED IN THE THEATER, EVERYTHING WAS DIFFERENT—AND TERRIFYING!
SO YOU DON'T BUMP INTO THE OTHER DANCERS OR WANDER BEYOND THE STAGE LIGHTS.
I FELT LIKE I WAS STANDING IN THE BELLY OF AN ANCIENT GIAN
...A FRIENDLY GIANT THAT'S HELD COUNTLESS OF BALLETS, CONCERTS AND FAIRY TALES. BUT A GIANT, STILL!

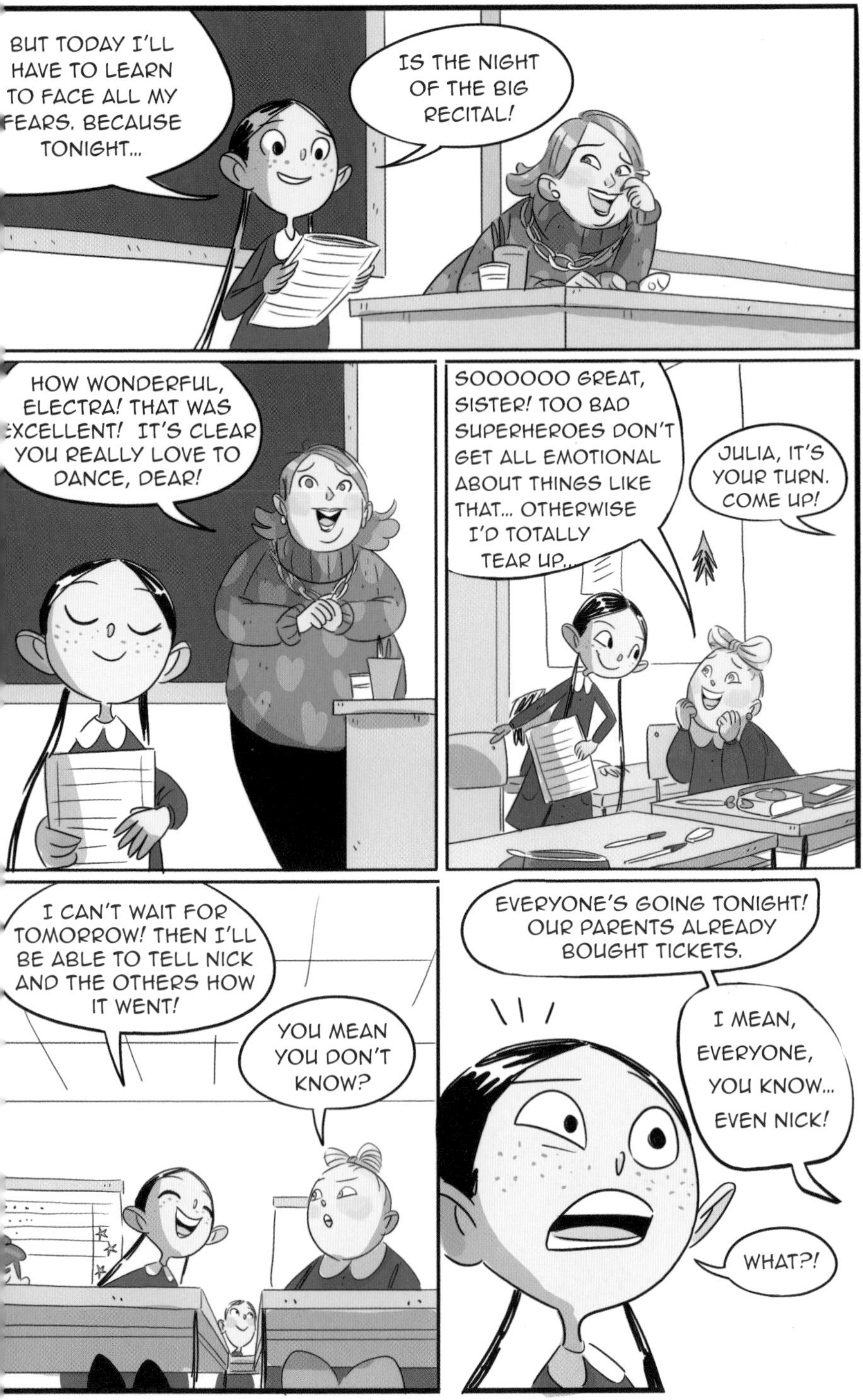
BUT TODAY I'LL HAVE TO LEARN TO FACE ALL MY FEARS. BECAUSE TONIGHT...
IS THE NIGHT OF THE BIG RECITAL!
HOW WONDERFUL, ELECTRA! THAT WAS EXCELLENT! IT'S CLEAR YOU REALLY LOVE TO DANCE, DEAR!
SOOOOOO GREAT, SISTER! TOO BAD SUPERHEROES DON'T GET ALL EMOTIONAL ABOUT THINGS LIKE THAT... OTHERWISE I'D TOTALLY TEAR UP...
JULIA, IT'S YOUR TURN. COME UP!
I CAN'T WAIT FOR TOMORROW! THEN I'LL BE ABLE TO TELL NICK AND THE OTHERS HOW IT WENT!
YOU MEAN YOU DON'T KNOW?
EVERYONE'S GOING TONIGHT! OUR PARENTS ALREADY BOUGHT TICKETS.
I MEAN, EVERYONE, YOU KNOW... EVEN NICK!
WHAT?!

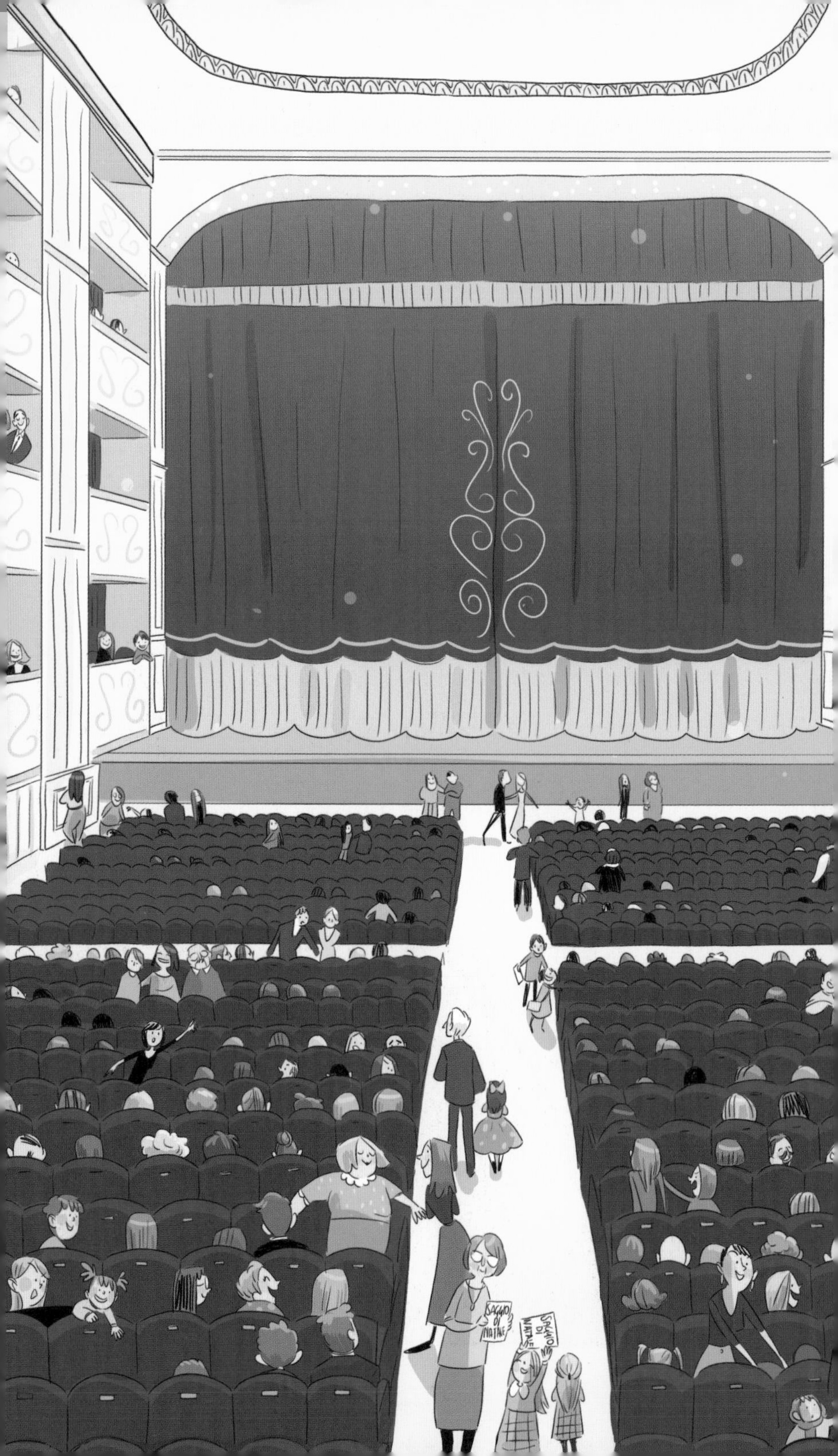
SAGGIO DI NATALE
SAGGIO DI NATALE

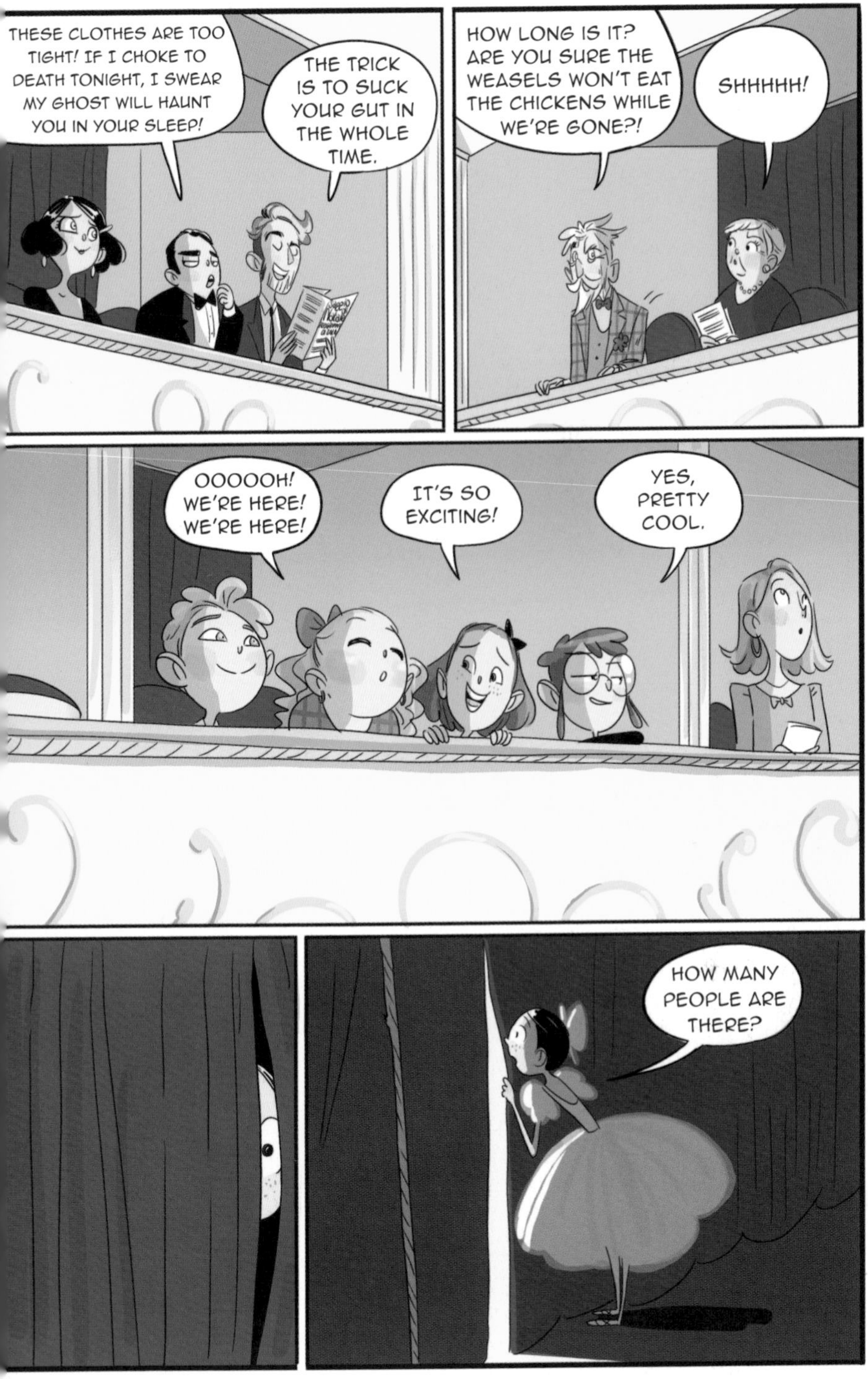
THESE CLOTHES ARE TOO TIGHT! IF I CHOKE TO DEATH TONIGHT, I SWEAR MY GHOST WILL HAUNT YOU IN YOUR SLEEP!
THE TRICK IS TO SUCK YOUR GUT IN THE WHOLE TIME.
HOW LONG IS IT? ARE YOU SURE THE WEASELS WON'T EAT THE CHICKENS WHILE WE'RE GONE?!
SHHHHH!
OOOOOH! WE'RE HERE! WE'RE HERE!
IT'S SO EXCITING!
YES, PRETTY COOL.
HOW MANY PEOPLE ARE THERE?

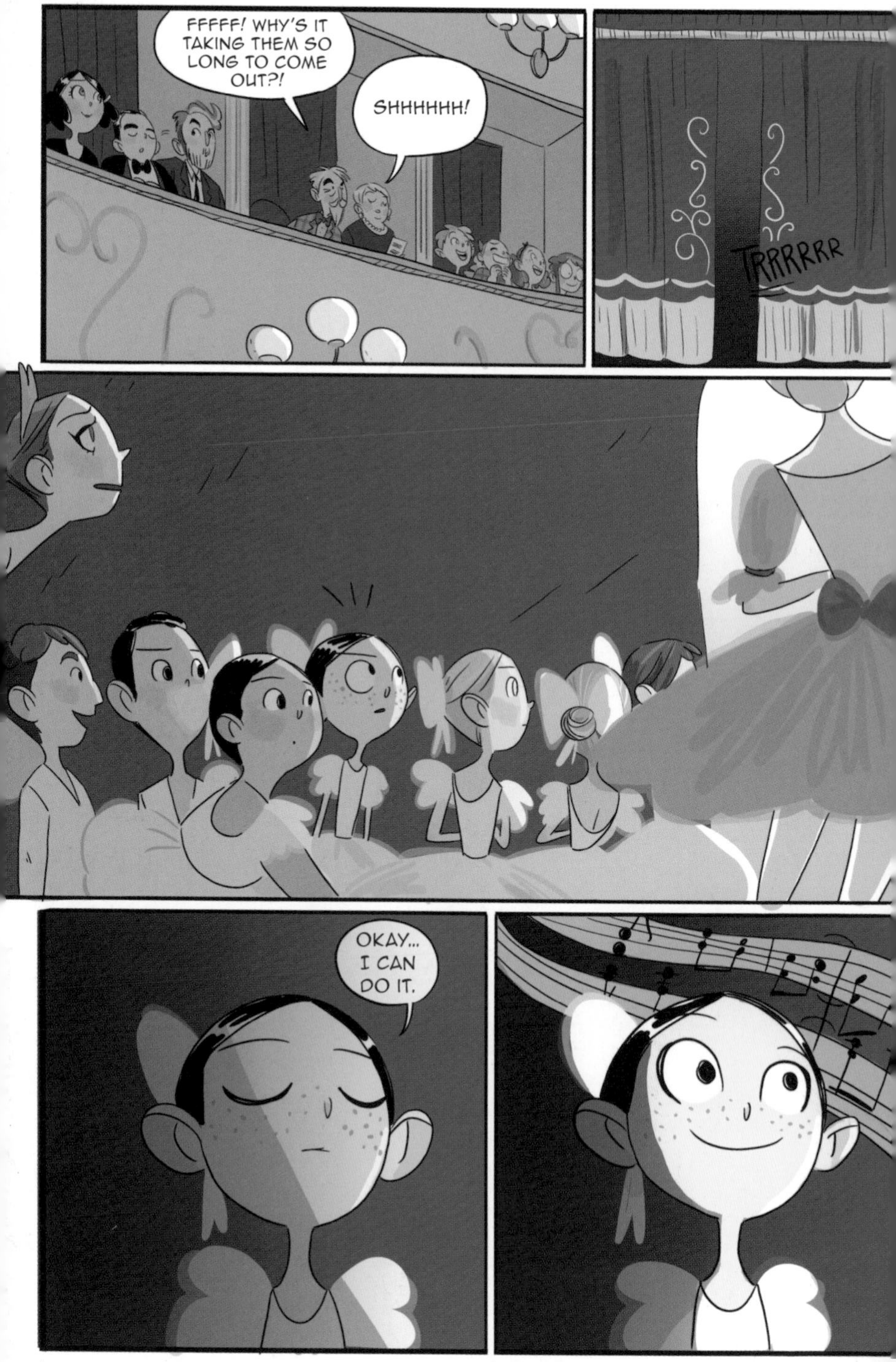
FFFFF! WHY'S IT TAKING THEM SO LONG TO COME OUT?!
SHHHHHH!
TRRRRRR
OKAY... I CAN DO IT.

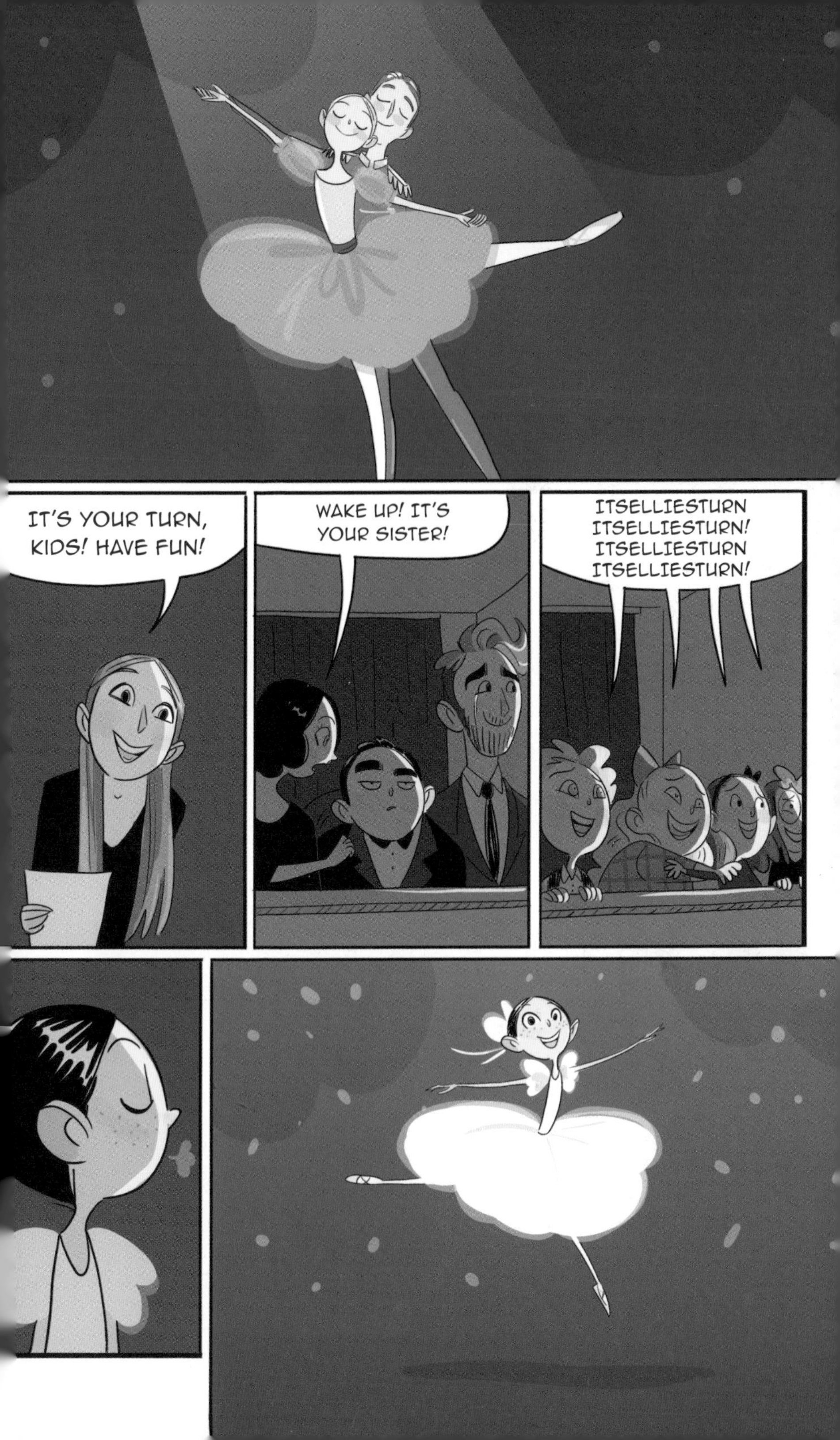
IT'S YOUR TURN, KIDS! HAVE FUN!
WAKE UP! IT'S YOUR SISTER!
ITSELLIESTURN ITSELLIESTURN! ITSELLIESTURN ITSELLIESTURN!

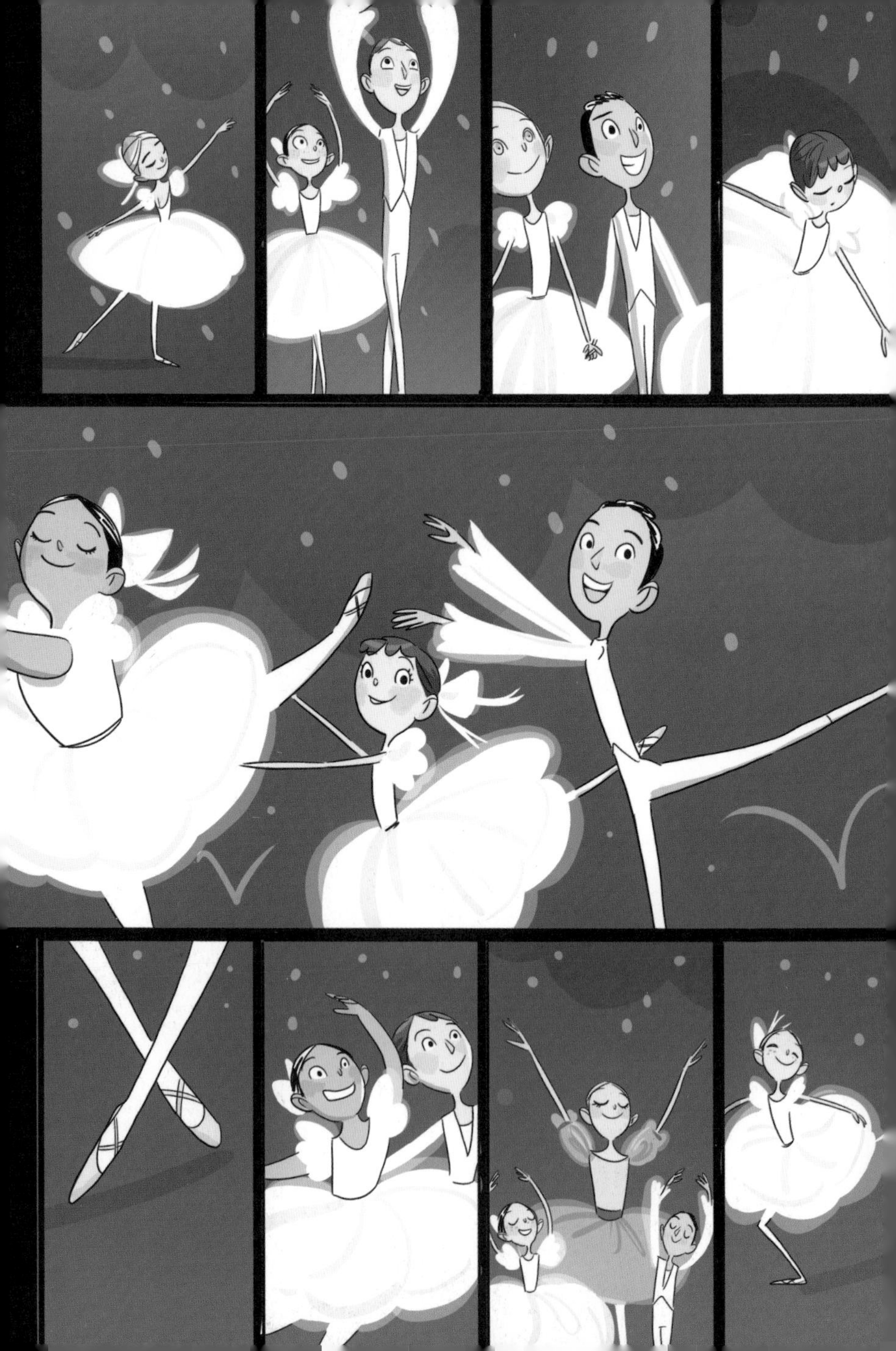

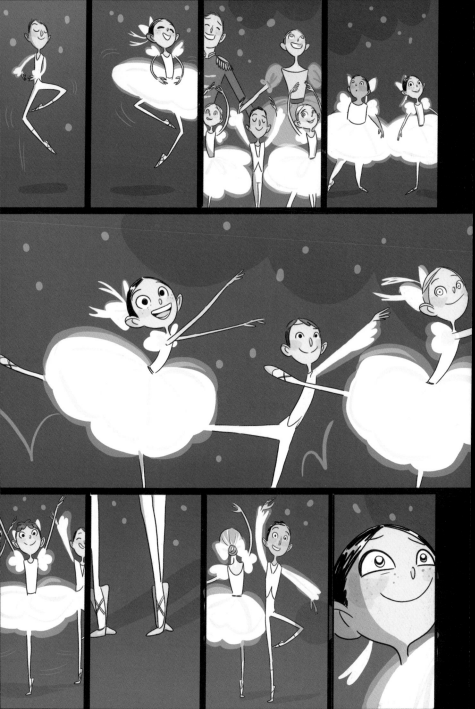

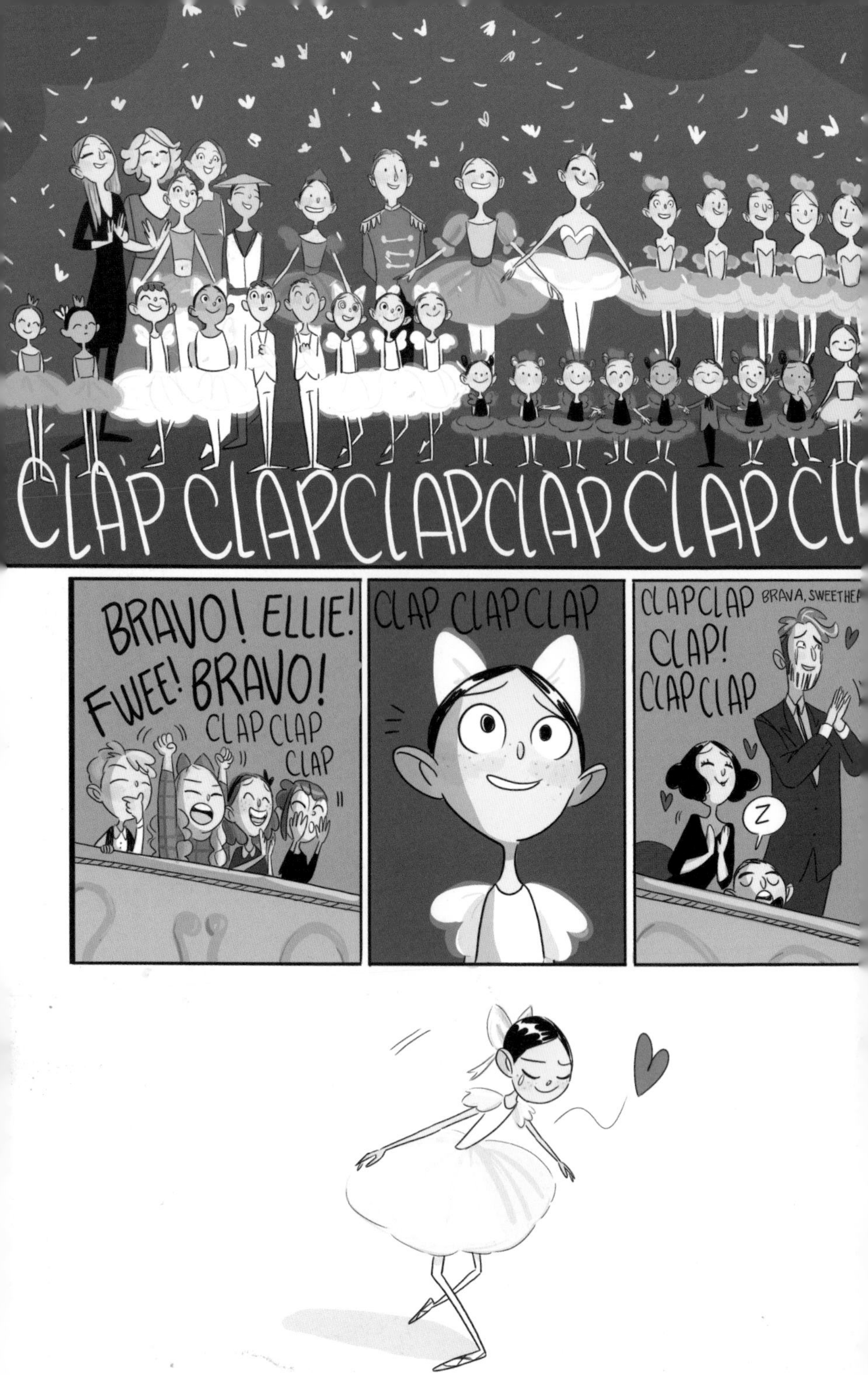

CLAP CLAP CLAP CLAP CLAP
BRAVO! ELLIE!
FWEE! BRAVO!
CLAP CLAP CLAP
CLAP CLAP CLAP
CLAP CLAP
BRAVA, SWEETHE
CLAP!
CLAP CLAP

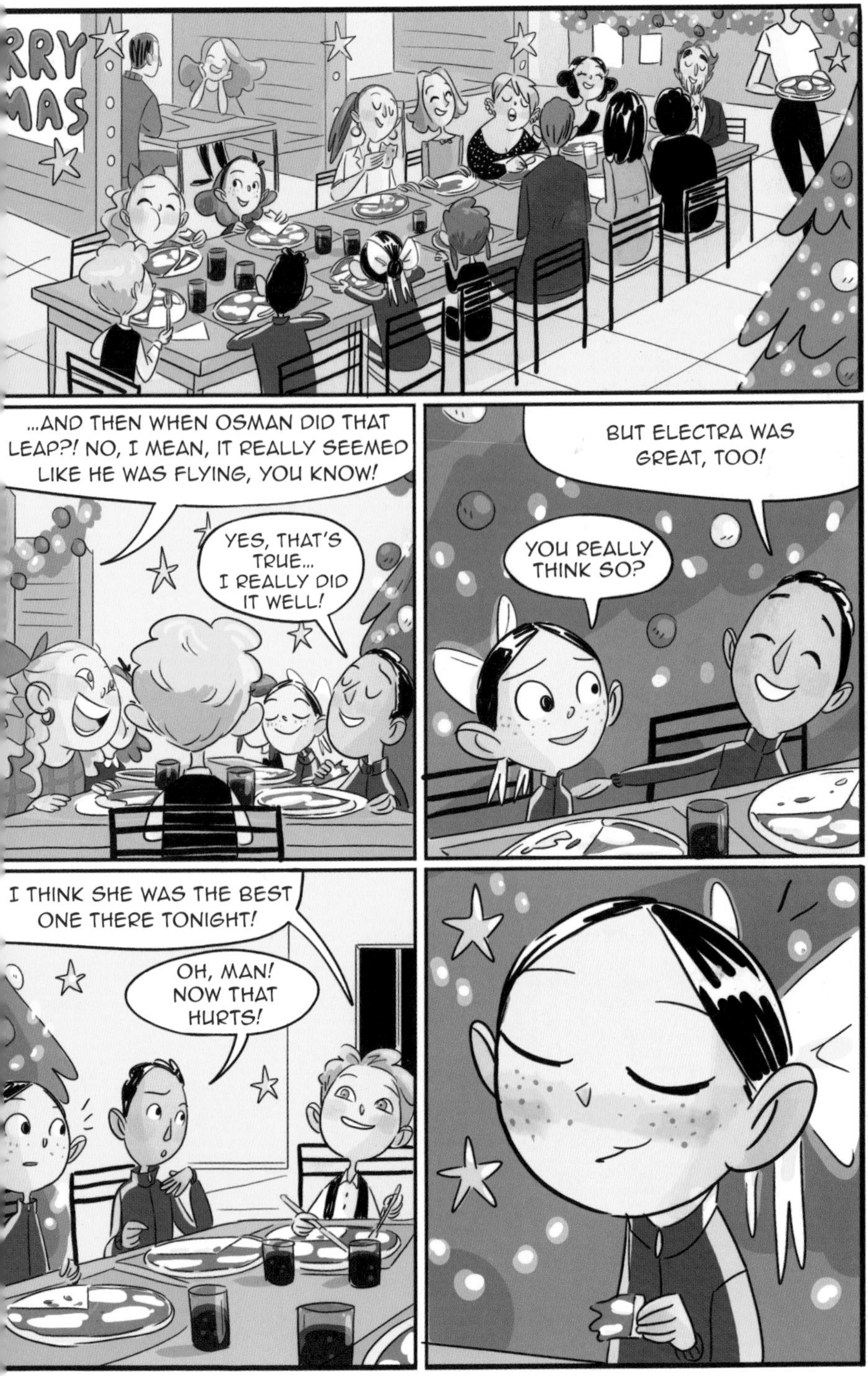
RRY
MAS
...AND THEN WHEN OSMAN DID THAT LEAP?! NO, I MEAN, IT REALLY SEEMED LIKE HE WAS FLYING, YOU KNOW!
YES, THAT'S TRUE... I REALLY DID IT WELL!
BUT ELECTRA WAS GREAT, TOO!
YOU REALLY THINK SO?
I THINK SHE WAS THE BEST ONE THERE TONIGHT!
OH, MAN! NOW THAT HURTS!

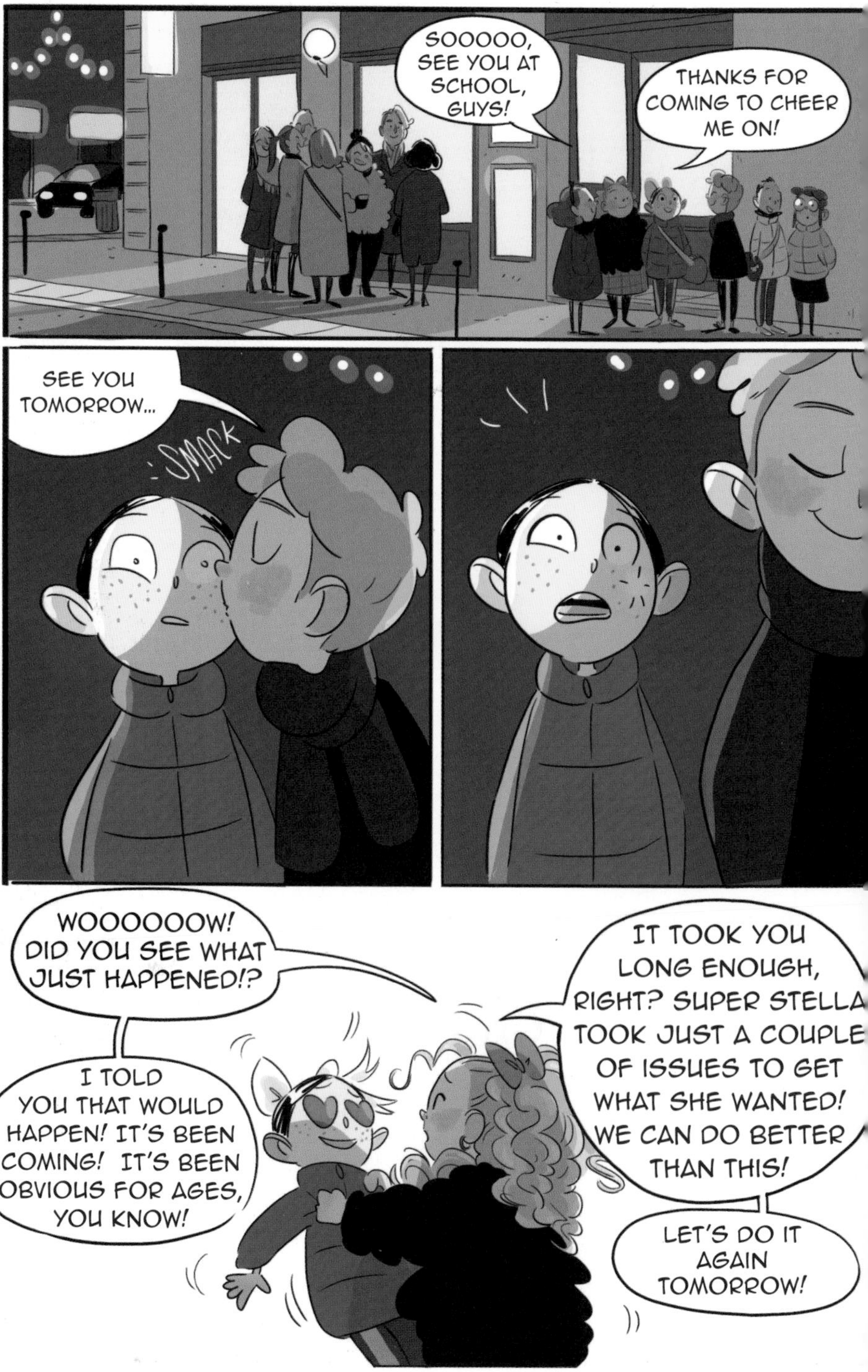
SOOOOO, SEE YOU AT SCHOOL, GUYS!
THANKS FOR COMING TO CHEER ME ON!
SEE YOU TOMORROW...
SMACK
WOOOOOOW! DID YOU SEE WHAT JUST HAPPENED!?
I TOLD YOU THAT WOULD HAPPEN! IT'S BEEN COMING! IT'S BEEN OBVIOUS FOR AGES, YOU KNOW!
IT TOOK YOU LONG ENOUGH, RIGHT? SUPER STELLA TOOK JUST A COUPLE OF ISSUES TO GET WHAT SHE WANTED! WE CAN DO BETTER THAN THIS!
LET'S DO IT AGAIN TOMORROW!